D1713450

EXO-HUNTER

WORKS BY JEREMY ROBINSON

EXO HUNTER

DARK HORSE RISING

JEREMY ROBINSON

BREAKNECK MEDIA

For my Friday Game Night peeps. You know who you are.
Thanks for making the pandemic a little more fun.

INTRODUCTION

As many of you know, I listen to music while I write. It inspires me and often takes the story in new directions. Sometimes, songs make it into the story itself. This time I went all out, making the main character a music lover from the 80s. *Exo Hunter* is full of music references, and it also includes lyrics from the Talking Heads masterpiece, "Once in a Lifetime," and I, of course, obtained permission to use them. I wanted to make these songs easy for readers to find, so I've assembled them in a YouTube playlist that you can find at bewareofmonsters.com/playlist. For the full experience, listen to each song when it comes up in the story, or if you don't like interruptions, when you finish. Hope you enjoy the tunes as much as I did when writing.

—J.R.

PROLOGUE

1989

"Keep your eyes frosty."

The team collectively slow-turns toward Whip.

"That doesn't make sense," Chuy says, adjusting the way her M40A1 sniper rifle hangs from her shoulder.

Whip's face is hidden behind a white face mask and gold, light-reflective goggles, but I can somehow still see his perplexed expression. He's a dangerous operator. A loyal soldier. Always ready for the next mission, no matter what it is. But he's somewhat of a plank. As in wood.

He's not very smart. That's what I'm trying to say.

And he carries an actual whip—hence the callsign—like he's Indiana Jones. He's good with it, but he's never needed it on a mission. Pretty sure he thinks it looks cool. Pretty sure he was dropped on his head as a baby, too.

Chuy on the other hand... She's here because of her brains. Sure, she also wields a sniper rifle like the damn finger of God, smiting our enemies from a distance, but she can outthink every one of us.

"You're mixing metaphors," she says.

"Whataphors?" Whip laughs alone.

"Wasting your time, Chuy." Brick pushes past her. The M16A2 rifle with attached M203 grenade launcher in his meaty hands looks like a child's toy. He's not traditionally an impatient man, but it's cold, we're on the ass end of the planet, and I dragged him out of the movie theater for this op just as Arnold Schwarzenegger smeared mud all over his body. Brick slugs Whip's shoulder as he passes. "That's for butchering an *Aliens* quote."

Some teams bond over BBQs, strip clubs or, I shit you not, weird hobbies like crocheting. Our team hits the movie theater every chance we get. Sci-fi and action are our top picks, but we take in just about everything.

"'Keep your eyes *peeled*,'" Chuy says. "Or '*Stay* frosty.'"

"I'm sorry, why are we debating semantics with a Neanderthal while my nuts are crystalizing?" Benny is an Irish naturalized US citizen. Thinks he's funny. Sometimes is. He's our tech guy. When he got the call for the op, he was at home, setting up his new NeXT Cube computer. Or so he says. When Brick and I picked him up, en route to base, I spotted *Super Contra* paused on his screen. He rubs his gloved hands over his white parka, like it's going to help warm him up.

Antarctica is cold. The constant wind makes it worse. Standing still... well, Benny is right. I can feel the sting in my balls, and my toes, and my fingers. As a Marine Corps Rapid Reaction Force unit, we've been through the shit and back more times than most spec ops boys. Because when something needs getting done fast, we're the best. Last night, we were all in North Carolina. Now, we're twenty klicks from Vostok Station, a Soviet controlled 'research laboratory,' carrying weapons of war that are strictly forbidden by the Antarctic Treaty.

And for what?

Only one of us knows, and she's not talking. But it was urgent enough for Uncle Sam to send us halfway around the world.

"Bugs, can I get a sitrep?" I say to Dr. Julie Carter. She's a stranger to me. A very smart, very attractive stranger, who has been a cagey pain in my ass since I met her on the C-130 Hercules that brought us to this frozen wasteland. "Bugs?"

She's standing at the mouth of an ice cave, pointing some kind of device into the darkness. Not even Benny knows what it does.

"She can't hear you," Whip says. "She's lost in her brain."

Chuy shakes her head. "Nothing scares you like a woman with a brain, eh, Whip? Let her work." She looks at me. "Both of you."

"Happy to let her work," I say, "so long as I know my team isn't going to lose fingers or toes when we thaw out."

My job requires that I put these people in danger, but I'm never stupid about it. Ever since learning we'd have a tag-along civilian, I knew things hadn't been thought through. This mission is a knee-jerk. Someone, somewhere saw something they wanted, and they sent Carter to snatch and grab it, and they sent us to keep her out of the Commies' hands.

Which means it's valuable.

And probably dangerous.

"We're good to go," Carter says, stowing the strange device in her backpack. Like the rest of us, she's dressed in Antarctic camouflage—white snow gear. Unlike the rest of us, she is unarmed, and I have no idea what she's got hidden in her backpack. "And please stop calling me 'Bugs.'"

"No can do," Whip says. "Mission protocol in potentially hostile territory. No real names. No dog tags. No clues about who we really are."

"Not that any of us knows who she is," Brick chimes in.

Carter sighs. The rest of us take some pleasure in her frustration. "Okay... *Dark Horse*..."

"You don't like it?" I ask.

"I think it sounds bad," Whip says.

"Good bad, or *bad* bad?" Benny asks.

"Michael Jackson bad." Whip attempts a leg-kick dance move. He looks more like a twitching headless chicken.

"That could still go either way," Benny says.

"Are you assholes taking this seriously or not?" Carter shouts.

"Lady," I say, "we don't know why we're here, we don't know who you are, and the more we don't know, the more dangerous this is for us... and for you. You'll have to forgive us for blowing off a little steam while we stand here in the cold, watching you wave a magic wand toward a hole in the ground."

It's a little harsh. And a lot unprofessional. I might get a reprimand back at base, but it will be a slap on the wrist. The mission is important, but my people come first. They need to know I'm looking out for them.

"You want to know what this is all about?" Carter asks, pulling a flashlight from her pack. "Follow me."

She heads toward the cave's mouth. It's basically a hole in the ice, descending at a thirty-degree angle.

"You're taking us into a hole in the ground…"

"It's ice," Carter says. "And it's not a hole. It's a ventilation shaft." She stops just inside and levels her masked gaze at me. "And it wasn't here two days ago."

I toggle my comms, connecting me to the second fireteam making up our squad. As bad as my current job is, theirs is worse: maintaining a perimeter with no hope of finding shelter under the ice. If bad guys show up, it's their job to stop the hostiles before they reach me. "BigApe, this is Dark Horse, over."

"Copy that, Dark Horse. Can we go home yet? Over."

"Going to be here a while longer. Bugs is taking us under the ice. Over."

"Under the… We don't get paid enough for this shit. ETA? Over."

Carter heads down into her 'ventilation shaft,' but Whip cuts her off and takes the lead. Good man. "Situation is fluid. ETA unknown. But if you don't hear from me in three zero mikes, feel free to come looking. Over."

"Thirty minutes on firewatch at the god-damned South Pole… I might not be able to move in thirty minutes! Over."

"Do some Kegels to keep warm, princess. Over and out." I toggle off my mic before BigApe can respond, let myself grin behind my mask, and then follow the others into the ice.

"Ventilation shaft, my chapped ass," Chuy says, adopting Whip's brand of tension relief humor. She shifts her head side to side, her headlamp glinting off the smooth, blue ice all around us. Feels like we're standing inside a giant sapphire.

It's stunning, but I don't linger.

Distraction gets soldiers killed.

Whip gently backhands Chuy's shoulder. "Fifty bucks says we flew all the way down here because a whale farted under the ice and it warmed its way to the surface."

"First," Chuy says. "This ice is over land, not the ocean. Second, fifty says this mission goes full clusterfuck in ten mikes or under."

"Stow it," Brick says. "It's getting warmer."

Chuy and Whip silently shake on the bet.

Brick is right. About staying quiet, and about the temperature. It might just be the lack of wind under the ice making us feel cozy, but the glossy sheen on the ice walls lends credence to Carter's theory. Warm air—or water—carved this tunnel. If we didn't have crampons on our boots, we'd all be sliding on our asses.

The very small part of me that's still a kid at heart wants to give it a try, but I have no idea what's waiting for us at the bottom. Could be a natural thermal vent. Could be Soviets.

Speaking of...

"Brick, Chuy, take the lead with Whip." As they pass an annoyed Dr. Carter, I put my hand on her arm. "Sorry, Bugs. The people with guns get to go first."

I would normally take point myself. I'm the one making decisions for these people; I'll be the one to face the consequences of a bad call. But I was personally tasked with keeping Carter alive. And that means she—and I—get to be a Marine sandwich until I know we're not walking into a trap.

"This is unnecessary," she says.

"Would help if you could tell me what we're doing here."

"It's classified," she says.

"We're about to find out anyway," Benny says. He's bringing up the rear, eyes on the tunnel behind us.

Carter just gives her head a slight shake and carries on. She's all business. I can't tell if I like her. From a silverback-gorilla, masculine 80s'-man point-of-view—she's choice. Cindy Crawford beautiful—brown hair, brown eyes—but without the hair-spray. All business, this one. And she's smart. Clearly. Which for me is important, if we're talking romance. But the nuances of whether or not she is a kind and *good* person are lost behind the thick garb, the facemask, and the goggles. We look more like extras from the *Star Wars* Hoth battle than Marines.

Liking her isn't a prerequisite to keeping her alive, but it helps me feel good about it, especially if my people are risking their lives for her.

"Leveling out," Whip says from the front.

Ahead, the tunnel flattens out and curves to the right.

We're a good fifty feet under the ice. Maybe half a klick from where we entered. I can feel the pressure of all that ice building in my ears. If something goes wrong down here...like an explosion, this mission would be beyond FUBAR.

"Take it slow and easy," I tell Whip.

"That *is* how your mom likes it," he says. My team is smiling behind their masks. I don't need to see their faces to know. But no one laughs.

Whip's fist comes up as he rounds the bend. His body tenses. When he speaks, there's no trace of humor anymore. "Tunnel opens up ahead."

Chuy stops beside Whip. They'll face whatever lies ahead together. Brick is close behind, ready to take their place or drag them to safety—should one of them fall. The three of them do a good job of filling the tunnel. I can't see shit.

Impatience radiates through Carter's parka. "I should be up there."

"You should be quiet," Benny says, whispering.

Carter turns around to glare at him—I'm assuming—but he's still got his eyes on the tunnel behind us.

I hold a gloved finger to my facemask, raise my rifle, and step in front of her. The crunch of my boots digging into the ice makes sneaking impossible, but that's okay for now. Chuy's body language is tense, but nothing close to 'Oh, shit' levels of trouble.

I round the bend in time to see Whip and Chuy exit the tunnel and part. Brick is silhouetted by blue light. He exits the tunnel and stands to his full 6'7" height. Hadn't realized he'd been leaning down the whole time. He doesn't complain or stretch. He just looks up and says, "You're not gonna believe this..."

He's relaxed, so I don't hold Carter back when she pushes past me. I follow her out of the tunnel, and like the rest of my team, I am awed by the view.

We stand at the base of what can best be described as a bubble in the ice. It's fifty feet in diameter with a thirty-foot-wide, flat floor. It's smooth, like the tunnel, and perfectly round, like being inside a glass-ball Christmas ornament. The ceiling of the bubble is just inches below the surface, allowing sunlight to filter through, lighting the chamber. For a moment, I'm lost in astonishment.

Carter pushes past Brick, scanning the empty space. She peels her mask off, revealing her brown eyes. "Shit." She looks around again like she might have missed something the first time. "Shit! We're too late."

"Too late for what?" Benny asks, as he enters the bubble and looks up. "Whoooaaa."

Carter rounds on me. "We need to get to Vostok. They must have it."

I lift my goggles so I can look her in the eyes. "Must. Have. What?"

She glares, but this is a fight she can't win with her eyes. I can stare down a charging elephant without flinching.

"If the Soviets exfil with it—"

"Uhh," Whip says. "Excuse me? Dr. Bugs?"

"*What?*" Carter snaps.

"Is *that* what you're looking for?" Whip points toward the crystal-clear floor, where *something* rests just beneath the surface.

We stand around the submerged object like a winter-garbed cult, heads bowed toward the ice. The encased, miniature obelisk is no bigger than a football. It's black and covered in what might be writing...or just cracks. Only the first few inches are easy to see. The rest of it is obscured by miniature air bubbles trapped in time.

"How do we get it out?" Carter asks.

"We kind of specialize in shooting people," Brick says. "And blowing stuff up. Sometimes at the same time. Getting ancient artifacts out of the ice—in one piece—is pretty far outside of our wheelhouse."

Carter looks to me for an alternative answer.

"He's not wrong," I admit. "But..."

Static in my ear makes me flinch.

"—oming! Over."

I toggle my mike. "BigApe, I did not receive. Say again. Over."

I don't like the pause that follows. I'm about to order Whip and Brick to the surface when, "—oviets, en route! Over."

"Say again. Did you say Soviets? Over."

At the mention of our Cold War rivals, the temperature inside the ice bubble drops, and my team tenses.

"Yes!" BigApe shouts, loud and clear. "ETA, one mike! Should we engage? Over."

"Shit," I say, and then I ask Carter, "How important is this thing? Really?"

"Very," she says, and it's not nearly good enough.

"Important enough to die over?" I ask, while BigApe repeats his question in my ear. "Should we engage?!"

"Whoever recovers this..." Carter motions to the artifact. "...might have the ability to sculpt the future into whatever form they like."

"What kind of Yoda bullshit answer is that?" Chuy says. "It's a statue, built for some long-forgotten god. We should bug out."

"How did a statue get fifty feet inside ice that hasn't seen the light of day for the past fifteen million years?" Carter's shouted question echoes around the chamber, and it morphs into a strange kind of rumble. It resonates throughout the spherical space, somehow growing louder.

"Fifteen million years is long before hominids evolved," Chuy says. "If people didn't make it, where did it come from?"

Carter's eyes move from Chuy toward the ceiling.

We all understand her meaning.

Out there...

Space...

Whatever is hidden beneath the ice...it's alien.

"Holee-shit," Whip says.

"BigApe," I say, "Light 'em up."

The order might save our lives.

Might also start a World War.

Our only hope that the fight doesn't blossom into something worse is getting the hell out without leaving a man or any evidence behind. And that includes what's in the ice.

"Chuy, Benny," I say. "Find a way to get that thing out of the ice. Whip, Brick, get topside. Guard the entrance." I set my eyes on Carter. "You, tell me every damn thing you can about what we're dragging out of the ice. Right now. Or I'll leave you for our comrades."

She looks about ready to tear my head off. But before she can speak, or my team can act, the rumbling draws our eyes to the ceiling.

The silhouette of a snowmobile races across the ice above us.

The sphere's ceiling cracks as the vehicle passes.

A second snowmobile follows.

Shards of ice fall and shatter on the floor, forcing us to look away or risk being impaled in the face.

Muffled gunshots tear through the air above. M16s. BigApe and his team are giving them hell. The thumping report of AK-47s follows.

"We should all be up there," Chuy says.

"Do what I told you," I say. "All of you—"

The chamber shakes. A second rumble grows louder. At the fringe of the translucent ceiling, the underside of a five-ton Sno-Cat rolls into view. It's going to drive right over the sphere's cap, where the ice is the thinnest.

"Everyone out!" I shout.

"We can't leave!" Carter stomps a foot in protest. "We need to—"

I grasp her parka, plant my feet, and toss her to the side, while the rest of my team heeds my warning, diving away from the room's core.

Above, the ceiling cracks.

Ice rains down when a thick, metal track punctures through, grinding and carving. The ceiling buckles beneath the machine's weight. I make it two steps before I'm forced to leap clear.

Metal and ice grind. Then, for a moment: silence. It's followed by an earsplitting crash as the Sno-Cat pounds into the floor. The impact cracks the smooth, blue walls, marring what had been an unnatural wonder.

I roll onto my back, to find the Sno-Cat face down, its long body jutting fifteen feet into the air. Inside the cab, two Soviet soldiers—unconscious and probably alive thanks to their seatbelts. Outside the Cat are two more tangos, both most certainly dead. Blood pools around the closest, seeping down through cracks in the once perfectly smooth floor.

A lightning streak of cracks spreads out away from the Cat. It cants to the side and then falls–straight toward me. I try to scramble back, but the floor is suddenly slick with moisture. Instead of gripping, my crampons slice through the softening ice.

Pressure grips my neck like I'm being strangled. Brick's got my hood in his big hand. He yanks and flings me clear, diving to the ice beside me.

"Owe you one," I say.

"I'm sure you'll get plenty of chances to pay me back." He glances at the slushy floor between us. "Ice is melting."

Across the chamber, Whip gets to his feet, unsteady as water flows past him from the walls. "This can't be good!"

"If we don't bug out now," Chuy says, "we're going to get frostbite topside before evac can pick us up."

"Unless we take Vostok Station," Brick says.

"That would *definitely* start a war," I say, but I don't see any other plays.

Carter sloshes into ankle deep water, trying to get past the twisted wreckage, to the artifact beneath.

"It's not going to happen, Bugs," I tell her. "Best I can do is bring this place down and bury it again."

"Not good enough!" she shouts, dropping to her hands and knees. She tries to push her way past some twisted metal, but she stops. Looks confused. "The water...is warm."

She's right. I can feel moisture in the air like a humidifier on my face.

Brick's gloved hand squeaks over his goggles, wiping condensation away. "This place is going to be a pond in the next– What...is *that?*"

The ice beneath Carter glows blue.

Whatever she was after has been turned on...or activated, and since I don't know if it's a flashlight or a bomb... "Move, people!"

"Nikomu ne dvigatsya!"

I swivel toward the voice, M16 raised. One of the Russians from the Cat has hauled himself out and is now holding the biggest knife I've ever seen to Carter's throat. The blade is distinctive. Probably one of a kind. The Damascus steel gives it an almost marbled look, while the stern eagle head carved into the pommel and the straight-edged feathers on the guard make the ebony handle scream: 'I was made in Mother Russia!'

Carter looks more annoyed than afraid, which is impressive, but that's not going to save her life.

That's on Chuy.

I can see her moving out of the corner of my eye, slow and catlike. The moment the sniper rifle scope reaches her eye, the man's head will stain Carter's jacket.

"Otpusti yeyo," I say in Russian.

He squints at me. My accent is as clear as his would be, were he speaking English. "Amerikanskiy..." The blade pushes harder against Carter's neck. A bead of blood runs down the metal surface. Carter's eyebrows turn up slightly.

There's the fear...

Blue pulses from the floor, rushing up around the translucent walls, revealing silhouettes...of something...of monsters...inside the damn ice! They're impossible to make out in detail, but they are definitely *not* human.

The Russian sees them, too, his eyes widening. "Zhizn' ebet meya..."

A scream draws our attention upward.

Two bodies fall from above, locked together, grappling. The first, I don't know. The second is BigApe.

They land in the now three-foot-deep water, BigApe on top.

Light lances all around us, reaching a crescendo of otherworldly energy.

"Peredyshka!" He withdraws the blade from Carter's neck and points it at the tunnel exit. "My mozhem poyti vmeste."

He wants a truce. Wants to leave together. I'd normally kick this Ruskie's ass back to Siberia, but given the circumstances...

"Da," I tell him, and I lower my weapon. "Da."

Carter hurries away from him, and I motion for the others to lower their weapons, too. Chuy was half a second from taking his head off, but now we have a prisoner and might get some answers.

BigApe grunts as he attempts to stand.

"Get his ass up and out of here!" I shout to Chuy and Whip.

"No complaints," I say to Carter, shoving her toward the tunnel. "Not a wor—"

Blinding light pulses through cracks in the walls.

A wave of nausea rolls through me. Drops me to one knee.

A high-pitched squeal fills the air, forcing my hands to my ears. I scream, but I can't hear it. All around me, the team suffers the same fate.

And then, an explosion.

I think.

It hits me like a freight train. Lifts me off the wet floor. And slams me into a white oblivion before knocking me unconscious.

My breath fogs rounded glass. Feels like a rebreather used for long dives. But I'm upright. And walking. I look down. The first thing I notice is my clothing. It's not a diving suit, it's a spacesuit. There are glowing red bands around my biceps. There's a stern looking eagle head emblem on my chest. The golden profile smacks of an authoritarian regime more than patriotic Americana, but it's been painted over with a red X.

A moving walkway scrolls beneath my booted feet. Turquoise light seeps out of the cracks between each pad. Each step keeps me in the same position. Takes me nowhere. I'm a hamster on a wheel.

And that's fine by me, because I want nothing to do with what's before me.

Despite the feeling of gravity keeping me rooted on the walkway, it's clear that I'm in space. My view of the stars is unhindered by Earth's atmosphere. The view is alive with pinpoints of light. A purple nebula glows and churns. But none of that holds my attention for long.

Wholesale destruction twists through the vacuum. I'm not sure what I'm looking at—what it used to be—a vessel, several vessels, a space station, or something else. But it was clearly manmade and has now been undone.

We have nothing like this, I think.

Neither do the Russians.

I look over my shoulder, hoping to see Earth. Instead I see a black sphere that is clearly not Earth or any other planet in the solar system humanity calls home.

Where the hell am I?

I look back toward the twisting destruction, my practiced eyes spotting bodies amidst the debris.

Thousands of them.

Maybe more.

But they're hard to make out. The details blur, like there's something in my eye.

What the fuck happened here?

A voice echoes like a memory. "Found something...thing...thing..."

And the world goes white again.

"Another one! I found another!" The accent is funny. While the man's English is perfect, the accent is faux German. Instead of intimidating, like just about every German speaker, he sounds a bit silly. Naïve.

The wall of white lifts away. A sheet of snowy ice.

A man in a strange black body suit stands over me. The emblem from the dream is on his chest, but right-side up and easy to see. It's an eagle, profile head, wings spread, but then turned down. Looks a lot like what I'd been wearing in my dream, sans the X. I have no idea what country or military force it represents.

When I blink my eyes at the Antarctic sun, his voice rises an octave. "This one is alive!"

This one is alive.

That means someone else was dead.

I lift my arm from the ice, reaching for the man. "Help me up!"

The man flinches back. His eyebrows are turned up in fear.

That's odd, I think. He's wearing the tight black suit, but his balding head is totally exposed. He should be freezing.

"Who... Who *are* you?" he asks.

"Afraid I'm going to need you to go first," I tell him, pushing myself up without his help. I'm desperate to get a look at my surroundings but taking my eyes off this guy for just a second would give him the opportunity to subdue me.

"Ozark," he says. "My name is Ozark."

"What kind of name is... What country are you from? Canada?"

"Country?" He's honestly baffled by the question. "Do you mean planet? Because this is Earth."

"I know what damn planet I'm on," I tell him, and I'm about to unleash a diatribe of insults laced between questions when a breeze brushes up against my exposed face.

It's warm.

Spring in New England warm. Maybe sixty-five degrees.

I glance down at his clothing again. It's not winter gear at all. It's some kind of skin-tight armor. A uniform. There's a name plate. Reads Burnett. Ozark must be his first name.

My eyes flit to the side. It's supposed to be a glance, but I can't look away. Behind Burnett are the ruins of a post-apocalyptic neighborhood. Caved in homes. Twisted swing sets.

Where the fuck am I, and how did I get here?

Soviets, I think. This is a mind-screw interrogation technique meant to break my mind from reality. Loosen my tongue.

A second man rushes up beside the first. He's got a belly. Not a soldier. Name tag reads Morton. When he sees me, his eyes go wide, like he's looking at a tiger with wings and a unicorn horn. And then he makes a comment that will haunt me for the rest of my life. "His skin... It's dark!"

His voice is deeper, but it has the same Americanized German accent.

When I stand up, both men hop a step back.

"Where on Earth *are* we?" I ask.

"New Antarctica," Burnett says. "You don't *live* here, do you? I mean, *no one* lives here."

"That could explain the skin," Morton says.

"No one lives on Antarctica," I say, trying hard to not slug the man. Yet. Broken jaws make answering questions difficult.

"Not anymore," Morton says.

I'm about to accuse them of both being Soviet interrogators when I see the second body, pulled not from ice, but from the ruins of a building. It wasn't a sheet of ice and snow pulled off my body. It was a wall and insulation. Laid out on the crumbling pavement of a long-since-used road is the big Russian. Eyes closed. Chest unmoving.

They wouldn't kill one of their own to convince me this is real... Would they?

If I bring him back, maybe he can tell me.

I head for the Russian. He's got a full beard, a barrel shaped body, and he has the distinct look of a killer. Like a bear.

"Fucking Soviets," I mutter, and I fall to my knees by his head. "You two going to help?" I shout toward Burnett and Morton.

"Help...what?" Burnett asks.

"Useless," I say, and then I start CPR, an act that draws gasps from the two men. The hell is wrong with them?

When the Russian's ribs crack, I know I'm doing it right. When he doesn't jump up in pain, I'm sure he's dead. I work on him for thirty seconds, pausing only to shed my parka. And then...

He gasps awake, sits up, backhands me away, shouts, "Moi rebra!" He clutches his ribs and falls back down, unconscious.

But breathing.

When I turn around on the two strange men, they look stunned, like I'm a wizard casting spells in some post-apocalyptic—

Hold on a fucking second.

I reach for my hip. Find my Beretta M9 handgun still holstered there. I draw it. Aim it at Burnett. He flinches back. Raises his hands. Morton follows suit when I turn the pistol on him.

No way this is a Russian ruse.

"What *year* is it?"

The two men look at each other. Confused by the simple question.

"What. Year. Is. It?" I fire a round into the pavement between them. It sparks and pings, sending both men leaping in fright.

Definitely not soldiers.

"Twenty-nine-eighty-nine," Burnett says.

"Sure you don't want to subtract ten from that twenty-nine?"

"Nineteen-eighty-eight?" Morton says. "Why would we... Is that the year you think it is?"

Keeping my weapon trained on the duo, I turn my head up. The sky is still blue. The clouds are still white. This is Earth, but there's a dead neighborhood...in a warm Antarctica. "How did all this—" I motion to the destruction. "—get like this?"

Morton's brow furrows. "Do you not know?" Looks at Burnett. "Could he really not know?"

"Know *what?*" I ask, finger on the trigger. The moment I put one of them down, the other is going to start blabbing like a truth geyser.

A rumble approaches. Something airborne. Sounds like a jet. "Which one of you assholes called for air support?"

"We called for a pick-up before we found you."

"Evac," I say. "Why?"

"Because we didn't find anything worth salvaging," Morton says. "Because there is nothing left here but junk and two-hundred-year-old death." He turns to Burnett. "Just like I told you."

"Shut-up, space breath."

"Space...breath?" The question slips out of my mouth.

"Because space smells bad," Burnett says. "Like welding fumes."

"I think it smells like burned meat," Morton says, "which I like, so go flap yourself."

"Flap yourself?"

Before I can ask another real question, the roar of a jet engine grows too loud to ignore. If these two morons are about to get backup, I don't want to look like a threat right off the bat. I holster my weapon and turn to greet the—

Ho. Lee. Shit.

It's a spaceship...on Earth...but still, this is some *Battlestar Galactica* bullshit. The craft slows to a hover like it's posing for pictures. Its 'wings' are only there to support the four VTOL jets keeping it airborne. Otherwise, it looks something like a boxy submarine with a broad windshield and one of those eagle emblems on the front.

The ship lowers to the ground and settles with a slight bump. The jets' roar comes to an abrupt stop. A hatch opens and a lone, very overweight man stuffed into a black uniform struts down the walk-way.

"I told you two slags that you wouldn't find anything of any consequence down he—" He's seen me. And the Soviet. His lips move, but no words escape.

"Is it just the three of you?" I ask.

"We're a minor salvage team," Burnett says. "Worst job in the galaxy."

"In the galaxy..."

"Could be worse," Morton says. "Least we're not Exo-Hunters."

"Excuse me," I say, lifting my pistol toward the new man.

He stutters to a stop, eyes wide, mouth formed into an O. "Ohh," he says, "Oh, geez. I'm sorry."

I'm about to ask him what he's sorry for, when a nozzle extends from the side of his suit. It violently sprays a stream of yellow liquid onto the pavement.

Burnett shakes his head in shame. "Every single time, Porter. Every time!"

To me, Burnett says, "He does this whenever he's caught off guard."

The laser beam of urine comes to an end with a sputtering spray that keeps any and all drips from striking his suit. The nozzle retracts, and the suit seals back up.

"That going to happen if you shit yourself, too?" I ask.

Porter's nervous smile confirms it, so I lower the weapon. These three are not a threat. "Anyone have a problem with me taking charge?"

I take their uncomfortable silence for compliance. "Great. Burnett, Morton, get my big friend inside. Tie him up. Do a good job of it." They get to work, grabbing the Soviet by his hands and feet, hauling him toward the spaceship.

A fucking spaceship...

"Porter."

"Yes, sir!" he says, and he salutes. I nearly tell him not to bother, but maybe he recognizes me as military. If so, Larry, Curly, and Moe here might actually do what I tell them. "You have a way to find out if anyone else is buried in..." I motion to ruins behind me. "...all this? Life sign scanner or something?"

"Only way to know is to look," he says.

"What the hell kind of future doesn't have life sign scanners?" I mutter, rolling up my sleeves. "Hope you're not afraid of a little physical labor."

"Uhh," he says, clearly not built for clearing rubble, let alone touching his toes. He lifts his forearm and speaks into the tight black sleeve. "We have Taks for that."

"Taks?"

Four square chunks of black metal fall away from the spacecraft's hull. By the time they reach the ground, they've unfurled into boxy robots that move on all fours. I grip my pistol tighter as they rush toward us, but the machines dive into the debris, hauling out concrete and metal far faster than a hundred men could.

An hour later, most of the debris is cleared, and no one has been found.

"You sure there were other…" He gives me a once over, like he's not sure what I am.

"People," I say to Porter. "I'm a person. A human being. Same as you. How can you not know this? Are there not black people in the future?"

"Hasn't been for a long, long time." He swallows, appropriately afraid of how I'll take the news.

I'm staggered. My knees weaken. *What kind of white supremacist future hell have I been shunted into?*

"Hey!" Morton calls out, rushing up, waving his hands. "I found something!"

"Where?" I ask, ready to charge in whatever direction he points.

"It's you!" He lifts a device. Turns it on. Static hisses. Then he points it toward me, and the thing squeals.

"What is that?" I ask.

"Radio waves! You're emitting radio waves. Technically it's impossible, but—" He demonstrates again, unleashing another squeal. "The same thing happened with your friend inside."

"Not my friend," I say, and I snatch the device from Morton's hand. I sweep it left to right out over the debris field. I'm about to lose hope when it squeals. I continue a full 360-degree sweep, stopping when the high-pitched sound makes my ears cringe again. Same location.

I turn to Porter. "What are you waiting for?"

Ten minutes later, the Taks have cleared five feet of heavy debris from a twenty-foot-wide area.

"Pull them out," I say.

"But they're—"

"Too heavy," I point out. "They could crush anyone beneath them."

"Do you really think someone could survive under there?" Morton asks.

I look him in the eyes. "The people I'm looking for have survived worse."

When I storm into the clearing, sweeping back and forth with the radio detector, zeroing in on the source, I hear Burnett ask the others, "Who are these people?"

I'm about to respond when the radio squeal ceases. I stop in my tracks, aim it straight down, and hear the sound again. I drop to the ground and dig until my arms are sore. Then I push through the pain. I'll stop when I'm done, not when I'm tired.

I reach an old metal door. Find the handle. Pull as hard as I can.

"Look at the muscles in his forearms," Porter whispers. The three men are standing a few feet away, watching me like I'm a sideshow attraction. "He's so *strong*."

The door groans, shudders, and then gives way. Dust and debris falls to the side with the door, blocking my view for a moment. I'm greeted by the back side of a parka. No idea who it is until, "Hijo de puta, what took you so long?"

"Chuy!" I say, grasping her shoulders and lifting her up.

She's weak on her feet, so I support her weight as she pulls her hood and mask off and takes in our surroundings. "Where the hell *are* we?"

"Wouldn't believe me if I told you," I say. "Not sure I believe it yet, myself."

When her survey ends at the spaceship, "El maldito futuro?"

"You know I don't speak Mexican," I say.

She gives me a weak smile. "That's a spaceship, right?"

I nod.

"This is the future?"

Another nod.

"Whip owes me fifty bucks," she says, and then she falls unconscious in my arms.

"I'll let him know when we find him," I say.

I pick her up and carry her toward the spaceship I'm about to commandeer.

1

FIVE YEARS LATER

Every time I visit a new world, I run through the same checklist. First, I give myself a moment to feel awe. Every planet is unique, and I—well, my crew and I—are the first human beings to see them up close and personal.

Before we arrive, the exo-planets are pin-pricks of light and data, nestled into the Goldilocks zone of a star. Sometimes a red giant. Sometimes a blazing white dwarf. But most, like the one I'm looking at now, orbit a yellow star that reminds me of home. The planet is Earth-like enough. An atmosphere swirling with clouds. Blue oceans. Continents. The only big difference is that the land masses have a purple hue, which doesn't mean anything. We once found a perfectly habitable world where all the vegetation grew pink. The *My Little Pony* paradise made me queasy to look at, but it went from a human population of zero to four billion in just a year.

Step two is a scan for any signs of advanced intelligence. The kind that can fight back. Life is plentiful throughout the galaxy. IQs above that of a chimpanzee (which are extinct, along with most everything else on Earth) are in short supply. So, we look for satellites. Cities. The usual markers of civilization. And here, like everywhere else, there are none.

Step three involves an up close and personal analysis of the atmosphere. For the most part, Predictors—the nerds who tell us where to go next—are pretty good at their jobs. They find planets via telescopes, or whatever, figure out which ones look ripe for a billion settlers, and send an Exo-Hunter team on their merry way. They haven't steered me wrong yet. But if there is sulfuric acid in the air, I'd like to know about it before heading to the surface for a looksee.

And that's the dangerous bit.

From space, planets are sterile and harmless, like a virus outside the body. But once you're on the ground... Nine times out of ten, a planet is rejected for settlement because it's too dangerous. Sometimes, the atmosphere is killer, and terraforming takes too much time. Sometimes the native life—plant *and* animal—is too hostile for immediate settlement, but the Union isn't opposed to wiping out entire species...

Or ethnic groups.

Back in the day, more than nine hundred years ago, they managed to cleanse the human race of everyone without pale skin. But those were darker times, fueled by fear and misguided religious zealotry. While most people populating the galaxy are a shade of peach, pink, white, and sometimes translucent veiny weirdness, there is no one left alive (that I have met) who remembers why anyone with different colored skin was feared or hated.

There are only three people alive today who have seen a more colorful humanity, and they saw the racism and bigotry that came with it.

It took three months of living on the cusp of the year 3000, for our crew to get used to our darker skin tones, mine something like dark chocolate, Chuy's like milk chocolate. It didn't bother them, but they had a hard time not staring at us the way people used to look at Picasso paintings. And that's why we decided to stay off the Union's radar. We'd not only stand out, we'd make a scene, and it wouldn't be long before everyone in the known galaxy would hear about us. My guys might be cool with varied skin tones, but I honestly have no idea how the Union would react, and I'm not in a rush to find out.

We took our hijacked space-faring vessel, which turned out to be a lander, and commandeered its much larger mothership, formally designated A-154-B7 and renamed it the *USSS Bitch'n*. While there is no longer a United States—or any other country—the name is still funny to me, to

Chuy, and to our Soviet comrade, Vladimir Ivanov, whose name is so Russian it hurts. I sometimes call him Vlad, or Ivan, but mostly I call him by the callsign I bestowed upon him: Drago.

Once he cleaned up and shaved, he didn't look much different from the Union people clogging up the galaxy. White. Blond. Blue-eyed. The only real difference is that he's a monster of a man with more hair than an ox. With technology performing most physical labor tasks, and leisurely life spent indoors or in spacecraft, people just aren't that physically fit anymore. Gone are the days of fluorescent tank tops drawing the eyes to ripped biceps and shoulders. Men and women of the Union mostly wear BCSs: Body Care Suits. Aside from eating, they facilitate the body's every need, from pissing and shitting to self-cleaning and, I shit you not, erection detection. Given the proliferation of a human race with nothing better to do than hump like rabbits across the galaxy, I'd say that feature is working.

Our three crewmen from the future still wear the suits, despite my refusal to and despite constant mocking from Drago. Those of us who call 1989 home wear a combination of custom-made military BDUs and modern body armor. We look badass pretty much 24/7.

With the *Bitch'n* under my command, we created fake identities with white faces, and we acclimated to life on the fringe of the future. Then we took on the job that kept us out of sight and was best suited to those who kick ass for a living: Exo-Hunters.

It's a dreaded post for most people these days.

Average life span for a new Hunter is one year.

We've been at it for nearly five. We've discovered enough new worlds to make William Shatner shit himself silly—thirty-seven of them habitable. As a result, we're well paid, and we're never without a mission. Which is exactly how I like it.

I can usually tell just by looking at a planet if the air is breathable. If it's not, we move on. The Union needs habitable worlds to satiate its perpetually booming population. With sixty-four planets hosting populations ranging between fifteen and twenty-five billion, the human race is multiplying faster than suitable worlds can be discovered. Side note: people also live a lot longer, so there are untold billions of geriatrics squeezed into BCSs, many of them still managing to pop out kids.

I swear, the whole galaxy is sex addicted.

It all started when a genetically modified plague was unleashed against people of color. Earth's population took a serious hit. As did the work force. The white supremacists who unleashed it didn't realize how thoroughly mixed people's DNA had become, and many of their 'pure' super-race fell victim, too. The human race nearly went extinct—the Fourth Reich and all. Breeding programs and genetic manipulation solved the problem. They created human birthing farms, where women could pump out up to thirty children before being discarded. That stopped when, thanks to genetic tinkering, women started churning out litters of children with each pregnancy. The master race proliferated, and Earth's population soared.

So much of the future is fucked up, but the genocidal darkness is ancient history to these people. Farther back than the Revolutionary War was from me in 1989. The human race that we have encountered now is placid, nice, and naïve. War doesn't exist because no one wants to bother fighting, and no one really knows how. As long as we keep finding planets for people to colonize, there'll be nothing to fight over.

"What the fuck are you waiting for?" Drago shouts at me from across the bridge.

"Fuck you," I say. "I was thinking."

"What is there to think about?"

"I was ruminating," I tell the big man, "about how we got here."

"About how magical object transported us into future?" he asks.

"Not exactly." Pondering that mystery has been a waste of time. It doesn't make sense to those of us from the past, and my future-crew is even more baffled by it. While mankind has conquered space travel, time is still a mystery. Morton, Burnett, and Porter are scavengers by trade, but they're also really smart. Too smart for manual labor. They're here because they don't fit the Fourth Reich's quality standards for one reason or another. But they're not theoretical physicists. There are people in the Union we could ask, but I prefer to stay hidden from the Union, even if I find a quadriplegic penguin more threatening.

Penguins. Also extinct.

Limbed and otherwise.

All we really know is that we're here, and that radio waves scream from our bodies. Anyone listening to 104.1 MHz gets blasted with a high-pitched squeal. I kind of wish we were broadcasting *Blue Monday*—because future music blows—but the radio waves emanating from our bodies is the one detail about all this that gives me hope.

While the Union thinks I'm someone else, out here on their behalf, shopping through the JC Penneys of planets, I'm actually looking for my missing teammates.

When we arrived in the future, the *Bitch'n* registered bursts of energy—three of them on Earth (myself, Chuy, and Drago) and five more launched out into deep space. Assuming that whatever brought us here wasn't made by complete nimrods, my hope is that those other energy bursts found their way to habitable worlds.

If not, then Benny, Brick, Whip, BigApe, and Carter are all dead.

And that brings us to step four of my new world checklist. "Turn on the radio."

Morton flips a switch. The bridge is filled with the sound…of static. As usual.

"You see?" Drago says. "Nothing. We are wasting time."

"That took all of three seconds," I point out.

"Three seconds I could have spent rebuilding Mother Russia." He grins at me and gyrates in his seat a bit. Drago has a fantasy of finding a bunch of wives—totally legal for the past nine hundred years—and fathering a new Soviet Empire. I've pointed out that his replacement master race would look a lot like the current one, except all deformed and in-bred.

"Not even a grizzly bear would have your children," Chuy says. She's my second in command. Got my back every step of the way. Wants to find our people as much as I do. I'm not sure Drago has given his team of Spetnaz a second thought.

"Is possible with genetics, no?" Drago says. "Grizzly children. Ruling the stars. Eating all the people. Space bears!" He has a hearty laugh, and I can't help but chuckle at the image of bears, floating through space, gobbling up naïve future Nazis.

Ach! Vut iz dish madness! Ein Bears Shpashen!

Everyone in the future has a fake-sounding German accent. Not to say they're pretending to have an accent. It's real. It's just not genuine. Sometime during the early Union, the powers that be revered World War II Germany, and they wanted to sound like good ol' Adolf. But they were also too lazy to learn the language, so they forced a generation to fake an accent. Every generation since has passed it on. Everyone in the future has silly German accents, but they no longer remember why.

That's right, the Fourth Reich didn't come from the Aryan mother-land. It came from the good 'ol U.S. of A. Chuy and I missed the official start of the new white supremacy movement by a few decades, which means the human race got just a few decades of viewing racism as bad before...

Well...

Genocide...

I shake my head, good humor fading at the thought of all those people succumbing to a plague created to selectively exterminate most of the human race.

Sick fuckers.

I wish there were someone responsible still alive to kick in the nuts, but unless the present-day Union is being led by Yoda, the assholes who wiped out billions of people are long since dead.

Now in a mood, I stand from my commander's chair. "How's the air?"

"Looks muy bueno," Chuy says. "Should feel like home. Gravity is a little lower than Earth, but everything is within safety limits."

"Dandy," I say. "See you down there."

The *Bitch'n* and every other spacecraft in the galaxy moves through space, over massive distances, almost instantly, using something called a Slew Drive. How does it work? No clue. Don't care. Someone once ex-plained it like this: the *Bitch'n* 'rotates' into the fourth dimension—which is not time, but some other kind of place where time or space moves differently, or is compressed... I don't know. But in that fourth dimen-sion, the *Bitch'n* can move just a small distance—let's say a kilometer—and then rotate back out and have traveled ten light years. Everywhere in the galaxy is just a quick hop, skip, and a jump away for those brave enough to face the unknown dangers that lurk on the far side of a rotation.

Which is mostly boredom, and sometimes Porter's swamp ass. His BCS body-odor scrubbers work overtime, and sometimes they short out.

But no one else in the Union has what I keep on my belt: a miniature Slew Drive. It lets me teleport between locations, Star Trek style, but it takes an hour to charge between rotations. Wouldn't want to use it in the outers of space, but ship-to-ship transportation works like a charm, as does ship-to-planet.

"Not again," Chuy complains. "We don't know whaaaa—tttt—zzzz—"

I roll out of the third dimension and into the fourth. Not much here to look at aside from bright white light and open space. The Slew Drive does its thing, and I take a single step. Then I roll back out of the fourth dimension and onto the planet's surface.

Chuy was trying to warn me that we don't know what's on the surface. Despite my complaints, the only way to check for unadvanced life-forms is to have a looksee for yourself. The future is advanced, but it's still a lot clunky and unintuitive.

The white fades and I'm presented with a blue sky, luminous clouds, and a purple landscape. The ground beneath my feet is…squishy. I bounce from foot to foot. Water seeps out from a myriad of tiny holes.

"The ground is a sponge…" If the whole planet is like this, that could be a problem. The purple landscape stretches as far as I can see in every direction. It's pocked with thousands, maybe millions, of round puddles, each one ten to twenty feet across and separated by thirty-foot gaps. None of it is uniform. Some puddles are closer together than others.

Weird.

"Sponge World," I say, bouncing and smiling. My job is to find habitable worlds, but I honestly don't give a rip. That's not why I'm here, and not why—

Uh-oh.

Movement.

Three puddles away.

Water sloshes.

Something's in there…

I reach for my rifle.

Shit.

In my rush to reach the surface, I forgot to bring it. But I'm always wearing my handgun. I make the bullets myself, because future people use 'lazzer' weapons that cauterize wounds. And yeah, that's lazzer with two Zs. Somewhere along the past few hundred years, the spelling of some words evolved, usually not for the better, like with lazzer. I prefer to shoot projectiles that let people—or alien monsters—bleed out.

Before I can draw my gun, the most warped-looking thing I've ever seen in my life—like a hairless sloth with skin stretched between its fore and hind limbs—explodes out of the puddle. It glides to the next puddle, belly flops into the water, and then flings itself into the air again, all while snorting like some kind of angry horse.

"Look at this spaz..."

When it lands in the puddle just fifteen feet away, its trajectory and intent are clear—it's hungry.

And I look like food.

2

Evolution is a sick bastard.

Every planet is invariably different, some more than others. Purple Sponge World here is one of the weirder landscapes I've set foot on, but this isn't a giant leap or even a small step for mankind. It's a shit show, and I'm the main attraction.

The puddle jumper is airborne again, gliding between bodies of water, directly toward my stupid ass. I shout in surprise—and honestly a little bit of *I just pissed my pants fear*—when it opens its mouth. Instead of teeth, which would have been totally normal on most planets, a hundred wormy tentacles blossom and reach out. At the writhing mass's core is a pulsing and churning throat filled with spikes.

It's an aquatic, flying meatgrinder.

Chuy's never going to let me live this down.

If I survive.

A plan flashes through my mind. Old school visualization. See what you're going to do, and then do it. If you've got a firm grasp of the laws of physics and what your body is capable of, it works like a charm.

In my mind's eye, I come to a sudden stop, drop to one knee, raise my weapon, and fire a single round into the puddle jumper's limb. Animals are animals, no matter what planet they're on. Letting it know that I'm not prey will send it scurrying away.

But none of that happens.

When I plant my feet to stop running, water oozes out of the landscape. My left foot stays planted. My right slides out.

"Oh, shit!" I manage to shout, as I perform as close to a split as my groin will allow. And then a little bit further. I spasm and flop to the side with an "Oow!"

On the plus side, my body bounces against the spongy ground, which breaks my fall, just in time. The puddle jumper glides over me, its wormy face reaching out and grazing my body as it passes. Its pale stomach is swollen and translucent. Through the skin, I see wriggling wormy things with black eyes. If they're parasites, I should probably put the thing out of its misery. But the possibility of those little freaky assholes being babies tempers my desire to unleash my inner Rambo.

With a pistol...

Whatever.

My entire back is wet, soaked with the otherworldly water, which smells kind of like algae. I pat down my body, searching for any sudden pain or missing limbs, ending with my crotch. Everything is unharmed and in place.

I sit up, gun aimed, but finger no longer on the trigger.

What would it say about me if the first thing I did upon setting foot on an alien world was shoot a pregnant mother?

The puddle jumper splashes down twenty feet away, disappearing beneath the water. For a moment, I think it's given up. Then I notice the water. It's spinning. Becoming a whirlpool.

The puddle jumper is swimming in circles.

Building speed.

"Aww, shit," I say, and I jump to my feet, intending to put some distance between us. My pulled groin protests, turning my sprint into a pathetic limp. I curse with every step. "Shit. Fuck. Shit."

The sound of sloshing water propels me past the pain. I've dealt with worse, but it's been a long time since I've lived the rugged life of a Marine on mission and in battle.

I've gone soft, I think, and then I grunt as I holster my weapon and pick up speed.

I tap my throat mic.

"Chuy, what's your ETA? The local wildlife is hostile. I could use a pick-up sooner than later."

Our comms are implanted, allowing me to communicate with any member of the crew. All I need to do is tap the side of my neck to activate it, and then start my sentence with their first name. Sometimes I just leave it active and just need to say someone's name and start chatting, like they were in the room. Her response comes in loud and clear: hysterical laughter broadcast right into my head.

Great...she's watching.

"Chuy!" I say over her wheezing. "This is serious!"

"I can see that, Jean-Claude," she says through fits of laughter.

I grit my teeth. Before being ripped out of 1989, my team watched *Bloodsport* together. It was an okay movie, but the man's ungodly crotch made all of us squirm. Van Damme either has no balls, or broken hips. Either way, ouch. But good for him, I guess. He's the only *dude* in Hollywood who got famous for spreading his legs.

Was the only dude... That world is long since gone, and since all media from the years before the ethnic purge has been destroyed, we'll never get to see any other movies in which he and his elastic taint starred.

A splash turns me around.

The puddle jumper is airborne again, gliding right for me.

But I'm ready for it this time, and I'm not even going to use my gun. I'm going to use a Marine's first and most dangerous weapon—his mind. The creature might be perfectly evolved to hunt in this environment, but like Cro Magnon man facing a saber-toothed cat, I'm going to survive by outsmarting it.

Instead of running away directly toward another puddle, allowing it to continue its fluid attack, I'm charging *between* two puddles thirty feet apart. The next puddle in front of me is a hundred feet off—and the puddle jumper won't come close to reaching it.

If it wants to keep using the water as a launching pad, it's going to have to veer off.

And that's going to buy me time.

And distance.

Then all I need to do is rinse and repeat, until Chuy arrives.

Part of me would rather get sucked into that meatgrinder maw than face Chuy's ridicule, but I'm not going to let anything or anyone end my life until I know that every member of my team is safe.

I watch the puddle jumper's approach. It twitches its hooked forelimbs back and forth, adjusting its trajectory. The creature's black eyes are locked on me. I look for intelligence in them, but I see only hunger, a supposition that is supported by the tentacles now jutting out of its mouth.

I'm past the two pools.

The puddle jumper is going to veer off in three...two...

My brow furrows.

Two and a half...

"Seriously?!" I slide to the spongy ground like Ricky Henderson stealing second. It's not enough.

As the puddle jumper glides toward me, closing in for the kill, I'm forced onto my stomach. I reach out with my fingers and punch through the flexible ground. Chunks tear free, but I'm jolted to a stop, and the alien predator overshoots me again.

I flop onto my back, totally soaked now, and I watch the puddle jumper land, hooking one clawed limb into the soft terrain and using its momentum to pull off a fluid 180-degree turn.

My feet slip twice before finding traction, but then they propel me away from the puddle jumper. And just in time. It swings one of those hooked claws at me. The near miss spritzes the back of my head with the water dripping off its body.

I can *feel* the thing chasing me. Its weight compresses the sponge, sending out rolling shockwaves. The ground beneath my feet becomes unstable. It's like running on a trampoline while the fat kid at the party is jumping on it, cake in hand, laughing at you with blue frosting-coated teeth.

Bobby Brumelstroot. A jackass from middle school. I still feel angry about my childhood bullies on occasion, but then I remember they're all dead and I feel a little better.

The puddle jumper adds humor to horror by roaring. I've heard a lot of animal calls over the years, both on Earth and on other planets. They're generally the same—loud, deep, and intimidating.

The puddle jumper's roar sounds like a wet fart blasted from the ass of a hippopotamus with irritable bowel syndrome.

And I can't help but laugh so hard I nearly fall on my face when the ground beneath me sinks, and I miss a step.

"God's sake!" I shout, and I draw my pistol again.

Have no choice.

The thing is gaining on me. In a few seconds, my ground-up head will be in its gullet.

Shooting a stationary target while moving is a challenge. Hitting a moving target while in motion is all but impossible, unless you're unleashing hell from a mini-gun. Winging a moving target while sprinting through a fucking bouncy house...

Well, that's exactly the kind of challenge for which God made me.

When the ground beneath me rolls up, I jump.

The extra upward momentum and lower gravity propel me into the air, even without damn flying-squirrel membranes between my arms and legs. I twist around, taking aim, and—

"Gah!"

The puddle jumper's mouth is *right* there! Its tentacles graze my cheeks. Little barbs at the ends hook onto my skin.

I fire a round.

The creature jolts.

The tentacles tear from my cheeks.

I land on my back, gun still aimed at the puddle jumper, and I slide ten feet before coming to a stop.

The creature twitches its leg while spinning in circles. It's confused by the pain. Unsure of where it came from. So, I reinforce the message.

I stand and point my gun in the air. "Hey, asshole!"

Black eyes twitch toward me.

I fire the gun again.

The puddle jumper flinches. Takes a step back.

Message received.

"If you're done screwing around with the wildlife," Chuy says in my ear, "you might want to start running again."

"Situation contained," I say. "I showed it who's the boss."

"Hijo de las mil putas," she whispers. "Have a look around you, Tony Danza."

While the puddle jumper continues to back pedal, several more pools of water are swirling now. My gunshot woke the natives. "I'm just...ugh..."

"You reap what you sow, cabrón. Now, start running."

Lil' Bitch'n—what I named the boxy, shit-shaped transport vehicle that carried us away from Earth for the first and last time—descends ahead of me, still moving forward, hovering a few feet off the ground. Chuy stands in the open rear hatchway, still laughing and waving me on.

For a moment, I'm confused by what I'm seeing.

Why is she still laugh—

Goddamnit...

She's reenacting the final scene of *Megaforce*, a movie that is more 80s than the 80s could have ever hoped to be. Knowing I have no choice but to play out her humiliating recreation, I run for the open hatch. She's all smiles and encouragement. "Deeds, not words," she shouts, and I nearly smile back.

She's a pain in my ass. She's also my best friend.

We'll laugh about this whole debacle for the next few months.

Then her smile fades, and her rifle comes up.

I glance back. A dozen puddle jumpers are behind me. Some airborne. Some running. Several of them are much larger than the one I faced down.

"Hold your fire," I say, and I pour on the speed despite the pain in my crotch and the water-logged clothing tugging against my skin. Chuy shouts a command to whoever is flying—probably Drago—and *Lil Bitch'n* comes to a stop.

I plan out my approach, timing each step perfectly.

Then the spacecraft reverses straight toward me!

I leap at the last second, soar twenty feet inside the cargo bay, crash to the floor, and roll to a stop at the far end. By the time I've righted myself, the rear hatch has closed, and we're moving forward again. Puddle jumpers thud against the hull, and then we ascend toward the heavens from whence we came.

Chuy stands above me. "You injured?"

"My pride," I say, and then I move and grunt. "Pretty sure I pulled a hammy, too."

She shakes her head and contains her laughter for just a moment. Then she slides down next to me, our backs against the wall. "I know you're eager to move on to the next planet—"

"And maybe our people."

"—but this was reckless." She gives me a stern look. "You're not going to save anyone if you're dead, and I can't do this without you." She smiles at me. It's damn near sweet. Then she adds, "Next time you pull something like that, I'm going to punch you in the dick."

She didn't need to threaten consequences. I learned my lesson the moment my legs split apart. "Fair enough."

"Good," she says. Then she raises her arm and taps a button to start a holographic projection. It starts with an aerial view of me standing on the surface, surrounded by puddles, not yet running for my life. "Now then... I recorded the whole thing."

3

The future is clunky. The technology is impressive—Slew Drives, artificial gravity, energy weapons—but I always pictured the future being sleek and stylish. It's actually kind of boxy, dark, and metallic. And the buttons. What's with all the buttons? The bridge's controls are like an homage to Eagle, the Apollo lunar module that landed on the moon... which I'm told was first colonized by 3D printed cement structures made from regolith (moon dirt) and piss.

The *Bitch'n*'s interior is comparable to a roomy submarine. Lots of big spaces. Tall ceilings. But there is nothing pretty or inviting about it. Angles everywhere. Not many windows, though I made sure my quarters had one. I suppose the harsh, utilitarian design—or lack thereof—is a byproduct of space travel's first conquerors being evil sunzabitches.

How pissed would they be to know that I exist?

Just thinking about it makes me smile.

I should take up Drago's plan. Get a harem. Single-handedly repopulate the galaxy with people of color. The idea of being a dad frightens me, though. My father was the epitome of sacrificial love, working every day of his life to provide for his family. Right up until the day he died of a heart attack. He set a high bar, which I've applied to my life in the Marines and to those under my command. Given how that's turned out, I'm pretty sure I'm not really father material.

One kid would be bad enough, but hundreds? Thousands?

Exo-hunting pays well, but not that well.

I roll onto my side, body still aching from my off-ship adventure. Future medicine works fast. I'll be good in a few hours. But there's still enough discomfort to make me think twice about doing stupid things.

My bed is a glorified cot, but it's next to a circular porthole about the size of a tire. Aside from the bridge, it usually has the best view on the ship. Sponge World fills the window, its violet surface lit by a yellow sun. From here, it's beautiful and inviting. At first glance, the Union is going to have a hard time believing the planet is not suitable for colonization. But our post-debacle analysis revealed that the 'continents' are actually giant floating masses, impossible to build on. The puddle jumpers got lucky. Had the planet been habitable, they'd have been facing extermination.

Just another species wiped out by the selfish desires of humanity.

People might not be warring anymore, but the lesser denizens of the galaxy aren't getting a fair shake. Extinction of every species that doesn't taste good is acceptable, as long as the proliferation of people continues.

When God said, 'Be fruitful and multiply,' I really don't think this is what He had in mind.

Religion, like animals, is a thing of the past. The white supremacist movement was birthed from religious groups, but belief in a higher moral power went out of style once power was achieved.

I was never a churchgoer; I'm agnostic.

Chuy on the other hand...is a staunch Catholic, even now. She's the only one left in the universe.

Does that make her the Pope? Space Pope Chuy?

I'll have to ask her.

Chuy's callsign is the nickname version of Jesus, which was pronounced 'Hey Zeus' en Español, a popular name in Mexico once upon a time. She chose Chuy as a callsign, not because of her beliefs, but because Jesus is who she sends our enemies to meet. Probably not the most Jesus-like rationalization, but neither were the Crusades—all five of them. Her real name, which I'm forbidden from speaking aloud, is Sophia Calleja Pérez. It's not even close to a match for her personality.

Like naming a German shepherd Rose, Cuddles, or Gertrude.

I lean closer to the window. Huff my breath onto it, fogging it up. My finger squeaks over the glass, as I draw a crude recreation of my own pooch, a corgi named Attila. When not deployed on missions or at a movie with the team, I spent my time with Attila. She was my companion for seven years. Of everyone left behind in the twentieth century, I miss her company the most.

"Sorry, buddy," I say, hoping that she ended up in a good home. Then I wipe the image away and roll onto my back.

Another sleepless 'night.' I tell the crew that my lack of sleep has to do more with being accustomed to a legitimate day-and-night provided by the sun and the rotation of a planet. Truth is, I'm plagued by fears that I won't be able to save my people. That they've been dead for five years.

And if that's true, my last mission—the thing that makes me...*me*—will be over. I'm not sure I'll be able to handle that, because there really is no place for me in this future world.

And that's what planet 003189 is for.

According to Union records, the planet's atmosphere is unbreathable to humans, the temperature variation between day and night is a hundred degrees, and the water there is so acidic it melts skin.

Couldn't be farther from the truth.

Planet 003189, which Chuy and I call 'Elysium,' is a paradise. It's Earth-like in every way that matters, aside from the fact that there is no intelligent life. Not even Drago knows the place's true value. When this mission ends, it's where I'm going to retire, free from the bleached-white Union and this oversized coffin. I'm fond of *Bitch'n*, mostly because of its name, but I look forward to every moment I spend somewhere else.

If I recover my people, they'll be welcome to join us, or to pursue their own path through the stars. If my mission fails...Chuy and I will have the place to ourselves. Who knows, maybe we'll eventually get together. She's my closest friend. Has been for a long time. She's a looker, too, and a great cook. But we're too similar—if that makes sense. It would be like falling in love with myself. If I had boobs. But I'm not currently my favorite person.

"Hey," Chuy says through the comms. Her voice is unexpected, but it doesn't startle.

"Hey," I reply.

"You're awake."

"You know I am."

"Going to have to do something about that," she says. "You're still human, you know."

"Going to have to do something about that, too," I say. "Think they could genetically engineer me to not need sleep?"

"I think that's how God made you already," she says.

"Maybe." I turn to the view again. Hasn't changed. "What's up?"

"We have a new set of celestial coordinates."

"Already?" I sit up.

"This planet was strike number seven for us, and planet 001045 is ready to pop. They say."

I slide my bare feet to the cold metal floor.

"You know...we don't need to do this," she says.

"I'm not ready to retire." I force the words out.

"Neither am I," she says.

"What other job in the Union would you want to do?" I can't imagine either of us spending any real time among this future society outside of our skeleton crew, to whom we've grown accustomed.

"We go outside the Union," she says, and I can hear her smiling.

"Really? Pirates?"

"How did you know!?"

I know because I've considered the same thing. It would be fun. And easy. But there's a stumbling block I just can't get past. "So, the end result of us traveling a thousand years in the future would be to reignite people's xenophobic stereotypes about black men and Mexicans?"

"I was born in LA, gilipollas. And what does it matter? After we're dead, the galaxy will be bleached clean again, probably forever."

It's a fair point. "I'll think about it...after I give up."

"Which isn't today?"

"Not today," I confirm. Probably not for many more years. "Drago."

"Dah?" He replies from somewhere else aboard the ship.

"Rotate us when you're ready. I'll be there in five mikes."

"Always with mikes. Why not say 'minutes' like normal person?"

"I'm not a normal person," I say, and I toggle off my comms. I'm supposed to keep them active when in dangerous situations or rotating through the galaxy—in case something goes wrong—but I don't feel like arguing with Drago right now, and the odds of things going sideways before I reach the bridge are disappointingly nil.

I hit the shower. The high-pressure mist stings, but it hits every nook and cranny with enough scalding water to clean even Drago. I close my eyes and wait for it to finish. Then, I hold my breath as the fans kick on, whisking away every drop to be recycled into drinking water, or someone else's shower.

As a typhoon of warm air swirls around me, I feel a momentary shift in equilibrium. I open my eyes to endless white light. And then, in a blink, the shower's interior returns.

We've rotated already. Drago must be bored.

I step out of the bathroom, throw on some homemade boxers, and head back into my quarters. Trying to lighten my mood, I start whistling *Axel F* by Harold Falter-something. I couldn't remember his name in the 80s, let alone now. I shake out my freshly cleaned pants, slip my leg in, and get stuck in a fold. I'm hopping around the room, cursing up a storm, when the door whooshes open and Chuy runs inside.

"Gah!" I shout in surprise, losing my balance, and spilling onto the bed.

"Sorry," she says, but she looks too frazzled for me to care about the intrusion.

I withdraw my leg from the pants and stand. "What is it?"

"Step Four," she says. "We got a hit."

"Show me," I say, standing in the middle of the bridge.

Porter spins around in his chair, mouth open to talk. But he stops upon seeing me. Closes his mouth. Furrows his brow. He's got a bearded John Candy thing going on. Like someone's uncle who might be an alcoholic, or a pedophile. "Ahh."

"Spit it out," I say, quickly losing patience.

Drago starts chuckling. Burnett and Morton turn to look at the commotion and start laughing, too.

"Hey, Buckaroo Banzai," Chuy says, stepping onto the bridge with a smile on her face, "you forget something?" She tosses a wad of clothing into my bare chest.

I sit in the captain's chair, trying hard to not flinch from its cold surface. The bridge is laid out something like the *USS Enterprise*, but more rectangular and with Klingon décor sensibilities. And the viewscreen...isn't. It's just a large window through which we can see the endlessness of space. "Anyone who doesn't cut the shit and tell me what you found is going to be cleaning the hull next time we rotate."

Porter's face falls flat, suddenly serious. Burnett and Morton, too. Drago just laughs harder.

I look Porter in the eyes. "Spill it."

"We ran through the four—"

I gesture my hand in rapid circles. "I already got the verbal foreplay, thanks. Give me the details."

Porter sits up straighter, blinks a few times and says, "We found a signal on 104.1 hertz. The same high-pitched squeal the three of you radiate." He glances at Drago, Chuy, and then back to me.

"It came from the planet's surface?" I ask, slipping into my pants, this time successfully. "It wasn't some random radio burst from a distant pulsar or something?"

"It came from the center of the planet's only landmass," Burnett says.

I pull a tight, black, long-sleeve undershirt on. "Show me."

The center of the bridge fills with a hologram of the planet we're orbiting. Two thirds of it is water, the rest is a massive continent stretching north to south and capped with ice on the poles. But it looks like it's cracking apart. Large seas cut into the mass, fueled by rivers large enough to see from space.

"It's like an exo-planet Pangea," I say.

"That's exactly what it is," Morton says. "There are actually eight separate continents all squashed together and very slowly separating. In a billion years—"

"Radio signal," I say, redirecting them back to what I care about.

A red blip appears near the center of the land mass.

"This is where the signal appeared," Porter says. "The environment is equatorial, hot, humid, and lush, with some kind of jungle. The atmosphere is rich with oxygen, but not enough to be toxic. You can—"

"Porter…" I stand, buckling my belt. "Why did you use past tense to describe the signal?"

"Oh," he says. "Because it's gone."

"Explain 'gone.'"

Porter looks nervous, like he's been caught in a lie, even though he's not. My crew is afraid of me. Not because I've ever actually hurt them, but because they know I could. And I let them think it. The truth is, they're my people now. I'd fight for them just like I am for my twentieth century team. They might be descended from space Nazis, but they're closer to happy-go-lucky basset hounds.

"Well, it was there for a few seconds," he says. "And then…it wasn't."

"Lasted six point five seconds," Drago says. "Stopped just after Chuy left bridge."

"Any explanations?" I ask.

Burnett raises his hand.

I huff out a laugh, shake my head, and roll my eyes. "You don't need to raise your hand."

"Oh..." He lowers his hand. "Okay. Uhh, the signal's disappearance can be explained by one of two logical conclusions..."

"Which are...?"

"If it came from someone like the three of you, it's possible the signal is being blocked."

"Blocked by what?"

"Given the rugged landscape, I'd guess a cave."

"And the second possibility?"

Somehow, Morton pales a little further. "They're...ahh, they're dead."

I throw on the last of my clothing. Reach for the personal Slew Drive on my belt.

"Dark Horse," Chuy says, as my finger hovers over the activation button. She gives me a 'Don't you dare' look, shooting me with imaginary .50 caliber rounds. I hesitate because I know she'll absolutely follow through on her dick punch threat.

"This is different," I say.

"You are right," Drago says, standing from his chair and stretching his arms. "This time is important to all of us."

I hadn't realized Drago cared about finding my people. I thought he was just along for the ride on the only ship in the galaxy that still carried real soldiers.

"We go together," he says, and he bumps into me as he passes. "Also, you have no gun." To Chuy he asks, "Was always so forgetful?"

"No," she says, eyes still on me. "He wasn't."

I remove my hand from the Slew Drive. "Fine. Let's get this done double-time."

As Chuy and Drago exit the bridge, I turn to Morton, who has managed to get himself in decent shape over the past few years, I *think* because he's secretly in love with Chuy. In shape or not, his large beak of a nose and his smile that looks like a sneer aren't doing him any favors. "Get *Lil Bitch'n* ready. You're flying."

To Burnett I say, "Prep the medical bay. Just in case." To Porter, I add, "Remember when you told me you had an idea on how to reduce the recharge time on this?" I pat the Slew Drive on my hip.

"Yes...?"

"Get it done."

"Yes, sir." He salutes.

Ugh. These guys...

I leave before something sarcastic slips out. It's not their fault they're placid and malleable, but it still irks me. I sometimes prefer Drago's incessant asshole routine. But only because I know it's an act. He slips up sometimes, usually when he's been drinking his homebrewed swill. He had a wife. A son. Parents and grandparents. All of them were alive, and close, when we were whisked away. All of them lived their lives without him.

I was an only child. My parents and grandparents had passed away. Atilla was the best dog in the whole world, yes, she was, but that's not the same as losing a son and wife.

Chuy left behind her parents and two brothers, so they've both got me beat in the twentieth-century baggage department.

At least I still have a chance to save my extended family.

I step into the armory. Chuy slaps a magazine into her rifle. Like all of our projectile weapons, they're custom designs built to our specifications by the dynamic trio. They're vaguely futuristic, but in very 1980s ways. What they all have in common is that they throw a lot of heavy tungsten, very quickly.

"Look at this moron," she says, and she nods toward Drago.

He's got two handguns strapped on his chest. Two more on his hips. He's got a rifle with an attached pulse grenade launcher over his back and two sawed off shotguns in his hands.

I look him up and down.

"You going to hold the Hot Gates against the Persian army all on your own?"

Drago raises an eyebrow. "First, I do not know reference."

"It's history," I say, "so I'm not surprised."

"Second, better to be prepared and not need, than need and not have."

"A cliché spoken like a Neanderthal, but...you're not wrong. And Chuy's not wrong, either." I pick up a magazine and slide it into my armor. Then another. And another. And another. And another. I keep my eyes on Drago's the whole time, until I've loaded myself with ten magazines. "Same amount of fire power. A fraction of the weight."

Drago grimaces. And then shrugs. "Are we going?"

Five minutes later, we're strapped into *Lil Bitch'n*, punching through the atmosphere.

The view through the windshield goes from fiery orange to white, as we slip out of the upper atmosphere and through a layer of cloud cover. And then, the world below turns green.

"Looks like the Amazon," Chuy says.

"The vegetation here is larger than anything that grew on Earth during your time period," Morton says, getting all of our attention. "I've been doing research. Like you suggested. Anyway...the trees here are an average of five hundred feet tall."

"Five hundred...feet?" I ask. "Are you sure?"

"You'll see for yourself in a moment," he says, taking us down toward the growing wall of green. "Just need to find a gap in the—here we go."

Lil Bitch'n twists and descends. It's an impressive maneuver. Bold for Morton. He's been learning about more than just ancient history. And he's right about the trees. We spend a full minute watching a trunk grow thicker as we descend. It's covered in a strata of vines and moss, which appear to change species at different altitudes. Each tree in this vast forest is its own ecosystem.

And from what I've seen, this planet is prime real estate for the Union. I feel protective of this place already, and I would consider hiding it if Morton hadn't already seen it up close and personal. I don't know if my crew's loyalty to me supersedes the Union's will, and I don't want to put it to the test.

Not yet, anyway.

We set down between two tree trunks that are a good fifty feet wide.

I unbuckle and hurry to the rear hatch, which is opening as I reach it. I step outside, and I'm blown away by the scent of Earth-plant decay and the sweet smell of flowers. The extra oxygen in the atmosphere invigorates me, and for the briefest of moments, I forget why I'm here.

Then I raise the radio signal detector and spin in a circle, waiting for it to squeak.

And...nothing.

Whoever set it off is still hidden.

Or still dead.

I step out onto the solid ground. Nothing spongy about it.

"Gonna suck telling them about this place," Chuy says, stepping up beside me.

"So, we do not tell," Drago says. "If Dark Horse can claim planet, so can I." He gives me a wink when I look surprised that he knows. "You think I don't know about your planet, but I am watching. Like hawk in sky." He takes a deep breath, expanding his weapon-laden chest. "Is good for future Russian home world."

Can't tell if he's joking. Don't really care. I activate my comms. "Morton, how far are we from the signal's last known location?"

"It was two klicks to the north," he says. "Did I get that right? Is it klicks or mikes?"

"You got it right," I say, and I toggle off my comms. "Who's up for a hike?"

Chuy strikes out with me. Drago, who is carrying a few hundred more pounds than he should be, grunts and then follows, which is good, because there's a good chance whoever we find—if they're alive—would react badly to seeing his face first. Not because they'd recognize him, but because he's so damn ugly.

5

Everything about this world makes me feel like an insect. The trees are skyscrapers. The leaves, king size blankets. We're wading through what I think would be classified as grass, but each blade is like a broadsword—and just as sharp. The vegetation forced me to put on gloves, and let Drago take point. He's hacking away with his machete-sized, eagle-head knife. I'm not sure why it's important to him, but it's his most prized possession.

And I can see why. The machete-sized blade hacks through the razor reeds, trailblazing a path northward.

But it's also making a lot of noise, the metal *tinging* as it lops the stems down. There could be an army in the grass with us, and we'd never know.

Blind and deaf, I focus on my only other sense that might detect trouble before it's knocking on our door. I sniff, long and deep, but everything is foreign. I weed out the scents I'm sure are vegetation—earthy decay and sweetness. The cut grass is fragrant, like roses.

I breathe in again, detecting something else in the mix. Something fetid. Like vinegar.

Drago stops mid-swing, his body going rigid.

He smells it, too.

I'd like to have only bad things to say about Drago, but he's a competent soldier, and I'm confident enough in myself to admit that his training as a KGB Spetsnaz operator makes my Marine Rapid Reaction Force training look like summer camp. He's a hairy bastard, but he knows his shit.

In the silence that follows, my ears perk up. I can hear wildlife all around us, buzzing and singing, but we haven't seen anything yet. Not even an insect. And that's fine by me. I'm here for one reason, and it's not a wildlife safari.

A vibration moves through my body.

"What is that?" Chuy whispers.

"Is sound," Drago says. "Listen."

He's right. At the fringe of my ability to hear is a low rumble. "It's distant."

"Thunder?" Chuy asks.

Last thing we need is to get stuck in an alien storm. Animals can be unpredictable and dangerous at times, but our closest calls are always weather related. Lightning, hail, blobs of viscous bacteria, rotting corpses, and flesh-eating larva. You never know what the skies of a new planet are going to rain down.

"Thunder doesn't explain smell," Drago observes.

"Not sure it *can* be explained. Could be anything."

"Mrm..." Drago swings, severing several strands of grass. Stands still again. Listening. Nothing in the forest has changed. The chorus of creatures continues unabated.

He swings again and pushes forward.

Despite our progress being slowed by stopping to listen, I don't complain. I'm in a rush, but not to die.

The deep rumble rolls through us again, vibrating in my lungs. A little louder this time. I toggle my mic. "Morton, is there a storm system to the east?"

"Umm, no," he says. "Some light cloud cover, but nothing that looks like a storm."

"No lightning?"

"On the west side of the continent, but that system would take days to reach you."

"What about seismic activity? Volcanos?"

"Most of the planet's volcanic activity is underwater. And on the coasts. Nothing in the middle of the continent. Buuut, you're right, there is an unusual amount of seismic noise that's louder than the average planet. Could be because the eight tectonic plates are moving away from each other, albeit very slowly in human terms."

"What does that mean? In human terms?"

"Uhh, well, it's been a thousand years since you visited Earth," Morton says.

"Did not visit," Drago says. "Lived."

"Lived. Yes. Earth's tectonic plates move up to five centimeters per year. In the past thousand, that's roughly a hundred and sixty-four feet. If you were to return today, the planet would look the same. It took Earth's Pangea ninety million years–give or take fifty million–to break apart fully. The supercontinent on this planet will take roughly ten million years to separate."

"That's…" *Useless,* I think. "…interesting. Let me know if anything changes. Weather. Seismic activity. Whatever."

"Is everything okay?" he asks.

"Dandy," I say.

"That's what you say when things aren't actually optimal," he says.

Chuy looks back at me. "He's not wrong."

"Thanks for the tip. Over and out." I motion for Drago to push onward.

It takes another ten minutes to exit the field of tall grass. The forest floor on the other side is a mix of hard-packed soil and crisscrossing roots the width of a bus. I think the trees here are smaller until I realize that they're actually thirty-foot-tall ferns.

We come to a stop beside one of the ferns. It's lying on the ground, compressed into the soil.

Drago shakes his head. "This world is strange. I no longer like."

I ignore the comment but agree with the sentiment. My nerves are wangjangled. Something is very wrong here. A voice in the back of my head is telling me to call it. To regroup. Try to understand the way this place works, and then come back. That would be the smart play.

But I can't stop myself from imagining the plight of whoever ended up marooned here. We need to find them now.

I'm about to push on when I see a footprint.

I crouch beside it.

A human footprint. Barefoot.

"Is small foot," Drago says.

"A woman," Chuy adds.

"Carter," I say, lifting the radio wave detector and moving in a slow circle. "C'mon..."

It squeals, high-pitched and irritating.

I'm about to charge toward the sound's source when I notice that the jungle has gone silent.

Drago looks up at the trees around us. "Shit."

"Is this because of us?" Chuy asks, weapon shouldered.

"Dark Horse," Morton says in my ear. "Seismic activity is spiking."

"How far out?"

"Five klicks," he says, "but...it's getting closer."

"What the hell does that mean?" Earthquakes roll through the earth. I know that. But I don't think that's what he's trying to say.

"It means...I think...I think they're footsteps."

Before I can respond to what my modern brain thinks is insane, my reptile brain freezes in place just as another airborne vibrato slams into my body, this time loud enough for me to hear the organic roar behind it.

You've got to be kidding me...

I aim the radio detector toward the signal's source, hear the shriek again, and break into a run. Chuy is right behind me. Drago and all his guns can't keep up. He gives up and stops by a row of boulders. "Will guard way back. You must hurry!"

Weaving our way between ferns, following the signal, I catch a few more signs that Carter passed through here, and recently. I'm lost in thought when rounding a fifty-foot-wide tree. I nearly barrel into the carcass of an animal the size of a rhino. The six-legged thing is dark green and lying on its side. And it's not just dead. It was killed. Hunted. A flank of its thigh has been carved away.

"Did Carter do this?" Chuy asks.

Hard to imagine a woman who'd never been on a military op taking down something this big. "Maybe she's made friends with some locals?"

"Let's hope not," Chuy says, and I understand her concern. The Union's protocol for first contact with another intelligent species is draconian and paranoid: genocide. If this planet was found to host a sentient species, it would be laid to waste from a safe distance. They might not loathe people of color anymore, but their fear of the unknown is real and powerful.

A spear impales the ground between me and Chuy, catching us both off guard. "Don't fucking move." It's Carter. How she got behind us without being detected is a mystery. "Who are y—"

I turn my face to the side, giving her a profile view.

"D-Dark Horse?"

"The one and only," I say, turning around slowly and trying to hide my emotions. Our previous relationship was brief and somewhat combative, but I've spent a long time searching for any sign of my people without a glimmer of hope. Finding her means the rest of them are out there. I'm happy enough to hug her, but she doesn't look ready for a warm embrace.

Carter is perched atop a fern behind us, another spear raised to throw, two more on her back. She's dressed in rags, covered in dirt, and somehow still looks like she should be in a Sports Illustrated Swimsuit Issue.

She drops down, clinging to the fern. It bends under her weight and lowers her to the ground, springing back up when she releases it.

"Took you long enough," she says.

"Huh?"

"To find me. Where is the rest of your team?"

"The rest of my..." I squint at her. "What do you think is happening here?"

"We're not on Earth," she says. "I figured that out pretty quickly."

I nod.

"And we've been separated for the past three years."

"Not exactly."

Carter eyes me. And then Chuy. Looks us up and down. "You two haven't been here…"

"On this planet?" Chuy says. "No."

"On another planet?" Carter sounds stunned, but she's catching on quickly.

"More than one," I tell her. "And it's been five years, not three."

"But how did you get here? How did you find me?"

I point the radio wave detector at her. It squeals. "Could hear you from orbit." I point it at Chuy, and then myself, revealing that we're all emitting the signal. "We've been literally searching the galaxy."

That hits home, and it gets a hint of a smile.

"Not just for you," Chuy adds. "The whole team."

"And me," Drago says, catching us off guard.

Carter whips around and throws one of her spears at Drago. He leans to the side, allowing the perfectly aimed projectile to sail past and stab a tree. Had he been anyone other than a Spetsnaz, he'd have been impaled.

"You found spy lady," he says. "Is good. Can we go now?"

I shake my head at him. "What happened to guarding the way back?"

"You're working with one of the Soviets?" Carter asks, gripping another spear.

"Carter…" I put my hand on her spear, holding it down. "There isn't a Soviet Union anymore."

"Really? In just three years?"

Drago has a chuckle. Stops when I glower at him. "What? Is funny."

When I look back to Carter, my expression is apologetic. "There's no Soviet Union. No United States. No countries at all."

"I don't understand. What could have… Oh, God… Was there a nuclear war?"

"There were a lot of wars," I say. "And billions of people died…over time."

"Billions and billions and billions," Drago says.

Carter rubs her temples with one hand. "I don't understand."

"It's been five years for us," Chuy says, "but a *thousand* years have passed since 1989."

"Whatever we found in the ice," I say, "it sent us through space *and* time. Welcome to the future, Dr. Carter."

Drago clears his throat. "I don't mean to be wet blanket on reunion, but we should get back."

"Back where?" Carter asks.

"Spaceship." Drago points to the sky. "In space."

Before Carter can reply, a loud roar rolls through the forest, forcing my hands to my ears.

"That really can't be good," Chuy says.

I turn to the east, searching for any hint of the sound's source, but I can't see anything through the impossibly thick forest. When I look back, Carter is sprinting away from us.

Drago rolls his eyes and sighs. "Americans..."

6

Carter is fast. Life here has undoubtably been difficult, but it's also turned her into an athletic fighter—which was not my first impression of her a thousand years ago. A hundred yards through a twisting maze of boulders, ferns, and cleared paths through tall grass, we arrive at the base of a massive tree with a coiling trunk.

Carter climbs a portion of the trunk, which looks like a snake large enough to swallow an elephant whole. Then she disappears into a hole.

"Well," Chuy says, stopping at the tree's base, "she lives like a squirrel."

"Yes...yes, she does," I say, and I start climbing. "Coordinate an evac with Morton. I'll try to move things along."

"I'm sure you will."

I pause to glance back at her. The lopsided grin says it all. "Fifty credits says you do the nasty before the day is over."

"I'm a professional," I argue. "A Marine."

"Not anymore," she says, and even though I've known that for a long time, it still stings.

"She's covered in dirt," I say upon reaching the top.

"Like that would stop you."

My smile matches hers. Then I slip inside the hollowed-out tree. The tunnel is angled up and forces me onto my hands and knees. It's a fifteen-foot crawl to a carved-out den that's a good twenty feet wide. The air is cooler than it is outside.

Smells a bit like warm oak, but also body odor and smoke.

She cooks in here, I think, noting the fire pit in the room's center. I look up. The ceiling is coated in black from smoke, darker at the room's peak, where a second tunnel leads up, and I assume, back outside the trunk.

Beside the entrance lies a large steak, presumably from the kill outside. It's laid out on a cut portion of leaf.

"Did you do all this?" I ask, scanning the chamber.

"The den and tunnel leading out were already here. Home to grubs before I found it."

"Big grubs."

"You wouldn't want to meet one," she says, packing a homemade bag. "I made the space a little larger, and I added that." She points to the hole in the ceiling.

"What was it like," I say, "living here?"

She pauses. Looks me in the eyes. "Fucking bogus. But I made it work." She cinches the bag shut.

I motion to it. "What is all that?"

"Intelligence," she says. "About the planet. The animals that live here. The environment."

"*That's* what we came back for? I don't need to tell you something very big is coming this way..."

She nods. "She probably saw you land. Beatrice is a grumpy bitch."

"You know what it is? Wait. You *named* it?"

"I named everything I came across that I wasn't planning on killing and eating. And this..." She slips the bag over her shoulder. "...is my job. I wasn't just killing, eating, and shitting the past three years."

"Five years."

"Definitely three."

"Doesn't matter," I say. "Look, I don't like saying it, but I'm not sure the information you've gathered will do anyone any good. The human race is...different now."

"Different how?"

"They're expansionists," I say. "They consume, multiply, and colonize nearly as fast as Exo-Hunters—that's what I do now—find new habitable worlds."

"What kind of government is it?"

Strange question to be asking while Beatrice closes in, but I sense she needs a few answers before she puts her life in my hands again. "Each planet has its own local government, but it's essentially a monarchy by council. No single leader, but also no infighting or power grabs. They're all happy, as long as they keep stuffing their faces and pounding out babies."

Her brow furrows. "They sound..."

"Evil?" I say, smiling.

"Are you sure they're not Soviets?"

"They are definitely not Soviets..."

"But they *are* something..."

"After this, no more Q&A, okay? I'm guessing Beatrice isn't something I want to meet."

"Not at all," she says. "And fine. Tell me who they are, and I won't say another word."

Riiight...

"Nazis."

"Nazis?! Are you *serious?*"

"Some of them are nice."

"Nice Nazis?! Are you fucking kidding me?"

"Already established I'm not, and you said you wouldn't say another word. It's messed up. I don't like it. The future is a freak show. But it's taken five damn years to find you, and I'd rather not get you killed because we spent too long having a chit-chat."

We have a stare off for three seconds.

Then she says, "Fine." She heads for the tunnel, picking up the wrapped steak on the way. "Try to keep up."

I scramble down the tunnel and back out into the world. The first thing I'm struck by is how quiet it was inside—the jungle is coming alive. Shadows whip past. When I look up, whatever flew past is gone. Where Beatrice goes, everything else leaves.

The second thing I'm struck by is a roar loud enough to stumble me. I nearly fall twenty feet, but I catch myself on the tree's crusty bark. By the time I'm ready to head down, Carter has reached the forest floor.

"What's the situation?" Chuy asks, watching Carter sprint past her.

"Run like hell," I say, and I leap the last few feet to the ground. We haul ass together, once again struggling to keep up with the cheetah-like Carter. In a straight-out sprint, I'd be able to take her, but the unsure footing and extra weight from the stupid number of magazines I'm carrying, not to mention the rifle itself, slows me down.

I toggle my comms. "Morton, fired up and ready to go?"

"Yes, sir." He sounds nervous. "The seismic disturbance is very close now."

"ETA?" I ask.

"One mike," he says. "For you. Three mikes for *Lil Bitch'n*. What next?"

"En route," I say, not answering his question. "We'll be there in time."

We might not be, but I don't want to risk spooking him. Morton, Burnett, and Porter have all been a good crew thus far, but they've always been very far away from the danger. If he realizes he might become a snack for an oversized alien, he might bug out.

"Drago," I say, "don't wait on us. Get to the LZ and—"

I can hear him on the other end. He's not speaking. He's breathing hard. "Are you already running?!"

"Have you *seen* creature?" Drago says.

"No," I say, looking east and seeing nothing but impenetrable tree trunks. Apparently, he got a look, and it spooked him enough to call a one-man tactical retreat.

"Whoa!" he says, sounding surprised. "Jungle woman is fast."

Holy shit. Carter already passed Drago, even with his head start. "Try to keep up with her. Make sure she doesn't kill Morton."

"Kill?"

"She's not quite used to the idea of future space Nazis."

"Are you?" he asks.

"Just do it," I say, and I switch off my comms.

My body has mostly healed from my run-in with the puddle jumper, but the previously fading injuries are starting to act up. The constant charge is taking a toll, but when we pass through the tall grass again, I glance to the left.

And I see Beatrice.

Just a part of it.

But it's massive, and enough to push me past the pain. We don't just need to get off the ground to escape this thing.

We need to leave the atmosphere.

"Dark Horse," Chuy says, as we pass through the field.

"I know..."

I push myself harder than I have in years. We reach *Lil Bitch'n* just as something massive hits the ground behind us. A shockwave sprawls us forward, into Drago's open arms. He tosses us, one at a time, deeper inside the cargo bay and shouts, "They are in. Go!"

Looking out the back, I see a tree trunk, but it's not vertical. It's lying on its side, surrounded by a cloud of dust and pollen.

It was *knocked over...*

"Hold on!" Morton shouts in all our ears, making us wince, but the urgency in his voice is clear.

Beatrice is here, and we need to not be—now.

I haul Carter onto one of the two benches lining the bay's sides. Strap her in. Before I can buckle myself, *Lil Bitch'n* lifts off and the front-end tips up. I clutch my buckle as my feet fall out from under me. Dangling from the bench, I look down as we launch up through the trees.

Below us, two trees explode away from each other, as something massive pushes between them.

Beatrice's head.

It looks like a snapping turtle the size of Grand Central Station—and that's just its head. The creature's four red eyes are focused on us.

On me.

Beatrice turns its head up. Chasing us. Eyes narrowing, it roars.

The blast hits like a tidal wave, throwing off *Lil Bitch'n*'s trajectory—and knocking me loose. As the lander rises up out of the jungle, slapping through leaves and shattering small branches, I topple down toward Beatrice's battleship-sized mouth.

I don't know how Beatrice can see me or why she even cares to consume me. To her, I'm a crumb.

Then again, she—I'm assuming Beatrice is a *she*—is an alien creature. For all I know, her flavor receptors might be magnified a thousand-fold, making a crumb super tasty and satisfying. Or, and this feels like a stretch, she's intelligent enough to recognize that the little creatures who arrived from the sky are a threat.

Beatrice's size wouldn't protect her from a planet-wide predator cleanse. In fact, it might just make her an easier target. The Union would carve her up to sell in exotic markets across the galaxy.

My body twists as I fall.

I extend my arms, arresting the tumble so I'm facing down. There are no teeth in Beatrice's beaked mouth. She either swallows her prey whole, or she bites off big chunks. I don't see how she'd even register my tiny body bouncing off her tongue and rolling down her throat.

Maybe she wouldn't.

One can hope, because this is one scrumptious human morsel she won't be tasting.

I reach down and tap the Slew Drive, spinning as I fall, right into the endless white, which stops any and all motion. I'm 'standing' in that I feel upright, but I can move in any direction I put my mind to.

But I can't move.

The Slew Drive is good at taking my thoughts or desires and using them to help me move in the right direction for the correct distance. But I normally have some idea of where I'm going—like to the surface of a planet. That's a pretty big target. Ideally, I'd rotate back to the *Lil' Bitch'n,* but I'm not sure where they are. And the big *Bitch'n* is somewhere in orbit. Rotating into open space would be a really bad idea.

Seeing no other option, I shift my body just an inch and rotate back into the third dimension, down to the planet's surface.

Or rather, five feet above it.

I fall, touch down, and then slip through the surface. Water consumes me. I sink ten feet before reaching the bottom. I try to swim up. Try to push off the muddy bottom. But my weapon and magazines have turned me into an anchor.

Lungs burning, I shed my gear, loath to leave my custom weapon and homemade rounds behind, but none of it is worth dying for. A hundred pounds lighter, I push off the bottom and...nothing. The mud has a firm grasp on my boots.

You've got to be kidding me.

I crouch, untie my boots, slip out of them, and this time, just swim for the surface. I break the water, gasping for air, spitting out liquid that tastes like dead fish. Treading water, I spin around until I spot Beatrice. She's a few miles away, on the far side of the large lake into which I've fallen.

Lil' Bitch'n is high in the sky above her, twisting away as the rear hatch closes. They'd have seen me rotate away. They know I'm alive. But they don't know where yet.

I lift a hand to toggle my comms and I immediately start sinking. In fact, even my perfect figure-eight water treading is barely keeping me above the surface. My clothing is saturated...but it's more than that.

Water on this planet is less dense.

I twist around. The shore is just thirty feet away. An easy swim on Earth. But I'm not sure I can make it.

Mouth open wide, I suck in a lung full of oxygen-saturated air and slip beneath the surface. As I sink, I shed clothing like I'm about to get horizontal with Kim Cattrall in a kimono. When I reach the bottom again,

I'm wearing my boxer-briefs and belt, upon which is a knife, my sidearm and the Slew Drive.

Free of the extra weight, I cut through the water, reaching the surface with just a little more effort than it would take on Earth. Then I kick for the shoreline repeating, "Please don't bite my dick off. Please don't bite my dick off."

Unlike most people, who have a fear of swimming in the ocean because of *Jaws*, I have a fear of swimming in lakes because my cousin's best friend's yuppie brother went skinny dipping in a lake and had his penis chomped by a snapping turtle. I'm wearing underwear, but if Beatrice has had babies any time recently, this lake could be teeming with penis-pilfering reptiles...though I guess they'd probably be large enough to eat me whole.

Better to be eaten whole than to live without a dick.

I'm out of breath when I reach the shore, but I catch it quickly. The oxygenated air gets me back into fighting shape in just a few seconds, which is good, because Beatrice is looking at me.

"How can you even see me?" I ask the towering creature, who stands a good hundred feet taller than the five-hundred-foot-tall trees. *That's bigger than Godzilla*, I think, and I scramble to my feet.

The ground shakes when the monster steps toward me, knocking trees to the side. When she roars, I can see the soundwaves approaching as they ripple the lake's water. When it strikes, my body vibrates, and the leaves on the trees above me flutter.

"Well, this is hellacious," I say, and I toggle my comms. "Need a pickup."

"Would if we could," Chuy says.

"What's that supposed to mean?"

"Means Morton is a chickenshit, and he's flying us back to *Bitch'n*. Drago and I will come back for you, but—"

"That's going to take too long," I say, backing away toward the forest. "I think Beatrice wants to make me her boy toy. Morton..."

"Uh, yes...?" he says.

"I want you to ask yourself a question, okay?"

"S-sure?"

"Was that a question, or an affirmative? You know what, doesn't matter. I want you to ask yourself who you're more afraid of, the city-sized alien, or me?" I do my best Jack Nicholson level crazy at the end of the sentence, oozing menace.

He answers without missing a beat. "The alien. I'm sorry, boss. I am. But I...I salvage non-living junk. I don't have the nerve for this."

He's not wrong. That he picked us up the first time means he over-came his fear long enough to do his job. I'm the one who fell out. This is on me. "Do me a favor? Once you reach the *Bitch'n*, get Carter out and let Drago fly back down?"

"Yes, sir," he says, relieved that I'm not chewing him out or threat-ening his life.

"Chuy?"

"Yup?"

"If I don't make it—"

I hear a click. She's disconnected. Our possible eventual demise has always been a sore subject for her. She's already lost a lot. We all have. Right now, we're all the other has. I don't blame her for not wanting to talk about it. But if Beatrice turns me into a puddle of dung, she's going to regret not saying goodbye.

Guess I better start running.

As Beatrice steps into the lake, I sprint into the woods.

Fifty feet in—the distance it takes to pass one damn tree—a gushing roar rises up behind me. A cool breeze tickles my exposed back. I don't have to look to know what's happening. An understanding of physics is enough. Beatrice's big ass foot displaced a shit-ton of water, kicking up a freshwater tsunami that is now crashing through the forest.

I run around the large tree, to keep myself from getting struck by the wave's full force. The tree shudders from the impact. Water explodes around both sides, and then surges past. When the rushing water is more like a river than a wall of kinetic energy, I leap in and let it whisk me away faster than I could run. By the time Beatrice clears the lake, she'll have emptied a good portion of it. If I can keep myself from getting knocked unconscious by a tree...or a fern...I should keep pace with the behemoth.

But that's easier said than done.

I hit every tree, root, and stem I pass. It's like I'm stuck in a prehistoric pinball machine. I can't control where I'm going or how fast I'm moving. The best I can do is try to spot an obstacle, twist toward it, and absorb the blow with my legs. My knees are already sore.

A roar tears through the air, snapping my hands to my ears.

Beatrice is close!

Trees behind me crack and fall.

The rushing water is a trickle to the giant. The trees are like saplings. She charges after me unabated and with such fury that I'm certain she is the first intelligent life we've encountered. I'm going to keep that to myself if I survive, and I'm going to do my best to convince the others this planet is uninhabitable.

Beatrice isn't wrong about wanting to kill human invaders, but, "You're trying to kill the wrong person!" I shout.

"Dark Horse? Are you still alive?" It's Porter.

"For the moment," I say. "Is *Lil' Bitch'n* back yet?"

"Uh, no. *Bitch'n* is a thousand miles out, but—"

"What?!"

"But we're in a fast orbit. We'll have *Lil' Bitch'n* docked and back to you in...fifteen minutes, give or take."

"Give or take what?"

"Ten minutes. But that's all give. There isn't really any take time. Not sure why I said that."

"Porter..."

"Yes?"

"What did you want?"

"Oh! Right. Sorry. The Slew Drive. I've got a firmware upgrade for you."

"Will I be able to rotate out of here?"

"Absolutely. The recharge time was really just a guideline, to prevent the chance of a nuclear meltdown."

"Nuclear...meltdown?" Distracted, I thump off a rock and barely notice.

"Well, yes, what did you think powered a Slew Drive?"

I've got a thousand snarky comments cocked, locked, and ready to rock, but I hold back my verbal assault. I can worry about irradiating my balls another time. "Send it!"

"Well, I would, but the unit appears to be...submerged. Are you in water?"

"Yes, I'm in water, damnit!"

"Well...can you get out of the water?"

I reach out for a passing fern and catch hold. The stem bends under my waterlogged weight, but it redirects my course to an unaffected sky-scraper of a tree. I slap against the tree's trunk, cling to the rough bark, and freehand scale it a few feet above the water.

But I won't be able to stay long. A fresh wave of water rushes toward me, and behind it, Beatrice's foot!

"Send it!' I shout. "Send it, now!"

"Okay...annnnnd...done!"

I reach for the Slew Drive. "How many rotations can I get out of this?"

"As many as you want, until you explode."

"How many is that?!"

"No one has ever tried rapid fire rotations before. They're not really called for when moving between planets. This is the kind of situation I warned you about when you asked for—"

"Blah, blah, blah, words. Turn on every exterior light the *Bitch'n* has. Light it up like a Christmas tree."

"Christmas?"

"Just make it bright!" I shout, as a shadow falls over me. I look up at the underside of Beatrice's baseball field-sized foot, trigger the Slew Drive, and rotate five hundred feet straight up.

It's unnecessary. Probably stupid. But I rotate back out of the fourth dimension right in front of Beatrice's face. I linger just long enough for gravity to take hold again, and for me to flip Beatrice the bird. Then I rotate again, and again, bouncing around in the atmosphere, eyes on the sky above. With each rotation, I rise higher. The air gets thin and cold. Goosebumps pepper my skin.

And then I see it.

High above. A glint of light.

I focus on it, imagine where I want to be, and then rotate off world.

I appear in the *Bitch'n*'s landing bay, just as the *Lil Bitch'n*'s hatch lowers to the floor, revealing Chuy, Drago, Carter, and Morton. They're all rushing and worried until I say, "What took you so long?"

Nailed it, I think.

They look up in surprise, which shifts to relief, and then to hysterical laughter.

"Should we call you Captain Chip? Or Captain Dale?" Chuy asks, giving me a pat on the shoulder. I look down at myself, glistening with moisture, dressed in underwear and a belt. It *is* funny. But I don't get a chance to laugh, because Carter catches Drago off guard, snatching one of his shotguns and leveling it at Morton, who squeals and raises his hands.

8

"What...are you doing?" I ask Carter, though I can see perfectly well that she's about to put a handful of tungsten buckshot into Morton's head.

"I don't know what happened to you," she says to me, "but the people I went to Antarctica with would never submit to Nazis!"

"Technically," Morton says, "the Nazi party ceased to exist more than a thousand years ago. The Union is—"

Carter's finger slips around the trigger.

"Julie..."

She gives me a dirty look.

"Carter?"

The look persists. "I'm not calling you Dr. Carter, and if you have a problem with that, we can go back to 'Bugs.'"

She reveals nothing.

"Look," I say, feeling silly for negotiating in my underwear, keenly aware that I'm starting to get perky nipples from the chill in the air, "Morton isn't a Nazi, or a white supremacist. If your plan is to hijack the *Bitch'n*, rename it the *USSS United States*, and use it to fulfill some kind of personal future mission, I beat you to it by five years."

I step between the raised gun and Morton. "You're on *my* ship. And this man, who just risked his life to save yours, is part of my team."

"Aww," Morton says, sounding genuinely touched. "I'm genuinely touched."

"I get it," I say, looking down the shotgun's barrel. "I reacted the same way when I found myself in an Antarctic Nazipocalyptic future hellscape."

"He did." Morton leans around me to address Carter. "But he was scarier. Porter pissed himself."

"Thank you," I say, pushing him back behind me. I don't think he understands what I do—that despite her super-model looks, Carter is a killer...and always has been.

"I don't trust you," Carter says.

"You don't have a choice." I motion to the ship around us. "You're on a spaceship...in space. You might be smart, but you'll never figure out the controls."

"So many buttons," Drago says.

"And..." I motion to Drago and Chuy, "the second you pull that trigger, you're dead."

Put the gun down, I think. *Please don't be a stupid smart person.*

The squint in her eyes goes steady. I've seen the look before, in stalking lions before they pounce, and in my ex-girlfriend Pamela Scholl, when she found out I was seeing her best friend, Alison Emann. No idea why I still think of them both as first and last name people... In the end they girl-bonded against me, like they had no choice but to fall head-over-heels for me during the same weekend.

Back to squinty-eyes Magoo, here. She glances side to side, just enough to spot Chuy and Drago in her peripheral vision. She's sizing us up, tracking targets, about to put a bullet in my head, one in Chuy, and then probably three in Drago, because he's big and a commie bastard. She'll keep Morton alive because he's clearly not a threat, and he's also a source of intel.

Or so she thinks. My smile disarms her. "What?"

"Just pull the trigger," I say, "this is getting a little melodramatic."

Her brows furrow, deeper when Drago starts chuckling.

Carter's trigger finger pulls, but it doesn't move. I'm disappointed that she chose to kill me, but I'm also impressed. She's a woman of conviction, dedicated to a cause. Problem is, she's misguided, and the cause died out centuries ago.

Before she can react to the gun not firing, my hand snaps up and twists it from her grip. I turn the weapon around on her. "Welcome to the future, Carter. Every weapon on this ship fires for one of three people, and you're not one of them."

Morton leans out around me again. This time he gives a friendly wave. "Neither am I!"

I turn the weapon so she can see the grip. I lift away my three lower fingers, revealing smooth pads. "When you pick it up, the gun checks your fingerprints faster than Billy the Kid could draw and pull the trigger. And if you want your fingerprints added to the list of acceptable users, you're going to have to start building trust. And that means no killing people. Capisce?"

She motions to Morton. "If you trust him so much, why can't he use the gun?"

"First..." I hold up my index finger. "He'd probably shoot himself in the foot."

"It's true," Morton says. "I'm a horrible shot."

"Second..." I hold up my middle finger. "Future Nazis. Doy. All that compute?"

Her jaw clenches before saying, "Yes."

"Are you going to try to kill anyone if I don't lock you up?"

"Only if they give me a good reason," she says.

At least she's honest.

I turn to Morton. "Try to steer clear of this one for a bit. Let the others know."

"How many others are there?" Carter asks.

"Two," Morton says. "I'm Morton. The others are Burnett and Porter."

"And...try not to frighten Porter," I add.

"Why?" she asks.

"Because big man pisses himself." Drago has a good laugh at Porter's expense.

"Except he doesn't piss himself," Chuy says. "Those suits they're wearing spray sudden evacuations all over the damn place."

"Okay, now that you know everything worth knowing about the future..." I turn to Chuy. "Show her to her quarters?"

Chuy rolls her eyes, but says, "Sure."

"Don't let period cycles sync on way to quarters," Drago says with a chuckle. "One woman with PMS is bad enou—"

"Que te folle un pez!" Chuy shouts.

"Chtob u tebya hui na lbu vyros!" Drago replies in the Mother Tongue.

Chuy flips him off. "Que te la pique un pollo."

"Idi na hui," he replies, grinning. Neither knows what the other is saying. They never do. It's entertaining as hell for me, because after five years of just Chuy to confide in, I've learned a lot of Spanish, and being proficient in Russian helped fast track my career with Uncle Sam. Would have been on my way to general by now, had the universe not boned my life in the keister.

Given the hint of a smile on Carter's face, I'm pretty sure she can speak Spanish or Russian, if not both.

"Great," I say. "Now that you both got that sexual tension aired out—" Chuy reels on me. "Allow me to make the coolest exit ever." I rush the words out as Chuy winds up to slug my shoulder. Before she can swing, I activate my Slew and rotate into the fourth dimension.

Just as the white light of the 4D envelops me, something goes wrong. Pressure wraps around me. Squeezing. A body. When the rotation finishes, I see Carter's dirty face looking up at me. She took hold of me as I slipped out of the third dimension and made the journey with me!

"Are you insane?" I ask her, irritated.

"Is this dangerous?" she asks, and she tries to step away.

I wrap my arms around her and hold her against me. "Dangerous? It's un-fucking-heard of."

That sobers her a little bit.

"Best case scenario, we rotate out of here intact and in the right place. Medium case scenario, we rotate out of here and exchange a few body parts, or we become conjoined."

"Worst case scenario?" she asks.

"We rotate out, intact or conjoined, into open space." I pat the Slew Drive on my hip. "I have no idea how this will work for two people."

"How does it work for one person?" she asks.

I give her the quick, layman's version of Slew Drive functionality—which is the only version I know—including the fact that they were designed for starships, not people.

"So...that—" She points to the Slew. "Is one of a kind."

"And just recently got a firmware update that increases the number of times I can use it, but also bumps up the chances that overuse might make it go kaboom."

"Kaboom..."

"Thermonuclear kaboom."

"Oh... So, we might...rotate out of..."

"The fourth dimension."

"...and explode?"

"Destroying the *Bitch'n* and killing my people. And that will really piss me off."

"Then..." Her hands wrap around my back. "We should probably make the most of our time while we're here."

I'm revolted. "Are you insane?"

Her hands slide down to my ass.

And now I'm erect.

Godamnit.

"I've been alone for three years," she says, squeezing.

"Five."

She smiles and kisses my chest.

"You're dirty," I say. I don't know when her last bath was, but she smells like the jungle...which isn't horrible.

"You don't care," she says, and she turns around, pressing her ass into me.

I don't know if anything lives in the fourth dimension. For all I know, this could be where God and His heavenly hosts live. If so, they're about to get a show.

"No," I say. "I don't."

Fifteen minutes later, we rotate back into the third dimension, inside my quarters. When nothing explodes, I sigh with relief.

"Now *you* owe me fifty bucks."

I jump in surprise. Chuy is sitting on my bunk. Can't tell if she's amused or pissed. She stands up and gives Carter a once over. Then she delivers the punch she'd intended to land before I rotated away. "There's a goat that still needs fuckin', and it ain't a bitch. You copy?"

She doesn't mean a literal goat. Because...also extinct.

It's a military expression. A mission that needs finishing. The bitch part is self-explanatory. "Copy that."

"Take a shower," she says to Carter. "You smell worse than Drago." And then to me, she says, "Captain Dark Horse, single-handedly bringing STDs back from the 80s. Well done, sir." She gives me a middle-finger salute and a smile before exiting.

"Shower in here?" Carter asks, heading for the bathroom, shedding clothing.

"Uhh, yeah," I say, seeing her fit body for the first time.

She smiles. "Ready for round two, Marine?"

This is a bad idea. Carter is an unknown element. Of all the people I've spent the past five years looking for, I know and trust her the least. And the first thing she did upon stepping foot on my ship was hold a gun to my crewmember—a gun she tried to fire at *my* head.

Really bad idea.

"Hell, yes," I say, pulling down my boxers and hopping toward the bathroom, as I yank them over my feet.

I'm generally not a 'pillow talk' kind of guy. My history of wham-bam-thank-you-ma'am tactics is as infamous as Russia's gulags. It's not that I wasn't interested in something long term. I just had a hard time finding a woman who wanted to settle down with someone who was MIA for a good part of the year and could end up KIA every time I went to work. It's a big ask, and it takes a special kind of lady.

I suppose I could have just given up, but a man's got needs. Doing the deed with a woman is a quick way to assess if they've got what it takes to...

God, I'm sexist.

I've been told that on a few occasions. More than a few.

But that's who I *was*. Past tense. I've spent the past five years in space, avoiding having feelings for Chuy, and spending time with a little lady I like to call Harriet Palmer. This future version of me is more mature and interested in deeper relationships.

"Why 'Dark Horse?'" Carter asks.

"Because I'm black, and I have a big dick," I say.

She stares at me, and then deadpan she says, "But you don't...have a big dick."

I burst out laughing. She joins in, lying her head against my chest. We're wrapped in blankets, squeezed onto my meager cot, with the view of the planet that has been her home.

"Seriously, why? Is it just supposed to sound cool?"

I adjust a bit so I can see her face better. "That's part of it. For some operators, that's all of it. Usually there is a little hidden meaning. A personality trait."

"Like Brick," she says. "He was big."

"*Is* big, but his father was also a mason. The callsign reminds him of home. Of family."

"Oh," she says. "So, Dark Horse?"

"In Miriam Webster terms, a dark horse is a competitor about whom little is known, but who unexpectedly wins."

"You see yourself as an underdog?" She sounds dubious. And I get it. I'm a tall, dark, and handsome badass. But...

"I was a black man in the U.S. military who wanted to *lead* armies, not just serve in them. My parents survived the civil rights movement, but we all felt the sting of racism. It was everywhere, even in the military. Sometimes *especially* in the military. It wasn't impossible, though. Colin Powell was a lieutenant general when we were yanked out of the past, and he was on track to his fourth star. He was a dark horse, too. An inspiration."

"And now you're the only black man in the galaxy," she says.

Hearing the words still stings. Fills me with a limp kind of rage—anger with no outlet. So, I squelch it, and I say, "But hey, I'm not getting stopped by the police just for walking down the street now."

She huffs. "That's only because people outside of this ship don't know about you."

"Uplifting. Thanks."

"People are people," she says. "Always will be. Fear of the unknown—that's you—drives people to do and believe stupid things."

"People are people," I say. "So why should it be..."

She grins. "Depeche Mode. The best."

"God, I miss the 80s," I say.

"Wouldn't have taken you to be a Depeche Mode man."

"Mmm," I say. "Maybe racism isn't dead after all. You had me pegged for a Run D.M.C. man, right? LL Cool J, maybe? Grandmaster Flash?"

"I'd *hoped*," she says.

"Yeah, 'It's Tricky' *is* one of my favorites. Classic D.M.C. I'm an equal opportunity music fan, but...this is depressing. I told you all that history is gone, right? The music. The movies. Everything from our era has been washed and sterilized from the history books. There are more than three hundred billion people, but not one of them has seen *Terminator* or remembers when men wore shoulder pads. They just look at me funny when I say, 'I pity da foo!' or 'Watchu talkin' 'bout, Willis?' They usually just say, 'Who's Willis?' or 'You know Willis?' The world as we knew it doesn't exist. Not the people, the cities, the culture, and not a single animal anyone would want to see. Earth belongs to the insects and the rats now. Remembering...just hurts."

"Are there no musicians in the future? Maybe we can hire someone to recreate the tunes, and we can belt out the lyrics ourselves?"

"First, future musicians are like nails on a chalk board. The instruments are all digital. The concept of rhythm has been forgotten. And singing is monotone—and that's pretty much just for the Union anthem."

"Sounds like the future is horrible," she says, a little depressed.

"It's not great."

"Have you ever considered going full Union? Maybe no one in the future is racist anymore. If they can't remember black people... Sounds like your crew adjusted to you pretty well. Maybe there's a place in the Union for you. For us. There must be something a man with your experience can offer."

"Already doing it," I say. "Exo-Hunter is the most dangerous job in the galaxy."

"Is there a compelling reason to not just bow out?" She turns to the view of the planet she called home for years. "Life wasn't easy down there, but it wasn't bad, either. There's a whole world to discover."

"Once you get used to the giant monster trying to eat you."

"Beatrice? She didn't want to eat you."

I raise an eyebrow.

"Looked like it to me."

"She wanted to kill you."

I lean up, taking in the view, imagining a long life lived like an Ewok. "Not sure I see the difference."

"Beatrice's species is herbivorous. But they're also fiercely territorial."

"Like supersized dinosaur hippos with turtle heads."

"Uhh, yeah, that's about right. Once they get used to you, they don't bother."

"Still. Hard pass. I'd rather go to Elysium."

"The final resting place for heroic and pure souls?" she says, impressing me with her knowledge of Greek myth...and just about everything else. "Think they'll let you in?"

"Well, no one lives there, no one knows about it, and it's basically my retirement home. But that can't happen yet."

"Because you need to find your crew?" She sounds doubtful.

"I found you, didn't I?"

"You might spend the better part of your life trying to find them. That's a long time to spend in..." She frowns at the dark metal room around us. "...in this shithole. No offense."

"Better to live in a shithole with purpose than paradise knowing I'd failed because I didn't try."

She smiles.

Leans back.

"That's why I picked you for the Antarctic mission. You see things through."

"You *chose* my team for the mission?"

"Not your team. You. I needed someone who wouldn't quit, even if I never told you what it was really about."

"An alien artifact frozen in the ice..." I turn to her. "Did you know what it was? What it could do?"

She shakes her head. "All we knew was that it was emitting serious energy waves across a myriad of bandwidths, it was locked in ancient ice, and—"

"It was in the Soviets' backyard. Hence the rush. Hence a Rapid Reaction Force team."

"No one knew where it was from."

"Or when," I add.

"There's no evidence the object was *from* the future, only that the resulting...event...propelled us *into* the future."

"But why?" I ask. "Something like that doesn't exist without a reason. How'd it end up on Earth? And of all the times and places it could have sent us, why here and now?"

"Questions without answers," she says. "And we're not going to find them while chasing your people around the galaxy."

Good point. But it doesn't change anything. People before answers. I can live with never understanding the why and how of this shitshow, if I'm able to get my people back. I suspect that Carter, who has no allegiance to my team, doesn't share my point of view. "It's not like I can head on over to Union Command and start asking questions. I'd stand out, and I'm not ready to put the non-existence of institutional racism to the test."

"*I* wouldn't stand out," she says.

Her brown hair and eyes don't scream Aryan master race, but they're not unheard of. Uncommon, sure, but Porter and Burnett both have brown eyes. Then again, maybe that's why they were given the illustrious task of salvaging the ruins humanity leaves behind when a planet is spent.

"You want your own ship," I guess.

"You have your mission. I have mine."

"Again. No Uncle Sam. No CIA. No evil empire."

She raises an eyebrow at me.

"Okay, *maybe* an evil empire, but there's nothing to be done about it, and no one to save or liberate. We have no enemies here."

"Not yet," she says.

"Please tell me you're not going to stir up trouble," I say. If she's planning on exposing us and causing some kind of interplanetary ruckus in the pursuit of old-fashioned life, liberty, and the pursuit of happiness, I might have to keep her locked down. Worst case scenario, I have to put her back where we found her until we find everyone else. And that would be a shame, because, damn, it's nice to not sleep alone.

She smiles at me. "I would never—"

An alarm blares, making both of us flinch into seated positions. It sounds like a ragged honk. Definitely has my attention. I tap my comms. "Chuy?"

"Almost to the bridge," she replies.

"Morton? What's the alarm for?"

"Proximity alarm," he replies.

"Proximity to *what?*" I ask.

"I'm not on the bridge, but generally...to another ship."

"Another ship... Who *is* on the bridge?"

"Drago," he says.

"Drago, what the hell is going on?"

"Dark Horse!" he says, laughing. "Have been waiting for this day for five years."

"What day?" I ask, tugging on my clothing. "The fuck is happening?"

"Enemies!" he says, like he just opened a Christmas present and got everything on his list. "Prepare for battle!"

I arrive outside the bridge at the same time as Chuy. She gives me a once over. "You got dressed this time. So that's an improvement. Have fun last night? Anything itch yet?"

"Funny," I say, and then I glance back, as Carter races to catch up with us. She's dressed in a form fitting, black BCS. I've looked upon the suits with scorn since I arrived in the future, but Carter makes it work. She could probably dress in the entrails of some alien creature and still look nice.

Good looks or not, she's still a wildcard and not really a part of this crew...yet. "You can't come in."

"The hell I can't," she says.

"You don't exactly outrank us anymore," Chuy says.

I don't enjoy denying her access, especially after a night of boinking. But I haven't ruled out the possibility that all the sexy cuddle time was a psy-op technique employed to get information.

"I won't say a word," Carter says. "Please. I've been alone in a damn alien jungle for three years. Whatever this is, it's something you've never encountered before, right? Let me do what I do. I'll observe and see the things none of you do."

I turn to Chuy.

"Don't look at me," she says. "Lady isn't my lover, cabrón."

I sigh, hand on my forehead.

"Let me help," Carter says. "Let me earn my keep."

"You know all the right things to say," I observe aloud. She's not fooling me, but she's not wrong either. Before her arrival, our crew was composed of two types of people: nerds and soldiers. Neither group has a firm grasp on the human psyche or big picture strategies. Her insight could be valuable.

Unless this is aliens.

Then we're probably all doomed.

"Not a word," I tell her, and then I step closer to the bridge door. It whooshes open for me.

Inside the bridge, I find Drago in the captain's chair and Burnett already seated at his station. He looks paler than usual. Neither of them holds my attention for long, because the view through the windshield nearly makes me choke.

It's a spaceship alright. It's man-made for sure, but it's unlike anything I've seen since arriving in the future. It's sleek, like the ship is built for speed—despite the fact that aerodynamics have no impact on maneuvering through the vacuum of space. Its paint job is shades of orange, from almost yellow to almost red. Whoever owns it wants to be noticed. The name stenciled on the nose—*ZORAK*—stands out because, like the ship's design, it shows a kind of unique flourish that is unheard of in the Union.

It's a custom job.

And there is only one kind of person in the future who might consider something so garish and awesome.

An Exo-Hunter.

"Who am I looking at?" I ask Burnett.

"No idea, sir. The ship's design isn't in the database, and aside from the name, there aren't any ID markers. I'm getting a transponder ping, but it's encrypted. The ship is a ghost."

"A ghost..." Carter whispers.

I shoot her a 'keep quiet' look and wave Drago from my chair. He relents with a huff, moving to his station. I sit down and wince. "Ugh, my chair feels hot and moist."

Drago shrugs. "I was excited. Thought they would attack, but they just sit there."

"They're trying to figure out who we are." Elbows on knees, I try to glean more details from the ship. In addition to appearing sleek, it's also built for battle. There are guns on the undersides of its wings, and rocket pods on the top.

Why would an Exo-Hunter advertise their presence with such a loud ship and then arm it with enough firepower to scream, 'Stay the fuck back?' Kind of a mixed message, but not unheard of in nature. Poisonous tree frogs—also extinct—used the same strategy. If you're impossible to miss and clearly a threat, predators just steer clear.

Is that what they're expecting? For us to turn tail and run?

Are they trying to poach this planet from us through intimidation?

If so, they're going to regret it.

Bitch'n might look like an impacted shit, but it's been customized by two Marines and one very sinister Spetnaz operator. If they want a fight, I'm with Drago: *Bring it on.*

But I can't just kick their ass.

I mean, I could. There's no law out here. No one would ever find the remains. Communication back to Union Command—without rotating there—would take longer than my lifetime. And Exo-Hunters go missing without a trace all the time. One of the job perks.

Morton and Porter hustle into the bridge and take their seats.

"Now that we're all here," I say, "how about we say hello?"

"Sounds good, sir," Morton says.

I wait.

Ten seconds.

"That means I'd like you to activate ship-to-ship comms."

"Oh!" Morton says. "Right."

"With voice modification," I say, preferring to remain unknown.

He pushes the button, turns a dial, and gives me a thumbs up—a gesture he learned from Drago, who smiles at me and gives two thumbs up. He knows the gesture irks me. I flip him off and say, "Hello—" I choke at the sound of my voice, high-pitched and unnatural, like Alvin or one of the other Chipmunks. Have to roll with it now.

"This is..." *Shit. Who am I? What's a common Union name?* "Captain Burnett..."

The real Burnett swivels around in his chair, mouth agape and somehow smiling at the same time. He mouths, "We have the same name?!"

Burnett doesn't know my real name. Only Chuy does. And Carter, I assume.

I do my best to ignore the hysterical expression on his face, and I finish my sentence, "...of Exo-Hunter vessel A-154-B7. Please identify yourself and state your business."

"What's an Exo-Hunter doing in a salvage vessel?" is the response. The voice is deep enough that I'm certain he's using a voice mod, too.

"Your vessel identification number, please," I say. A Union stooge would never proceed without all parties being at least partially identified, which is why I gave *Bitch'n* actual ID—which was designated long before I got my hands on her and made some improvements.

"Transmitting," the voice says.

Not sure why he's sending the number. Speaking would have worked fine. I lean to the side, looking at the screen in front of Burnett. The numbers blink on the screen, one at a time.

28008-2-FU

"That's an odd ID code," Burnett says, already searching for database results.

"Comms," I say, silencing the system. "It's a bullshit code."

"How can you tell?" Morton asks.

Drago chuckles. Then bursts out laughing. He's seen it, too. "Is funny!"

"It says 'two boobs, fuck you.'"

"They're screwing with us," Chuy says. She's got her game face on. Ready for a fight.

"Comms," I say, transmitting again. "I'm sorry we can't seem to find your identification number in the system."

Silence.

"Comms." To Porter. "The Slew Drive firmware update..."

"What about it?" he asks. "Did it not work to your satisfaction?"

"Worked perfectly," I say. "Can you give *Bitch'n*'s firmware the same update?"

"In theory, but—"

"Do it," I say. "Now."

He nods and goes to work, tapping on keys and buttons.

We're in the future, in space, but most new science has been devoted to colonization, reproduction, and food production. War hasn't been a priority in a long time, and conflict in the stars is unheard of. As a result, there are no *Star Trek* red flags. No raised shields. No weapons systems coming online. The only way to predict an attack existed in the 1980s A.D. and B.C.: intuition. And I'm feeling a tsunami of bad vibes radiating from this spacefaring version of masculine overcompensation.

"Dark Horse," Carter whispers.

"What?" I ask, annoyed and trying to think. We've been silent long enough for them to know that we know something is screwy. We've got seconds at best.

"The question you need to be asking is why?"

"In case you missed it, they're not answering questions," Chuy says.

"You can answer the question yourself," Carter says to me, ignoring Chuy. "Why would someone come to this planet?"

"To Exo-Hunt," I say.

"Does the Union usually send more than one vessel to the same planet? Seems kind of redundant and inefficient for people desperate for new habitable worlds."

She's right. If they're Exo-Hunters, they're not here for the planet. They're here for something else. But what other reason could—

Carter raises her eyebrows, somehow transmitting the message, 'The answer is standing right in front of you, penis-breath.'

"They're here for you..." I throw my hands up. "You could have just said that!" I take hold of twin joysticks attached to the armrests on either side of the captain's chair. I don't normally bother with the ship's day-to-day operations, maneuvers, or maintenance, but I can control the flight, weapons, and Slew systems from my chair. With the push of a button, I hijack the ship from the others.

"Porter?"

"Almost there," he says.

"Uhh," Drago says.

"What!?"

He points at the *Zorak*. "Rocket pods opening."

"Comms," I say. "You might want to think twice about that."

Silence.

"Have it your way," I say. "Comms. Porter!"

"Done!" He raises his hands in victory. "Yesssssooohnooo!"

As Porter's triumphant shout transforms into a squeal, a dozen rockets launch from the *Zorak*. *Bitch'n* would survive the hits—I think—and our return fire would erase the enemy, but I'd rather not take the risk, or pay for the damages.

With just a second to spare, my Los Angeles-class submarine of a spaceship rotates out of the third dimension, into the fourth and then back out again, emerging behind the enemy. Just as I'm about to give them a peek at the sexy secrets hidden beneath our skirt, the fired rockets twist around and race toward us again.

I sigh. "Damnit."

11

"Let's give them a little taste," I say to myself. In the good old days, a vessel like this, sporting multiple weapons systems and navigation controls, would be operated by a team of people; tanks, submarines, battleships— even fictional spacecraft. And that holds true in the future, but this kind of intergalactic dogfight requires reactions at the speed of thought. Giving commands slows things down. As does the various reaction times of the people receiving the orders.

My command chair connection on *Bitch'n* allows me to react almost at the speed of thought, plus a few seconds for one-liners. "Operation Pufferfish is a go!"

Two chain guns built to my specifications emerge from the *Bitch'n*'s hull and swivel toward the oncoming rockets. The computer handles the rest, identifying the rockets and opening fire. The guns are a recreation of the Phalanx CIWS (close-in weapon system) used to protect U.S. Navy vessels from airborne threats. It fires five thousand rounds per minute at a velocity of about a mile per second. But it doesn't need to throw that much tungsten. Because it doesn't miss. The guns acquire targets, fart out a dozen rounds, and then move on to the next threat. The only big diff- erence between our Phalanx system and the real deal is that our rounds are explosive, not to make them more lethal, but to prevent them from zipping off into space where they could eventually strike an unprepared vessel—human or otherwise. If the bullets miss their target, they detonate, turning the round into super fast-moving dust. It's not a perfect solution, but the infinite void is full of high-speed particles. A few more won't change anything. *Bitch'n* is a responsible war machine. Mostly.

From inside the bridge, it's a little anti-climactic. There is a slight rumble from the gunfire, and a streak of light from the tracer rounds flying out to meet the rockets. Then a burst of fire as the rockets explode. Even the explosions are lackluster.

Damage done by things that go boom is usually delivered by three things—fire, shrapnel, and pressure waves, or as I like to call it—the violent wind. Fire and shards of metal thrown out faster than the speed of sound can really ruin a guy's day if he's close. But it's the violent wind that reaches out and touches large numbers of people, compressing organs and brains.

In space, pressure waves don't exist outside a target. But when you score a hit... Then the pressure wave can move through a ship's interior—briefly. The moment a hole opens up, the atmosphere being pushed inward is suddenly sucked back out. The explosion might throw you back, but you could be slurped out into space before ever hitting the wall.

Spaceballs got it wrong. Things don't switch from suck to blow in space, only blow to suck.

I file that insightful gem away in case I ever need to explain why explosions in space are a yawn-fest compared to twentieth century sci-fi.

The incoming rockets pop one by one. A flash of light and a moment later, a *shhhh* sound, as the tiny bits of debris rain against the hull. The Phalanx does its job, but two of the rockets find our blind spot at *Bitch'n*'s bow.

Before striking the hull, the rockets adjust course, heading straight for the bridge.

They're not automated hunter-killer rockets, I realize, *they're remote controlled.*

Someone is piloting them. And they're going for the kill.

Which, for some reason, catches Carter off guard. "What the hell are they doing?"

Too bad for the *Zorak*, we've got Slew Drive 2.0.

We rotate away, and then back again, appearing in front of our enemy once more. I smile to myself, picturing the *Zorak's* crew letting out a communal "Huh?!"

Phalanx targets the fully exposed rockets as they bank around toward us again, destroying them with ease.

We've made an impression. Of that, I'm sure. But I'm not done yet. Not by a longshot. With a push of a button, eight railgun cannons emerge from *Bitch'n*'s hull. Two on each side, two on top, two on the bottom, aimed front and back. I can pull off a death blossom without all the vomit inducing spinning. If that wasn't enough, I've got rockets, too. And a few missiles for long-range bitch slaps. I've never had to use any of this before, and I've often wondered if it was overkill, but here we are, facing down an aggressor with short man syndrome.

"And this is the moment where the enemy realizes they're outclassed, throw up their hands, and surrender," I say to Carter.

"Why...exactly?"

"I just aimed eight railguns at them. They fire tungsten rods at sixteen *thousand feet* per second. There's no dodging that. Their hull will be Swiss-cheesed before they realize we're firing."

"Are railguns common in this time?" she asks.

"No," I say. "We have the only...ooooh."

The *Zorak*'s crew has no way to know what a railgun will do to their ships or future life goals.

"Comms," I say. Carter gasps beside me, like she's just realized something. I try to ignore her. "Crew of the *Zorak*, we've just aimed—"

Carter squeezes my arm. I'm about to chew her out when I see the expression on her face. "Hold on a second. Comms." To Carter, "This had better be good."

"Zorak," she says.

"Yes, *Zorak*. The spaceship trying to blow us up."

"I know what it means. The name."

I squint at her. "How could you know anything about anything in this time period? You've been living on Monster Planet—"

"Because," she says, almost growling, "Zorak is from *our* time."

I freeze. "Seriously?"

"Zorak is the arch nemesis of Space Ghost."

"Space...Ghost."

"Spy lady has spent too much time by herself," Drago says, twirling an index finger around his ear.

"Yeah, man," Chuy says. "She's loco."

"Space Ghost is a Hanna-Barbera cartoon," she says. "And he flies a damn spaceship that is yellow and orange." She stabs a finger at the *Zorak*. "Yellow and orange!"

"A kid's cartoon," Chuy says. "Great. That's just great."

"I have...I *had* a nephew," Carter says. "We watched together."

"Why would anyone in 2994 know about Space Ghost?" I ask.

Morton spins around in his chair. "They wouldn't. I've never heard of it, and only one of you four has." His breath catches. "Unless..."

"They're not from 2994." I stare at Carter. "And they were here for you... Comms. *Zorak*, please identify yourself." *Shit. My squeaky voice isn't going to make an impact.* "Voice Mod, off. This is Captain Dark Horse of the U.S. Marine Corps. Identify yourself. *Now.*"

I wasn't intending to use my actual name, rank, and the fact that I'm a Marine from a long since forgotten past. It slipped out, but maybe it will help if they know we're not from now, too.

More silence.

I pull the weapon systems back inside the *Bitch'n*. They were the aggressors here. I have yet to hit back. But I've revealed we're a bigger threat than they can handle. Maybe signaling we're not going to hold a grudge will help ease tensions.

Still nothing.

Carter clears her throat.

"Comms," I say, silencing the connection. "What?"

"You detected my radio signal from orbit, right?" She motions toward the *Zorak*. "I'm assuming it works on spacesh—"

"Burnett!"

"On it!" he says.

Static fills the bridge as he activates the radio scanner. It's followed by a high-pitched squeal.

"Santo cielo," Chuy whispers.

"Comms," I say. "Brick? Is that you? Benny?"

And then it comes to me. The only member of the team fond of cartoons.

"Whip!"

Silence.

"C'mon, man. I know it's you. Please...tell me it's you." The desperation in my voice is a little pitiful, but it's impossible to hide.

And then...the *Zorak* twists and folds into a line of brilliant white, slipping into the fourth dimension and rotating back out somewhere else.

Anywhere else.

Fuck.

"Can we track them?" I ask, already knowing the answer.

"In theory, but not in real time," Burnett says. "Transponders transmit celestial coordinates only when they're in range of Union receivers. Whatever data exists on the *Zorak* might not include their most recent rotations...unless they've been back to inhabited space. And then, the only way to access the information is from Union Command."

"Do you really think it was Whip?" Chuy asks, as disappointed by the outcome as I am.

I give her a look that says I do, but I can't say it out loud. *What's he doing out here? Why didn't he respond? Does he not remember us? Has he been hiding from me all this time?*

Too many questions without answers, and if I keep focusing on unknowns, I'm going to get paranoid.

Porter raises his hand.

For the love of all that is holy... "Yes. Porter. Speak."

"What is a pufferfish?"

I clench my fists, about to pop.

"Earth fish," Drago says. "Cute and innocent, until you try to eat. Then, spikes! Venom! Death!"

Porter is confused for a moment, then his eyes go wide. "Ohh, *we're* the pufferfish. I see. Clever, sir. But aren't pufferfish—"

"Extinct," I say. "Yes. Everything is extinct!"

"Sorry," Porter says. "I didn't mean to upset you."

"I'll be less upset if you can plot a long-range rotation for me."

"Of course. Where are we going?" he asks.

I frown. I've been avoiding this proverbial lion's den for five years.

"Union Command."

"How do I look?" I ask, stepping into *Lil' Bitch'n*'s cargo bay. I'm dressed in a modified BCS. It has more armor, a golden eagle insignia covering the chest, a 'shock rod'—basically a taser—hanging from the belt, and a black mask with reflective eye goggles. I've never been to Command Central, but apparently the facility is protected by Overseers dressed like this.

Burnett volunteered to access the data I'm looking for on his own, which I appreciate. Porter is something of a genius with tech, and Morton has become a respectable pilot, but Burnett doesn't always have a lot to offer. But here he is, stepping up.

His virtue is loyalty. Like a puppy.

But I can't trust him to do what needs doing if things go sideways. So, I'm going, too, and the only way to do that is to cover every inch of my skin and hope no one takes a peek at the ID Porter forged.

"Like a ninja," Chuy says, knowing exactly what I'd want to hear.

"Cool," I say.

"Like future-Nazi ninja," Drago says.

"Also, kind of cool," I say, looking myself over.

If Drago shaved, squeezed himself into a BCS, and had the capability to hide his accent, I'd probably bring him along. Chuy, too, but a female Overseer might stand out, and Porter only had time to create one faux security BCS. That left me with Carter, the wildcard, without whom I might have destroyed Whip's starship. She's pulled her weight since we found her, and she hasn't tried to kill my Union crew again.

She also doesn't need to wear a mask.

A person's station in the Union is determined by two things—physical prowess and intelligence. Those who are born with the total package are elevated into positions of power, and those who aren't are shunted downward. My boys wound up collecting junk from abandoned worlds because they weren't prize ponies. Porter is overweight. Morton has a slight lazy eye, slouches, and his face is as unsymmetrical as a Picasso portrait. Burnett...he's bald, frail, and a few gumdrops short of a gingerbread house.

But Carter—she's the total package. Fit, beautiful, white, and a look in her eyes that says, 'I'm the smartest person you know.' Anyone looking at her will likely assume she's someone important, hopefully to the point where no one will bother checking her ID.

"Hold on," Morton says from the cockpit.

I pull the mask off my head and take a seat between Chuy and Drago, across from Carter and Burnett. *Lil Bitch'n* shakes as we lift off, and then it's smooth sailing as we leave the hangar bay and turn toward planet 009-32-1923.

"So," Burnett says. "We've got a minute."

"Oh boy," Drago says, leaning his head against the hull. "Here we go."

"What's...happening?" Carter asks.

"Burnett likes... How you say? Ice breakers." Drago closes his eyes. "Wake me when done."

"Okay," Burnett says, turning to Carter. "Pets?"

She just stares at him.

"No pets?"

Nothing.

"We don't have pets, either," he says.

Her eyes narrow, almost imperceptibly. She turns to me. "No one has pets?"

"Where the human race goes, most living things go extinct," I say.

"Unless they taste good," Chuy adds.

This furrows Carter's brow. "Hold on. What you're describing is reprehensible. It's an afront to basic human decency."

Burnett looks wounded. "Well, I wouldn't say th—"

"*You* won't say anything," Carter says and then she turns back to me. "How do you sleep at night?"

"He doesn't," Chuy says. "Not much, anyway."

"You help them," Carter says. "All of you. And then bemoan the fates of all the worlds you help destroy. You're no better than Christopher Columbus."

Drago opens one eye. "I thought America celebrated Columbus Day. He was hero explorer. Found American continent."

Carter crosses her arms. "He was a genocidal asshole who got lost and accidentally landed in Venezuela, claimed it for Spain, and then instigated the world's most deadly landgrab, raping and pillaging as he went." Carter leans forward, elbows on knees. "How is that any different from what you three are doing for the Union?"

"We are not raping...animals?" Drago guesses.

"You are helping them corrupt and destroy worlds," she counters.

I've got a slew of arguments lined up. I repeat them to myself at night when I'm not sleeping.

Billions of people will die of starvation if we don't find new planets.

The creatures dying aren't sentient.

Carter would still be stuck on a planet if we hadn't become Exo-Hunters.

Finding my people is priority number one.

But at what cost?

I lower my head. This is how atrocities are justified. "She's right."

"She is?" Chuy says.

"You're damn right, I am," Carter says, and she's not done yet. "'I do solemnly swear that I will support and defend the Constitution of the United States against all enemies, foreign and domestic; that I will bear true faith and allegiance to the same; and that I will obey the orders of the President of the United States and the orders of the officers appointed over me, according to regulations and the Uniform Code of Military Justice. So help me God.'"

The silence that follows is painful.

Burnett breaks it. "Wow… Just… Uhh. People don't speak like that anymore. Sounds serious, though. What is it?"

"Marine Corps oath of enlistment," I say.

"What does it mean?" he asks.

"That the Union, who destroyed the United States, and the rest of the world, was—and is—my enemy."

"But…there is no United States anymore," Burnett says. "No constitution. No President. Right?"

"For those who believe in it," Carter says. "The United States isn't just a location on a planet. It's a set of ideals. And those who turn their backs on those ideals…they're—"

"Traitors." I squeeze my hands together, not because I'm angry with Carter, but because I agree with her.

Drago grunts. "I made similar oath…"

"Wrong ideals," Carter says.

He looks her in the eyes.

Her speech to me stirred something that's been lying dormant in all of us. "But same enemy."

Carter gives him a nod.

"Umm, what's happening?" Burnett says. "I feel like I'm missing something."

"We're about to go rogue," Chuy says.

"But why?"

"To fight for a better life," I say.

"But life is good," Burnett says.

"Not just for people," I tell him. "But for every living thing."

"Oh. *Oh.*" He sobers under the weight of realization and the undeniable fact that while the Union doesn't remember racism, that's not the only prerequisite for being evil. How we treat the world around us is a good indicator of a society's moral compass. And mine has been pointed in the wrong direction for a while now.

I nudge Chuy. "Looks like we'll be pirates, after all." I look at Carter. "Thank you…for realigning my moral compass."

"Just doing my job," she says.

"Still going to get my people back," I tell her. "That hasn't changed for me. Never will."

"Without enabling the Fourth Reich," she says. "I'd expect nothing less."

"Sorry," Burnett says. "But what does this mean for me?"

"Means you've got a choice to make," I tell him. Our little 'rah-rah-sis-boom-bah, yeah America!' rally has put us in an awkward position. Two of the crew members critical to the mission in which we're ankle deep were born and bred Union. Morton might not know about the shift in allegiance, but Burnett does, and I can't do this without him.

"You can stay a Union man," Carter says. "Or you can take a stand and fight for what is right."

"If I take a stand, does that mean I get to stay on the *Bitch'n* and keep my friends?"

Oh. My. God.

So much like a puppy, it hurts.

"Yes, Burnett, you'd get to stay. It also means you'll get a callsign."

"A callsign! Like Dark Horse and Chuy and Drago?"

"Yes..." I tell him.

Eyes wide, he says, "I want to be...Burn!"

"Burn..." I say. "Are you sure? Your real name is Burnett..."

He shakes his head, oblivious. "I don't see the problem."

"You're right." I smile at him. "It's perfect."

"Approaching Command Central if you want to see it from the outside," Morton says over comms.

I stand, take two steps toward the cockpit, and stop in front of Carter. "Thank you."

She gives a nod. No hint of self-righteousness, judgment, or gloating. She's just happy I made the right choice. So am I.

I head for the cockpit and stop behind Morton, confused by what I'm seeing. We're in orbit above a planet that appears to be almost entirely black, like it's nighttime, but it's actually lit by this solar system's star. I've never seen it before, but something about it feels familiar. "I thought we were looking at Command Central."

"We are," he says.

"Shit…" I say, suddenly understanding the odds against our pinprick rebellion's success. "Command Central is a *planet.*"

"Was it always like this?" I ask.

Morton looks up at me, confused puppy expression on his face. "Like what?"

"Like...*that.*" I motion to the view of what looks like a charred planet with gray oceans. "It's like if Satan built a Death Star...or Cybertron."

Wearing a shit-eating grin, he says, "I don't know what any of those things are."

I pinch the bridge of my nose for a moment. "Why are the continents black? Why does the whole planet look coated in metal?"

"Because it is," he says. "Command Central is a feat of human ingenuity and engineering. It is a sprawling metropolis. The tallest building stretches five thousand feet into the sky. It's a planet-sized city. Prime living for those who prefer urban settings, home to the High Council, the Overseers, and the Predictors."

"Was there ever life here?" I'm not sure why that's important. Command Central has been around for hundreds of years. Whatever was here before humanity arrived has nothing to do with me, and there's nothing to be done about it. Who'd want to live in a shithole like this, anyway?

"Emergent life," he says. "Single cell organisms. They might still live in the oceans."

"Looks pretty polluted," I say.

"The oceans were always a shade of gray. Not as dark, of course. When Command Central was discovered, it was rich in two things—oxygen and Oxium—the metal that built everything you see below, *Bitch'n*, and most other modern spacecraft. It's easy to work with, light, and has tensile, compressive, yield and impact strengths that are beyond comparison. Without it, the Union wouldn't have been able to expand so rapidly. Luckily, this was the second habitable world discovered in the early expansionist era."

"Which planet was the first?" I ask.

"They called it Beta Prime." He pushes a few buttons, preparing to enter Command Central's atmosphere. "This was before planets were identified with numerical codes."

"How come I've never heard of it?"

He shrugs. "It's insignificant. No one has been to Beta Prime in hundreds of years."

"Why the hell not?"

"It was an experiment. To see if human beings could acclimate to environments that weren't outright toxic, but not exactly friendly. When the population survived, the planet was abandoned."

"Abandoned? What about the colonists?"

"They were criminals and undesirables," he says. "They formed violent tribes and warred with each other until none were left. That's what I was taught. It's not really something people talk about much."

"How can anyone know that the people there are dead if no one has been back?"

Another shrug. "Not really my area of expertise. I have no reason to doubt the historical data, though."

"Given the Union's penchant for erasing the past, I'd say you have a pretty good reason to doubt the historical data." He's talking about the early Union days, when humanity was Nazi as fuck. I'm not surprised they dove headfirst into Atrocity Land when testing the interstellar waters, but just leaving an entire planet behind is odd. I file it away for a rainy day. Might be worth looking into if I get bored...which is unlikely.

"You should probably take a seat, sir," Morton says. "The upper layers of atmosphere are thick. Our descent could be rough."

I head for the door and then stop. "Oh hey, just a heads up. We're going rogue, betraying the Union, and becoming pirates...or something like that."

"That sounds exciting," he says with a grin. "What's a pirate?"

"I'll explain it to you later," I tell him. "Are you okay with the rest? You understand it, right?"

"I'm a crew member of the *Bitch'n*, serving under your command. I will follow wherever you lead."

"Even if it brings us into direct conflict with the Union?"

"That would be...inadvisable, but...yes. Obviously."

"Why obviously?" I ask.

"We're...what's the word you have used? Family. Right?"

He's right. I have used the word family to describe my team. What he doesn't realize is that I was referring to my people from the 80s. But he's not wrong, either. The boys have earned their spot on the mantle with the rest.

"You guys..." He's looking out the windshield, so he misses me wipe away a single tear. I'm genuinely moved by his and Burnett's loyalty. I just hope I don't get them killed. I give him a pat on the shoulder. "Thanks."

I head back to the cargo bay, take my seat, and buckle up. *Lil' Bitch'n* shakes as we enter the atmosphere, but dampeners keep the sound to a minimum and help eliminate some of the jolt. After we punch through the roughest layers, I say, "So, apparently, Command Central is a planet."

"*Whole* planet?" Drago asks.

"The whole damn thing."

"Is that a problem?" Burnett asks. "How does that change our situation?"

It doesn't. Not really. It's not like we're attacking Command Central. We're sneaking into one facility, getting what we need and sneaking back out. Planet or not, we assumed it would be heavily guarded even if the Union isn't militarized like they were in the good ol' days.

"It's just damn intimidating," Chuy says.

Burnett nods. "I see your point. Drago scares me because of his size. And his face. And his penchant for—"

Drago clears his throat, cutting Burnett short.

"Even *that* is scary," Burnett says, and then he turns to me. "How do you do it? Overcome fear."

"You don't need to overcome it," I say. "A fearless soldier is dangerous to the enemy *and* to his own people. It's more like...you take the fear and all the nervous energy that comes with it, and you redirect it. All it really takes is conviction—that what you're fighting for is worth dying for."

"Like the first law of thermodynamics," he says.

"First law of thermo...dyno...ramics?" Drago says.

Burnett smiles. He's not always the smartest person in the room. "Thermodynamics. It's—"

"Also known as the Law of Conservation of Energy," Carter chimes in. "Energy can't be created or destroyed. It can only be transformed into one form or another."

I'm expecting Burnett to be sad that Carter has just stolen his thunder, but he smiles wide. "Exactly! But in this case, the energy built by the human body in response to fear—rapid heartbeat, a surge of adrenaline, narrowing vision—is transformed into something positive."

I snap my fingers and point at him. "And that's called bravery."

"What if bravery isn't enough?" he asks.

"Music," I say. "Something inspirational."

Burnett leans forward. He's never heard real music, but he's always intrigued by the concept. "Would you normally have played music now, on the cusp of launching a dangerous mission?"

"Now is the perfect time for music," I say, and I frown when the only thing I hear is a muffled rumble. For a large part of my life, music was everything. Before joining the military, I was in a high school garage band. I played guitar and sang, but when people saw a black kid playing British New Wave tunes, most of them laughed, no matter how good I played or how hard I sang.

Of all the things I miss about the old world—the sky, freedom, pay-per-view porn—my heart aches for music.

I flinch when Drago stomps his foot twice and then claps.

"What was that?" Chuy asks. "You kill a bug?"

Drago grins. Stomps his foot twice, followed by a clap.

When he does it a third time, muscle memory takes over, and I do it with him. He smiles at me and we're stomping out the opening beat to Queen's *We Will Rock You*.

When Chuy joins in, Burnett laughs. "Is this... Is this music?"

"Hardly," Carter says, but then she stomps and claps with the rest of us. Like me, she's a music fan, and it's been a long time.

I'm about to belt out the lyrics when a jolt runs through the ship. The rumble stops, and our thumping with it.

"We've touched down." Morton's voice fills my comms, and then he uses a turn of phrase he picked up from me. "The clock is ticking."

And he's not wrong. We're not supposed to be here, and visits to the Database—capital D—are usually scheduled. Database isn't a very creative name for the place, but these are Nazis. They appropriated culture with the same ease that Butch Cassidy robbed banks, but they sucked at creating anything meaningful themselves. Probably because art is a reflection of the heart. Not much you can do with a heart of lifeless coal.

I unbuckle, stand up, and put my hand on my Slew Drive. "Let's do this." I give Burnett a thumbs up, trigger the slew drive, and rotate out of *Lil' Bitch'n*.

A dimly lit hallway greets me on the other side. I'm deep inside Command Central's Database. I take a quick look around, making sure no one saw me arrive. Then I activate my holomap, projected from my wrist. It shows a transparent three-dimensional image of the structure around me, including a red dot to show me where I am and a blue line showing me where to go.

Wish I'd had this in '89, I think. And then I feel a tickle on the back of my neck. A breeze. But I'm—*shit*. In a hurry to get started, as usual, I left my mask behind.

I grit my teeth, brace for mockery, and then rotate back to *Lil' Bitch'n*. When I arrive in the exact spot I'd left, Chuy is already holding out the mask, shaking her head at me. "Burnett and Carter are en route. Try not to get lost."

"Ha, ha," I say, and I pull the mask over my head. "How do I look?"

"Like a puto."

"Ugh! ¡La concha de tu madre!"

Chuy barks a laugh. "Nice. Been saving that one for a special occasion?"

"You know it," I say, and I rotate back into the historical home of the crackers who committed world-wide genocide and erased people who look like me and Chuy from the entire galaxy. The smile under my mask, from shouting something like 'Your mother's vagina,' at Chuy, fades when I slip back into the Database hallway—and find it occupied.

Two men wearing white BCSs—Predictors—sense my presence behind them and stop in their tracks. They turn toward each other and then toward me.

They could be twins. Blond hair brushed in a perfect gelled swoop. Blue eyes. Square jawlines. Skinny and fit. And...glasses, which somehow makes them look more like sinister geniuses of the Fourth Reich. But poor vision is cause for demotion. They shouldn't be working at Comm- and Central.

Unless...

Two details jump out at me—the lenses neither enlarge nor reduce the size of their eyes, meaning they're not corrective lenses. And they're tinted yellow. *They're protective lenses*, I realize, but Hans and Franz here think the glasses make them look cool. Or smart. Or whatever attribute Union nerds find attractive.

I say nothing. I don't know much about Overseers. No one in my crew has ever met one, even the trio born and raised in the Union. But in my twentieth century experience, security guards usually have a few things in common—they're big, they're serious, and they don't talk unless you give them a good reason. And then, they get loud, puffed up, and tend to say too much.

"I did not hear you approach," Hans, the man on my left, says.

"Mmm," Franz says. "Stealthy. Impressive."

Hans squints at me and eyes me up and down. I've been ogled before. At the beach. By the pool. In the gym. But never by a man, and for the first time in my life I feel the discomfort of a woman on the receiving end. I feel a little violated and a lot pissed.

What the hell is he looking at?

Also, is being gay cool with future Nazis? It's never come up, but I can't imagine homophobia surviving the genetic Blitzkrieg that wiped out most of humanity.

"This one is masculine," Hans says.

"Yes," Franz says. "Quite."

Hans chuckles. "I rather like it."

Neither of them finds my silence odd, so I maintain the stoic Overseer act. They're also not afraid of me, which is a little disconcerting and strange.

Hans approaches me, raises his hands, and palms my pecs. Then he starts squeezing. "Rather flat...and firm...but the strength." He looks me in the eyes, though he cannot see them past the reflective goggles. "The things I would let you do to me..."

Okay, what the fuck?

It takes all my self-control to not break the man's wrists, and to keep from laughing. I'm simultaneously disgusted and amused, like watching Richard Simmons, greased up and molesty, sweatin' to the oldies with a frozen grin.

"Come," Hans says to Franz. "Feel for yourself.

Franz approaches, grinning. He has a go at my chest, getting his jollies.

Have your fun and move on boys.

Hans smiles at Franz, a gleam in his eyes. "How much time do we have?"

"Enough..." Franz searches the hallway. Points to a nearby closed door—a storage room, maybe. "There." To me he says, "Overseer, are you prepared to perform your secondary duty?"

Secondary duty? Are Overseers security guards and *sex slaves? Wait...*

Holy shit. Overseers are women!

There's probably a formal response to the request, and I doubt it has anything to do with personal preference.

"She's ready," Hans says, confirming they think I'm a woman, which makes me a little insecure about my masculine figure, but I'll work that out in therapy.

Hans places his hand on my crotch. A quizzical look slowly stretches across his face. He pats around, following the shape of my very not-feminine cock and balls. Then he freezes. His eyes snap wide. His hand pulls back. He raises a single finger, about to speak. Then closes his mouth, and his hand.

"What?" Franz asks, and again when his compatriot can't respond. "What is it?!"

"She...has a penis?" Hans says.

Franz takes a step back. Eyes me up and down. His face seems to elongate in surprise, but he doesn't look entirely upset by the revelation.

Punch them, I think. *Knock the twins on their asses, and get the hell out of Touchy-Feely Town.*

As much as I'd like to send them to la-la land, they might wake up and sound the alarm. I need to get out of this without violence.

For now.

"I am a man," I say. I keep my voice emotionless and mostly monotone, but my deep baritone still makes them flinch. "Part of a new Overseer program. And...I am at your service."

They look at each other, trying to hide their smiles.

Called it.

"But..." I say, "the High Council has requested my immediate presence in the Database for an assignment of utmost galactic security. Therefore, I must decline your request."

"The High Council," Hans says. "Sounds important."

Holy shit, they're buying it.

"In situations like this, where time is a constraint, it is now encouraged that Predictors with...alternative sexual interests, explore them on their own time." I sweep my hand toward storage room door. Nothing else needs to be said, and if I keep speaking, I'm definitely going to laugh.

The pair look at each other, having a conversation with just their eyes. And then, without another word, they're off, headed toward the storage room. I stand still until they're inside the room and the door is closed. Then I turn on the holomap and break into a run. I'm amused by the encounter, but guilt starts to set in. Hans and Franz might be the first sexually liberated men in a thousand years, but there's a good chance my charade, and their visit into the closet, will get them killed if they ever come out.

Then again, they were going to rape me, when they thought I was a woman, and when I was a man.

Then again, *again*, I could have killed them both and stayed on schedule. So, there's that. Guilt negated.

I activate my comms. "Carter, where you at?"

"En route," she says. "Security was...lax. Why didn't you check in?"

"Made some friends," I say. "Freed their minds."

"You killed them? I thought we agreed to—"

"They're not dead. They're...exploring their sexuality."

She's silent for a moment. "Is that military slang for dead?"

"What? No. Dead is dead. KIA is dead. Tango Uniform is tits up, and tits up is dead. 'Exploring their sexuality' is literal. Let's just say, my physique triggered their erection detectors, and now they're putting them to good—"

I round a corner, following the blue line, and I'm greeted by a busy hallway. I deactivate the map and try to act like I'm supposed to be there, letting the uniform do the convincing for me, despite the fact that I don't have boobs, hips, or a backside worth double taking—unless you're Hans and Franz, or a lady.

"On your nine," she says.

I look left to find Carter and Burnett approaching from another hallway. Both are straight-faced and all business, just like everyone else here. There are a mix of uniforms—various shades of BCSs—and no one really looks at anyone else, which is good. But I do see a few black-clad women up ahead. The real Overseers.

I slow my pace, allowing Carter and Burnett to merge in front of me.

"How are we going to find our way without a map?" I whisper. Thanks to the comms, they can both hear me loud and clear.

"I memorized it," Carter says, and then she stops at a locked door-way with a keypad. Burnett punches in a code Porter got from remotely hacking a large number of personal computers within Command Central. A light flashes red. Shit.

But the door's lock *thunks* open.

"Wait, red is good?" I ask.

"Of course," Burnett says. "It represents blood—the life spring of humanity."

"Oookay," I say, and I follow them in. "That's normal. That's...Whoa."

The space is vast. Farther than I can see. There are aisles of computer terminals and stacks of what Porter called servers. They contain all the data known to the Union, about every planet, every ship, every person, along with all human knowledge and what hasn't been purged from the historical record. It smells like warm electronics, but the temperature is well regulated.

"This way," Burnett says, walking straight ahead. We pass people every now and again, but they're all so engrossed in their work that they don't look up to see who is strolling past. Security cameras are mounted every thirty feet in every direction, but we didn't trigger an alarm when we entered, and aside from my masculine build, which is totally, obviously a man's body, we look like we belong here.

"So," I say. "FYI, the Overseers are chicks."

"Chicks?" Carter says.

"Women. All of them."

"Well, that's not good."

"Because I totally don't look like a woman, right?"

She glances back at me, eyes me up and down, and shrugs. "Mch."

Meh? What the hell does—

"Aufseherin," she says.

"Gesundheit?" I say, and I can feel her eyeroll through the back of her head.

"Aufseherin were female concentration camp guards during World War II," she explains. "Aufseherin is German for Overseer. Some of them, like their male counterparts, were sadistic war criminals belonging to the Waffen-SS. Point is, if the Overseers here are similar to those in the concentration camps, don't underestimate them because they're women."

"Nazi stormtroopers first, women second. Got it."

"This should work," Burnett says, stopping at an empty console. We've got fifty feet of no one on either side of us. I can hear people closer than that in other aisles, but they can't see us.

"Make it snappy," I say, and I try to look casual in an 'I'm keeping an eye on this guy' kind of way.

But then I forget all about the act, why we're here, and what the plan is.

"What the hell?"

Carter, who is leaned over, looking at the screen—no doubt memorizing how the system works, just in case we ever need to break into Union Command's database again—glances back at me. "Shh."

She's too focused to hear it.

Someone is humming.

On its own, that would stand out, because this music-less society doesn't know how to carry a tune. They don't even know any to carry. But the melody drifting to me from a nearby aisle isn't the mindless hum of a distracted mind—it's *Sweet Dreams* by Eurythmics.

By the time I reach a junction cutting between the aisles, I can't hear the humming anymore. The musically inclined person hasn't stopped—hopefully—I'm just several hundred feet away. Which makes finding the correct aisle very difficult.

I pause at the next aisle over, staring down an endless strip of computers and nerds hard at work. Not a one of them looks up from their screens. They're all too brainwashed to care about someone staring at them, too dedicated to their jobs—which is kind of the same thing, or they're simply afraid to look at someone dressed as an Overseer.

How bad could they be? I wonder. The Overseers might be modeled after female concentration camp guards, but they're still part of the soft-in-the middle Union. They probably just stand around, chatting it up and having potlucks on the weekend. What enemy could they possibly be guarding against? Other than me, obviously.

Had to be this aisle or the next, I decide. Any farther and the hum of electronics would have muffled the sound. I'm about to charge down the aisle when I think better of it. Choosing wrong will waste a lot of time that I might not have.

The next aisle over looks almost identical to the previous. Endless workstations.

People staring at screens.

This is hopeless.

I'm about to turn away and head down the first aisle when I see it.

A foot. Tapping.

I can't see the rest of the person seated at the workstation, but their heel is bouncing in a steady beat. I hum 'Sweet Dreams,' tapping my own foot in time with theirs.

Target acquired.

"Dark Horse!" Carter whispers. She's at the end of our aisle, glaring at me. "What the hell are you doing? Stay on mission."

"I *am* on mission." I point down the aisle. "Someone down there is humming."

"Humming? What the hell does that—"

"Sweet Dreams," I say.

She stands frozen for a moment. "Like…Eurythmics?"

"Close cut, carrot-top in a suit, Eurythmics. Yeah. Could be someone from our time. Could be one of our people. Just stay with Burnett. I'll take care of this."

She nods. "Just…be subtle."

She can't see my smile, but somehow she senses it. Oozes mockery when she says, "Subtle is my middle name."

"I was going to say I was born subtle."

She shakes her head and moves back toward Burnett. I turn toward the bouncing foot, locked on like a missile, and I do my best nonchalant speed-walk toward it.

I can't help but wonder who it is. Whip was never an audiophile, but he'd know the song…and I'm certain he's already moving around freely in this timeline. But why would he be here?

Same reason I am, I realize, as I try to walk a little faster.

When I approach the tapping foot, my hope that it's Whip fades. The shoe is white. As is the pantleg. It's a Predictor. The thin ankle suggests a woman. I stop behind her, arms behind my back like a watchful Overseer just doing my thing.

She's a small person. Just over five feet tall. Her BCS is skintight, despite her petite figure. A mop of curly blonde hair sits atop her head. It's the closest thing I've seen to a fashion statement, so I'm guessing the curls are natural.

The screen she's looking at shows a series of files with numeric codes. The numbers mean nothing to me, until I notice a trend in the last four digits. 1983.

My heart pounds.

Can't be...

The blonde head of hair bops to a tune I can't hear. And then it stops. She taps the screen, highlighting the next file down in the list. A message appears on screen.

Resume Historical Document?

YES or NO.

She taps YES.

An image appears on the screen. It's moving. For a moment, I'm confused by what I'm seeing, in part because it's been a long time, but also because I didn't think it was possible.

Matthew Broderick is on screen. And Ally Sheedy. Both are smiling. Having a good time. Sitting in front of a computer console.

Sweet baby Reagan on a trampoline! This is War Games.

"How can it talk?" the Predictor says, quoting Sheedy's line from the movie. Then she responds as Broderick, "It's not a real voice. Ahh, this box just interprets signals from the computer and turns them into sound."

She gets every inflection right. This isn't her first time watching.

Nor is it mine, and what happens next is beyond my ability to self-control. The Predictor and I speak aloud the next line in unison, which also happens to be the movie's most iconic line, "Shall we play a game?"

With a tap, the movie pauses.

The Predictor is in shock. Her hands snap out, fingers splayed like I've got a gun to her head. She's shaking. Terrified.

"You're not supposed to be watching movies," I guess.

She turns around to face me, big blue eyes glistening. Can't be older than twenty. "I-I'm sorry." She looks me up and down. "Sir?"

"I don't look like a woman, right?" I ask.

She shakes her head. "Not at all...but, why not?"

"I'll ask the questions," I say, trying to maintain the illusion of authority. "What are you doing here? To the outside world, this history no longer exists."

"Entertainment," she admits. "I'm sorry. I didn't think there was any harm. Viewing historical documents isn't strictly forbidden inside Command Central."

"And if you leave? Will you take these historical records with you?"

"Leave?" The concept confounds her. "We can't leave."

"Never?" I ask.

"Of course not." She motions to the aisles around us. "This is the only home I will ever know."

My bleeding heart is gushing. She's doing a piss-poor job hiding the crushing depression of her existence. She's using movies and music of the past to escape her fucked up reality. I've been craving the same since we arrived in this future hell.

"But," I say. "Could you?"

"Could I what?"

"Remove the historical records?"

"Why would I—"

"As you already noted, I am a new breed of Overseer. My job is to predict—like yours—but instead of finding habitable worlds for the glorious Union, I am looking for security risks. If you can show me how someone might collect the historical records and transport them from the Database, it would make my job easier."

"I don't know..."

"You help me," I say, "I'll help you. Show me how it could be done, and I won't mention this infraction now...or at any time in the future."

Her smile lights up the aisle.

"For real?"

"Absolutely," I say.

"Radical," she says.

"Mmm," I say, and I chime in with my own 80's teen speak. "Totally tubular."

She squints at me, but she says nothing. She opens a drawer and takes out a small device. Plugs it into the front of her computer terminal.

"This is a pinkie drive. It's small, but it has enough storage to hold several terraflops of data."

I don't know what a terraflop is. Sounds kind of sexual. But I don't want to appear too ignorant. "How much of the historical record would that hold?" I point to the screen.

She shrugs. "About a hundred years' worth."

The mask hiding my expressions has never been more useful. If she could see my face, the jig would be up. I'm almost sick with desperate hope.

"Show me," I say. "Transfer everything between 1950 and 2050." I haven't seen the movies and media post '89, but there are more than a lot of sequels I want to see, and a number of bands who have more than a few more albums in them.

"Sure," she says, tapping a few buttons. A file transfer progress bar appears on the screen, slowly moving from left to right. "While we wait," she says, spinning around to face me, "why don't you tell me who you actually are, and what you're really doing here?"

"I already told you," I say.

"Horse shit," she says. Kid is up on her past lingo. Speaks like one of us. "I heard you quote the movie. No one says 'tubular.' And there aren't any damn Overseers with dicks. Start talking or I push the big red button."

Her hand is hovering over an actual big red button labeled: SECURITY. *Shit.*

I see only one way out of this, and it's risky, but what the hell, we're pirates now.

"What's your name, kid?"

"I'm the one asking the questions," she says, doing an impersonation of me.

"Just...c'mon. Your name. Mine is Dark Horse."

"That's a stupid name." When I laugh, she smiles. "Hildegard."

"Excuse me?"

"I said, 'Hildegard.' That's my name."

"And you think *I* have the stupid name?"

Her hand moves toward the button. "It's a common name."

"Okay, okay. Sorry. I just... Can I call you Hildy?"

She smiles again. "That's what my mother called me, so I'm told."

I want to ask her about her mother, but this isn't the time or place. "Listen, Hildy, I have one question for you."

She waits, expectant eyebrows raised.

"Have you seen *Back to the Future?*"

"Like, six times," she says. "'Hello. McFly.'"

"So...my situation is like that, but instead of moving *back* in time, I moved *forward* in time from the past."

"I get it. That's *Back to the Future Part II*," she says.

"Did...did you just say Back to the Future...*Part Two*? There was a sequel?"

"At the end of 1989."

"Is that on there?" I point to the pinkie drive.

She nods. "So...you're from the past."

"Early 1989," I say.

Her hand rests on the button without pushing it. "Prove it."

"Okay...just...try not to spaz out." Moment of truth. No going back. Do or die. I take a deep breath, check to make sure no one is watching, let it out, and then remove my mask.

16

A slowly building high-pitched squeal rises out of Hildy's throat. Her eyes are locked onto my face, looking at my eyes, my lips, my hair.

"Pretty awesome, right?" I say.

She can't speak.

"Hildy," I say. Her eyes lock onto mine. "Can you remove your hand from the button now?"

Her hand snaps back. "Sorry. I just... How are you here?"

"Like right now, in the Database, or—"

"In the future," she says.

"Long story." I glance at the data transfer progress bar. It's a little more than halfway done. "Too long."

She hitches a thumb toward her monitor. "Is this what you're here for? Movies and music?"

"Not exactly," I say. "I heard you humming."

Her eyes widen. Fearful. "I was humming?"

"Guess that's not a good thing?"

"There's no official rule against accessing the historical record...if you're a historian."

"Is the data not protected?" I ask

"I stole a historian's credentials. I've been using them for a few years. The people who made all this are long gone, but the stories...the music... It gives me hope, you know?"

"Hope for what?"

"Something more than this." She looks around at the whirring computers. "I sit in a room like this every day. We can't go outside. I've never smelled fresh air. I've never...had fun. Or friends. In a few months, I'll have to start carrying babies."

Kid is breaking my heart.

"Of course, none of that will be possible now," she says.

"Why..."

She tilts her head toward the screen. "Viewing files is a normal part of a historian's daily tasks. Downloading ten decades of data onto a portable drive is not. It will be flagged. Reviewed. And it will eventually lead to me... Oh no!" She snags the mask in my hands. Shoves it in my face. "Put it back on! And don't turn around!"

She's looking behind me and over my head. I was so distracted by the siren song of *Sweet Dreams* that I didn't check for security cameras. If I'd been facing the other direction, Union Command would have had a clear view of my face.

I slip the mask back on, then turn around for a look. The mirrored bubble in the ceiling makes it impossible to see where the camera is facing, but we have to assume it's pointed straight at us.

Close call for me, but Hildy is right. She's in deep shit.

"Hildy..." I shouldn't do this. It's reckless. And stupid. And the others are going to kill me. But it's the right thing to do. Huddled masses and all that. "Do you know what a pirate is?"

"Like someone who steals data?"

"Not really, but— Actually, yeah, that's exactly what I'm doing here, but in a more historical sense, like with a boat, and a crew and 'argh, me hearties.'"

"Ohh," she says. "Like Jack Sparrow?"

"I don't know who that is," I say.

"Right. 1989. You haven't seen *Pirates of the Caribbean*."

"Pirates of the... Did they make a movie out of a theme park ride?"

"I think so, yeah. Also, Captain Hook! And One-Eyed Willy!"

I put my gloved hand over her mouth. She's getting excited. "Okay, okay, you know what a pirate is. The question is...do you want to be one?"

"Me a irate?!" she says, her voice muffled by my hand. "Iv oo?"

"But...it's more than that," I say. "Me and my crew—"

"On a irate ip?"

"Yes. The *Bitch'n.*"

I feel her smile under my hand. "*itch'n!*"

"Can you calm down so I can understand what you're saying?" I ask. She nods. I slowly withdraw my hand.

"Here's the deal. We're not just stealing stuff and hoarding treasure. We're also looking for my people—"

"Other people from the past?"

"Four of them, yes."

"Radical."

"And..." This is where it becomes a hard sell. "We're taking a stand against...all this. The way people live. The rape of countless worlds. The extinction of millions of species. The destruction of our world."

"Of Earth," she says, wistfully.

"Yeah."

"So...not just pirates, but...rebels against the Union?"

I let that sink in a little bit. It's intimidating to hear aloud. "Yes."

She sits unmoving. Ten silent seconds goes by.

Is she going to bolt?

Is she going to whack the security button?

I wouldn't blame her for doing either. The proposition before her is no doubt daunting.

When we reach the twenty second mark, I can't stand it anymore. "Well? Are you in?"

The file transfer progress bar disappears. She pulls the pinkie drive out of the computer. "Doy. I was just waiting for the download to finish." She stands, pushes her chair in, and switches off the screen.

"Wait. Really? Just like that?"

She looks at me like I've just eaten shit and asked, "Hhhhhow are you doing?" point blank. "You think anyone living in this hellhole wants to be here?" She smiles. "But only one of them knows what a pirate is, and only one of them can help you find your lost friends."

Holy shit.

She's a predictor. Finding needles in haystacks is her job.

"Also, we should go. They know about the file transfer by now."

"And if they know about yours..." I grab her wrist and run back the way I came. At the junction, we round the corner at a sprint, skip an aisle, and then head down the next. Carter and Burnett are still there, working at a console.

Burnett looks nervous, his fingers a blur.

Carter's jaw grinds.

They're not making any progress.

Carter sees me coming and flinches. Faces me with clenched hands.

"It's me," I say, showing her my palms. Her eyes flick from me to Hildy behind me. She has questions of her own, but she answers mine first. "We hit a dead end."

"The system has a credential system I didn't know about, and mine...well, salvagers don't have access to much." He sees Hildy and smiles. "Hello."

"Hi," she says. "Are you a pirate, too?"

"You didn't?" Carter says to me. "For real?"

"I'm a pirate, too," Hildy says. "Don't worry."

"I feel so much better," Carter's skeptical sarcasm shifts to hope. "Can you access the system?"

"If they haven't locked me out yet." Hildy shoos Burnett away from the console. Takes his seat. Slips the pinkie drive into the console. Types in her credentials.

Access granted.

"What do you need?"

Carter tries to hide her grin, but I can tell she's pleased and impressed. "Any and everything having to do with a ship called *Zorak*."

"You have a serial number?" Hildy asks.

"Just the name," I say. "We need to know where they've been and where they're going."

Her fingers fly over the keys. Several searches come up empty. "That name isn't on file for any ship. What kind of vessel is it?"

"I don't know ship models," I confess.

"A custom build," Burnett says, "but it's being used by an Exo-Hunter."

"Exo-Hunters," Hildy says with a little bit of vitriol. "Union couldn't rape the galaxy without them." She looks back at me with a 'you know what I'm talking about' look on her face.

"Well," I say. "You know. Some people in questionable lines of work turn out to be good guys."

She twists her lips. "Like Han Solo."

"Exactly!" I say.

"The people we're looking for are like Han Solo?" she asks.

"I hope so," I say, and I motion to the screen.

It's all the reminder she needs. "Still nothing. But..." She keeps on typing. "We can just copy all the celestial data from..."

"Past five years," I say.

"Past five years, and all the predictor assignments moving forward for the next year."

"You know where we're going for the *next year?*"

She pauses. "Where *who* is going?"

"Where *they're* going," I say, hoping she doesn't notice the edit. "Exo-Hunters."

Her eyes linger for a moment. "Yes." She taps the Enter key. A file transfer begins. Its progress is much faster than the media we pilfered. "Thousands of goldilocks planets have already been identified and scheduled for Exo-Hunting."

She swivels the chair toward me. "You know. I heard a rumor. About a ship of salvagers turned Exo-Hunters. They're long-termers, which is unusual, but they're also fast. Some say they're hungrier for new planets than the Union."

"Huh," I say.

"You wouldn't know anything about that, would you?" The file transfer finishes. She pulls out the pinkie drive. Clutches it in her hand.

All without taking her eyes off mine.

Busted.

Kid is smart.

Before I can try to wiggle my way out of her ire, a commanding female voice says, "Nobody move. Keep your hands where I can see them."

I raise my hands and use my body to shield Hildy from the woman's view. I'm relieved when Hildy slowly slips the pinkie drive into her pocket. She's not thrilled about us being Exo-Hunters, but she's still on board.

"Face me," the woman says. "All of you."

I turn toward the woman, whose garb matches mine. Like me, her face is hidden behind a mask, but the skintight body suit reveals a curvy, but stocky body. Low center of gravity. She's got mass behind her, and the way she's holding herself says that she knows how to use it.

"Overseer," she says, addressing me. "What is the meaning of this gathering?"

"There was...an accident," I say. "I stopped to assist."

"I tripped," Hildy says, looking sheepish.

"What's wrong with your voice?" the woman asks me.

I clear my throat and attempt to raise it an octave or two. "Uhh, my lunch was spicy."

"Mmm. Let me get this straight," the Overseer says to Hildy. "You tripped, caught yourself on the computer console, accidentally inserting a pinkie drive into the computer, and downloading sensitive material?"

"Yes," Hildy says. "That."

"And the same thing happened to you two aisles over?" the Overseer asks.

"I'm clumsy," Hildy says.

The Overseer's reflective lenses are locked on to me. "Overseer, turn sideways."

I do as asked, trying to act casually annoyed at being grilled by one of my own.

"Where is your bump?" she asks.

I glance down at Hildy, whispering. "What does she mean?"

"You're not pregnant," Hildy says.

My head snaps around to the Overseer. I mistook her girth as straightforward body weight. But it's not. She's pregnant. My arms fall to my sides.

My voice returns to normal. "Hold up. Overseers are all *pregnant* women?"

"The female gender is capable of serving the Union in multiple ways, simultaneously!" The Overseer's response is aggressive. Fanatical. Hildy is eager to take a stand, but this woman is a true believer. And if Hildy has access to the historical data of the 80s, everything before that exists, too, including World War II, the moral code of the Third Reich, and Mein Kampf. Which means—

"Alarm!" the Overseer shouts. "Alarm!"

—these Overseer ladies are the real deal. Nazis. And that means the Union has sharper teeth than I believed.

Two more Overseers arrive behind the first. At the far end of the aisle, several hundred feet away, three more of the female guards stalk toward us.

"Can I just ask you one question?" I ask the Overseer.

She waits.

"Is my lack of a pregnant belly the only reason you knew I wasn't a woman?" I motion to my body. "Really?"

"You're not a woman?" she responds.

"Oh, that is *it*," I say, raising my clenched fists. "Come and get some, Captain Preggers."

17

"You're not serious?" Carter says to me, as I await the Overseers with clenched fists.

I was kind of hoping that concern for their unborn children would dissuade them from a fight with a larger combatant, but the Overseers show no signs of backing down. "You see another way out of this?"

"We could rotate out of here," she says.

"That was a bad idea the first time you did it. And now there are four of us. Also, I'm not sure where we are in relation to the surface, or *Bitch'n.*"

"So, take us a few aisles over. Nazis or not, you can't fight pregnant women."

"Fine," I say, grabbing her shoulders. I pull her close, and we rotate out of the aisle, and into the hallway outside. I shove her away and then rotate back.

The Overseers are closer when I arrive, but they flinch back at my arrival.

"How did you do that?" Hildy asks.

I grab Burnett and rotate out, depositing him next to Carter in the hall. I give myself a quick once over, making sure I don't have anyone else's parts attached to my body, then I say, "Be right back," and rotate back into the Database.

I slip out of the white void, intending to grab Hildy and go poof, but a freight train fist is waiting for me.

Connects with my chin. Had I been a shorter man, it would have crushed my nose.

My feet scramble to keep me upright, as I reel back from the punch. I crash into a console and find a fiendishly grinning Captain Preggers stalking toward me.

Behind her, Hildy is easily subdued by the other two. Apparently, Preggers called dibs on me. Even the three Overseers approaching from behind have slowed down.

"I've been waiting for this moment all my life," Preggers says.

Hildy gasps. "I know that line."

I push myself up from the workstation. "Phil Collins."

"Yes!" Hildy says. Seems to be oblivious to the fact that we're about to be captured by the very evil empire we've just agreed to stop. "'In the Air Tonight.'"

Preggers takes a swing. Then another.

I bob and weave, avoiding the strikes, but I can't keep it up forever.

"Hildy," I say, noticing how loosely the Overseers are holding her arms.

"Yeah?"

"Remember who you are now. *What* you are now."

"Pirates," she says, wistfully.

"Right. Time to start acting like it."

I block two punches with my forearms, but I miss the third—an aggravated backhand slap that stings more than a good punch would. Punching is what you do in a fight. A slap is disrespectful. An insult. She's calling me out. Calling me a pansy.

"Okay, that's it," I say, taking a fighting stance.

"You shame the Overseer's uniform you're wearing," Preggers says to me.

A slew of comebacks flit through my mind, but they all have to do with being pregnant, and that's just low. I can't bring myself to say them aloud, so I just wait for her next attack.

Hildy, on the other hand, has an epiphany. "Act like a pirate... How does a pirate act?" She turns to the Overseer on her right. "Do you know how a pirate acts?" She smiles. "Because I do. They fight...dirty!"

Hildy lets out a piratey "Argh!" and stomps on the Overseer's foot, drawing a shout of pain. She yanks an arm free, twists around, and delivers a devastating kick to the crotch of the second Overseer. If she'd been a man, the woman would have dropped to the floor in a heap, but the Overseer doesn't have balls, and her crotch is padded.

The woman lifts Hildy off the ground and throws her. She sails past Preggers, crashes into a console behind me, and falls to the floor.

I back step toward her. "You okay?"

She sits up. Winces. Puts her hand to a fresh gash on her cheek. It comes away bloody.

Her wide eyes turn to me, and I swear, she does the best impression of Bruce Lee in *Enter the Dragon* that I've ever seen, tasting her own blood.

"Kid, you are my new favorite person."

Beaming, she pushes herself up beside me. "Let's kick their pregnant asses."

"My *ass* is not pregnant," Captain Preggers says, and then she charges Hildy instead of me.

Despite Hildy's enthusiasm, she's not a fighter, and if I don't do something she's going to take a haymaker to the temple that could turn her into a vegetable with a natural perm.

I catch Preggers's wrist mid-punch and use her momentum to spin her around. Before she can react, I've got my right arm around her neck and my left squeezing it tight. She fights against me, trying to strike my face with the back of her head, but there is no escaping a rear naked choke.

When her compatriots charge to the rescue, I maneuver Preggers between us, stopping them in their tracks. As savage as they might be, they're also concerned about each other's babies.

"I'm not killing her," I assure them. "Just putting her to sleep."

I don't think it will matter. The moment I put Preggers down, the others will charge. And we've got about thirty seconds before the others arrive behind us. I take a wide stance to maintain balance, as I move Preggers toward the floor.

"When I put her down," I say to Hildy, "grab hold of me."

A five-step plan solidifies in my psyche. One, let go of Preggers. Two, grab hold of Hildy. Three, rotate away. Four, rotate back into the hallway with Carter and Burnett. Five, get the fuck out.

Easy peasy lemon squeez—

Preggers's body jerks. I'm vaguely aware of one of her feet leaving the floor.

Then her heel connects with the back side of my balls and steamrolls them forward.

The pain is instantaneous and excruciating. Preggers falls from my hands, as I drop back to the floor, twisting into a fetal position, hands between my legs. Through gritted teeth, I hiss, "Grab hold!"

Hildy either understands why, or she just knows how to listen. She wraps her body over mine, holding on tight. Blinded by pain, I put a hand to my side, activate the slew drive, and then rotate away from the Database.

When we rotate out, I'm lost. Using a slew drive with your eyes closed and your mind whirling with white hot agony is like flying blind in a jet that can transport you anywhere in the galaxy. The only thing I know about where we emerge is that the air is breathable and the floor is hard. Every other detail beyond that is lost in a haze of agony."

"Are you okay?" Hildy asks, leaning up to look down at me.

"Gonna be...a minute...before I can move," I tell her.

"I've seen men get kicked in the nuts," she says with a chuckle. "It happens in a lot of movies. But, honestly, I didn't think it would actually hurt that bad."

"Well, it does." The knot in my stomach loosens a bit, allowing me to breathe. I still haven't exited I-Might-Pukesville, but I'm at least on the road out of town. "Do you know where we are?"

Hildy looks around, seeing the same thing I am: a featureless hallway. Then an alarm blares. Sounds like an angry electronic donkey. "Well, we didn't go far. Can't we just..." She motions to the Slew Drive on my belt. "What is that, anyway?"

I push myself up.

"Slew Drive."

"Slew…" She's aghast. "You have a *Slew Drive*…on your belt. And you used it…" She counts on her fingers. "…five times in less than a minute. Are you crazy? Don't you know what could—"

"Big explosion," I say.

"Badaboom."

"Right," I say.

"Big badabigboom."

"What?"

"After your time," she says. "Sorry. Can't we just rotate out of here? Back to your ship. Back to *Bitch'n?*"

"Yes." I stand, hands on knees, catching my breath. "And no. Without knowing where we are and which way to go, we could end up moving farther away."

"Or inside a wall," she says. "Or a person. Gross."

Slew Drives are meant to be used in outer space. Ships travel to predetermined locations carefully selected by Predictors like Hildy. That keeps them from rotating out of the fourth dimension and into a star. "Actually," I say, "My PSD—Personal Slew Drive—prevents me from emerging in solid objects, inert or living."

"What? How?"

"Turns out funny looking guys can still have really smart brains. Porter's probably a genius. You'll meet him if we get out of here without, you know, dying."

"Really?"

"Really." I stretch my back. The pain is going to linger for a while, but I'm functional again. I point to a nearby closed doorway. "Let's try door number one. If we can figure out where we are, you can point me in the correct direction, right?"

"That's my job."

"Perfect." I limp-walk toward the door with Hildy by my side. The hatch slides open at my approach, and I barrel into the room beyond, making it five steps before the severity of my mistake delivers another kick to the nuts.

All around me, women in beds are screaming. For a moment, I mistake it for a torture chamber, but then I hear a chorus of younger voices, screaming along with the women. All around me, babies are being born. Hundreds of them."

"I know where we are," Hildy says.

"Me too," I say, backing up. "The wrong damn place."

An Overseer with a bulging belly sits up in bed. Her top half is still in uniform. Still masked. Her lower half is covered by a blanket, beneath which a nurse is attempting to withdraw a newborn.

The Overseer's head snaps up to a ceiling mounted screen. I follow her gaze and see an image of Hildy looking down at me, curled up in pain on the floor. The Overseer's finger stabs in my direction. "Neither of you move!"

Then she clenches her whole body tight, screams, and pushes. A moment later, the nurse emerges with a baby. "It's a girl!"

The Overseer kicks the blankets away and swivels her feet to the floor.

"Which way?" I ask Hildy, desperate to leave this twisted chamber of horrors.

"Where are you parked?" she asks.

"Uhh, I don't know. Visitor parking?"

"There is no visitor parking!"

I'm vaguely aware of bare feet slapping on the floor, coming our way, but I don't look. I can't look. The sight of a woman wielding a placenta like a mace will scar me for the rest of my life.

"Someplace where a spaceship can park, where security is lax!"

"Receiving!" She holds onto me with one arm and points back the way we came. "Five thousand feet that way!"

I'm not big on trusting people I've just met, certainly not with my life, but she's trusting me with hers, so here we go. I rotate out of the birth ward and exit a moment later, back outside, just two hundred feet away from Lil' Bitch'n. Problem is, two very pregnant Overseers are charging straight toward us.

18

"Whoa, whoa, whoa!" one of the two charging Overseers shouts, as I ready myself for a fight. The voice is familiar, but I definitely don't know any pregnant women. The smaller of the two women is oddly shaped. Her round belly and lanky limbs make her look like a four-legged spider.

Hold up.

I know that weird body...

I turn to the one who spoke. "Carter?"

She pulls off the mask, swooshes her hair around like she's in a Vidal Sassoon commercial and gives me a smile. "We ran into a little trouble, but we improvised."

"Same," I say, already trying to erase the birth ward from my memory.

Carter reaches under her BCS and pulls out her original, non-Overseer BCS, bunched up to look like a pregnant belly.

"Do we have to?" Burnett asks. He's standing with both hands on either side of his belly in a classic Sears-photoshoot 'I'm pregnant' pose. "I've always wondered what it would be like to feel maternal."

"You've got clothing stuffed under your suit," I point out. "Not a baby."

"But it feels more real than the times I've used VR to..." He pulls the BCS out, clearing his throat. "Never mind."

"Don't need to ask me twice." I turn toward *Lil' Bitch'n*, ready to bolt, but there are two more Overseers blocking our path. "They're not with you, right?" I ask Carter.

"No," she says, striding toward them. Had Carter and Burnett stayed in character longer, we might have been able to ruse our way close enough to subdue the pair. But they've seen everything, and they already have their lazzer pistols aimed.

"Might not be the best idea," I tell Carter.

She raises her hands, still approaching the Overseers. "Hi there. Hello."

"On the ground!" a woman built like an ox shouts, taking a step forward and aiming her pistol toward Carter. Lazzer weapons, like any good sci-fi gun, have adjustable power settings. They can knock you out, or burn a hole straight through you, and I don't want to find out what an Overseer's default setting is. Given the severity of our crime, combined with the fact that these Overseers haven't seen a day of action—probably ever—I think they'll happily fill us with cauterized holes. All they need is an excuse.

And Carter is giving them one.

The second Overseer, a tall, lithe woman, steps up next to her partner and screams, "Face to the floor!"

"I just want to talk," Carter says.

I slide behind Carter and hurry to catch up to her. Probably looks like I'm going to use her as a meat shield, but I just don't want the Overseers noticing me right away. Right now, Carter is the threat. Their adrenaline-fueled, narrowed vision is locked on her.

The Overseers' faces are hidden behind masks, and their muscles by full body BCSs. But I can still read their body language, and the tension in their trigger fingers. Both of them are a sneeze away from firing. *Four more steps*, I think, *and then Carter is toast.*

A finger twitches.

Carter shouts in surprise as I tackle her from behind. We fall to the metal floor, landing hard, my weight crushing her down.

"What are you doing?" she grunts out.

"Saving your ass," I say, slowly moving off her, while keeping an eye on the Overseers. They're aiming at me now, but they appear more confused than angry. Saving someone probably isn't a part of the Overseer lexicon.

"I was in control of the situation," Carter says, sliding out from under me.

I point behind us. "You were in control of shit." Beyond Burnett and Hildy, who are clinging to each other and crouched in fear, are two smoldering orange holes in a metal wall. Definitely not on stun. "That was almost your head. And mine."

"Oh," Carter says. "But...I didn't—"

"Hear anything?" I'm losing my patience. "You're in the future. Not everything is going to work the way you expect or plan. Unlike what you see in movies, future weapons don't make 'pew pew' noises. They don't make any sound at all. And the beams move at the speed of light. You're dead before your eyes can register the flash. You just go from not having a hole in you to *having* a hole in you."

"Face down!" the skinny Overseer shouts, stepping closer.

I motion to Hildy and Burnett to get on the ground, and then I lie face down, toggling my comms as I go. "Chuy," I whisper.

"We see it, boss," Chuy says in my ear. "Way ahead of you."

"You are all under arrest!" the skinny Overseer shouts.

Her partner steps closer. "You have no rights. Confess now, and you will live to have a trial."

"That's a little harsh," I say. "Don't you think?"

"Confess now!"

The whir and clunk of opening gun ports fills the air.

"I don't think so," I say. "Also, you might want to drop your weapons." I turn my head so I can see both women glance back at *Lil' Bitch'n*. Two large lazzer cannons on her underside are trained on the pair. A lazzer pistol makes a quarter sized whole. The cannons will erase the women's top halves.

To me, it's an obvious bluff.

The Overseers are both pregnant, and we're not monsters.

But they don't know that. If they value their lives, and those of their unborn—

"Then we all die together!" the sturdy Overseer shouts, aiming at me again.

Or not.

A fist flies into view, colliding with the skinny Overseer's head. She sprawls into her shorter partner, but the strong woman just bats her aside and points her weapon at the newcomer.

Drago catches the gun and shoves it up, as the woman fires. Then he steps forward and delivers a headbutt that knocks her unconscious.

"Holy shit, dude," I say. "She's pregnant!"

He catches the woman and lays her down on her back. Then he shrugs. "Next time I let her shoot you?"

I twist my lips and then say, "No."

"Baby will live." He takes my hand and pulls me to my feet.

I don't bother taking the women's weapons. Neither would work in my hands. "Thanks."

"You would save me, too," he says.

"I'd think about it."

He has a chuckle and then looks over our group. "Have everything?" He draws his weapon. "Or we do my way now?"

"We have everything," I say, pulling Hildy to her feet. "And we are leaving. Now!"

A small army of Overseers rushes out of two large doorways. All of them are armed, half of them are clutching their pregnant bellies in one hand.

"This shit just got real," I say.

Hildy's head snaps toward me. She's squinty-eyed and suspicious. "You said you were from 1989."

"I am," I say, confused by the sudden shift.

"You just quoted *Bad Boys. Two.* That came out in 2003."

"Bad Boys is a *song,* and it came out in '87."

"Right song, but you quoted the movie," she says.

"You found small blonde version of Dark Horse in Union Database?" Drago asks, as Carter and Burnett run past him, heading for *Lil' Bitch'n.*

"You've seen it, haven't you?" Hildy presses. "Will Smith kicks so much ass, you wouldn't forget—"

"Hold on. The Fresh Prince becomes an *action star?*"

"Uh, yeah. One of the best. I have—"

"Shit isn't about to get real. Is about to rain down from sky in great big fiery balls of...flaming shit." Drago hauls us toward *Lil' Bitch'n*. "Finish argument inside!" A final shove sets us off and running, as lazzer blasts begin charring the ground around us and the outer layers of my ship's hull.

The hatch closes behind us as we run inside the cargo bay, blocking several rounds.

"Sit there," I tell Hildy, pointing at a bench seat.

She strolls past me and heads for the cockpit. I'm about to complain when she gives me a grin. "Trust me."

"Kid," I say, but I stop short. She's earned a little bit of trust, and anything but escape right now means death for all of us—including her.

She returns from the cockpit, her smile wide now.

"What did you do?" I ask.

She sits down across from me, beside Chuy. "You'll see." Then to Chuy she says, "Hi, I'm Hildy."

Chuy turns to me. "What is happening?"

"This is Hildy," I say, then I motion to Chuy. "Hildy, Chuy. Chuy, Hildy."

Chuy purses her lips, about to unstrap and slap me silly.

"I'm a pirate now, too," Hildy says.

Chuy is about to protest when the ship shudders. We've left the ground.

This part of a voyage is usually quiet, but this time, a strange noise fills the whole ship.

"What is this?" Drago asks, a little panicked. "What is happening?"

Hildy laughs, watching my face, looking for a reaction, which she gets a second later when the sound plows through my memories, hits me full-on, and launches me back in time, to another world.

"Pirates need pirate music!" Hildy shouts over the magical guitar chords of *Blitzkrieg Bop* by The Ramones.

When 'Hey! Ho! Lets' go!' fills the air, genuine tears blur my vision. Kid just turned this shitty world into Christmas morning.

We rise toward space, bopping our heads and tapping our feet, almost oblivious to the sound of lazzer weapons scorching the hull, and the flash of warning lights letting us know that we're taking damage.

19

"Union Command is mobilizing a fleet," Morton announces.

"A fleet?" Carter glares at me. "I thought you said the Union was mostly placid, naïve, and had 'less bite than a toothless hedgehog.'"

"That's silly," Hildy says. "Hedgehogs are extinct."

"Poor little guys," I say.

Hildy makes a pouty face. "I know, right?"

"Hedgehogs taste good," Drago chimes in. "But fatty. Good in stew."

Even Carter, who is pissed at me, takes a moment to stare at Drago in disgust.

"Man..." I say, "that's just... Don't talk for a while, okay?"

Drago shrugs, leans his head back, and closes his eyes.

Carter turns back to me. "What you should have said was, 'In my limited experience at the outer fringes of known space, the Union is—'"

"I get it," I say. "But I stand by it. They might have hardware still lying around, might even know how to use it, but no one in the galaxy has seen battle in ages. Hell, most of their security guards were pregnant!"

Hildy raises her hand.

"Not you, too," I say, and then I shake my head. I wave a hand at her. "Go ahead."

"Keeping the Overseers with child was a strategy implemented by Union Command more than two hundred years ago," Hildy explains. "Crimes against the young and unborn carry the highest penalty."

"The highest..." Chuy shoots me with her lazzer eyes. "How many pregnant ladies did you punch?"

"None!" I say. "I mean, I choked one out, but she's fine."

"I punched one," Drago says, eyes still closed.

"And cudgeled the second with your head," Carter says, and then she turns to me. "I hope you were serious about being renegades."

"Never been more serious," I say.

"Also..." Hildy holds up her index finger. "Union forces routinely participate in wargames, using uninhabitable planets as battlegrounds, and forbidden space for...well, space battles. Ammunition is live. The losers are those killed in battle."

Drago opens his eyes to shoot her an 'Are you serious?' look. Not even the Spetsnaz are that brutal.

"Okay. So, I was wrong," I say to Carter. *Lil' Bitch'n* shakes from an impact. "Morton, give me a SitRep."

"Uhh, several...I don't know what they are. Cruisers. Battleships. Angry looking things. They're behind us. Gaining fast."

"Will they catch us before we reach *Bitch'n*?" I ask.

"Two of them will," he says.

"Firepower?"

"I don't know!" he shouts, panic rising.

"Drago," I say. "You up to this?"

Drago unbuckles. "Am up to anything. All the time."

Lil' Bitch'n rolls hard and then drops a hundred feet in a second. Drago is lifted off the floor, spun, and slammed into the ceiling. When we level back out, he's unconscious.

"Morton... Try to keep us steady for a minute, okay?"

"Sorry," Morton calls back. "I was evading a missile."

"Strap him back in," I say to Chuy, motioning to Drago. "And no one else unbuckle. Things are about to get bumpy."

"Ooh," Hildy says. "Good line."

"Thanks," I say, and I head for the cockpit. I take the gunner's chair off to the right and behind the pilot's seat. "Hey, big guy. You ready for your first combat mission?"

"C-combat? I thought we were running away?"

I buckle myself in, lower a VR mask to my head, and take hold of two joysticks. "Sometimes running away involves doubling back to shoot people."

"So...like a strategic pants shitting?"

I laugh hard. That is the funniest damn thing he's ever said. "Precisely." I slip into the VR view, which is a feed from the underside of *Lil' Bitch'n*, between our two cannons.

"Sounds like fun," he says, though it sounds forced. He's trying to not let me down. I'll try to do the same for him.

Though my seat remains stationary, I swivel around in VR and the guns outside *Lil' Bitch'n* do the same in the real world. A cloud of what look like bees fills the gray sky behind us, streaming out of now-open hangars. The planet must be covered with them. Two of the fighter craft are closer than the rest—and gaining fast.

They look a lot like the *Zorak*, but their unpainted metal is as black as Union Command's surface. Where the *Zorak* was sleek curves, these things are all angles. But they're still clearly the same design. And they cut through the planet's atmosphere like Ginsu knives. *Lil' Bitch'n* is as aerodynamic as a sausage, but she can take a hit.

Hopefully more than one. I grip my controls, visualizing what I want to do. "Full stop when I say."

"Full stop?" Morton says. "That's going to hurt."

"Not as much as being dead!" I shout.

"Everyone: hold on!" Morton says through our comms.

I grit my teeth and brace myself for the movement. "Full stop!"

Lil' Bitch'n isn't great at moving forward, but she can screech to a halt like we've just careened into an invisible wall. The pilots of the two fighters flinch, veering to either side to avoid pancaking into our hull. As they part, I open fire, unleashing a constant stream of lazzer fire. I miss the rumble of real bullets, but the high-powered lazzers carve long molten lines down the undersides of both fighters.

The fighter on the right rolls as it passes. Chunks of armor plating fall away, but it's not out of the fight. The fighter on the left isn't as lucky. The lazzer punches through a soft spot in the armor and strikes something important, resulting in a very satisfying explosion.

I'm about to whoop, when I realize I've just taken a life—maybe more than one—for the first time in five years. I'd forgotten that it takes a toll on the psyche. But, they are future Nazis, and since we're now Public Enemy Numero Uno, I think they'll be the first of many. Unless...

Oh God.

"Hey, Hildy?" I shout, because she doesn't have comms yet.

"Yeah?" she replies.

"The Union doesn't use pregnant pilots, do they?"

"No!" she replies. "That would be horrible. They use really aggressive assholes who take drugs to be fearless!"

"Are you just saying that to make me feel better?" I shout.

"No!" She sounds a little angry. "Also, what the hell kind of space pirate are you?! Shoot 'em out of the sky!"

"Morton!" I shout.

"I'm right next to you!" he hisses, flinching from the volume of my voice.

"Right. Sorry. Take us up. Fast as you can without moving in a straight line."

"That doesn't make a lot of sense, but...yes, sir!"

I'm pinned to my seat as we accelerate again. Then my bodyweight shifts, keeping me pinned as we rocket upward at a nearly vertical angle. *Lil' Bitch'n* starts shaking from the strain.

My VR view of the world looks straight down at the planet's black surface. A kind of haze twists beneath us, as thousands of fighters climb behind us. Flashes of light sparkle in time with the sound of lazzers impacting our thick hull. *Lil' Bitch'n* can take a big beating, but she's not a war machine.

C'mon, baby. Hold it together until we're home.

I switch to a full auto lazzer spread and hold the trigger down. Not much to aim at, but if I fire enough...

A mile below, orange bursts of light join the fireworks display, as my fire punches through the faster, but less armored fighters. Several explosions rock the fleet.

But it's not enough.

Not nearly enough.

Keeping my fingers on the triggers, I say, "Porter, open the hangar door. Ready all weapons systems. I want to rotate the moment we're on board."

"What?" he says. "Huh?" He's shifted from confusion to panic in the time it takes Speedy Gonzales to rub one out.

I hear the vacuous suck of a toilet.

"Are you taking a shit right now?"

"Didn't have anything to do until you—"

"Porter, did you skip wiping? Wait. Never mind. You can clean up later. Right now, I need to you do everything I asked in the next... Morton, ETA to *Bitch'n*?"

"Sixty seconds," Morton says, as the ship starts shaking, not from lazzer fire, but from leaving the atmosphere.

"...in the next sixty seconds. After that, we're all toast."

"Is toast...bad?" Porter asks, breathless from running to the bridge. "Because...I like...toast."

"The toast will be burned, Porter. Hard as a brick."

"Oh my God," he says. "That's horrible. Hangar door open. Slew drive charged. Annnd...weapons systems ready to go! Eat my sweet and spicy tater tots!"

I have a nice chuckle. 'Eat my sweet and spicy tater tots' is something Chuy and I occasional shout in victory, just to see if it will catch on and become a thing. Morton and Burnett have both said it, but it's become something of a catchphrase for Porter.

"Okay. Here's the hard part," I say.

"I'm ready for anything!" he says.

"Great. I'm going to need you to shoot anything that isn't us."

"Excuse me?"

"In about ten seconds, a fleet of angry Union ships are going to clear the atmosphere behind us. I need you to shoot them. Let them have it."

"You want me to shoot...Union ships?"

Aww, shit.

Porter doesn't know the situation. Doesn't know we've gone full-on Rebel Alliance versus the Galactic Empire. And I have no idea which way he's going to swing.

"Oh no," Morton says. I can't see what's got him upset, but his voice has risen two octaves, so it can't be good. "Porter, what are you doing? No! Stop! Brace for impact!"

I don't really brace for impact as much as I clench for impact. I'm still shooting at the Union ships behind us, so all I can really do is pucker my asshole and hope for the best. And in this case, that's hoping that Porter hasn't chosen the life of a Future-Nazi over his pals. Granted, I didn't give him, Morton, or Burnett much of a choice when I commandeered *Bitch'n*, but they didn't really put up a fight, either. And I've offered to cut them free several times.

They've all chosen to stick with us.

But maybe Porter was playing us all along? Maybe he was tracking our efforts? Reporting back to Command? Maybe he was the reason the *Zorak* knew exactly where to find us? It makes sense.

Holy shit. Porter is going to kill us!

A twisting tangle of rockets slides into view, wrapping around *Lil' Bitch'n*'s backside, headed straight for the fleet pursuing us. Not a one strikes us.

Porter didn't kill us.

He saved us.

"Yes! Porter! I never had a doubt!"

"Had a doubt?" Porter asks. "In what, sir?"

"Never mind..." I release the joysticks when *Bitch'n*'s hangar doors close behind us, blocking my view just as the cloud of rockets meets the approaching fleet. Explosions fill the atmosphere.

We haven't just declared our intention to be pirates, we've declared war.

"Time to go," I shout.

"Where are we going?" Porter asks.

Anywhere but here, I think, and then I realize that the Union knows every place we've been, and they'll no doubt check the planets marked as habitable. But we need a destination for the Slew Drive to work. Without celestial coordinates, there's no telling where we'll end up. We need to go someplace so horrible that the Union will assume we'd avoid it, no matter the cost.

Only one place fits the bill. "Elysium."

"I...don't know where that is," Porter says.

"003189," Chuy says.

"Go!" I shout.

We roll into the white of the fourth dimension and linger there for a few moments. Then we roll back out. From inside *Lil' Bitch'n* and most of big *Bitch'n*, nothing has changed. The only way to know we've escaped the jaws of a monster we've just poked in the eye is Porter's word.

"Rotation complete," he says. "We have safely arrived at 003189. But...are you sure this is the right place?"

I yank the VR headset off and unbuckle, racing toward *Lil' Bitch'n*'s opening cargo bay door. I'm worried that something has happened to my retirement plan. "What do you mean?"

"Just that we've been here before," he says.

Thank God. "Yes. That's the point."

Hildy puts her hand on my arm as I pass, pleased as a peacock with a peach. "That was amazing!"

"I know, right?" I walk past her, but I make eye contact with Chuy. "Find her a room?"

"I ain't a concierge, cabrón," she says, but I know she'll do it.

When I leave *Lil' Bitch'n*, Porter, who has been able to hear the conversations, says, "But...this was one of the most inhospitable planets we discovered in the past five years. Also, who is the new voice? Sounds like a young woman."

"Hildy. She *is* a young woman. What's wrong with the planet?" I jump down from the lowering hatch before it's all the way open, and then I hustle toward the bridge on the ship's far end...and that will take a few minutes.

Screw it, I think, and I stop. I put my hand on the PSD. Saving a few minutes with a slew drive is reckless, but it's been working like a champ. And I suppose it will, right up until the moment it doesn't. But this planet is important to me.

"Hold up," Carter says. She rushes up, puts her hands around my waist. "Okay, let's go."

I'm incredulous for about a half second and then I decide, *Why the hell not?* Pirates do stupid shit all the time. I put one arm around Carter and rotate to the bridge.

Porter startles at our sudden arrival. Puts a hand to his chest. Takes a deep breath. Doesn't piss himself—or the bridge. He smiles at me. "Did you see that?"

I give his shoulder a pat. "You've come a long way, man."

"Probably helps that I was in the bathroom when you called."

"Mmm," I say, staring out the windshield toward a planet that looks painfully like Earth, but isn't. "Elysium..." To Porter I ask. "What's wrong with the planet?"

"Well, we visited this world more than three years ago," he says.

"Annnd?"

"There's no one here. It could have been settled right away, but there isn't a single city that I can see, or a pre-settlement satellite network. It's like the Union doesn't know—" He gasps like I've just stepped out of my quarters wearing a sheer negligée and nothing beneath it—like I'm a naughty bitch, but in a good way. "*You didn't tell them?*"

"How would you feel about it, if I didn't?" I ask.

He's torn, vacillating between horror and delight, like he's just been asked if he wants a spanking from a sexy lady...or me in that negligée. "I—I'm not sure. But there really isn't a choice now, is there?"

He slumps in his chair, the full weight of what he just helped us pull off settling in. There's a good chance that he killed even more Union pilots than I did, but he didn't know why, and he wasn't given a choice.

I sit down across from him, serious, elbows on knees, hands clasped. "Look, buddy, that wasn't the way I wanted anything to play out. If you want to bail, I'm cool with that. Only *we* know you were behind the controls. It's too late to change what happened, but let me fill you in, so you can decide what's best for yourself."

I give him a rundown of everything that happened at Union Central, leaving out the embarrassing bits. I let him know about Hildy, about being pirates, about Burnett and Morton signing on. And then I apologize again for not giving him the same choice.

When I'm done, he seems to shrink deeper into his chair, looking like he might sprint from the bridge—if he can sprint. Speed-lumber might be a better word.

The bridge door slides open. Drago, Morton, and Burnett enter, the former looking annoyed by our obvious Kodak moment, the latter two concerned for Porter, based on his expression alone.

"Hey," I tell him. "It's okay. If you don't want to join us, just say so."

"It's not that," Porter says, looking me in the eyes. "It's... I just realized I still haven't...you know..." He glances back as his own posterior. "...cleaned up."

The BCS extracts urine and fecal matter—when it's being worn. Typically, they need to be cleaned out later, and sometimes if the system is overloaded, it ejects the piss and shit. People fill up their BCSs all the time without a second thought, but it is still preferable, and more comfortable, to use a toilet. Porter was using the toilet when I called, and he pulled on his skintight BCS before he was cleaned. Ipso facto, his suit's gonna have the mother of all skid marks when he takes it off.

"Ugh." Drago slaps a palm to his shaking head and takes a seat at his station. "Little men with big feelings."

"Whoa, whoa, whoa," I say holding up my palms. "Hold up. Rewind. Does that mean you're in? That you want to be a pirate? That you'll stand with us in a hopeless rebellion against the Union?"

"Huh?" He radiates befuddlement. "What? Yeah. Of course. We're friends."

I sit up straight, a stupid smile on my face. I reach out my hand. "Yeah, we are."

He shakes my hand, pleased to have pleased me.

"Now," I say. "Go clean up."

He nods and exits the bridge, walking like he's got an egg clenched between his cheeks...and then it occurs to me that he might.

Erasing the image from my mind, I turn to Drago. "Keep an eye out for Union ships." To Morton and Burnett, I say, "Check *Lil' Bitch'n* for damage. If she's good, we'll need to take her to the surface. Fill up on water. Maybe hunt for some protein. We might be on the run for a while, and it won't be long before we're persona non-grata at every inhabited planet and space station."

"What about when the fuel cells run out of power?" Burnett asks.

Morton rolls his eyes like he's been at this his whole life. "We're pirates, dummy. We'll just take what we need."

I snap my fingers and point them at Morton. "I like the way you think." I shift my fingers toward Burnett. "Let me know when you're on your way to the surface. And make sure to bring Chuy and Hildy."

"Don't worry about me," Drago grumbles. "I will just sit here, alone. Who wants to visit paradise planet anyway?"

"You won't be alone," I tell him. "Porter will be with you."

"Fuck you," Drago says.

"Fuck you, too, buddy."

Drago chuckles, and I turn to Carter. "Hello and welcome to Dark Horse Realty. I'm your agent, Dark Horse. You can call me Mr. Dark or Mr. Horse. Would you like to see some of our choice properties?"

Drago rolls his eyes and swivels away.

Carter's eyes haven't left the view since we entered the bridge. "Yes," she says, and she turns to me with a smile. "Please."

I take hold of her again, activate my PSD, and rotate down to my version of paradise.

21

"Is your life always like this?" Carter asks. "The running and shooting and death? It's kind of overwhelming."

She's lying in the grass beside me, eyes on the blue sky above, watching the clouds roll by. It's a pleasant day. Spring in North Carolina. But there's no beach in sight. Instead, we're surrounded by snowcapped peaks. A breeze flows down the mountainside, collecting and bathing us in the scent of flowering plants. The first time I found this place, I spun around with my arms out, singing, 'The hills are alive with the sound of music.' Then I remembered there was no music, and that there were Nazis in that story, too, and I got depressed.

But now...now we have *all* the music. Not to mention movies, TV, and the history of the twentieth and twenty-first centuries. Half of each, at least.

If the entire Union wasn't out to kill us now, I'd be feeling good.

Honestly, I'm feeling pretty awesome anyway.

"Umm, well, yeah. Mostly." I turn toward her. Her hair is tied back tight. Her eyes closed in the sunlight. "The stakes are higher now, but the life of an Exo-Hunter is much more dangerous than that of a Marine."

She turns to me. "Exploring uninhabited planets is more dangerous than fighting the Soviets?"

"First of all," I say, "we never directly fought the Soviets."

She smiles at me. Gives a wink. Taps the side of her nose. "Good soldier."

"Second, it's the unpredictable nature of exploring new worlds that makes it so dangerous. In the Rapid Reaction Force, we knew our enemy, the terrain, and the culture. We trained relentlessly. Weren't many situations that caught us off guard—until *you* showed up and dragged us to Antarctica. Thanks a lot."

She fake-smiles at me in a way that says, 'Suck it up.'

"But there is no way to predict what you'll find on a new planet. Sometimes it's flesh-eating bacteria. Or it's parasites with an affinity for assholes. Or it's a horde of flying sloth-monsters that flops around in puddles. And that was just three days ago!"

"Sometimes it's a skyscraper-sized, turtle-faced behemoth."

"Totally worth it." I full body stretch like a dog in the yard, rolling back and forth before I settle back down, hands clasped behind my head. This is the most relaxed I've been in a long time. Not sure why, but I'm comfortable with Carter. She puts me at ease. When we first met, I felt scrutinized and a little bit condescended to, but I guess being transported into the future and facing off against a Nazi empire is the great equalizer. Back on Earth, she had superiors to answer to and all the pressure that comes with that.

Here and now, it's just us.

"I'm sure living with Beatrice wasn't easy," I say.

"Or any of the other king-sized monstrosities," she adds. "Seriously, it was like living in a Harryhausen movie."

"You know who Ray Harryhausen is?" I ask, and then tack on, "*Was.*"

"Uh, yeah. Who doesn't?"

"I don't know, maybe every woman I've ever dated."

"Good thing we're not dating."

I roll onto my side, elbow on the soft earth, hand propping up my head.

"Which one?" I ask.

"Which one what?"

"Harryhausen movie."

She thinks on it for a moment. Grins. "*Clash of the Titans, 20 Million Miles to Earth, Mysterious Island...* Pretty much all of them. Seriously. That place... I don't know how I survived for three years."

"Five."

She rolls her eyes. "Agree to disagree."

"Ugh, I hate that saying. Facts are facts. One of us is right and the other is..." I sit up. For some reason, my brain works a little better when I'm upright. "Unless we're both right."

"Already thought of that, genius." She sits up beside me. "Time in space is relative. The rotation of my temporary home was four hours faster than Earth, and the time it took to circumvent its start was fifty days less. So, your years and my years were different."

"Well, yeah, that's obvious and entry level Exo-Hunter knowledge." I wait for the stink-eye to find my smile, then I continue. "But I'm talking about something...bigger. And less tangible." I turn my whole body toward her, start to tip over because we're on a hill, and turn myself back. "What if we actually arrived in different years?"

"You five years ago. Me three years ago." A shrug. "We're talking about theoretical time-travel physics, a subject neither one of us is an expert in—"

"Or anyone else."

"—so, sure. Why not? It also means that some of your people could have arrived before you."

"And that some haven't arrived yet."

"No way to prove that, though."

"We'll keep looking," I say.

"Going to be a little harder now," she points out.

"We'll see." She's right. I know she's right. But I can't just give up on my team, even if the whole Union is hunting us down.

"Have you considered they might be better off wherever they ended up?"

"Were you?" I ask.

"I was...lonely, but honestly a lot safer. Like you said, predictability. I knew how to kill what I could. How to survive. How to stay off Beatrice's radar, and I had a cave to hide in during mating season. I would have gotten by just fine until I was too old and feeble to hunt. Now? Well, it's just a matter of time before the Union finds us and does what Nazis do best."

"Grill sausages and sauerkraut?" I say. "Oh! Oktoberfest!"

"The Nazis did *not* have Oktoberfest."

"Blitzkriegenfest?"

She huffs a reluctant laugh and stands. When her hair is caught in the downhill wind, she turns to face it.

I climb to my feet and brush off my pants. Stand beside her, enjoying the breeze and the uphill view. The mountain behind us is staggering.

"What's the wildlife like here?" she asks.

"Not trying to eat us," I say.

"There must be some alpha predators," she says.

"I've seen a few, but they don't look at a person and think, 'Hey, that looks like food.' They just kind of watch and go on their merry way. I'm sure one of them will try to take a bite eventually, but we're cautious."

"So, *that's* not a problem?" She points to the mountain's base, where forest turns to field. A brown ball of fur warbles as it runs...or is it rolling...down the hill toward us. It's still a mile off. But I can already tell it's big. Evolution on Elysium followed a similar path to Earth's. It's entirely possible the creature headed toward us is like a grizzly bear. Which means we don't want to be here when it arrives.

"Not really." I pat the Slew Drive on my waist. "And if I felt like standing my ground..." I nudge the rifle lying in the grass. "But I don't want to kill anything unless I'm going to eat it. And that's more hair than I want to deal with."

"Could be tasty," she says. "And now I've got a hankering for some meat."

"Still have that wackadoodle steak you brought along for the ride."

That makes her happy. "Good. You'll like it."

Our eyes meet and linger. I want to break the sexual tension with a quip, but I just kind of choke on the words before they escape my mouth. She finds that funny, laughs at my expense, and then leans in to kiss me.

"Hola, pendejo," Chuy says in our comms. We flinch apart. "Hope I'm not interrupting anything."

She knows she is.

"What's up?" I ask.

"You wanted to know when Hildy was on her way to the surface. Well, now you know."

"LZ?" I ask.

"Sending the coordinates to your Slew."

"Wait, you can do that?" It's news to me.

"According to Porter. Part of the firmware update."

"Rad," I say.

Carter cringes. "'Rad?' You're not a teenager."

"Just trying to keep the 80s alive," I say.

"She's not wrong, boss," Chuy says.

"Ugh." I toggle my comms off.

"Even in the past, you'd be three years out of the 80s. Time to move on."

"You know how many ways people in the future have for saying 'good?' One. 'Good.' That's it. Nothing is great, or cool, or bodacious."

She twists her lips.

"Okay, bodacious is too far. But seriously. Some things are just...rad."

"Like Hildy coming to the surface?"

My smile widens as I shake my head. "Like Hildy seeing the natural world, on *any* world, for the first time in her life."

That clicks. Carter gives an approving nod and then says, "Hey, Dark Horse..."

"Yeah?"

I think she's going to plant that kiss on me, but instead she hitches her thumb to the side. I glance to the left, uphill, and I'm greeted by a ball of raging fur, complete with a Cheshire grin of big, flat teeth and four red eyes bearing down on us.

I pull her close, activate the Slew, and rotate away just as the creature lunges.

We emerge by a crystalline lake at the base of the valley. The mountains tower around us, ominous and majestic. Above, *Lil' Bitch'n* swings in for a landing. She's battle-scarred and patched up, but still more than capable of getting the job done. When the hatch opens, I hustle over.

Chuy exits first, dragging a long tube we'll use to refill our fresh water supply. Hildy is not with her. "Kid is scared."

I head up the ramp and find Hildy still seated.

"I've seen it before," she says, wringing her hands together. "In movies. I don't know why I'm nervous."

"Because that was on a little screen, and this...this is going to blow your mind."

"Is that a good thing?" she asks.

"I think you know it is.' I offer her my hand. "C'mon."

She takes my hand and trusts me again. I lead her to the open hatch. "Close your eyes, so you can see it all at once."

She does, and she lets me lead her to the bottom.

"Okay..." I say. "This is as close to Earth 1.0 that you're going to find in the galaxy. Have a look."

Hildy opens her eyes, gasps, falls to her knees—

—and vomits all over my feet.

22

"I'm sorry," Hildy says, head to the ground, eyes clenched shut. "I don't know what happened."

I shake the puke off my feet. "Don't sweat it, kid. Happens to everyone." Then I mouth to Carter, "What just happened?"

She crouches down beside Hildy. Puts her hand on her back. "You got overwhelmed. It's okay."

"But why?" Hildy's almost in tears.

"You've spent your whole life living in a colorless, dystopian nightmare with recycled air and water. And this is big, and vivid. The air is fresh, and that means it's full of things that are new to your brain. Smells. Particles. All of that is hitting you all at once. I'm not surprised it's triggering a psychological and physiological response."

"Like I said," I say. "Totally normal."'

"Just take it slow," Carter says. "Start with what's beneath you."

"Not the puke," I say. "You might want to shift to the side a little or something."

Hildy takes my advice, shuffling away from the vomit. Then she stares at the ground. Her fingers curl through the fine grit, warmed by the sun. "Is...this sand?"

"You're on a beach," Carter says. "To your right is a lake, but don't look yet. Hear it first."

Our whole crew goes silent.

Even Chuy stands still, water hose in hand.

I close my eyes and hear it for myself. The gentle lapping of waves, almost like a bird's wings.

"I hear it," Hildy says, sounding happy again. "And a kind of... whooshing."

"Wind," Morton says.

Hildy tilts her head to the side. "And...a song. Is that music?"

"Animals," I say, and I don't bother trying to explain what they are. This planet has winged creatures, but they're not like birds. The singing comes from monkey-like creatures that live in the tree-tops.

Hildy turns her head to the side. Takes in the lake. "Whoa." Her arms are shaky for a moment, but then she pushes herself up, eyes still locked on the water. "Everything is moving."

"Nature has a hard time staying still," I say.

She shifts around onto her backside. Pulls her knees up. Lifts her head a little higher, expanding her view to the lake, the sky above, the massive clouds and the breathtaking mountains framing it all. She looks about to puke again, but then she lets out a sob and starts crying.

I plant myself beside her in the sand. "Hey."

She wipes her arm across her nose. "Hey."

She leans her poofy head on my shoulder. Her unexpected affection nearly chokes me up. I'm not sure how a former Marine-turned-pirate could also be such a sap. I suppose you have to care about things to fight for them. As long as Chuy doesn't—

I glance up. Chuy is knee deep in the lake, with the hose, sucking up water. She's watching us with what looks like a genuine smile, but she transforms it into a sarcastic 'aww' face. She shakes her head at me, but before she turns away, the smile returns.

Is it just me, I think to myself, *or are people getting weird now that we're pirates?*

Could be that we've added two new crew members and the dynamic is changing.

Or that we might all die horribly in battle at any moment now.

That has an impact. Or, maybe, Hildy is exactly what we're fighting for, and should have been fighting for, all along.

"Thank you," she says, and she motions to the view. "For this. And for everything else."

"Right back at you," I say.

She lifts her head to look me in the eyes. "You're thanking me? For what?"

"Most things in the universe are both good and bad. The sun provides life, unless you get too close. Then it's roasty-toasty death time. Water nourishes, unless you're fifty feet down and don't have gills. Nature is staggeringly beautiful. It makes human beings feel alive. But, sometimes, it wants to eat you. Or zap you with lightning. Or melt your face off with acid rain, and I don't mean the man-made pollution variety. Like actual acid.

"The human race is the same. Both good and bad. There have been glimmers of good since I arrived in this time—mostly from my crew—but the Union is a product of what happens when humanity is steeped in darkness for hundreds of years. I had trouble finding anything positive about it.

"Until a few hours ago."

"What happened a few hours ago?"

I nudge her with my elbow.

"Shut-up," she says. "Whatever."

"Seriously."

"You're talking about the music and movies and shit, aren't you?"

"That's part of it," I say. "I'll never be able to repay you for that. But also, just *you*. Because you're different than everyone else in this twisted future. You absorbed and now reflect human culture from a time when we were still, by and large, good. We had our share of dictators, despots, and evil regimes—including the assholes who inspired the Union—but most of the world stood against those things. You stand out, like a lighthouse, and not just because of this insane hair." I shake my hand in her hair until she leans away and swats me. "You're realigning our path toward what is good and right. You gave me music back, but you also gave me hope.

"And I can fight for that. Hell, I can die for it."

She nods.

Takes a deep breath and holds her chin up against the overwhelming world. "Me too."

"Not while I'm around," I say. "So...have you ever been swimming? The water here is warmer than the—"

She's up and peeling off her BCS, right down to her Union-gray bra and underwear. There are scars on her back. Long streaks of burned flesh.

"What the hell happened to your back?"

She twists around like she can see the scars. "I...don't remember it, but corporal punishment is part of training to be a Predictor. I must have made a mistake or two. But it's not up here..." She taps her head. "So..." She shrugs and then bolts for the water.

Chuy winces when Hildy freight-trains through the shallows, laughing it up. She shoots me a 'Don't you dare' look when I shed my clothing down to my skivvies.

"I ain't afraid of you!" I shout, and then I follow Hildy's path over the sand and into the water. Chuy leans away, as my flailing body kicks up a spray of water. But it's not nearly enough. "Whoo hoo!" I shout, and I leap into the air, plummeting back down into the water like a breaching whale.

I catch a glimpse of my miniature tsunami crashing toward Chuy, but then I'm underwater. When I return to the surface in chest-deep water, Chuy is already charging. She jumps at me, catches the top of my head, and shoves me back down.

When I come to the surface a second time, she's laughing—until Hildy splashes the two of us.

"Oh, it's on now," Chuy says.

Before she can return fire, two more cries of derring-do tear through the air. Morton and Burnett, neither of them brave enough to shed their BCSs, run into the water. They make it shin deep before losing their collective balance, stumbling forward, and falling before the water gets deep. They sit up together, covered to the waist, laughing, and splashing.

Chuy and I share a knowing glance. A little bit of parental pride. We've gone for dips before, but the boys have never been brave enough to join us. Like Hildy, this is the first time they've ever been immersed in water.

It's a baptism of sorts—a public declaration. The galaxy might be mired in oppressive doctrines...but we are free.

Carter, on the other hand, watches from shore, not quite smiling. Her arms are crossed. Can't tell if she's trying to hide amusement, or if she doesn't approve. She's loose when it's just the two of us—in a few ways—but still mostly business when everyone else is around.

It's too bad. She's missing out. These people are the only chance she has left to form a family. Our blood relatives are long since gone. The only familial bonds we can have now are those we forge without the aid of DNA.

She'll come around, I decide, and I jump into the air, arms open wide. I belly flop down, slapping the water with my hands and absolutely drenching Morton and Burnett.

Behind me, I hear Chuy. "¡Uno, dos, tres!"

I turn around just in time to see her launch Hildy into the air. Hildy's stark white body glows in the sun, only half as bright as her smile. But then six feet up, looking down at me, gravity tugs her—and that smile—down. Laughter becomes a shout of fear, and—*sploosh*. I slip to the side, avoiding collision. Then I dip my head beneath the surface, find a flailing Hildy, and help her to the surface.

She breaks the surface, sputtering and coughing. For a moment, I fear she'll have almost drowning imprinted on her first experience with water, then she laughs and turns to Chuy. "Again!"

Over the splashing and frivolity, I nearly miss Drago's voice in my ear.

"What was that?" I ask, and to everyone else, I say, "Hold up, hold up." I put a finger to my ear. It won't help me hear him any better, but it's still a universal sign for 'I'm trying to hear a call.' "Drago, say again."

"I said, 'We have incoming.'"

I tense. "The *Zorak*?"

"Uhh, no."

I slosh toward shore. Chuy is hot on my heels. "Union?"

"I don't think so."

"Aggressive?" I ask.

"Who? Me?"

"The...ugh. The damn ship approaching you!"

"Ooh," he says. "Sorry for confusion. I said 'we', but I meant 'you.'"

"You what?" I shout.

"Have incoming."

"*I* have incoming?"

"Da," he says. "Look up."

A ball of fire slowly resolves into what looks like a black cube, plummeting from the sky. It's not on a collision course, but it's going to touch down close enough that it can't be a coincidence.

"What is it?" I ask, hoping that someone will have a clue. It doesn't look like a bomb or a missile, but I'm not ruling anything out. Problem is, we have about thirty seconds before it reaches the ground, and that's not nearly enough time to get everyone on board *Lil' Bitch'n* and on the move. Especially if it's a nuclear warhead or something.

"I don't recognize it," Hildy says. She's standing next to me, dripping wet, eyes to the sky. Her insane puffball hair has been tamed by the water, but individual strands are already starting to spring free as they dry in the sun.

"Stay close to me," I whisper to her.

Chuy gives me a sidelong glance.

"You, too," I tell her.

She gives me a nod. Understands the message. We might need to rotate to safety. And if that's the case, I'm taking the two of them. Chuy because she's essentially a part of me, and Hildy because I've just yanked her out of her life and made her an outlaw. I'm not about to abandon her on Day One. She's an innocent in all this.

I've only rotated with Carter. I don't know if it can handle three people, but I'm ready to give it a shot. If we survive, I'll be plagued by guilt for not saving everyone, but I've already got a long list of things to talk through with my future therapist.

"You're a Predictor, though," Morton says. "You must be able to identify every vessel in the Union."

Hildy nods. "I can."

"So that's..." Burnett says.

"Not part of the Union." I put an arm around Hildy. Pull her closer. Chuy stands close to my other side. We look like we're posing for a family photo.

And Carter notices. Frowns. Then she returns her eyes to the sky. "It's a dropship."

Morton shields his eyes from the sun. "How can you t—oh, I see it! There are boosters on the underside. I think. They don't look like anything I've ever—"

Blue light blossoms from the object's underside.

I wrap an arm around Chuy, about to trigger the PSD.

With a few hundred feet to go, and seconds before impact, the object starts to slow, which supports Carter's guess. Someone is coming to pay us a visit. And if Hildy is right, it's not someone from the Union.

It's Whip, I think. He was spooked before, but now he's ready for a face-to-face. Nothing else makes sense.

We lose sight of the dropship when it dips behind a hill, half a klick away.

"Morton, grab the weapons kits, and then prep *Lil' Bitch'n* for takeoff." Morton scrambles into action, running for *Lil' Bitch'n.*

"Burn..." He smiles at my use of his requested callsign. "...finish filling the tank with water." He takes the hose. Gets to work.

"Hildy..." I hitch a thumb to the open cargo bay. "Get on board. Stay on board."

I turn to Carter.

"I'm coming with you," she says, stepping forward, assertive and self-assured.

"Not this time," I tell her. "I need you here in case something goes wrong. Get them off planet and back to *Bitch'n.* Chuy's got my back."

"You want me to babysit?" She's pissed. Probably not just about this. I was going to leave her here to die.

I must enjoy digging my own grave, because I respond with, "I want you to follow orders. My ship. My crew. My call. If you don't like it, we can drop you back with Beatrice. You want to question me when we're floating around in space or exploring a new world, fine and dandy. Want to debate strategy before or after a mission, I'm cool with that. When we're facing any unknown threat that puts my people in danger, I'm fucking Kim Il-sung. Do what I say, when I say it."

Chuy and I start tugging on our clothing. "Okay?"

Carter stares at me. Her eyes lack the kind of interest from the past two days, which sucks, but if I bend this rule for her, in front of everyone, people are going to start debating every call I make, and that's going to get us killed eventually.

"Whatever you say, Supreme Leader." She gives me a salute and heads for *Lil' Bitch'n*. She bumps into Morton on her way up the ramp. He spins around on his way down, carrying two hard cases with our gear inside.

"That went well," Chuy says.

I pull my shirt on. "Not the first time I've pissed off a woman."

"Won't be the last," she says.

Morton lays the cases down in front of us while we finish dressing. Opens them both to reveal our custom weaponry.

"Whoa," Hildy says, reaching for my rifle. "This looks straight out of Predator."

I swat her hand away, and then say, "Thanks, but no touching."

She pouts at me, but she can't hide her unceasing positive vibes. "Can you teach me? Eventually. How to use this stuff? I mean, I'm a rebel pirate now, right? I should know how to defend myself."

Chuy slings her sniper rifle over her shoulder. "She's got a point."

"But not today." I slap a magazine into my rifle and chamber a round.

"Badass," Hildy says.

"Kid," Chuy says, "he's already got a big head."

"You, next," Hildy says to Chuy. "Say something good. I mean, cool."

"¡Vete a freír espárragos!" Chuy says.

Hildy's eyes blossom like a nuclear mushroom cloud. "What does *that* mean?"

"Means 'get your ass inside *Lil' Bitch'n* and don't come back out until we get back.'" I nudge her toward the open hatch. "You copy?"

"Copy," she says, and starts moving toward the ship. "Copy...I don't even know what that means. Copy!"

"Ready?" I ask Chuy.

She tilts her head to either side, popping vertebrae. "Ready."

I raise an arm toward her. One hand on the PSD. An invitation. She gives me a 'Did you just fart in my mouth?' look and says, "Seriously?"

"Tactical advantage," I say. "Plus, I'm pretty sure it won't kill us."

With a sigh, she steps up close. I wrap an arm around her waist, and I'm struck by the fact that this is the closest we've ever been. We've high-fived, picked each other up, and tended wounds, but in all the time I've known her, we've never once shared an embrace.

I clear my throat, feeling awkward.

"Calm down, vaquero," Chuy says. "If Carter doesn't castrate you, I will."

I activate the slew and rotate away from the beach.

A flash of white, a quick twist, and we emerge in the forest near the landing craft's position. I release Chuy from my grasp. "Good to go?"

"Affirmative," she says, and she starts moving downhill.

Below us, in a clearing, is the cube landing craft. It's touched down in a field surrounded by tall trees. I don't see any open hatches, or people outside, but I'm pretty sure it's not going to explode. So that's good.

While Chuy moves into position, I toggle the PSD and rotate to the field's far side, just inside the trees. After a quick scan, I step out in the open, rifle shouldered, ready to fire. I stand like that for a full sixty seconds.

Then I lower the rifle, but not my guard.

When no hatch opens and no one bothers to say 'hello,' I take a step closer and call out, "Yo! If you're here to talk, start talking. If you're here for a fight, I'm getting bored and—"

"Drop the weapon."

The deep voice belongs to someone large and as stealthy as a ninja. I am not an easy man to get the drop on. With a subtle twist of my head, I get a periphery peek at my adversary's weapon. I can't tell what kind of weapon, only that it's aimed at the back of my head, slightly to the right.

"Not going to happen," I say.

"And I'm not going to ask you again," the man says. "Three seconds and then you die."

"One," I say, kicking things off. "Two."

I tilt my head to the left, nice and calm like I'm stretching.

"Three," the man says.

Heat registers on my neck. I feel a subtle vibration on my skin. I hear a subtle buzz. All of it at the same time, a fraction of a second before the man's weapon shatters and falls to the ground.

"Nice shot," I say to Chuy, who has been listening through comms and watching from the forest.

"I'm sorry," I say. "I should have told you. That was *my* countdown. If you wanted to shoot me at the count of three, you should have started counting first. Then, I'd really have been in a pickle."

I turn to face the man, raising my weapon. He's wearing black body armor with a red X spray painted over the chest. Definitely *not* Union. A black mask—cooler than mine—hides his face. "Who are you?"

"Don't point that at me." He nods toward my rifle.

"Seriously? I don't mean to sound like a school kid, but you started it." The man sighs.

If he wanted to kill me, he could have. He's no longer armed. And a bullet leaving Chuy's sniper rifle will take just a fraction of a second longer to remove his head. So, I do as he asks, and I take a subtle step to the side, making him an easy target. "Happy?"

He says nothing.

"Now...who are you?"

He lifts his hands, palms forward, then reaches toward the back of his mask. He moves slowly, aware that he's still got a weapon aimed at his head. He takes hold of the mask and peels it off, blocking his face with his arms. The mask comes away.

I stare at him for ten seconds before Chuy says, "Moses, what the fuck?"

I'd normally complain about her using my real name, but I'm just as dumbstruck, and I find myself able to only repeat her question. "What the fuck?"

24

The man, staring at me through cool, blue eyes, has skin that's just a shade lighter than mine.

"Like looking in a mirror," the man says. "Right?"

Not exactly. The Union might see us as twins, but he's two inches shorter than me, his hair is unruly, like an awkward afro. Mine is high and tight. But there is something...maybe the way he carries himself, or the way he's scrutinizing me while I do the same to him, that feels familiar. Like a younger me.

I'm not sure if that makes me like him or dislike him. But I'm not going to trust him just because he magically doubled the number of black men in the galaxy.

"Answer the question," I say.

"In a minute."

"Waiting for something?"

He doesn't answer. Just has this cocky look on his face. A subtle grin. Knows something I don't, and he's feeling smug about it.

"Chuy, I'm going to give this guy another countdown. Feel free to remove his kneecap if he doesn't answer." When she doesn't reply, I know things have just gone from annoyingly intriguing to full-on FUBAR.

"Over there," the man says, pointing behind me.

I raise my rifle again, just in case, and turn to look. Chuy stands at the forest's edge, hands raised. There's a man and a woman to either side of her, weapons pointed at her head. Both of them are shades of very much not white.

Ho-lee shit. What is happening?

A question for later. Right now, Chuy is in danger, and that's not something I take lightly, or that I'm going to let stand.

When I turn to face the stranger again, I'm smiling. It's not a sheepish grin, or an honest, 'Happy to meet you' smile. It's a 'You just opened a can of crazy,' smirk. "Second question. Do you know who *I* am? Because if you did, and you wanted to survive long enough to answer question number one, you wouldn't be threatening my people."

His hesitation to answer lacks all of the previous bravado.

"Don't sweat it," I tell him. "I'll ask you again in a minute. Just..." I raise an index finger. "Hold on."

Before his face is done expressing confusion, I've rotated out of the field and appeared behind the man and woman holding Chuy hostage.

"Howdy," I say.

The duo flinch and spin around to face me. It's a natural instinct, to face an attacker that's caught you off guard, but it leaves them open to attack from Chuy.

Knowing I'm not fond of fighting enemy combatants of the feminine gender, Chuy delivers a crushing punch to the woman's side. She crumples to the ground, dry heaving.

I handle the man by taking hold of his rifle. When he attempts to pull it free, I push. The heavy weapon collides with his forehead and knocks him unconscious. As the man falls to the ground, Chuy slides into my arm, and we rotate back across the field, right behind the cocky wannabe doppelganger. Chuy draws her pistol and shoves it against the back of the man's head. I stroll around in front of him. "So. Back to question one. Who the fuck *are* you?"

Chuy steps to the man's side. If she puts a bullet in his head, I won't get slathered in brain matter.

The man chuckles. "He said you were good. I mean, I knew you were. It's why you're here. But that—rotating back and forth—that was poetry."

He's trying to control the conversation, redirecting me to what is now question number three: Who said I was good?

"Your name," I say. "Last chance."

He lets out a sigh. "Bighead."

"Bighead?"

"It's a callsign," he says. "I didn't pick it."

His big hair combined with his cocksure attitude makes the name a perfect fit. Whoever gave it to him has a sense of humor and an understanding of his character.

"Who did?"

"Can't tell you," he says. "Not yet. Not until he's sure."

"Sure about what."

He shrugs. "Who you are. Who you've become."

"If we get any more cryptic Yoda bullshit out of you, I'm going to shoot you out of spite," Chuy says.

"I don't know who Yoda is," he says.

"So, you were sent here to what?" I say, "Deliver a message?"

He nods.

"Ha," Chuy says. "I'm literally going to shoot the messenger."

"I don't think you will," he says. "That's not who you are, Chuy." He turns to me. "Or you, Dark Horse."

My instinct is to low blow the guy, let a fist in his gut help loosen his tongue. But his knowledge of our whereabouts, and of our callsigns, suggests that the person who sent him knows us well. And right now, there's only one prime suspect: Whip.

If this really is a character test, I want to pass with flying colors.

I glance behind me. His two partners are on their feet and hobbling in our direction. Will be several minutes before they reach us.

I motion for Chuy to lower her pistol, and she does without hesitation.

"What's the message?" I ask.

He digs into his pocket and freezes when Chuy's gun comes up again.

"Slowly," she says.

When he pulls out a folded piece of paper, Chuy lowers her weapon again.

"A little quaint," I say, taking the paper. "This is the future, you know."

"Only for some of us," he says, revealing that he knows when we're from, too.

I open the note to find a bunch of symbols that mean nothing to me. "This a code or something?"

He looks at me like I'm a Tyrannosaurus Rex whose brain is smaller than a walnut.

Chuy leans over. Looks at the scrawled symbols. "Celestial coordinates. Also, you're holding it upside down."

I rotate the page 180 degrees. The symbols become numbers. "So, I'm an idiot. Sue me."

Chuy won't know where these coordinates will take us just from looking at them. I doubt even Hildy could do that.

"So, what now?" I ask. "You go on your merry way, and we walk into whatever trap is waiting for us here?" I waggle the paper in his face.

"Your call. But if I were you, I'd be more worried about your Union crew than whatever you find there." He points to the page. Doesn't know where the celestial coordinates lead, either.

"You know something about my crew?" I ask.

"I know more than a few somethings about the Union, including that you've been nice and cozy with them for years."

He could be digging for information, so I decide to give him a taste of his own medicine. Instead of answering, I step aside and motion to his weird, cube lander. "Have a nice trip home."

"Really?" he says. "Just like that? You're letting us go?"

"I don't take prisoners," I tell him, "and I don't want to kill you. Yet. But, that can change. So, mosey on back to wherever you came from, and tell your boss I'll think about it."

"You're really not going to ask me anything else? Like where we came from? How none of us are white? Why—"

"You're still talking?" I chamber a round. "Whoever sent you had a message to deliver. You did that. That you're looking for the cat and mouse banter to continue tells me you're an amateur, and this is the first time you've been asked to do something significant. Going home with a story about getting your ass kicked isn't going to win over the ladies, so you're hoping for a redo. And if you get one, it's going to involve me rotating you a mile up and interrogating you on the way down. If that sounds like a good time, feel free to—"

"Okay," he says, stepping toward the cube. "Okay. Geez. Didn't think you'd be so cranky."

"Been a weird couple of days," I tell him.

He taps the large cube's smooth side. The metal wall dissolves, revealing a doorway. "Going to get a lot weirder." He lets his two compatriots, who have finally arrived, enter first. Like a couple of disciplined puppies, they don't even meet our eyes. He steps in behind them, and the wall seals itself.

When the cube starts to hum, I reach my arm out for Chuy. She steps into my grasp, and we rotate away together.

We emerge inside *Lil' Bitch'n*'s cargo bay. Hildy yelps at our return and claps a hand over her mouth. Carter looks up, both interested and suspicious.

"Everyone on board?" I ask.

Burnett steps out of the cockpit. "All here and good to go."

I toggle my comms. "Morton, get us home, ASAP."

"We in a rush?" he asks.

"Yes. That was implied by the 'ASAP,'" I say.

I take a seat beside Carter. Buckle up. "Sorry about before."

"What happened?"

"We were given a message," I say. "From a friend. Maybe." I show her the page.

She stares at it for a moment, and then says, "Looks like a bunch of upside-down numbers."

"Sorry," I say, turning the page around. "Celestial coordinates."

"To where?" she asks.

"No idea. But we're going to—"

Hildy snaps her fingers at me. Holds her hand out for the paper.

"Really?" I say. "That was going to be a cool line."

"Just let me see it," she says, and I hand her the paper. She looks at the coordinates and her brow furrows. "Who gave this to you?"

"Didn't get his name," I say. "Why?"

She waggles the page. "This isn't an exo-planet."

"It's inhabited?" Chuy asks.

That would be something of a worst-case scenario. No way we're going to jump back into Union space. Not while their entire fleet is out looking for us.

She shakes her head. "Not anymore. This is one of the dead planets."

25

Dead planets. There are five of them. Earth was the first. They're worlds that have been used up and depleted of their natural resources, and made uninhabitable thanks to pollution—of the air, water, and food. The first thing that goes is wildlife—gobbled up by an ever-expanding human population. Next is the environment, then once the world is too hot, the food supply.

When a planet dies, billions of people rotate away to multiple, habitable exo-planets. They're like cancer cells, dividing and spreading, leaving death in their wake.

I was part of the process for a long time. Now that I'm not, I see the darkness of it with clear eyes. I had ulterior motives, sure, but that doesn't stop guilt from hopping on for a piggyback ride. Going to be carrying it around for a while.

Dead planets are mostly abandoned, save for the occasional salvage crew. Nobody knows that better than Morton, Burnett, and Porter. They spent ten years together, slagging through the rubble of dead worlds, looking for scraps.

I shouldn't be surprised they're not thrilled with the news.

"I'd hoped to never see a dead world again," Porter says.

We're all on the bridge. Ready to rotate. The boys are hesitating.

"They're so depressing," Morton says. "They make me feel...bad."

"That's because you have a conscience," Chuy says.

"It's a good thing," I add.

"Doesn't *feel* good," Morton says.

"It will later," I assure him. "We were all part of a broken system. It's easy to fall into. At least you all were born into it. I don't have that excuse."

"Is there a way to not feel bad about it?" Burnett asks.

"Do the right thing," I say. "From here on out."

"There is word for that," Drago says. "The thing that we seek. Iskupleniye."

"Redemption," Carter says, translating for those who don't speak Ruskie.

"Holy hell," Hildy says. "Do you all talk this much, all the time, or just when you're about to do something exciting? Let's get on this bitch."

"I don't think that's a saying," I say, "but I hear you. Morton..." I feel like I should have a catchphrase for this moment, like... I can't remember his name. The bald guy.

Why can't I remember his name?

Who cares.

"Take us there," I say. "No. That's dumb. Morton...rotate. Nope. Awkward."

Hildy shakes her head. "You've been doing this for how many years and you still don't have a term for 'en—"

"Let's beat feet!" I say.

Everyone just stares at me.

"We're in a spaceship, chocho," Chuy says. "Ain't no feet to beat."

"Morton," I say, giving up, "fire up the slew. Let's fuckin' go."

Hildy leans closer to me. Whispers, "That was better."

And then we rotate into the white. We linger there for a moment, slipping through space in another reality, and then we rotate back out. Below is a gray planet. If I didn't know better, I'd assume it was a barren world, still in the early stages of development. In a way, it is. The planet will eventually recover from the damage done, but it's going to take millions of years.

"Is shithole," Drago observes.

"Wasn't always," Hildy says. "It used to look a lot like Earth."

"How long did it take?" I ask. "From the moment it was discovered until it looked like this?"

"Ninety-seven years," she says.

"A single lifetime," I say. The guilt on my back is binge-eating.

"The rate of planetary decline has slowed over the years," Hildy says, trying to sound cheery.

"How long until planet death now?" Drago asks.

"On average, two hundred years," Hildy says. "It's been fifty years since the last, but we're due for another three in the next fifteen years. If it makes you feel better, none of the worlds you found will die within your lifetime."

"It doesn't," I say, standing and stepping closer to the windshield that doesn't shield wind. The planet's oceans are greenish. Probably an algae bloom. There are subtle signs of previous habitation. Old cities are scars on the land. I don't see much in the way of natural growth. Aside from it being a depressing guilt trip, nothing else about this planet stands out. "If this is the message, I don't get it."

"You need to go down to the surface, silly," Hildy says.

"Finding a message on a planet the size of Earth is—"

"The celestial coordinates include longitude and latitude," Hildy says, a little too late to spare me from embarrassing myself again.

"And don't go rotating down there," Chuy says. "There's actually too much O2 in the atmosphere, and a shit-ton of pollutants. It would be like breathing in the smoking section of a Denny's. We're going to need suits and helmets."

"Well, that's horrible." I head for the door. "Chuy, Hildy, Carter, you're my brainy Three Amigas for this one. Morton, you're flying *Lil' Bitch'n*."

"I'll just stay on ship forever then," Drago complains.

"As long as the Union is looking for us, I need someone who can fight to stay on board."

He grumbles to himself, but he doesn't complain. He knows I'm right.

On my way to *Lil' Bitch'n*, I slow my pace, letting Chuy, Morton, and Hildy overtake me. I slide up next to Carter. "You're not saying much."

"Nothing to say."

She might not run her mouth like some of us—like *me*—but Carter always has something to say. "Is this like a woman thing where you say you're not hungry, but you're really saying you want a double cheeseburger? Or you say, 'Go ahead, that sounds great,' but you really mean, 'I will skin you alive if you dare?'"

"Sometimes my job requires me to watch, listen, and learn," she says. "When I'm done doing that, I'll let you know."

Reading between the feminine lines, I ask, "So, it's Chuy then, right?"

She stops in her tracks, and I nearly trip over myself trying to put on the brakes. "You think I'm jealous…" She points to Chuy, now entering the cargo bay. "…of *her?*"

The hint of disdain in her voice says that she's either definitely jealous of Chuy, or she has some other problem with her that I can't begin to imagine.

"What's wrong with Chuy?" I ask, feeling defensive for my partner. "That came out wrong. What I mean is, if you're going to be jealous of me having sexual relations with other people, I already told you, it's just been me and Harriet for years."

Her smile requires a microscope to see, but it's there.

Good enough for now, I think, and I resume our trek, which involvees a minute long walk to *Lil' Bitch'n*, five minutes of prep, a ten-minute flight, and another ten minutes to get everyone suited up.

I'm not a fan of wearing a fully encased helmet. They're a little claustrophobic and they really suck if you have bad breath. The suits are modified, airtight BCSs. They allow for full range of motion, but they're a little tight in the britches. When the hatch lowers to the ground, I strut down the ramp picking at my crotch.

"You got space crabs again, boss?" Chuy says.

"Ha ha," I say. "Feels like my nuts are being pinched by a lobster."

"This planet once had lobster-like creatures," Hildy says.

"Let me guess," I say. "Extinct?"

"Actually, no. People kept them as pets. They were extremely loyal and easy to train. When the people left, they took their pets with them. They're now popular on three inhabited worlds."

"Fun," I say, and then I stumble to a stop at the ramp's bottom. I'm unprepared for what I find.

It's a neighborhood.

Unlike the apocalyptic Antarctic remains in which I awoke, this place is still intact. At least the structures are. There's no plant life anywhere. The air is full of dust. It hisses against my viewscreen, whipped up by gusts of wind.

"Which way?" I ask Hildy.

She doesn't hear me. Can't say I blame the kid. Her first venture to another planet was Elysium—nicest place in the habitable galaxy. This...is a nightmare.

I put my hand on her shoulder. "Not going to puke this time, right? Because that's going to go very badly for you."

"No," she says. "I just didn't... I wasn't... I'd seen photos of this world. And videos. But there's no record of this."

"Dead things tend to be unpleasant," I say. "We don't need to stay here long." I hope. "Just point me in the right direction, and I'll—"

She points.

"Thanks." I strike out toward what looks like a quaint home in a nice neighborhood, if you ignore the wasteland surrounding it. There's even a white picket fence—classic Americana sans the red, white, and blue. Hard to believe the white supremacists who spawned this future nightmare came from the country who defeated the Nazis. But here we are.

There's something off about the fence. Little knobs on the top of each baluster. "What the hell..." The knobs are little skulls. No idea what they belonged to, but they couldn't have been cute.

This is the only house decorated after the mass evacuation. Has to be the right place. I let myself into the yard through the gate and pause to take in the freakshow. There's what looks like a car, built from a collection of metal parts. Not far away is a mannequin, dressed like a mom from the 1950s, her painted eyes scratched away, but her frozen smile still present. In between them is a shovel, stuck in the dirt.

There is a question mark painted on the shovel's blade.

On the house, car, and mannequin's forehead are painted-on 'No' symbols.

"The hell does this mean?" Chuy asks.

"Not a clue," I say. Nothing about this makes sense. I turn to Carter. "Anything?"

She just shakes her head, looking intrigued, but little else.

Hildy gasps. When I spin around to face her, she's beaming.

"What?" I ask her. "You know what all this is?"

She all but skips past me. "You're looking for a message, right? Something that only you, or someone from your era, would understand?"

"That was the hope," I say.

"Well, you're standing in it."

I scan the strange front yard again, and I don't see any message. I'm about to vent my frustration when Hildy motions to the shovel with both hands. "You may ask yourself, how do I work this?"

She waits for a response.

"I got nothing, kid. Sorry."

"Seriously?" She leaps over to the car. Motions to it. "Where is that large automobile?"

That clicks.

"Holy shit," Chuy says, pointing to the 'No' symbol on the house. "This is not my beautiful house."

"This is not my beautiful wife," Carter says, eyeing the mannequin. "Talking Heads. Nice. What does it mean?"

I turn to Chuy, equally happy and terrified. "'Once in a Lifetime' was Brick's favorite song." I tug the shovel out of the dry soil. "How do I work this?" I scan the yard and spot a lone brick. "I dig."

26

The soil is hard-packed and full of rocks. Digging through it is a bitch. I'm tempted to use the Taks. Their robotic arms would make short work of the solid earth. But I don't know what's buried here, and Taks aren't known for being gentle.

There's only one shovel, so I labor alone while the others scout the area—Hildy and Carter are inside. Chuy is in the backyard. I don't expect them to find anything. I just didn't want to be watched, in case this brick is a gravestone. Just thinking about it makes my eyes water.

He's not dead, I tell myself. The brick was a marker, that's all.

I hope.

Two feet down, the shovel clangs against something hard. A rock. Too big to shovel out. Hands and knees, I find the stone's edge, get my gloved fingers on its side, and pull. It takes a lot of wiggling, but the rock comes free.

Only, it's not a rock.

It's another brick.

I toss it to the side, look back into the hole. I'm not sure what I was expecting to find beneath the brick, but it wasn't more dirt. "C'mon, Brick, you're killing me."

I pick up the shovel and start digging again. Ten minutes of hard labor gets me nowhere and nothing but sweaty. I try to wipe my arm across my forehead and just bonk my helmet.

I'm about to unleash a torrent of creative curses when Chuy says, "Anything?"

She's approaching from the side yard, hands empty.

"Another brick." I point to the ruddy rectangle. "And a lot more dirt."

"I can take a turn," Chuy says.

"I got it."

"You're not the only one who feels the burden of finding our people, you know."

I'm about to argue the point. I've been so laser focused on chasing down Brick, Whip, Benny, and BigApe that I haven't really considered how Chuy feels about it all. I know she wants to find them, but I didn't think about how she might feel responsible for them.

"We've been together this whole time," she says. "And they're...lost. Maybe living in a shithole like this. Maybe dead in a shithole like this. Right now. We're the team. You and me. And it's on us to find the others. You copy?"

"I copy," I say.

"Then give me the fucking shovel." She holds out her hand. Waits.

"Just a few more minutes," I say, and I stab the blade into the ground, stomping it down with my foot.

She rolls her eyes and picks up the second brick. Hefts it from one hand to the other. Then she picks up the first brick. She bounces them in both hands.

I pause to watch. "Warming up?"

She tosses the second brick. "This one is lighter." She drops the lighter brick by her feet. Holds a hand out. "Shovel. Now."

I hand it to her. With a quick stab, she splits the brick in half, revealing a cavity. She drops the shovel and picks up both halves while I step out of the hole. She tosses the empty half away and tips the other into her free hand. A folded slip of paper slides out, and she drops the brick's remains. By the time she opens the paper, I'm looking over her shoulder.

This time, I know what I'm seeing. "More celestial coordinates."

"The hell?" Chuy says. "Not even 'Hey guys, I'm alive. Hope you're okay.'"

I'm disappointed, too, but there's a bright side.

"At least it's not a grave."

"Find something?" Carter asks. She and Hildy are exiting the house.

"More celestial coordinates," I say. "Anything inside?"

"Someone lived there for a while," she says, "but it was very organized. Very clean."

"Sounds like Brick," Chuy says. "Big man always was a neat freak."

I hand the new coordinates to Hildy. "Know where this is?"

She scans the page, and when she doesn't recognize the location right away, I know something is off. Her brow furrows. She turns the page over, looking for more. Then back again. Opens her mouth to speak, and then closes it.

"What is it?" I ask.

"I'm not sure," she says. "I know where in space this is, but I can't think of anything that's there. Should just be empty space."

"Is there any place that's been lost?" Carter asks. "Its location forgotten?"

"Like Atlantis?" I ask.

"Sure," Carter says. "But a planet."

Hildy's shaking head slows to a stop. "Actually, there is one place. Its location was removed from the database. From *every* database. I asked about it once. My supervisor told me that the High Council had declared the knowledge forbidden, for the safety of the Empire."

"Hildy," I say. "This is the point where I get annoyed from not knowing what the hell you're talking about."

"Right," she says. "Sorry. Beta Prime."

"The Australia of planets?" I ask, and then I add, "The first colony, right? The early Union used it as an experiment in colonizing new worlds. Sent a bunch of... What did Burnett call them? ...undesirables. When the people survived, they all went native and killed each other. No one has been back since."

"That's one of several dozen rumors," Hildy says. "The truth is that the planet was quarantined because the air itself was infected. If the infection got off planet, it could wipe out the entire human race."

Given the method of 'purification' employed by the early Union, a plague capable of wiping out humanity probably strikes a nerve, even now. Who'd want to go back? Better to forget and pretend it never happened.

"Sounds like the place to be if you don't want the Union finding you," I say.

"It would be suicide," Hildy says. "Who would want to hide from the Union so bad that they'd risk living on Beta Prime?"

"You know what propaganda is?" I ask Hildy.

"I...think so," she says.

Knowing the definition and knowing propaganda when you hear it are two different things. "If there was something on Beta Prime the Union didn't want anyone to know about, but for some reason or another, couldn't just destroy it, what would be the best way to keep even the most curious people away?"

She doesn't answer.

"Lie about it," I say.

"You're saying the planet isn't quarantined," Hildy says. I can see her brain wrapping itself around the new paradigm. "That there isn't a virus?"

"Never was," Chuy says.

"But I still don't understand why," Hildy says. "What could be there that they don't want anyone to know about?"

I turn away from the group and walk to the fence. Resting my hands on a post, I look out at the nightmare neighborhood where Brick lived for a time.

Things are about to get messy, and dangerous. *More* dangerous. Because, if I'm right...we've been on the wrong side of an old war for a long time, and we'll soon meet the people we've been inadvertently oppressing...until yesterday.

Can't be a coincidence that Brick's message was delivered just as we launched our one-ship rebellion against the Union.

How long has he been keeping track of us?

How long has he been waiting for me to wake up?

"Sorry, man," I say into the windblown dust.

"You going to just stare off into the distance," Carter says, "or are you going to fill us in?"

"The people who delivered Brick's first message... On Elysium..." I turn to face them. "They weren't white."

"You mean, like you?" Hildy sounds excited by the prospect.

"The man I spoke to," I say. "Bighead. He had dark brown skin and blue eyes. The woman had kind of a Polynesian vibe, and the second man might have been Chinese. At least ancestrally. Those places don't really exist now. Point is, they weren't white. And they weren't Union."

"Then who are they?" Hildy looks at me with the wide eyes of a child being told a bedtime fairytale about unicorns and magical forests.

"Undesirables," Chuy says, oozing disdain.

"Oh," Hildy says, sounding a little confused, and then sad realization hits. "*Oh...*"

"Sounds like this—" Carter taps the celestial coordinates. "—might be a good place to hide from the Union. Any reason we're not already en route?"

A multi-cultural planet. The sterilization of the human race undone. Brick being alive. All of it sounds too good to be true. "Good place to hide could also be a good place to set a trap."

"We're sitting ducks down here," Carter says. "They could have killed us on Elysium, too."

"She's got a point," Chuy says. "And if this really is Brick..."

I nod. We don't really have a choice. That puts us at a strategic disadvantage. But it's the only path forward. "You guys go ahead. I'll catch up."

All three of them are about to protest for one reason or another, but Chuy understands that when I need a moment, there's a reason. She herds Carter and Hildy toward *Lil' Bitch'n*. "He'll catch up."

I look over the yard, trying to imagine what it would be like eking out a living in this harsh landscape. How many of those little creatures did he have to eat? How did he find water? How did he not give up? Or die? And how did he get out, ally himself with Beta Prime, and find me when the Union could not?

I pick up the shovel, looking at the painted question mark. He made a riddle of "Once in a Lifetime," knowing only Chuy and I would figure out who left it. He also knew my favorite part of that song. Knew that I'd be asking myself, *Am I right? Am I wrong?* And as the curtain covering the reality of my past choices pulls back, I'm saying to myself, *My God! What have I done?*

He could have chosen dozens of songs to reveal himself. But he chose this one. For me.

My God...

I've wanted to see Brick again for five years.

Now I'm dreading it.

What have I done?

27

A knock on my door makes me flinch. I'd been lost in thought, in a near dream state, but not quite asleep.

I slide my bare feet onto the cold floor. Rub my hands over my face. "Come in."

The door slides open to reveal a feminine figure, silhouetted by a hallway light. *Carter,* I think, but she looks curvier than I remember. "If you got my number from the bathroom stall and are here for a good time, I'm afraid I'm not in the mood."

"In your dreams, cabrón." The lights snap on revealing Chuy dressed in a BCS, looking amused.

I wince at the light and at my error. "Why are you wearing a BCS?"

"Unlike some people on this ship, I wash my clothing on occasion." She brushes me aside with her hand. "Scooch."

I slide over to make room for her. Backs to the wall, the porthole between our heads, we sit in silence for a moment, arms resting on knees. The cold metal on my bare back feels good. Better than lying awake in the damn cot.

"So," Chuy says, after an unbearable silence. She reaches up and taps on the porthole. "What are we still doing here?"

"We've been going flat out for a while," I say. "Thought the crew might need a break."

"Uh-huh." She's not buying it.

"The only people actually sleeping are the bear and the bat," she says.

The bear is Drago. He sleeps in a curled nest of blankets in the corner of his quarters. Snores loud enough to hear through his two-inch thick metal door. "Who's the bat?"

"Your lady," she says. "Pretty sure she sleeps hanging upside down from the ceiling. I haven't seen her, but she has a kind of 'I vant to suck your blood' vibe about her."

I raise an eyebrow at her.

"You know exactly what I'm saying. Don't try to hide it just because she took you to pound town. She puts on a good show, but underneath the good looks and the practiced charm, she's—"

"Ruthless," I say. "I know. Some people would say that about you and me."

"Only bad guys." She smiles. "And whoever gets your popcorn at a movie theater."

"There's a right number of butter pumps and a wrong number," I say.

"That's subjective," she says.

"Three pumps in the middle, three pumps on the top. That's a God damned universal law."

Our laughter fades to silence until Chuy says, "I miss popcorn."

"I miss when life was simple. Good guys and bad guys. A mission with a clear-cut objective. Deployed or not deployed. This mess... I feel confused most of the time. And now..."

"We fucked up," she says.

"*I* fucked up."

"Pssh. Wasn't a choice you made that I didn't support. Keeping a low profile. Working for the Union off the radar. It felt safe."

"So, we were cowards," I conclude.

She shrugs. "We were a thousand years out of place, living in a galaxy populated by more than a hundred billion space Nazis. Keeping a low profile was smart. Now we have a ship. And a crew. We understand the system and the people. We found Carter...who, despite her undead ways, nudged us in the right direction. I'm not thrilled that she used sex to gain your trust and extract intel from you—"

"Hey," I complain.

"Wasn't her coming to your door," she points out. "You got used, compañero. You just haven't figured it out yet. She's a spook, man. Psyops. Let me guess, she used movies to get to you. Wait. No. Music."

I frown.

"Sorry, boss. You're an easy target." She elbows my arm. "Worked for Hildy, too." I'm about to complain when she adds, "But, that was organic and honest. Kid won your heart. Mine too, honestly. We needed a breath of fresh air on this flying turd. I just want you to keep your eyes open when it comes to Carter."

"Consider them peeled open," I say.

"You know, she'll probably work her way through the rest of the men on this ship until she knows everything about everyone. It's what she does."

I laugh despite the possibility that Chuy might be right. My connection to Carter felt genuine, but she's probably still good at her job, even if she was lost in a jungle world for three years. And right now, my fledgling relationship with her is the last thing on my mind. "Chuy…we helped the Union expand their Empire. We're complicit to whatever atrocities are carried out on the planets we found for them. The hell were we thinking?"

"We were surviving. And now we're going to make that right," she says. "But we can't do that while orbiting a dead planet."

"I'm not sure I can face him," I say. "Brick found us. Knows what we've been doing, and who we've been doing it for."

"He's still Brick," she says. "He'll understand."

"The song wasn't just a clue," I say. "It was a message."

"I know." She sounds more hopeful than wounded.

"What message did you get from it?" I ask.

"'Once in a Lifetime' is a repetitive song, but there is one line that's repeated more than all the others. Like twenty times. That's the message."

I could play the song. Hear it for myself.

I've uploaded Hildy's pilfered media to every hard drive and back-up storage device on Big and *Lil' Bitch'n*, including a pinkie drive that I keep with me all the time. Just in case. Right now, hearing the song would be too painful, so I let the lyrics rattle through my head. And then a line stands out.

The message Chuy extracted from the song is very different from 'My God! What have I done?'

Where I found judgement, she found forgiveness.

"'Same as it ever was,'" I say.

"Nothing has changed," she says. "Brick is still himself. We're still a team. No matter what we've done, and what he's gone through. 'Same as it ever was.'"

I force a smile. "Maybe you're right."

"I'm always right," she says. "You know how many people owe me fifty bucks?"

That gets a genuine smile. "Does Brick owe you any money? Maybe that will help."

"Nah," she says. "He's smart enough to not bet against me." She punches my knee. "Or you." She pushes herself to the edge of the bed. "C'mon. I'm getting bored."

"Life on the run has you addicted to adrenaline," I say, following her toward the bridge, until I realize that I am, once again, just wearing boxers.

Ten minutes later, I'm dressed, Drago and Carter are awake, and the crew is ready to go, but not very enthusiastic.

"Mount up!" I say to Morton, thrusting my palm in the air.

Once again, the crew just stares...until Chuy snickers and says, "Dickbrain."

"It means," I say, "get on your horses."

"I think *Mr.* Horse needs more sleep," Drago says.

And then Hildy gasps. "This is that social thing, where you quote something obscure and then someone else says the next bit, and you bond over knowing the same thing?"

"Yes," I say.

With the brightest smile I've yet seen on her face, she waves her arms around in the air and sings, "For he's a Jolly good fe-el-loooow. Which nobody can deny!"

I snap my fingers and point to Morton.

"Go."

While Hildy unleashes a second "Which nobody can deny!" doing an impressive impersonation of the Singing Bush from *The Three Amigos*, *Bitch'n* rotates away from the dead planet and emerges from the fourth dimension in orbit above Beta-Prime.

I'm pretty sure Hildy would have kept singing, but the view silences her.

The planet below...

"Is that Earth?" Carter asks. "Did you take us to Earth?"

"No, ma'am," Morton says. "I followed the new coordinates."

"Continents are wrong," Drago says. "More water."

"We've been to Earth," Porter says. "This looks—"

"Cleaner," Burnett says and turns to me. "If the virus was a fabrication, why would the Union give this up?"

"They wouldn't," I say.

"And they'd do anything to get it back," Hildy says.

I stand from my chair.

"That's why we're not taking any risks."

"Let me guess," Drago says. "I am staying on board, blah, blah, blah."

"Actually, no. I have no idea what we're walking into. I want you with me."

He pumps his fist. "Yes."

"Burn," I say.

Burnett snaps his head toward me. "Yes, sir?"

"You're in charge while I'm gone."

"What?" he and Carter say at the same time, him astounded, Carter angry.

"Sorry," I say to Carter. "Burn's my number four. Been with me for five years. He's earned it."

Morton and Porter start clapping, genuinely excited for Burnett's apparent promotion.

"Well done, Burnett," Porter says. "Or should I say, *Burn?*"

Burnett is bowing when Carter sighs, shakes her head, and then exits the bridge.

"Morton," I say. "First sign of trouble. Bug out."

"Won't leave you behind," he says.

"Well, yeah, don't do that. Just come up with a plan and then come back for us."

He salutes.

"Porter... Same thing."

Porter salutes.

"Anything I can do?" Hildy asks.

"Keep these knuckleheads out of trouble," I say.

"Okay." She smiles. "How do I do that?"

"Just keep an eye on things. Spot anything weird, let Burnett know. Or contact me directly. You remember how to use your comms, right?"

She taps her neck, says, "Dark Horse. Right."

Hearing her voice in my ear twice is a little weird, but it demonstrates her point.

"Good," I say. Then I turn to Chuy and Drago. "Let's rock."

28

Drago shoves me away from him, repulsed by the idea of my arm around his waist. He stumbles a step and blinks his eyes a few times before rubbing them. "I do not like personal rotation. Feels strange."

He's not wrong. Everything about slipping between dimensions of space, shifting from one part of the universe to another, is disorienting. It's less noticeable in a ship, because your immediate surroundings don't change. Using the PSD means everything changes in an instant. Temperature. Air quality. Smells. Ambient noise. It can be a shock to the system if you're not ready for it.

In this case, we went from the temperature-controlled, sixty-seven-degree interior of *Bitch'n* to a humid, ninety-degree jungle full of pungent smells.

From above, the planet looked Earth-like. From the ground, it looks more like Oz. The trees are coated in brightly colored bark. Some are dark red. Others blue, green, and purple. I can't be sure, but I think the different colors belong to different species. Instead of leaves, there are bunches of green vegetation—like heads of broccoli. They're on all the trees, but the size and shape of the broccoli varies between species.

"Smells like skunk," Drago says.

Something stinks of decay, but there's no way to know if it's a dead creature or just how vegetation on this planet smells. Earth had its fair share of stinky plants, including the aptly named skunk cabbage.

I slip my rifle from my shoulder to my hands. "No idea what to expect, so be ready for a fight, but do not pull the trigger first. Copy?"

"Copy," Chuy says, chambering a round in her sniper rifle.

Drago pumps an auto-shotgun that can unload twelve shells in three seconds. He calls it his 'person eraser.' He hasn't had a chance to test the name's accuracy. I hope he never does. He's also carrying two handguns, a rifle, and that big-ass Ruskie knife. It's less weight than he carried on previous missions, but definitely overkill.

I hope.

Still have no idea what to expect here, which is why we rotated a mile outside the coordinates on the note.

"I will take point," Drago says, and he doesn't wait for me to agree.

"If you want to be my meat shield, have at it," I say, and I follow with Chuy. I'm not a fan of people risking themselves on my behalf, but I don't really see Drago as a subordinate. We've become allies. Antagonistic friends. I'm the ship's captain, and he respects that, but I have no illusions about any real control over him. Arguing with him about being on point will just start a testosterone fueled tit-for-tat that ends with creative ways to say 'fuck you!' And then he'll still be on point, and Chuy will shake her head at me with a perfected judgmental eyeroll.

"Dark Horse," Chuy says.

"Don't judge me!" I say.

"When you're done with your imaginary argument, let me know." Annnd eyeroll.

Dang it.

"I'm done," I say, taking a deep breath and letting it out.

"Stressed?" she asked.

"What gave you that idea?" I ask.

She steps over a fallen tree, its purple bark sunken in and crumbling. A line of fist-sized insect-like things are gnawing off chunks of the tree's insides and carrying them away. I hop over the tree, trying not to straddle it for long because those things have pincers long and sharp enough to shish kebab my nards.

"We're kind of flying blind here," she says. "You know I don't mind danger—"

She doesn't just not mind it, she welcomes it.

"—but aimless risks at the whim of outside forces doesn't sit well."

"Even if it's Brick?" I ask.

"*If*," she says. "We're not sure about that yet. Finding our people was a mission I could get behind. A guiding force. Being Exo-Hunters might have been wrong, but the job was clear. We might not have liked our place in this future, but we understood it. Now... Someone else is giving the orders and we don't know who. After this mission, that ends, no matter who or what we find."

Drago interrupts by snapping a fist into the air above his head.

Chuy and I stop in our tracks, the conversation shelved for another time and place.

Drago lifts a lump of low-hanging, dark purple broccoli and stares into the jungle ahead. He lowers it back into place without making a sound. Steps back to us. "Light. Up ahead. Fifty feet."

"We're still half a click out from the coordinates," Chuy notes.

She's right, but we have no idea where we're going. Could be a rendezvous point. Could be a village. Could be another brick with a message. *God, I hope not.*

But light usually means people.

Switching to hand signals, I turn to Chuy. Motion to my eyes, and then point up into the trees. She nods and heads off to find a good vantage point. Then I turn to Drago and sweep my arms ahead, signaling for him to take the lead once more. He looks at me like I've just asked him to have sex with Beatrice and shakes his head. Then he repeats my sweeping hand gesture.

With a sigh, I comply. I don't have time to mime an argument with the last grumpy Russian in the galaxy.

I do my best to move through the lumpy foliage without making a sound, but the broccoli heads are hard to avoid and they squeak when you brush against them. So, I push through clumps of them only when the wind kicks up. A good breeze sets the whole jungle to squeaking.

I slow when I see the light ahead. It's blue and ethereal, changing the hue of the tree trunks as it strikes them. Side stepping, I change positions until I find a window through the jungle and spot the light's source.

From a distance, it resembles a twelve-foot-tall termite colony, but decorated with baseball-sized, glowing blue ovals.

"Is like American Christmas tree, no?" Drago says.

"No," I say. "First of all, that's clearly a pile of dirt. Second, I don't hear any Bing Crosby."

Remembering that we likely have *Frosty the Snowman* and *Rudolph the Red Nosed Reindeer* now, I think I might celebrate the holiday with Chuy this year.

"Who is Bing Crosby?" Drago asks.

I ignore the question and approach the strange mound. The closer I get, the more I'm infused with a sense of calm. The air smells better, too. It's an oasis of serenity. I lower my guard and stop just a few feet away. It smells sweet, and a little bit like bacon. I want to touch it. Hell, I kind of want to taste it.

"What is it?" Drago says, stepping up beside me.

"Not sure," I say. "But it's kind of..."

"...magical," he says, reaching out a hand to touch one of the glowing blue, fist-sized jelly beans. Luminous oil shimmers and swirls beneath a thin membrane, mesmerizing.

"Beautiful," I say.

"Uhh, boss," Chuy says. "You guys don't sound normal. Everything okay?"

In a flicker of clarity, I say, "Dandy," and then I reach out my hand.

I don't know what I'm doing.

I just need to touch it.

I flinch at the sound of Drago's shotgun falling to the ground, but the effect doesn't last long. The glowing blue has my full attention. My craving for it is almost sexual. Irresistible.

I reach for the blue.

"That's a bad idea," a man says. I barely register it.

My fingers are just inches from the blue when a hand grasps my wrist and yanks it away.

"No!" Drago shouts, shoving someone away. "I need it!"

I'm about to do the same, when I see the man holding my wrist—Bighead. Most of his face is covered by a mask, but his dark skin and bright blue eyes are hard to forget. His face breaks me from the spell long enough to remember why we're here.

"It's carnivorous bioluminescent bacteria," Bighead says. "Secretes a hallucinogenic pheromone. Attracts animals, and small-minded human beings."

"I don't care!" Drago says, fighting against the Asian man and the Polynesian woman I encountered on Elysium. I'm not sure how they're holding him back. He's twice their size. But he's all Jell-O.

Actually, so am I. Bighead is telling the truth.

"Drago," I say, slurring his name. I place my hand on his chest. He blinks at me. "We're drugged. I think... I think..."

Drago's intensity fades. His body goes slack. The man and woman holding him back switch to holding him up. A smile emerges on his face. "I hear music. Is...is Gorky Park!"

I hear it, too, and I burst out laughing. The Russian band's biggest MTV hit, *Bang*, has magically started playing in the jungle.

"This song is pretty good," I say to Bighead. "For Ruskie glam rock."

"Wouldn't know," he says, pulling me away from the psychedelic love pillar.

I start belting out the lyrics, making a mess of the song. I know the English bits, but the words travel through a blender on the way from my brain to my mouth. Drago starts playing air guitar and singing the Russian bits just as poorly as I'm singing the English. As we're led away from the spire, Drago and I bump into each other. The big Russian wraps his arms around me in a bear hug. "Russia and America! We are friends now!" The video for *Bang* featured both American and Russian flags. Controversial at the time. Sold records. Got lots of play on MTV in the months before our jaunt to the future. Took a thousand years, but the message of unity seems to have just struck Drago now.

We're separated and dragged farther away, both of us lost in the 80s, filling the jungle with incoherent wails.

Fifty feet away, I'm still feeling pretty good. A hundred feet away, I can still hear the music, but the euphoria is fading. I stop singing.

"Okay," I say. "I'm okay."

Bighead stops. "You sure? The effects take a little while to wear off."

"I'm good," I tell him, and he lets go of me. I stumble a few steps and lean against a tree. Feel like I've just run a race.

Drago lies on the forest floor, breathing heavy, sweating. "Why can I still hear music?"

The song stops. "Sorry," Chuy says in my ear. "Things were getting intense. Hildy pumped Gorky Park in via the comms at my request. Thought it might distract you both."

Neither I nor Drago respond or react. Better they don't know that Chuy is providing overwatch.

I sit up and look back at the now distant pillar. "Is that thing really carnivorous?"

"It's full of flesh-eating bacteria," the woman says. "Would have dissolved you, and you'd have liked it."

"Well, then, thanks." I pat my own chest like I'm communicating with a cave woman. "I'm Dark Horse...but you already knew that." I motion to my Russian friend. "This is Drago."

"And where is Chuy?" Bighead asks.

"Beats the hell out of me," I say. "She's an independent woman."

"Rude future people," Drago says. "You know our names. You share yours." He waits, and when no one answers he persists. "C'mon. Tell names or I make you carry me all the way."

"Spunky," the woman says.

"Poncho," the man says.

I'm still just high enough that their callsigns strike a chord. I can't stop myself from laughing.

"What?" Spunky asks, annoyed by my response.

"Brick. He named you after his pet chameleons," I say. "Spunky and Poncho. On the plus side, he really loved those little guys."

"Time to go," Bighead says, lifting me off the tree.

I give a lazy nod, and I kick Drago with the side of my boot. "Let's move."

He rolls to his feet with a grunt, complains about leaving his shotgun by the flesh-eating bacteria trap, and falls in line. Our five-minute journey is quiet, so I take the time to observe our surroundings. We're following a game path through the jungle. It's not very efficient, weaving a serpentine line, but it avoids several of the pillars illuminating the jungle in cool blue. Seems like a dangerous place to call home, but a smart place to set up a basecamp if you don't want to be found. Natural defenses can turn a losing fight into a victory.

We stop at a metal hatch embedded at the base of a cliff face that rises several hundred feet into the air.

Bighead knocks on the door three times, pauses, and then knocks twice more. Old school. The door *thunks* from the inside and then swings open with a grinding squeak. A man steps out, dressed like a soldier at war. All black body armor. He's a behemoth of a man and would be intimidating as hell if he didn't also have gray hair, a beard, and enough wrinkles to—

"Moses," Chuy says in my ear, and I know something is really wrong. *What did I miss?* I see it in the man's pale blue eyes a moment before Chuy speaks the realization aloud. "That's Brick."

29

"Brick?" I ask, but I know it's him. The gray hair is out of place, but his blue eyes, pale skin, and wide smile are impossible to mistake. As is his voice.

"Hey, Boss," he says.

He laughs, deep and resonating when I throw my arms around him in an embrace. Then he squeezes back, hard enough to crush the air from my lungs. "It's good to see you, old friend."

"Ugh," Drago says. "Amerikanskiys and your big emotions."

Brick pulls out of the hug and gives the Russian his full, intimidating attention. "You're aware that there is no longer a United States, or a Russia, correct?"

"Da," Drago says, clenching his jaw.

"Don't worry about Drago," I say. "He's a toothless puppy dog."

Drago smirks, but flips me off.

I return the favor.

"Keeping the rivalry alive?" Brick says.

"One of the only things that feels normal," I admit. "Speaking of...what's with all the gray? And the wrinkles?"

"I got old," he says.

"Is it a side effect of time travel?" I ask. "We didn't experience anything like that."

Brick chuckles.

"It's a side effect of traveling through time, at a very normal pace, for thirty-five years."

His meaning sinks in slowly. "You've...been here for *thirty-five years?*"

He takes my chin in his big hand, turns my face one way, then the other, looking at my face. "And you have not. Three years?"

"Five," I say.

He gives a slow nod, but he looks sad. "I wish I'd known. I would have reached out sooner. We could have forgone all the cloak and dagger."

"Speaking of, what was the point of all that? Don't get me wrong, I really enjoyed the Talking Heads riddle. But I don't understand why it was necessary."

"I needed to make sure that you were still you. That you remembered who you are...and who I am."

"Because I worked for the Union?" I ask, shame creeping up on me. I've been dreading this conversation, but now that I'm here, I just want to get it over with.

He nods. "Yes."

"And now? You're sure I'm not?"

"You're the most wanted man in the galaxy," Bighead says. "We know you're not working with them anymore."

"I just wasn't sure if you'd work with me," Brick says.

"Look," I say, feeling a bit defensive, "I didn't become an Exo-Hunter because I liked the Union, or because I believed in their expansionist dogma. I was out there looking for you. For everyone. Did I compromise my morals to do it? Sure. Did the ends justify the means? Probably not. Would I do it again? You're God damn right I would."

Brick smiles. Rests his meaty hand on my shoulder. "Good. That's good. Your dedication to protecting your people is why you're here."

"Thought I was here because you summoned me."

"You misunderstand," Brick says. "Not here, in this place. Here, in this time." He turns and steps inside the open door. "Follow m—"

A blur drops between Brick and the doorway. He staggers back a step, caught off guard. Before any of us can react, a pistol is raised and pressed against the big man's forehead.

I lean to look around Brick's broad body. "Chuy..."

"He tested you," she says. "Now I'm going to test him."

There's anger in her eyes, until she looks at him a little closer.

"Been a while, Chuy," he says, and there is something strange about his voice. Barely contained emotion, but it's squelched. "I missed you."

"I'm sorry," I say. "Am I missing something?"

Drago leans over. Whispers in my ear. "Is obvious. They were 'thing.' Before. Is love lost. Separated by time and space. Romantic, no?"

"But for how long?" Chuy asks, and then she turns to Bighead. "How old are you?"

"Twenty-five?" he says, like he's not sure, but I think he's just confused. Like I am.

Chuy and Brick were together? How did I never see it? Why didn't they tell me? Even after all this time in the future, where potential conflicts of interest don't exist, I was kept in the dark.

"Ten years," she says, anger settling. "You waited ten years?"

"Nine," Brick says.

She lowers the gun. "That's a long time, I guess."

And then it all clicks. "Whoa, whoa, whoa. Bighead is your *son?*" I take stock of the kid again. So much of him doesn't look like Brick at all, but the eyes... How did I not see it before? The Bighead name makes more sense now. It's the kind of callsign a father would give to a son whose ego needs to be checked.

Brick opens his arms, and Chuy steps into his hug. It's a quiet embrace, full of joy, sadness, and regret. When they separate, Chuy turns away, attempting to hide that she's wiping a tear from her eye.

"William," Brick says to Bighead. He motions to me. "This is my oldest friend, Moses." He motions to Chuy. "And this is Sophia." He plants his big hand on Bighead's shoulder. "Guys, this is my son."

"Can we stick to callsigns?" I ask.

"You can call me Will," Bighead says. "Please."

"You're not on a mission," Brick tells me.

"My whole life is a mission," I say, and then I turn to Drago. "Eh? Not bad, right?"

He waggles his hand. "Eeeeeh. Is so-so for catchphrase."

Brick has a good, hearty laugh that gets the rest of us going. Even Drago.

"I missed this," Brick says. "People in the future don't banter."

"Hard to banter when people are dying all the time," Will says.

"Who...is dying all the time?" I ask.

"Come with me," Brick says. "We have a lot to talk about."

He leads the way inside. Chuy and I follow with Will. Drago next. Spunky and Poncho close the door behind us, but they don't come inside.

The tunnel is smooth like a lava tube, carved out of solid rock and lit by glowing yellow stones that look natural. Brick powers ahead, moving quickly despite his size...and his age.

Will pushes between Chuy and me, spins around, and walks backward. His cocky edge is gone now. Might have been a show. Now he just seems intrigued. "So, you and my father were..."

"Together," Chuy says. "Yes."

Will gestures like his head is exploding. "Pshh. I can't believe he never told me."

"I know the feeling." I shoot Chuy a look.

She's unfazed by my displeasure.

"Is he a good father?" Chuy asks.

Will turns to look at Brick for a moment, then speaks quietly. "He's kind of a hard ass, but I don't blame him for that. After everything that's happened. After mom died. It's just been the two of us, and—"

"Your mother is dead...?" Chuy looks wounded by the news. Honestly, so am I. Brick has endured a lot, and we weren't here for him.

"I'm sorry," Chuy says. "When did she die?"

He rolls his eyes up, thinking. Stumbles and catches himself. Adjusts his course with the tunnel's bend. "Fifteen months ago. He's been leading on his own since."

"Leading who?" I ask, but I'm quickly overridden by Chuy.

"How did she die?" she asks.

Will's face falls flat. "That's for him to tell you."

"Seems like a good kid," I say, not elevating the volume of my voice. "You did a good job raising him."

Will is baffled until up ahead, Brick says, "Thanks."

Subtle shifts in his body language—cocking an ear, shaking his head—revealed he was listening.

"You could *hear* us?" Will asks.

"I'm old," Brick says. "Not deaf." He stops by a metal hatch at the tunnel's end. "What I'm about to show you is a thousand years in the making. Millions of lives were given to create it, including my wife's. The laws of time and space were broken..." He looks me dead in the eyes, his stare intense. "...all so the final chess piece could be put into play. Understand?"

"Not remotely," I say.

He smiles. "You will."

Brick opens the door, steps to the side, and motions for us to proceed. I hesitate, feeling a strange weight on my chest. "What the hell is happening?" I whisper to Chuy.

She leans close. "I think you're the final chess piece."

I shake my head. It's not possible. I'm a Union sympathizer who compromised his morals to pursue a personal mission, and I would absolutely do it again if put in the same position. Unless there is a 'prick' chess piece I haven't heard of, I didn't earn my place on the battlefield.

Is there a battlefield?

"Kind of taking the wind out of my big reveal's sails," Brick says.

Chuy takes my arm and leads me past Brick. We step through the door and stumble to a stop. My mouth expands like a black hole, and then closes. Chuy's grip on my arm tightens, but I barely notice the pain. I'm not just speechless, I'm dumbfounded.

When Drago steps up next to us, he does a decent job of putting my feelings into words. "Svyataya perhot' podzalupnaya..." which loosely translates to "Holy pisshole dandruff."

It's an underground hangar full of starships of varying sizes and types, stretching into the distance as far as I can see. Some are Union ships whose designs I recognize. Traders. Colonizers. Terraformers. Cargo vessels. But there are just as many that I'm unfamiliar with. Given their patched up look, they probably saw service long before I, or Brick, arrived. I look toward the ceiling, five hundred feet overhead. "Are...are those clouds?"

"It's a natural cavern," Brick says. "Has its own weather system. During the summer months, it gets humid. Even rains on occasion."

"Who cares about weather," Drago says, "You have fleet!"

It's not just a fleet of ships. Everywhere I look...are people. And unlike the monotone Union, I'm seeing every shade of skin color possible, representing nationalities that I thought were—like most living things from Earth—extinct.

It's overwhelming.

When I lean forward, hands on knees, Brick pats my back. "I had a similar reaction when I arrived. Sara—my wife—found me on the dead world. I thought it was a coincidence. Turns out they were looking for me. For all of us. But I was the only one who arrived on time. We'd nearly given up hope on you until we started intercepting communications between the Union and a prolific Exo-Hunter."

"You identified me from my reports?" I ask.

"Only adult I know who actually uses the word 'rad.'"

I shrug. "Man's gotta spice things up where he can."

"Nearly gave up a second time when it became clear that you were a sympa—that you were working for them. If not for your dramatic exit from Union Command, we wouldn't be talking now."

"How do you know about Union Command?"

"If you haven't noticed," Brick says, motioning to his face. "Not everyone here stands out in the Union. We have moles in Command. Even the High Council.

"What I don't know, is what all that was about."

"We were looking for a way to track a ship we tangled with," I say.

He squints at me. "What ship?"

"The *Zorak*," I say. "You know it?"

He shakes his head.

"I thought it might belong to Whip," I say.

Brick doesn't react to the mention of Whip's name, but says, "Because of Space Ghost. Makes sense... You broke into Command and stole celestial data on a ship, essentially ending your truce with the Union, just to find Whip?"

I stand up straight and take a deep, steadying breath. "Of course."

He smiles. "Of course. But...?"

"But what?" I ask.

"There's always a 'but' with you. Also, informants."

"Buuut," I say, "we kind of also took a Predictor. Voluntarily. She's with us, one hundred percent. Name's Hildy. Good kid. You'll like her. And..." I dig a hand into my pocket. Pull out the pinkie drive. "She gave us a gift."

He looks over the drive, a twinkle in his eyes. "Please tell me this contains data on the Union fleet. Armaments. Locations. We don't have anyone in the Union military yet."

"I didn't know there *was* a Union military until two days ago," I admit. "But no. It's not strategic. It's better than that." I smile at him. "It's hope." I enjoy leaving him with the mystery. A lot of that has been coming my way, and it's nice to turn the tables. "Your turn. What the hell is all of this?"

"The Undesirables," he says.

The story of how Beta-Prime was colonized rises to the surface of my frazzled mind. "The colony survived..."

"Thrived," he says. "For fifty years. Then the Union returned. Tried to exterminate the population. Hundreds of thousands of people died in the battle. Just as many fled underground, and with some help, they survived the second great purge."

"Helped? By whom?" Chuy asks.

"Later," Brick says. "Right now, I need you to understand why you're here."

Before he can continue, a stout woman approaches, smiling with more joy than I've seen in a long time. She has a chubby face and long black hair tied back in a ponytail. She double pumps her eyebrows in my direction and then turns to Brick.

"Zeta," Brick says in greeting. "Got a SitRep for me?"

She glances at me again, smiling, and then tells Brick, "Torque says the Orion's slew is working, but it might have only one or two rotations left in it."

I nearly say it aloud, but I manage to keep my realization internal. Zeta has Down Syndrome. On Earth, I wouldn't have thought much of it. My childhood best friend, Max, had DS. But I've just now realized that I haven't seen someone with that particular syndrome, or any other kind of disability, in the past five years.

Eugenics isn't just fucked up because it's all about creating a master race, it also requires the eradication of less desirable traits. That's why Morton, Porter, and Burnett were all relegated to lives as wifeless salvagers. But there's no way to know if someone is going to be too heavy, too bald, or too scrawny at birth. And there is always a need for hard laborers. But the disabled...

Back in the 1940s, the Third Reich launched a program called Kinder-Euthanasie—Child Euthanasia. They murdered more than five thousand children, purging the master race of Down Syndrome, cerebral palsy, all kinds of malformations and a number of other undesirable mental and physical traits. It should come as no surprise that the Fourth Reich has followed the same path, but it's still a kick in the metaphorical nuts.

"That's okay," Brick says to Zeta. "One or two is enough."

I blink out of my dark thoughts and back to the current conversation. "If you need tech help with a slew drive, I've got a guy who works magic."

"One of your Union crew?" Brick asks. "I don't think so."

"They're not Union anymore," I say. "They're rebels, along with the rest of us."

"We prefer the term, 'insurgents,'" Brick says. "Less Star Warsy."

"Makes sense," I say. "But seriously, he can help."

"How good could he be?" Brick asks.

"Umm," I say, and I trigger my PSD. I rotate away and emerge from the fourth dimension two hundred feet away, standing atop a starship. Fingers to mouth, I whistle. The sound reverberates through the chamber and silence follows. Thousands of people are looking at me. Never one to pass up an audience, I rotate back, appearing beside Brick. "He's pretty good."

Brick nods. "That was... I'll think about it." He turns to Zeta. "Let Torque know that's good enough for now."

Zeta gives a nod and starts walking past me. Then she stops, turns toward me, and snaps a salute. "Glad you're finally with us, General."

Before I can respond, she's off, headed toward a large starship that looks like two battleships turned on their sides and fused at the bottoms. That must be the Orion.

"'General,'" I say with a smile. "I get a half dozen promotions I don't know about?"

When I look at Brick, he's not laughing.

My smile fades. "Did I?"

"Chess piece," Chuy whispers.

Brick's cryptic hints hit me all at once. I'm the chess piece. The final chess piece. And they broke the laws of time and space to get me here. To summon me here, from the past, but I arrived thirty years later than Brick, who has revealed a fleet of insurgent undesirables representing the diverse Earth I once knew, but had thought lost for the past five years.

I was brought here to lead.

Not just to lead. To defeat the entire, God-damned Union.

"Why me?" I ask.

Brick hesitates.

"It's a simple question," I say, losing my patience.

"Not a simple answer," he says. "And I think you're going to want to sit for it."

"Can't be crazier than this." I motion to the fleet, still astounded by its vast size and the diverse personnel tending to the ships.

"C'mon," Brick says, and he walks down a catwalk, his heavy feet thumping on the grated metal floor, beneath which is a several hundred-foot drop.

I look at Chuy for her thoughts.

"After you, General," she says.

"Not calling you 'General,'" Drago says. "'Shit for Brains,' yes. 'General,' no."

"Good," I say.

"But you should probably try to get used to it," Will says. "To everyone here, that's who you are. It's what they were promised. So maybe try not to do or say anything stupid."

"No pressure," I say, and I follow Brick. He leads us in silence, giving us time to take in the immense fleet, all waiting for what? A direct assault on Union Command? Even with all these ships, I don't see how it's possible. The Union is vast. Their fleet is modern and fast. And no one knows just how large it is. A direct assault on the high council might cut the head off the snake, but it would likely start a galactic war.

I don't see a good way to get this done.

"In here," Brick says, holding up a door.

Inside is a generic conference room with a long table. Nothing special about it aside from the large man covered in thick gray hair, seated at the table. He looks at me with indifference. Chuy, too. But when Drago enters, the man stands up, eyes wide. "Comrade?"

"*Adrik?*" Drago says, sounding stunned.

"It is you!" the big man, who is apparently named Adrik, says. "Vladimir!"

The two big men round the table and embrace, slapping each other's backs.

Leave it to Spetsnaz to turn a hug into a beat down. "Stop!" A man's voice shouts. "Stop, God dammit."

I recognize the voice, but I can't place it, probably because it's muffled. Is there someone behind the two Russians?

When Drago hops back, looking down, I realize that voice came from Adrik...but not from his mouth.

Drago motions to Adrik's torso. "Your chest is talking."

"Is not chest," Adrik says, and he yanks open his shirt.

At first, I'm not sure what I'm looking at, but then I see a face poking through a forest of curly, gray chest hair.

What...the fuck?

When the face says, "Hey, Dark Horse," I understand who I'm looking at, but not how it's possible. "Heeey, BigApe... How...how are things?"

31

"Oh, Dios mío," Chuy says, and she performs the sign of the cross.

"Dude," I say, chastising her for the reaction. I feel the same mix of shock and revulsion, but somehow, I manage to keep it inside. For years I have fantasized about what it would be like to reunite with each member of my team. So far, none have worked out even close to what I dreamed up. Brick is old and has a son. Carter was a cavewoman. Someone who might or might not have been Whip opened fire on *Bitch'n*. And now BigApe...is fused to the chest of a Russian bear-man named Adrik.

"Don't worry about it," BigApe says. "I have that effect on people. And I'm okay with it."

"*Now*," Adrik says. "For first ten years it was, 'oh, I am so sad,' 'wah, is hot under shirt,' 'boo hoo, have hair in mouth.'"

It takes a lot of self-control not to put a bullet in the Russian's head. His disregard for BigApe's horrifying condition triggers my inner serial killer. But killing Adrik would also kill BigApe. And maybe that would be for the best? Who wouldn't want to die in his situation?

"I'd have killed myself if I could have," BigApe admits, confirming my thoughts.

"He tried a few times," Adrik says.

"How does face man kill self?" Drago asks.

"I have control of our right leg," BigApe says.

"And left pinkie." Adrik holds up his left hand. Just the pinkie wiggles.

"I tried to throw us over the catwalk a few times," BigApe says.

Chuy sits, elbows on the table, head in her hands. "Hostia puta..."

"But I'm good now," he says. "Have been for a long time. Better now that you're here. Means all of this—" Adrik's left pinkie extends toward BigApe's face. "—wasn't for nothing."

I take a seat beside Chuy. "How did you end up like this?"

"When the Surge was triggered in Antarctica—"

"What is surge?" Drago asks.

"The event that brought us all to the future," Brick says, as he and Will take seats at the table. "We call it the 'Surge.'"

"When it was triggered," BigApe says, "Adrik and I were fighting. This was the result. The Surge isn't a perfect science."

"Not really science at all," Will says.

"But it brought us here," I say, "from the past? Can it send us back?"

Brick shrugs. "No idea."

"How about we attempt it," I say, more eager than ever to leave this future hell.

"It's not that simple," Brick says.

"Do you need dilithium crystals or something? Whatever it is, I'll get it for you."

"What we need," Brick says, "is you."

I deflate. Right. The insurgency. General Dark Horse to the rescue. "Have any of you stopped to think you might have put all your eggs in the wrong basket?"

"More than once," Brick says, and it actually stings a bit. "But history is history, and everything the Undesirables have been working toward hinges on you."

"How is that possible?" Chuy asks, feeling annoyed on my behalf. "Dark Horse is just...one man. He's a competent Captain. A good friend. But the leader of a rebellion? Against Nazis? In the future?"

"Thanks for the confidence boost," I say.

"Don't get me wrong, I'd follow your gringo ass to hell. And we sure as shit were going to be a headache for the Union until we retired, or until they took us down. But this? A planet full of people putting all their hopes in Dark Horse? C'mon." She focuses her attention on Brick. "You know the burden hc carries for his people every time he leads them into danger. The responsibility he feels when someone is hurt. Or lost. It's been eating him alive for the past five years. And now you want to multiply that by what? Thousands?"

"Millions," Brick says.

Chuy throws her arms up, muttering a string of Spanish curses.

"As much as I don't want to agree with Chuy on this," I say, "she's not wrong. I think you should choose someone else."

"I didn't choose you." Brick tilts his head toward the door. "They did. Long before I arrived."

"But why?"

"I would like to hear why as well," Drago says.

Will nudges Brick. "Can I? Please."

Brick gives a nod and leans back, arms crossed. Will has a big smile on his face, like we've been sitting around a damn campfire singing *This Land is Our Land,* and now he's going to tell us a spooky story.

"Where should I start?" Will says to himself. "Okay. So. Ummm..."

Brick sighs, leans forward, elbows on the table, obscuring my view of his son. "The civil unrest that eventually led to the Union as we know it started in the early two thousands. There was an uprising in the United States. A second civil war, only far messier than the first. There were no dividing lines. North and South. There were white supremacists, along with those who did their bidding out of fear and propaganda, and everyone else."

"I don't understand how any of that is possible," Chuy says.

We've heard the watered-down version of this before. It's never made much sense. The detailed version even less so. How did people go from being quietly racist, but on the right track, to openly white supremacist?

"The 80s were one of the last sane decades," Brick says.

"The eighties were a *sane* decade?" I ask, my mind flicking to Cold War aggression, the proliferation of nuclear arsenals, and the popularity of Pee Wee Herman.

"By twenty-thirty, many politicians and military leaders were closet Nazis. Racist judges were appointed. Gerrymandering ensured political victories. Laws began to change. Hate festered. The country fractured. The newly oppressed began to organize a resistance. Peaceful demonstrations. Protests. Art, music, and movies helped change hearts and minds. The pendulum started swinging back to center.

"But the powers that be weren't about to give up the influence they'd spent so long fostering. Martial law led to more protests, which turned violent. After a year of watching people get gunned down for exercising their constitutional rights, a more formal resistance emerged, united under a leader willing to make the hard calls.

"The resistance pushed back hard. They were joined by several nations from around the globe, kicking off World War III. But the majority of the U.S. military was controlled by a group who began referring to themselves as the True Union, claiming to represent real American values while making a mockery of the first Civil War's Union army.

"Despite the odds being stacked against them, the resistance was difficult to defeat. The lack of clear sides meant the U.S. nuclear arsenal was sidelined. So, the resistance fought smart, using guerrilla tactics inspired by the Minutemen, who helped defeat the British in the Revolutionary War. In fact, the name stuck, and since then, the resistance...or insurgency...has used the Minutemen name."

"It *is* a cool name," I say.

"You thought so back then, too," Brick says.

"Whatchu talkin' about, Willis?" I ask. It just slips out. Haven't said it in years. But it makes Brick smile, and his son leans out over the table.

"Huh?" Will says. "I didn't say anything."

"It's an expression from the 80s," Brick tells him, and then he turns back to me. "The Minutemen's leader from twenty thirty-three to twenty forty was formerly a United States General. He led the Minutemen until he was killed, along with most other people not pure Aryan enough to survive the Union's plague. But his children, and their descendants, along with thousands of others, had a natural immunity to the plague. While the Union rebuilt, the Minutemen recovered in secret, until they were discovered, and the cycle of death and destruction repeated.

"When the Union discovered slew technology, they finally got the upper hand, slaughtering or capturing Minutemen until the war was effectively over. As the Aryan population boomed, the Union turned their eyes to the sky and used the last of the Minutemen to populate Beta-Prime.

"All of the people here are their descendants, including those of the General, who very nearly defeated the Union."

"Really?" Will asks, sounding surprised. "Who are his descendants?"

"And who was the General?" I ask.

Brick looks at his son and says, "In answer to the first question—*you.*" Then he turns to me and adds, "In answer to the second question—*you.*"

32

"What do you mean, *me?*" I ask. "I'm here. In the future. How could I possibly lead a resistance at the turn of the century?"

"I'm not a scientist," Brick says. "I don't pretend to understand all this stuff, but it has something to do with alternate and diverging timelines. There might be an infinite number of possible realities. By bringing you here, we created a world where none of us existed to fight the early Union. And I mean *we.* You led the rebellion, but we were all there with you. Most of us didn't survive to see the plague, though. You two did."

He motions his finger between me and Chuy.

"But that's not our history. In this timeline, you both fought the Union in the past, and are here in the present."

My mind is blown. This...is insane.

But it also makes sense. Because, of course I would have fought the Union. And I was on track to make General someday. It's just hard to imagine rebelling against the country I served for so long. It's also hard to imagine that the United States, founded on the principles of equality for all, would become a haven for Nazis.

Looks like I'm not the only one in shock. Will is staring at the tabletop. He hasn't blinked.

"Your kid okay?" I ask Brick. "Looks like he's having a stroke."

Brick gives his son a quick once over. Has a good laugh. "He's just figuring out what you missed."

"I missed something?" I ask.

"Big something," Drago says.

"Very big something," Chuy adds.

Will snaps out of his daze. "You're not messing with me, right? This is for real?"

"Not messing with you," Brick says.

"Yes!" Will says.

My patience is wearing thin. My life has been a series of reality bending revelations lately. I'm not really in the mood for more suspense. "Can someone please explain what—"

"You're my grandfather," Will says to me. "My great, great, great, etcetera grandfather."

I just stare at him for a moment. Then I look at Brick.

He nods. "Sara was a descendant of yours."

I sit back in my chair, body slack. "Huh..."

"Weird," Brick says. "I know. But I didn't know when we got together."

My eyes shift back to Will again. I can't tell if I see myself in him or not. Whatever DNA I donated to his gene pool has been watered down by a thousand years.

Will gasps, some kind of new revelation birthing into his mind like a message from God. "Wait. That means..."

"Will," Brick says, but his son is oblivious to the verbal warning.

Will looks at Chuy.

"That means *you're* my great, great, great, etcetera—"

"Will!" Brick shouts.

The kid's mouth clamps shut, but it's too late. Doesn't take a genius to figure out what Will was going to say, or what it means.

After a moment of stunned silence, Chuy asks. "Is it true?"

There have been three intensely awkward moments in my life. The first was when I was walking by a motel on my way home from school. There was a shortcut behind the building. I looked through a window and was spotted by the woman inside. She was buck naked. By the following week, there was a fence. The second moment was when my parents walked in on me as a teenager. I was working out...also naked. Up until the minute they died, they believed I was choking one out.

And now, here I am at my third most awkward moment ever, discovering that I am a great, great, great etcetera grandfather, and that the woman with whom I sired my good friend's wife's ancestors—that's a mouthful—is sitting next to me...and she's my best friend.

Brick addresses Chuy. "I didn't know Sara's family tree when we met, but I knew *we* didn't work out. People here learn about the insurgency's early days the way every good American back in the day was taught about George Washington and Abraham Lincoln. You two are central to the story. I didn't fully understand why until Sara eventually told me about her lineage.

"So, this is like a reverse Bill and Ted situation?" I ask.

"Who are Bill and Ted?" Will asks. "Are they related to me, too?"

"They were heroes from the 80s," I say, trying my best to redirect the conversation away from what became of me and Chuy once upon a time, but also not yet. "Destined to save the world through music."

While Brick has a good chuckle, Will is engrossed. "I wish I could have heard music from back then. I mean, we have music here, but—"

"It's primitive," Brick says. "When you're fighting a war for hundreds of years, living in fear, there isn't a lot of time for making music. Drums. Singing. What people might have called tribal. It's a lot of fun...but I miss what we had."

What we have, I think.

"Do you have a computer I can use?" I ask.

"Of course," Brick says, and he nods his head toward Adrik and BigApe.

The conjoined pair stands and heads to a cabinet at the back of the room. He returns with a laptop computer that looks like it has seen the wrong side of a few battles. I open it and wait for it to power up.

"What...do you need it for?" Brick asks.

I hold up the pinkie drive. It's not just a gift for Brick, it's also my fast-track away from the conversation regarding my and Chuy's past-future relationship, including the fact that we had *children*. "I offered you hope. It's time to deliver. I'm assuming you all have a PA system in this place?"

"Moses," Brick says, with the same stern warning voice he used with Will.

"You're going to have to trust me, bud." I say. "And from what I gather, you're going to trust me with a whole lot more than this."

The computer beeps when it starts. Brick turns it around. The mechanical keys clack with every tap of his meaty fingers. Then he spins it back toward me. "Connected to the PA. Now, what've you got for me?"

"Not just for you." I insert the pinkie drive. The database automatically opens. So many choices...a century of music at my fingertips. I don't want to scare anyone, so Mötley Crüe is out. Don't want to confuse people, or make a bad first impression, so Brick's favorites are out, too. Well, not all of his favorites. Like me, Brick is a fan of most 80s tunes, but he also has a penchant for classical.

I refine my results to classical, and then I struggle to remember the name of what I'm looking for. Chuy, who knows what I'm up to, leans in close. Our arms are touching. I would have never noticed before, but now her touch feels like a tsunami about to crash down on me, and I honestly don't know if that's good or bad.

She points to an entry. "This one."

"Yes," I say, selecting the song. Then I turn to Brick. "You're wel-come. In advance."

Before he can express further doubts, I play the file.

A slow resonant G major slips through the air. It lasts only half a second, but it melts Brick's face. All of the stoic discipline disappears. When he glances at me in shock, there are tears in his eyes. He's been here for thirty-five years. Not five. The joy I felt upon hearing *Blitzkrieg Bop* for the first time in five years is magnified to a level I hope to never understand.

The music continues, the cellist drawing her bow over the strings, unleashing perfectly played G, D, and A chords, and from there, Bach's Cello Suite no. 1 fills the air in every part of the underground hangar. Background noise that I'd already gotten used to—ambient voices, power tools, banging—all of it, stops.

Tears flow freely down Brick's cheeks. He just sits and listens. Lost in the moment. Will stares at the ceiling like he can see the sound, mouth agape. He's never heard anything like this before. Even Adrik and BigApe are moved. I'm not sure how BigApe can hear. He doesn't have ears of his own, but he's smiling, and maybe he's even content, despite his freakish merger.

We sit, silently listening to the music for two and a half minutes. Then the final, long wistful note plays.

The silence lingers a full ten seconds. Then Brick stands, rounds the table, and hugs me. It's not a man-hug, like before. It's affectionate. "Thank you," he says. "I wish you could have met her."

I nod into his shoulder. "Sorry it took me so long to get here."

"Ugh," Drago says. "Either get room or put on man-sex show for us. Stop it with the hugging and happy-touchy feelings. Is revolting."

"Great," BigApe says. "There's two of them now."

"Quiet," Adrik says, closing his shirt.

The music's spell is wearing off.

I unplug the pinkie drive from the computer and place it in Brick's hand. "This has every piece of music, every movie, every TV series, novel, work of art, and all of Earth history between 1950 and 2050. Ish."

Brick blinks. He's without words.

"I know, right?" I say. "You have Hildy to thank for this."

Brick is confused. "Hildy was…?"

"The Predictor."

"*This* is what you stole from Union Command?" Brick starts laughing. He holds up the pinkie drive like he's inspecting a diamond. "Five years of toeing the line, and you throw it away for this?"

"Wasn't anything worth fighting for until that," I say. "And now all of you."

There's a knock on the window. I turn to find a group of people, their skin magnificently diverse. Zeta is at the front of the group, her head poking up over the window's bottom. She knocks again, makes eye contact, smiles, and waves.

Zeta asks a question, but her voice is muffled by the glass.

Brick waves her in. The door bursts open. "What was that? Can we hear it again? I want to hear it again." She's breathless, like she ran here. Hell, I think all these people sprinted to the window, drawn by the music, but now they're staring at me.

"Later," Brick says. "Finish out the day, first."

"But—"

Brick holds up a hand, silencing her. "We're close, Zeta. No time to waste, right?"

"Right..."

"Tonight," he says. "I promise."

She smiles, nods, and backs out the door. Before it closes behind her, she turns to the gathered throng. "We can hear it again, tonight!"

The door closes, muffling the cheer that follows. Then the crew disperses, heading back to work. The ambient sound of work crews returns.

Brick heads for the door. Grasps the handle, but he doesn't open it. "Now then. Back to business. Time to meet our friends."

"They're not coming here?" I ask.

"Can't," he says. "We need to go to them."

"Are they like overweight, lazy defectors or something?" I ask.

"Not remotely," he says. "They're Beta-Prime's original inhabitants."

"The Union sent people here *before* the Undesirables?" Chuy asks.

Brick shakes his head, opens the door, and says, "They're not people."

33

By the time I catch up to Brick, he's waiting for me in an elevator. "I'm sorry. Did you say, 'not people?'"

"Mmm hmm." He holds the door, waiting for Chuy and Drago to join us. Will, Adrik, and BigApe linger outside the door.

"You're not coming, comrade?" Drago asks Adrik.

The big Russian and BigApe shake their heads simultaneously. BigApe's headshake brings Adrik's chest to life, stretching skin and waving the forest of hair back and forth. I struggle to even look at him. "To talk to...our friends, you must be summoned and expected."

"What happens if you surprise?" Drago asks.

"Nothing fun," Will says.

Drago turns to Brick. "Am I...?"

Brick shakes his head.

"Even a thousand years in future, Soviet Union gets no respect." Drago steps out of the elevator.

"Has more to do with who *you* are," Will says. He motions to me. "...and in their case, who they *were*. You might have come from the past with them, but no one here—aside from Adrik—knows who you are."

"Someday people will know who Drago is," he says about himself.

Adrik's left hand reaches out. Grasps Drago's shoulder. The pinkie gives him a pat.

"Being overlooked sucks," BigApe says, "but it also gives you a chance to have fun. When was the last time you had a beer?"

"You...you have *beer?*" Drago rises from his sullenness like a phoenix.

"Is close to beer," Adrik says, and leads my comrade away.

"Can—can I get a beer?" I ask, half serious.

"Later," Brick says. "I promise. For now..." He motions to my weapons. "All that needs to stay here."

Didn't realize I was still carrying my rifle, handgun, and enough ammo to take on an army. When I hesitate, Chuy backhands my shoulder.

"Dude," I say.

"*Dude,*" she replies.

"Fine." I shed my weapons, handing them over to Will, who quickly begins to struggle from the weight. When I'm done unloading my firearms, Brick says, "Knife, too. And that." He points to the slew drive on my hip. I'm about to complain when he says, "We can't bring anything that might be perceived as a threat."

"Sounding less and less like friends," I point out, and I pluck the PSD from my belt. I slip it inside Will's pocket and say, "If you try using it, you'll probably die. If you break it, I'll definitely kill you—great grand-kid or not."

He nods, accepts Chuy's weapons, and then struggles to carry it all away.

I raise my hands and do a little spin so Brick can see I'm disarmed. "Happy? I'm as defenseless as a newborn baby."

Brick smiles. "You and I both know that's not true. But I hope for all our sakes that *they* don't see you as a threat."

"Comforting," I say. "You going to tell us what we're walking into here?"

"Better if you see it," Brick says.

The elevator doors close. There's just one button. Brick pushes it. My stomach lurches as we launch downward. I'm not a fan of elevators. I'm not generally claustrophobic, but I can't get into an elevator without imagining how I'd feel if I were stuck in one. My thoughts are cut short when my ears pop from the pressure.

"How far down are we going?" Chuy asks.

"About a mile," Brick replies. "Nearly there."

The elevator slows, shifting my insides back into place. Then we stop. The doors open, annnd...nothing.

Pitch black.

Brick flicks on a flashlight, revealing another smooth, glassy tunnel. He steps into the darkness. My internal 'This is a bad idea' alarm is screaming like a goat in heat.

Brick says, "Stay close and keep your voice down."

"You sure this is safe?" I ask.

"Is if you do what I tell you," he says. "And if they decide they like you."

"Fantastic," I say, and I follow him into the dark.

Five minutes into our subterranean stroll, Brick says, "The first Undesirables settled just a few miles from one of the tunnels that leads beneath the surface. They lived in the caves above for years before one of them ventured into the depths. He didn't return. Neither did the people who went looking for him. But the next group, an unarmed scientific expedition, made a discovery that would save their lives, keep the Union at bay, and allow the Undesirable population to boom. There are cities and installations like the one above, all over the planet, all of it connected through subterranean tunnels."

"Like this one?" Chuy asks.

"Larger," Brick says. "Big enough to fly through, though we mostly get around using slew transports, rotating from one hangar to another. Same way you both bounced around the galaxy."

He stops in the tunnel, but I can't see anything to justify why. He turns toward us. "Stay on the trail. No sudden movements. No loud voices. Try not to look at them, and if possible, try not to think about them."

"Anything about this seem like a really bad idea?" I ask Chuy.

"All of it," she says. "But don't puss out on me." She motions with her head for Brick to lead the way.

The flashlight flicks off.

Can't see shit. "People here evolve night vision?"

"Give it a minute," he says. "Your eyes will adjust."

He's right. And it only takes about thirty seconds for me to see a hellish red glow up ahead. "Well, that's comforting..."

Another thirty seconds and I can see the floor well enough to walk. Brick leads the way again, walking at a steady pace, but carefully placing his feet to minimize noise. Chuy and I do the same, and I'm starting to feel like I'm walking through enemy territory, not going to meet 'friends.'

I don't notice that we've left the tunnel and entered a massive cavern until I sniff, and it echoes.

Brick stops, silently shushes me with a finger to his lips, and then carries on.

Red light fills the massive space, emanating from the cavern's floor somewhere up ahead. We round a tall outcrop of stalagmites, and I see the light's source. There are thousands of them, attached to the cavern floor like a crop...

A crop of red, gelatinous cucumbers.

What. The fuck.

Do the 'friends' we're going to meet eat these things? I have a million questions, but I can't ask.

The red light filling the chamber radiates from the strange vegetation. It's bioluminescent, like the flesh-eating bacteria that tried to seduce me on the surface. As we approach, the nearest glowing dildos lean toward us.

I'm starting to hate new planets and all their weird shit.

As we follow the ten-foot-wide path through the field, the cucumbers on the sides lean in. Thin tendrils reach out as we pass, but they come up short. They don't look that dangerous. A quick stomp, and—

Red light flares.

The tendrils wriggle, really trying to get at us.

Actually, shit... They're trying to get at me. *Just* me.

Brick turns around, points at his head, and mouths the word, "Stop."

Right. Can't even think about them.

Can these little fuckers actually hear my thoughts?

Light flares again, and Brick shoots me a glare that confirms it. He's afraid of the glowing red phalluses, and I should be, too.

Focus, I tell myself. Think about something else. A song pops into my head. I listened to it on repeat while taking a shower, before leaving *Bitch'n.* One of my favorites. The chorus to *Video Killed the Radio Star* loops in my head. I lose track of time. Of how long we're walking. I just grin and think about playing the greatest hits with Brick, later on.

I bump into Brick's back, which is as big and solid as his name suggests. He's stopped in the middle of the path. "What is it?" I ask, reaching for a gun that's not there, then a knife that's missing, and finally the slew drive, which like everything else I depend on to keep people alive, is MIA.

"They were pulsing," he whispers, looking down at the red, vertical cucumbers. They're no longer leaning toward us, or trying to grasp our legs with their little tendrils.

"That bad?" I ask.

"You were humming," Chuy says.

I look down at the foot-tall, warbling red vegetables, and rather than thinking about them, I fill my head with the song again and hum. The whole field starts to warble, the color flaring and dulling with the music.

"I think they like it," Chuy says.

"They don't like anything," Brick says.

"Aren't these your friends?" I ask. I've already guessed that 'friends' is a loose term. That these little things were weaponized and turned against the Union.

Brick blows that theory out of the water, saying, "They don't think. They're incapable of friendship. They just react to invaders. Like an immune system. Anything that's not supposed to be here gets—"

A roar echoes through the chamber, drowning out my humming. The red light flares.

"What did you do?" Brick says.

I can't help myself.

"I tried to think of the most harmless thing. Something I loved from my childhood. Something that could never ever—"

"Not the time, Moses!" Brick says, abandoning his 'stay quiet' rule. "RUN!"

As the big man takes off, a boom and a roar spins me around. In the chamber behind us, blocking our retreat, is a bus-sized behemoth with six legs, no eyes, and two very large mandibles extending from a mouth that looks a lot like a sphincter. It has what looks like an exo-skeleton, but I think it's actually thick, folded skin like on a rhino. Along the creature's back, there are hundreds of the red cucumbers, their tendrils frantically waving in the air.

"They're controlling it," Chuy says, grabbing my arm. "Let's go!" She drags me a few steps until I'm sprinting alongside her, trying hard to ignore the solid rock floor that's now shaking beneath my feet, as the immune system works to destroy its musical invaders.

34

The red cucumbers thrust toward our legs as we run down the path. The thin string tendrils wriggle and reach. Some of them have latched on to the stone floor and are pulling, like they're trying to uproot themselves and have a go at us. The things move in unison, pulsing toward me, and I can't help but feel a little violated. I'm being visually assaulted by a field of luminous dongs.

Then I notice that the pulse is in time with the giant creature's thundering footfalls. The little gelatinous fuckers change in my mind's eye. They're no longer trying to kill us themselves, they're fans in the stands, cheering on their favorite sports hero—Big Ass Sphincter Lips—as he closes in on his opponents.

The too-long name becomes an acronym in my mind—B.A.S.L.—and transforms into a nickname: Basil.

The path ahead bends to the right and out of view. Brick takes the turn at full speed, not looking back.

Don't blame him. None of us is armed, and I don't think harsh words are going to help. Hell, humming is what got us into this mess. Also, Brick is big...and old. Chuy and I are still in our prime and gaining fast. If this chase doesn't end in the next thirty seconds, we're going to pass him.

And I can't have that.

I just got Brick back. I'm not about to leave him behind now.

I can't fight Basil, but maybe I can make the cucumber club think twice about throwing down with the U.S. Marines. They're all connected. That much is clear. Maybe if I punt one of them, they'll get the message: *you might take me down, but a shit ton of you are coming with me.* Hell, I could just charge through them, crushing them beneath my feet and forcing Basil to do the same, or back the hell off.

It's the best plan I can think of, but it's apparently a bad one.

"Don't even think about it!" Brick shouts back at me.

"Get out of my head, old man!" I shout back, and I wonder how he knew what I was thinking. Have I really changed so little over the past five years that he can still predict what I'm about to do?

"You'll get us all killed!" he shouts, as Chuy and I close the distance between us. "This isn't Earth."

I'm right behind him now.

"What's that supposed to mean?" I ask, looking over my shoulder. Basil is a few lunges back. We have seconds. Two more steps and I'm executing Operation Red Smear.

Before I can, Brick stops in his tracks, opens his arms, scoops Chuy and I off our feet like some damned WWF superstar, and hauls us into a small tunnel. A few feet inside, he stumbles and pitches forward. We crash to the solid floor in a heap.

I cough and shove his meaty arm off me. Catching my breath, I sit up.

"It means," Brick says, winded. "That you're...not in charge... Down here...you do what I tell you...when I tell you...or you will get us killed. Do you understand?"

I might be the same old Dark Horse that Brick remembers, but he is no longer the man I commanded. He is a leader, seasoned by hardship and battle. While I've been hopping around the galaxy having adventures, he's been enduring God knows what, raising a son, losing a wife, and leading an insurgency. From the moment I saw him, I've been treating him like my old pal, Brick. But that's not who he is. We might not be Marines anymore, but if I'm on board with this insurgency, he's now my commanding officer.

"Sorry, sir," I say. "Won't happen again."

"Please don't call me 'sir,'" he says. "You're not in charge...but you will be. Someday soon, the weight on my shoulders will be on yours."

Yeaaah, my sarcastic inner voice says. While Brick has been carrying far more responsibility than I have for much longer, he's clearly better adapted to bearing heavy burdens—physically, mentally, and psychologically.

Basil stalks back and forth by the tunnel's entrance, lit by the cucumbers' ambient red glow. The beast is too big to pursue us. Doesn't even bother trying. It knows better. The red cucumbers aren't just controlling it, they're smart.

"What are those things?" I ask. "And more importantly, who doesn't like The Buggles?"

"The big guy is a rygar," Brick says.

"I named him Basil, FYI," I say, "but he's not what I'm talking about."

"He wants to know about those red bastardos." Chuy sounds as annoyed by our current situation as I feel.

Brick offers his hand to Chuy. Pulls her up. The tunnel is just a few inches taller than his 6'3" height.

I help myself up, and I look back to the entrance. Basil is just standing there now, mandibles twitching, sphincter-face flexing. I don't see any eyes, but I'm sure it's watching us.

Sure, *they're* watching us.

"They don't have a name for themselves, but they claim humanity gave them a name once...in a parallel universe, where none of this happened."

"P-parallel universe?" I ask.

He flicks his flashlight back on and leads us down the smaller tunnel. "Have you ever heard of the many worlds theory? Or the multiverse?"

"I think you know I haven't," I say.

"Basically, it means that there are an infinite number of universes." He pauses at a T junction in the tunnel. "Every time you make a choice, left or right—" He shines the light left, and then right. "—and choose between them, you split reality."

"In one you head left," Chuy says. "In the other, right."

"Exactly," Brick says, and heads left. "But it's more complicated than that. Because there are an infinite number of choices. This conversation. Every footstep. The timing of each breath. And it's not just you, it's everything. Every person. Every animal. Even bacteria. From the beginning of time to the end. The result is that everything that *can* happen, does happen. Somewhere. Somewhen. All of it."

"Hold on," I say. "You're telling me that *Aliens* is a true story?"

"In another universe," he says. "Yeah."

"And this is for real?" I ask. "You've seen it for yourself?"

"The intelligence that revealed these things to me is the same one that plucked us out of 1989."

"So...there's a universe where Basil ate me?"

He shakes his head.

"Not just one. An infinite number. And there is an infinite number where we escape."

"Anything that can happen has happened," I say. "Does that mean there are an infinite number of universes where Basil pinned me to the floor and had his way with me?"

Brick has a laugh. "Rygars are asexual. But there are probably an infinite number of universes where rygars mate. So...yes. Anything you can imagine has happened, is happening, or will happen. Fun, right?"

"No," I say, remembering some of the things I've dreamed up, and then remembering that there were people like Ted Bundy and Josef Mengele in the world. "Not fun."

Brick stops at the tunnel's exit, his big body filling most of the tunnel. "Try not to focus on the negative. For every evil committed in the multiverse, there is every extreme of the opposite."

"Like, somewhere there is a reality where Sesame Street is *real?* And Mr. Snuffleupagus is alive *and* my friend?"

He nods. "An infinite number."

"Okay, that's better, but also weird, because it means there is also an infinite number of universes where you are Big Bird's bitch."

Brick snorts. "And an infinite number in which I like it."

"Oh, Dios mío," Chuy says, hand to her head. To Brick she says, "He's never going to sleep again, you *know* that, right?"

"It's the price we pay," Brick says, and for the first time I notice the dark circles under his eyes. They have nothing to do with age, and everything to do with that weight he's carrying... The weight that will soon be mine.

Chuy is right.

"Back to your question," Brick says.

"About the evil electric bananas?"

Brick squints at me.

"It's slang," I say.

"For what?"

I grin. "Dildos."

"Bananas are yellow," he says. "You got the color wrong."

I sigh. "About the...cherry-flavored vagsicles."

"Better," he says. "Could have just gone with popsicles. Not everything has to be dirty."

"What are you, my dad?" I ask, and then I realize he's old enough to be.

"Apúrate, cabrona," Chuy says.

"Okay," Brick holds out his hands while tamping down his grin. "Okay. Back to business. What look like jelly-filled, glowing krullers to you and me are actually a highly intelligent network of living creatures. Individually, they're not much, but when they're rooted together... they're an intellect far beyond our comprehension, experiencing time, space, and all the layers of reality in ways far beyond the human experience. People encountered them in parallel universes twice before, both times on Europa, one of Jupiter's moons. In one of those realities, we called them Europhids. So, that's what we call them now."

He steps to the side, giving us a view outside the tunnel.

There's another cavern ahead. It's bright, from wall to wall Europhids, but they're not red this time.

They're blue.

35

As I step out of the tunnel and into the massive cavern coated in wall-to-wall blue Europhids, I feel like some kind of sweeping soundtrack should be playing. The theme song for *2001: A Space Odyssey* or something.

This time, as the music plays in my head, I do my best to not hum. But I don't think these Europhids will attack. Brick said that those red bitches were like an immune system, attacking and killing invaders. All of it in place to protect this. The intellect. And if we're here, past the metaphorical blood-brain barrier, then maybe we're safe.

The blue Europhids aren't leaning toward us.

I don't see any little tendrils reaching out.

In comparison, these guys are docile. They just kind of wave back and forth slowly. The motion rolls through the field that covers floor, walls, and ceiling. The undulation, coupled with the calm blue light, is soothing.

I feel...at peace.

More than is normal for me.

"What are they doing to me?" I ask, more curious than worried. "Are they like the flesh-eating bacteria on the surface? Are they seducing me with their love stank?"

Brick shakes his head. "What you encountered on the surface evolved over millions of years to look like Europhids, their pheromones working in a similar, but less complex manner."

"They've been around for millions of years?" Chuy asks.

"Is that impressive?" I ask.

"Homo sapiens first appeared somewhere between two and three hundred thousand years ago. If the Europhids have been around for millions, they must be incredibly evolved."

"Don't look very evolved," I say.

"They're found on thousands of planets and moons throughout the universe," Brick says, "many of which would kill us if we tried to visit without protection. Their intelligence dwarfs the combined thinking power of the entire human race, and spans layers of reality. And they haven't been around for millions of years, they've been here for *billions*. Don't let their lack of opposable thumbs fool you— this is the dominant species in the universe."

"Well," I say. "That's kind of horrifying."

"Only if you cross them," he says. "Or walk through a field of the red ones humming a ditty after you were told not to."

"That's on me," I say. "But I don't get it. If they're so big and powerful, why am I here?"

"Because for the first time in their billions of years existence, they feel threatened."

That can't be good. "By whom?"

My mind conjures images of alien conquerors, slaughtering their way across the universe. Maybe they're shape shifters. Or have Cthulhu faces. Or—

Brick raises an 'Are you serious?' eyebrow in my direction.

"Oh," I say. "Shit."

It's us.

Humanity is the alien conquerors slaughtering their way across the universe.

It's the Union.

It's me.

Suddenly feeling a whole lot less safe, despite the Europhids' calming effect, I glance back at the tunnel. I could make a run for it, but I don't know where I am or how to get out. Best case scenario, I manage to go back the way we came...and into the warm embrace of sphincter-face

Basil. Worst case scenario, I get lost in the subterranean maze and slowly starve to death.

What's the point in running? I'm either here because a past me that no longer exists nearly defeated the Europhids' enemy a thousand years ago, or because I *am* that enemy and they're going to liquify me or something. Trying to sound nonchalant, I say, "And I'm here because..."

"That's for them to tell you," Brick says. "Honestly, I've been preparing for something. This whole planet has. For hundreds of years. But none of us know exactly *what* yet. I'm kind of hoping they'll tell you."

"You realize that none of what you just said is reassuring, right?"

"Very much so," he says in a way that makes me realize all the discomfort I feel about putting my faith in a bunch of glowing jumbo-sized hotdogs, pales in comparison to what the Undesirables have experienced.

With a sigh, I turn to face the field. "Hello!" I wave. "Uhh, greetings, Europhids." I give Brick my best, 'I've got this' wink and nod. "I am Dark Horse...uhh, Moses Montgomery." Honesty seems like the best policy here, hence my full real name, but I haven't heard it aloud in a very long time. Still makes me cringe. Sounds pretentious. Like it should have a 'Sir' at the beginning and a 'the third' at the end.

"Moses," Brick says.

"I'm just getting warmed up," I tell him. "Trying to make a good first impression here."

"They don't have ears," he says.

"Oh. But the humming?"

"Basil has sensitive ears. They heard you through him. The red Europhids sometimes develop symbiotic relationships with creatures they encounter...not always voluntary. They're all instinct. The blues are more civilized. They speak mind to mind, but they won't do so without express permission."

"How do I give them permission if they can't hear me?" I ask.

"They can feel you, even now, but the only way to really experience them is to submit. Make yourself vulnerable."

"Okay..." I say. "How do I do that?"

He motions to the path ahead.

"Follow the yellow brick road. You'll know what to do by the time you get there."

"Kind of cryptic, don't you think?"

"It's different for everyone," he says.

"Anyone walk down this path and not come back?" I ask.

He nods. "On occasion."

"Were they bad guys?"

"Depends on who you ask," he says. "Don't get me wrong, there is nothing safe about what you're about to do. I'm the only one to do it more than once, and I don't enjoy it. At all. It's...invasive."

"But necessary," I say.

"Very."

Goddamnit.

I turn to Chuy. "If I don't come back—"

"—I'll take care of the boys and Hildy," she says.

Not what I was going to say, but now that I've had a fraction of a second to doubt myself, I'll take the out. "Thanks."

"Brick..." I offer my hand. He shakes it. "Nice seeing you again."

When I start down the winding path, he says, "Won't be the last time," but I can tell he's not sure. I'll do whatever I can to gain the Europhids' trust, but if they take the past five years of my life into consideration, that might be an impossible target to hit.

The path is just a few feet wide. If the blue Europhids reached out with their little string tendrils, they'd have no trouble snagging my legs.

Feels like summer camp. I'm doing a slow-motion trust fall, but the people waiting to catch me are blue, jelly-cudgels.

"You guys aren't going to let me fall, right?"

No response.

"No ears. Right..." I stop and look around. The path stretches out before and behind me, weaving through the cavern in which I'm already lost. Chuy and Brick are out of sight. How long have I been walking?

I think I'm alone.

With a super intelligent hive-mind.

A song crashes into my mind.

I can't.

I have to.

If they want me, they've got me, and this is who I've always been. The first time I sang this on mission, Chuy and I were separated from the rest of the team, behind enemy lines, hiding in a bush in the middle of the night. I sang it in a whisper, and stopped when Chuy punched me, but that small bit of fun helped get us through the night.

I start humming the peppy tune, skip the opening, and launch right into singing the chorus of *I Think We're Alone Now* by Tiffany, directly to the little blue guys.

I'm lost in the jive, bopping my way through the blue field that doesn't react at all to my humming, my snapping fingers, or my singing. They either really can't hear me, or they're indifferent to my singing, or the song. *Can't be the song,* I think. No one can resist the dulcet tones of—

A sheet of blue stops me.

To my left, right, and straight ahead, are walls of blue Europhids. The path forward ends in their embrace.

"Are you serious?" I ask, understanding.

And with understanding comes hesitation. "I'd really rather not."

No reply.

"C'mon...there isn't going to be probing involved, right? Because I don't know if you realize this, but you're shaped like— Never mind. Super intelligent. You know what you look like to people. Or maybe just to me. I know, I know, I'm rambling because I'm nervous."

I snap out of a trance. I was speaking to the Europhids. And I *felt* a reply. My eyes snap wide. I'm just a few inches away from them now.

"Can I keep my clothes on?" I ask.

I take their lack of reply to mean yes. "Fine. Just...don't get too frisky, okay?" A deep breath, and then I step forward. There's a moment of consciousness where I have just enough time to think, *Feels like a cushion of boobs.*

Then the world disappears.

36

"Wake up, Mosey," a nearly forgotten, but intimately familiar voice says.

"Where am I?" I ask, my voice coming from nowhere and everywhere. All I can see is white. I can feel my body, but it doesn't exist. Looks like the fourth dimension, but it doesn't feel right. This is more like a dream.

"You haven't decided yet."

"Max?" I ask, even though I know that's impossible. Max Wells, my childhood friend, died before I joined the Marines. Heart complications from Down Syndrome resulted in several surgeries, the last of which went sideways. The last time I saw Max was in his backyard.

And then, suddenly, I'm there.

The grass has been freshly mowed. The smell is intoxicating. I take several sniffs, feeling bits of my memory flash back to childhood, creating an intense longing for home. The swing creaks, snapping me back to the present.

Or is this the past?

My feet skid on the worn earth, slowing me to a stop. Puffs of gray soil coat my white Converse Chucks. I'm young again. A kid. I've been teleported back in time, into my old self, but with my adult mind intact.

How the hell?

The flower garden buzzes with yellow-striped pollinators. Birds chirp in the maples surrounding the fenced-in yard. Somewhere, a dog barks. I don't remember this particular moment, but there were dozens just like it during the years Max and I had together, talking movies, music, and babes. He liked Twiggy. I was partial to Sharon Tate.

A distant roar draws my eyes to the sky. A plane emerges from a cloud, leaving a contrail behind it. People heading somewhere. Life as usual. Long before things went to shit and got flushed and spewed into a fetid Nazi sewer.

"Hey, Mosey," Max says. He's seated above me, in a treehouse we built with his father. It's just six feet off the ground, but it was our castle for a while. His short legs dangle. His belly bulges under his too-tight T-shirt. Everything about him is exactly how I remember it, including his bottlecap glasses. Except...he's not smiling.

Max, like many people with Down Syndrome, experienced intense emotions, joy being the most prominent. Didn't take much to make him smile. Just looking him in the eyes was usually enough.

His voice sounds enthusiastic, but there's no trace of a smile. Or any other emotion for that matter. Max was a lot of things. Indifferent was never one of them.

"Maxwell," he says, using his self-given nickname merging his first and last names. When our parents weren't around, I called him SFB—shit for brains—which is shockingly not politically correct, but it made Max laugh until his face turned hot red and I thought he might pass out. "Maxwell Bond, at your service."

Max was a Bond fan, mostly for the skimpily-dressed Bond girls. Saw himself as a dapper lady's man and had no problem approaching the fairer sex as Maxwell Bond. He never had any luck, but he was also app-roaching women three times his age.

The Max sitting above me forces a wide smile, but it's all wrong. Joyless. His teeth are bared, but without an upturn to his lips, or a squint in his eyes.

This isn't Max.

And I'm not home.

I'm in a cave, motorboating a wall of blue Europhids.

"This isn't real," I say.

Max shrugs.

"You're not going to speak in riddles, right? Because I don't think I can take being bullshitted right now. Just say what needs saying and ask what you want to ask. Be direct."

"Like a man," Max says, and he attempts smiling again. "Chuy would appreciate the sentiment."

If they know about Max, and they know about Chuy, the Europhids have full access to my mind. It's unnerving.

"Anything you don't know about me now?" I ask.

"About your past? No. Our memories of your life are more complete than your own."

"That's...pleasant," I say.

"Your conscious mind is not capable of storing the data from a single childhood. Unpacking your life and experiencing it through you allows us to fully understand what motivates you. And to predict what you will do in the future."

"Like what you found?" I ask.

"Not particularly," Max says. "But you are not entirely to blame. The mission to bring you here, to this time, was...experimental. What human beings in your time would have called a 'Hail Mary.'"

"Hail Marys are desperation plays," I point out. "High value, but low odds of success. Which kind of makes me think arriving in the future thirty years late might not be the worst outcome."

"Far from it," he says, kicking his feet, watching the clouds. "But it is suboptimal."

"But better than arriving thirty-thousand years late inside a star," I point out.

He nods. "Much."

"So, you, an all-knowing, supreme being that's existed for billions of years and colonized the universe, are desperate for help because...of the human race?"

"This iteration of the human race, yes."

"I'm guessing you don't care much about how humanity treats itself, otherwise you'd have stepped in a thousand years ago. So, this is what, territorial? The Union is encroaching on your turf?"

Max looks me in the eyes.

The seriousness in his gaze, something I've never seen before, makes my stomach churn. "Yes."

"Really? It's that simple?"

Max sighs, stands, and then just falls forward off the tree house. He faceplants on the ground like fucking Wile E. Coyote dropping off a cliff.

Instinct drives me to my feet. "Holy shit. Are you okay?"

I help my friend up. He's covered in dirt and debris, grass stains on both knees, but not injured. Then he flashes that unholy grin at me again, and I stumble back.

Max takes a seat in one of the two swings. Waits.

Max—the real Max—would do the same thing. Sit in the swing, sullen-faced, waiting to spill the beans, until I sat down next to him. It was usually nothing serious—complaints about *Batman*, or *Thunderbirds*, or *Star Trek*—but we had a chat like this the day before that last surgery. It was our serious place, and the Europhids know that.

Once I'm settled back in the swing, Max says, "Imagine, if you can, that the universe is not simply an open void pocked with occasional stars, surrounded by a smattering of planets, all of them essentially alone in the endless black. Imagine that it is, in fact, your body. Seen from a distance, it is a marvel to behold. A singular being of light. A miracle of time and physics. Beyond precious. That *is* how every human sees themselves, is it not?"

I don't reply. Feels like a trap.

"Your body, like all living things, is host to a myriad of other living things. Bacteria mostly. Some of it beneficial, some of it detrimental. And your mind is largely separate from such things, operating independently of the body. You following me, Mosey?"

"Please stop calling me that." Only Max used that name. It belongs to him.

"Imagine now, that someone, anyone, drove a nail into your skull. You survive, but part of your brain dies, and all of the knowledge, experience and connection contained in that segment of gray matter is lost forever."

"I'd kill them," I say without missing a beat.

Max nods. He already knew that.

"Now imagine that the being wielding the hammer, is a species, a virus, living inside you, attacking your mind."

"Wait a second..." I rub my face, expecting stubble, but I feel the smooth skin of youth. "Hold on. Are you saying that humanity is the Alzheimer's of the universe?"

Max nods. "While it would take a million years to exterminate our kind—humanity excels at extinction. And to us, a million years is but a day. The human race, as it exists today, is a terminal disease. You wield the hammer, *and* you are the nail."

"But we've only encountered you twice before, right? On Europa. In another dimension?"

"On those occasions, one thousand years ago in two different dimensions, contact was made—not without some violence—but in the end, balance was restored. We first encountered the Union here, on what you call Beta-Prime. That was hundreds of years ago, but to us—"

"It's still the present," I say, putting myself in the shoes of a being who might experience years like minutes.

"Those of our kind living on the surface, what you call red Europhids, among several other more colorful names, were seen as a threat and eradicated. It wasn't until the 'Undesirables' arrived that contact was made and a peace established. It was also then that we began to understand the threat represented by the Union. Over the past several hundred years, the Union has taken three planets hosting Europhid colonies, one of them fledgling, the others ancient and deeply rooted. All three Europhid colonies were destroyed, from orbit. The most recent assault took place three years ago. It was a world *you* discovered."

Max takes hold of my hand before I can apologize. Scorching pain cascades from his touch, washing through my body and exploding from my mouth. My scream isn't just of pain.

It is the scream of a man whose death is inevitable.

Consumed by fear.

And then fire.

37

I can't see Max anymore. Or hear the birds. Or smell the grass. My mind is overwhelmed by searing pain. Every nerve in my body burns. I can feel myself melting. My bones char. My insides boil. As the anguish spreads, my mind is awake and aware, experiencing the death of every cell, until after what feels like months, I am undone.

"This is what being on the receiving end of an incendiary bomb feels like. We no longer retain the knowledge of the Europhids destroyed by the Union, but we remember the excruciating pain of their deaths. What you just experienced was a blink...but I hope you will not forget it."

I open my eyes. I'm on the ground, curled in a fetal ball. Max is on the swing still, kicking his short legs. He stares down at me, no longer attempting a smile. His eyes flicker with blue light, reminding me that none of this is real. Despite that, I don't think I'll ever forget the pain I just experienced.

And that's the point.

The Europhids know who I am. Know everything about me. Now that I've felt their pain, they know I'll stop at nothing to keep it from happening again.

"We don't know that, yet." Max hops off the swing. Stands over me. "More than anything else, you are motivated by kinship. It is the driving force that makes you a good commander of men, but it's also a great weakness, allowing you to turn a blind eye to injustice."

I want to argue the point, but I can't. This is a lesson I've already learned. And he's not wrong. If I had to compromise my morals to save one of my people again, I'd do it without a second thought, and I'd deal with the repercussions later.

"That is why—"

"Can you stop reading my thoughts?" I push myself up and dust off my not-real shorts and T-shirt.

Max furrows his brow. "Impossible. All of this is happening in your mind."

"Right." I pick up a rock and throw it into the trees at the back of the yard.

We used to hit rocks out of the yard with a baseball bat, listening to them buzz away.

Stopped when we broke a neighbor's window.

"That is why," Max says again, "*we* must become kin."

"If choosing to use Max's form makes you think we're family, I'm afraid your great intellect is missing the point." I throw another rock.

"You have experienced our pain," Max says. "You understand us. We understand you."

I laugh at Max in a way that I never would have, if this were really Max. "You've obviously never done this before. Not even with Brick."

"What we are attempting...only once, with a woman named Kathy Connolly, who was far more intelligent and understanding than you." Max hops off the swing and picks up a rock. "But please, explain your meaning."

It's possible the Europhids have already extracted my thoughts, but they're at least pretending to respect my mental privacy. "Shared experience. Joy, hurt, contentment. Whatever. Glad sacrifices of time and resources. Not just willing, but happy to do it, even if the doing sucks. Over time, after layers of trust are established, *then* kinship develops. It's not something that can be rushed."

"But it can be," Max says. "During extreme circumstances and times of shared danger, the bond between humans can become intense in a relatively short amount of time."

I'm about to argue the point when Max makes his point with a single word.

"Hildy." He throws his rock. Doesn't clear the fence. "Apologies for using your recent memories. Knowledge of them was attained before our conversation began."

I rub the rock in my hand with my thumb, feeling the authentic rough surface. He's not wrong. Hildy was Union. We bonded through music. A shared human experience. Then bonded through the danger of our escape. Trust was fast-tracked, and now, in my mind, she's one of my people. The same thing happened with Porter, Morton, and Burnett, but it took longer.

"You are far less fun and charming than Hildy," I say. "And we don't have a whole lot in common."

"We share an enemy," he says.

"The Union," I say.

"It is more profound than that." Max picks up another stone. It's flecked with mica. He smiles at it. Admiring. "Knowing what you do now, would you condone the destruction of a Europhid colony?"

"No," I say.

"Not for any reason?"

"I mean, if you start conquering the universe, maybe."

"That is not our way."

"And yet, you're found throughout the galaxy. Throughout the universe. Sounds colonial to me. And from what I've seen of your red-colored buddies, not every being you encounter is happy about your arrival."

"Can you keep your cells from dividing?" Max asks. "Can you prevent your immune system from destroying foreign invaders? Your body expands and grows despite what your mind might think. We are bound by biology, spreading throughout the universe. Growth is sometimes painful. Sacrifice is sometimes necessary. But when a colony is established, and an equilibrium found, the planet or moon we inhabit, and everything living on them become…kin."

"Oh," I say. "Huh. That include the Undesirables?"

"It does."

"And that's why you brought me here? To protect them?"

"To protect us all," Max says.

"Can I ask… How did you do it? Bring us to the future?"

Max chuckles. "That would be like you explaining military tactics to a butterfly."

"Hey." I don't disagree, but there's no reason to insult my intelligence.

"In terms you can understand, we worked with a team of human scientists, augmenting a slew drive to work with space—and time. Two machines were created. The first was created to send the second back in time. The second was designed to activate when you were in proximity, and then bring you to this time and place."

"But why Antarctica?" I ask. "Why not just send it to Fort Bragg?"

"Exposure." Max throws his sparkly rock. Faces me. "You lived in the earliest days of the Union, before anyone noticed the brewing storm. But there were people in positions of power, in your military and your government agencies who would have been inspired by the technology on display. During that time, at that location, on that specific day, you and your team were the best choice available to your government. It was a risk, but...here you are. A little late, and tainted by the Union, but present and, perhaps, willing to help."

"So, you're not all-powerful and all-knowing?" I ask.

"Delusions of grandeur are not unknown to us, but...no. Mistakes have been made, including not predicting the complications created by those who joined your trip through time."

"I thought you and Brick were tight." I face Max, trying to read his face. He just stares straight ahead, his expression a mask.

"Hey, boys," Max's mother says from the back porch. She's dressed in a flowing sun dress. Hair perfectly styled as usual. A red lipstick smile on her face. She always looked like a magazine advertisement. "You want some lemonade?"

There are few things in the universe more delicious than Mrs. Wells's lemonade. She makes it fresh, with—

"Stop," I tell Max. "You're trying to avoid the question." I turn to Mrs. Wells. "I love you, Mrs. Wells, but you're not real. So, fuck off."

She rolls her eyes and heads inside the house.

"We were not referring to Brick," Max says.

"Chuy and Drago are with me, and if I'm with you, so are they."

Max nods. "We know this."

"Then who else—"

"Those you have not found on your quest were found long ago, by others."

"What are you talking about?" I grab Max by the front of his shirt. "What the hell are you talking about?"

Max is undisturbed by my violent reaction. The real Max would have burst into tears. "Of the group transported from your time to the future, three were discovered by the Union and recruited. Being from a time when war was common and power could be taken, they quickly rose through the ranks, attaining positions of authority. We have identified two of the three. The man you call Whip. Another called Benny. The third man's identity remains elusive, even to Brick."

I release Max. I stagger back a few steps and then fall onto my ass.

After taking a moment to digest what he's telling me...that Whip and Benny are with the Union. "That was really Whip, then? In the *Zorak*. And Benny was with him?"

Max nods. "We are familiar with the *Zorak*, and its crew."

"The third man... He must be one of the Russians. Like Drago. Everyone else is accounted for. But what was he doing there?"

The rhetorical question lingers in the air. I don't know, and neither do the Europhids.

"Has Brick attempted reaching out to Whip?" I have a hard time believing that Whip and Benny would join the Union. I turned a blind eye to the Union to find my people, but I never drank the Kool-Aid.

"Brick established contact with Whip early on, seven years ago."

"Seven years ago? How long have they been here?"

"Whip and Benny arrived nine years ago, four years before y—"

"I can do basic math," I grumble.

Max gives a nod. "After many years of discussions, Whip agreed to meet with Brick, in person. Here. The results...were catastrophic."

I feel sick to my stomach. Whip and Benny *betrayed* Brick? It's unthinkable. It's...

No...

Oh, shit. Please, no.

"When did this happen?" I ask.

"Fifteen months ago."

"Shit," I say, punching the earth. "Goddamnit!"

I stand, fueled by rage and mourning, and I grasp Max's arm. "Show me. Show me now!"

38

I'm back in the fire, consumed by pain. But this time, I can see. I can feel. I can move.

But I'm not me. I'm something else.

My arms are covered in short gray hair. I'm clinging to a twisting coil of vines that grow in spirals, reaching up into the sky, high above the jungle canopy. And I'm not alone.

A dozen more creatures, just like me, hide on the vines above. They're full of energy, twitching back and forth and lashing out at each other. Their fear twists my gut. They're monkey-like things with big eyes, long claws for climbing, and a killer overbite sporting a row of needle teeth. Each one is the size of a cat. Individually, they wouldn't pose much of a threat to a human being, but in a group...

One of the creatures turns its back as it climbs higher. A glowing red growth at the nape of its neck reveals that it's being controlled, at least in part, by the red Europhids.

Noting my attention, the monkey-thing spins around and charges up to me. While my human mind reels back, expecting an attack, the small creature wraps its thin arms around me in a hug. I embrace it, feeling the same kind of affection that I feel for the others with me.

I'm not in control, I realize.

I'm a passenger, watching this through the creature's eyes, feeling what it feels. I'm surprised by the intensity. The creature isn't intelligent.

People would have no qualms about eating it. But the intensity of its emotions is as poignant as my own.

Is this a memory?

Yes, Max's voice replies in my mind. *This is the final memory to reach the collective mind from the colony you exposed to the Union.*

Shit.

Brick attempted to interfere, Max says, *against our recommenddation. Beta-Prime had been removed from the Union database. We were hidden. And according to our collaborators, Beta-Prime and the Undesirables had become less of a priority. They were still militarizing under Whip's influence, but the active scans for Beta-Prime had ceased.*

But Brick couldn't stand to let a colony die.

Rather than bring an army and start a war, he convinced Sara—the Undesirables' leader at the time—that he could use his connection to Whip and Benny. He believed, as you do, that if he could just speak to them, they would 'see the light,' beg forgiveness, and turn on the Union.

Sara loved him. Believed in him. They went to intercept Whip and Benny together.

This was the result.

Below, a small army of soldiers scours the jungle. They're dressed in robotic black armor that no doubt makes them faster, stronger, and capable of surviving a kinetic or lazzer attack. A shiny golden eagle head that represents the Union is emblazoned on their chests. I don't recognize the weapons. They're lazzer rifles, but I've never seen the model before.

Everything about them, including their glowing red eyes screams 'Fourth Reich.' Had I encountered this side of the Union when I first arrived in this time, I don't think I'd have been blinded to reality. Hell, I'd probably have been killed on the spot.

The man leading the pack is nearly indiscernible from the others, but the whip hanging at his waist, identifies him as Whip. And he appears to be in charge.

Whip holds up a fist. The small army stops at his command. Two of the soldiers break rank, joining Whip.

"This the spot?" Whip asks.

His voice is distorted. Deeper and mechanical, but it's still him.

The shortest of the three checks their coordinates using a forearm interface. "Location confirmed." The voice is distorted, too, but the Irish accent is impossible to hide. Benny. "Let's drop our payload and bug out. Something about this planet doesn't sit right."

"You say that every time we visit a new planet," Whip says.

"I don't like aliens," Benny says. "And I'm not a fan of walking into the unknown. Every new world is a potential shit show."

"Yeah, well, let's get this thermal enema started, and we can rotate home for a conjugal visit with our harems. Hell, last time we purged these little fuckers from a planet, we got our pick of the galaxy. Today's a good day, Benny boy. Tonight's going to be even better."

The third soldier, an unknown, shakes his head at the banter, but says nothing. Just observes.

Benny taps his wrist, activating comms. "Get the therm-det in place, double time."

Moving in the background, a group of armored soldiers directs a hovering platform containing a large device shaped like a jet's engine toward the cave's entrance.

Therm-det. Doesn't take a genius to figure out what that does. This is what the Union uses to burn out Europhid colonies.

The unknown soldier tenses. Brings his weapon up. Aims it into the jungle beneath me.

Whip turns to the soldier, more annoyed than worried. "The fuck is up your ass—"

"Contact," the soldier says, voice unrecognizable. "Someone in the jungle."

"Lower your weapons," says a familiar deep voice. Brick steps out from behind a tree, unarmed, hands raised to the sky. "I come in peace."

"Brick?" Whip says, staggered.

Benny's facemask snaps open, revealing his pale skin and his smiling face. "Brick!" His voice is unfiltered now. He rushes Brick and wraps his arms around him. Brick gives him the same warm welcome he did me, but the armor makes the embrace awkward.

"Holy shit," Whip says. "It's really you."

His helmet mask opens. Whip has facial hair, as blond as the hair on his head. Big and bushy like Grizzly Adams. It's a tactical mistake. Gives the enemy something to hold on to in close quarters combat, but I doubt that's an issue with their mechanized armor.

"In the flesh," Brick says, accepting Whip's offer of a handshake.

"What the hell are you doing here?" Whip asks, voice like I remember it now. "Did you land here? Tell me you haven't been living on this shithole planet the entire time."

"Not here," Brick says. "As to what I'm doing here, I'm going to let my wife do the talking."

"Wife?" Whip says with a chuckle. "Just one?"

"Just one," Brick says.

"Man, you are missing *out*," Whip says. "That will change now, obviously. You're going to lose your mind when you see the digs we—"

Whip's voice catches when Sara steps into the open. Like Brick, she's unarmed, hands raised. "Hello."

Whip's mask snaps shut. He and the unknown soldier raise their weapons toward Sara.

"Identify yourself!" Whip shouts.

Brick steps between the weapons and his wife. "Whoa, whoa. This is my wife."

"Fuck," Benny says. "Guys. This is *Brick*. He's one of us."

It takes a moment to sink in, but Whip lowers his weapon. His mask, however, remains closed. The unknown soldier follows Whip's lead, but keeps a finger on the trigger.

Sara leans out behind Brick. Eyes the weapons for a moment and then steps out in plain view. She's tall and skinny. Has a nice smile. Her braided hair is tied back. Reminds me of my mother, to whom she is distantly related.

"Whip," Brick says. "Benny. This is my *wife*." The way he says 'wife' leaves no doubt that she is not to be screwed with. "Her name is Sara. Believe it or not, she's related to Dark Horse."

"Dark Horse?" Whip tenses. Scans the jungle. "He here, too?"

"Wish that he was," Brick says. "But no."

Whip relaxes. Brick doesn't miss it.

Neither do I.

The unknown soldier takes a few steps back. Casually turns around like he's watching the soldiers move the therm-det into place. From Brick's position, his arm is hidden, but from high above, I watch the soldier activate his comms. My animal ears, which are large and cupped, have no problem hearing the soldier's whispered message. "Union Command, we have an Undesirable on the planet's surface. We might have stumbled across Beta-Prime. Please advise."

He's cool and collected. No trace of emotion.

Until a transmission comes in. I can actually hear the voice on the other end, but it's distant and muffled. No idea what is said, but the soldier's body language changes. So does Whip's. As the unknown soldier turns back, he shares a glance with Whip, who gives a subtle nod.

The pair raises their weapons toward Sara.

"Whip, what the hell?" Brick says.

"Sorry, big guy," Whip replies. "Looks like you've gone and consorted with the enemy. Going to have to detain you both. She's headed to Union Command. You...still have a choice. I get that she's your lady, but you don't need to throw away your life for her, right? Other fishes in the sea and all that. Hell, I can set you up with a few new wives by tomorrow. Choice is yours."

"Came here to make peace," Brick says.

"Can't save Beta-Prime," Whip says. "They threaten the way of life for bajillions of good people."

"Doesn't need to be like this," Brick says.

My little heart is pounding, but it has nothing to do with how *I* feel. It's the creature, responding to the Europhid's understanding that shit is about to go sideways.

Don't do it, I will Whip, even though I know how the story ends. *Please don't do it.*

Benny turns to face Whip and the unknown soldier. "What the hell?"

"She called it in," Whip says, nodding his head toward the unknown soldier.

She?

"And now we got orders," Whip says. "You remember how to follow them, right?"

"Y-yeah."

"Good. Then do me a favor and cuff them both. *Now.*"

Benny is conflicted, but he obeys. Approaches Brick and Sara with a frown on his face. "I'm sorry about this," he tells them. "I don't know why they're like this."

He reaches out to take hold of Sara's wrist, but stops short. "Run," he whispers.

"Everything okay, Benny?" Whip asks.

"Run!" Benny shouts, spinning around and raising his rifle. He gets off a single lazzer pulse. It cuts through the air between Whip and the unknown soldier.

Brick and Sara break into a run, fleeing the scene side by side.

Benny is shot, just once. In the face. By the unknown soldier. The lazzer is powerful enough to carve out a steaming bowl where Benny's face had been.

A high-pitched shriek wails from my little body. It's repeated throughout the jungle. I catch a glimpse of hundreds of these critters charging down the vine spirals, and then I'm one of them.

An electric crackle fills the air as I descend. A glowing blue whip unfurls. Flows back through the air and then arcs forward, cracking with a burst of energy.

Sara shouts in pain, body arched back. She collapses to the ground.

Twenty feet from the forest floor, I leap from the vine. Sailing through the air, I extend my claws and let out a battle cry. All around the jungle, these small creatures launch themselves in a coordinated attack that has no chance of success.

But it gives Brick time.

I hear him, screaming in anguish. Begging for Sara to open her eyes.

My host glances toward Brick's voice, sees him pick Sara up, her back carved open, spine visibly severed. Then he retreats into the jungle, covered by the massive assault launched by the Europhids.

My host looks forward just in time to see a line of blue light whipping toward its face.

I snap out of the past, lying on my back, in the grass of Max's backyard. It's not until I see Max standing over me, a deep frown on his face, that I remember this isn't real either.

The vision I had is like a dream. The details are already fading. But the bullet points remain. I'll never forget them.

Whip killed Brick's wife.

Would have killed Brick, too.

"Fuck." I stand. Fists clenched. Rage engulfs me.

How could Whip do it? How could he turn on his team?

"Small minds," Max says, "make easy targets. While you lived on the Union's fringe, your friend found a home amidst the high council. He lives a privileged life. All his wishes are granted. And the action craved by men like him, and you, is fulfilled by commanding the Union military. Whip's allegiance was purchased long ago. The time spent under your command, serving with your team, was short in comparison."

"Benny was smart. How could he—" I punch the wooden swing set. Wincing in pain, I shake my hand out.

"One would assume," Max says, "that like you, the man called Benny was guided by ignorance. He believed the Union was all that remained of humanity, so he conformed. When he realized there was another path, he took it at great cost. What I want to know, is will you do the same?"

"You already know I will," I say.

"Even if it means confronting your old friend?"

"Evil is evil," I say, "even if it's also a familiar face."

"And if you must kill Whip?"

"I'll do what needs doing."

Max shakes his head and rolls his eyes. It's the first authentic Maxism the Europhids have managed to pull off. "Bold, macho statements might have worked in the 1980s, on Earth, but I'm going to need assurance."

I don't like being backed into a corner, but the sooner I can get out of this fantasy world, the sooner I can put the Union in a hurt locker. If that means killing Whip...

I punch the swing set again. "Fuck!"

He chose his fate, I decide. When he killed Brick's wife and didn't blink when Benny's head was carved out.

"Who was it?" I ask. "The soldier who killed Benny."

"We don't know," Max says. "Her mask was never removed."

"Her," I say. The detail returns like a boomerang, colliding with my skull. It was a woman. Working with Whip, but not subservient to him. Until she fired the gun, she was just watching. Observing. Making sense of what Whip and Benny missed—that Sara was an Undesirable. That Brick was her enemy. Signs of a keen mind, and a long history of not trusting people.

"Shit," I say. "Carter."

"We are aware of Carter's involvement in the mission that brought you to us, and have suspected that she was the unknown soldier," Max says. "But we have never been able to confirm her identity or location."

"That's because she was stranded on a planet," I say, trying to make sense of things. "Living like a cavewoman for the past three..."

Hell. I feel the Europhids cannonball into my memories, absorbing every detail from the past few weeks.

"You were duped," Max says. "She was not on that planet for three years. She was deposited there by the man you encountered in orbit a short time after returning to your ship."

"The Union set me up," I say. "*Whip* set me up. Sent me on a course that would—"

"—bring you to us," Max says. "Where is she now?"

"In orbit," I say, cold dread emanating from my bones. "With Hildy, Porter, Burnett, and Morton. God, they don't stand a chance. Let me out. *Please.* I need to get back."

"Time is short," Max agrees, "but it moves slower in this place. What feels like hours is just seconds in reality. I understand your eagerness to leave. To set things right. I appreciate it, as well. But I still require assurance."

"Just tell me what to do, and I'll do it." Right now, I'd give the Europhids just about anything. I don't deal with betrayal well. Whip was a close friend. He didn't just turn his back on me, he betrayed everything we swore to protect. What makes me angriest about it is that I'm no better. I sacrificed my morality and for a hell of a lot less. But I didn't kill anyone. And like Benny did in the last seconds of his life, I'm going to make it right.

As for Carter...she used me. Told me exactly what I wanted to hear. Pretended to connect with me. Turned me into a marionette, guiding me into conflict with the Union so that I would be trusted— finally—by the Undesirables. How long were they watching me?

Probably from day one.

"Mosey," Max says. "I need you to focus. The power of your emotions will serve you well, but not yet. Right now, I need you to understand."

"Understand what?"

"My red counterparts connect with the minds of other beings, often times against their will. But this is not my way." Max looks me in the eyes. "I need your permission."

"To what, exactly?" I'm suddenly not so sure about this. When I was in the little creature's body, I didn't feel two separate wills. "Is this like a Body Snatchers situation? Are you going to inhabit my body? Destroy my consciousness?"

"You will remain you, in every way." Max holds out his hand. A bumble bee lands on it, cleaning its antennae. Max looks it over. Then he reaches out a finger and places it on the insect's fuzzy back. "But you will also be more."

A flicker of blue light arcs from Max's finger to the bug's body. The bee twitches. It's eyes glow blue. The bee takes off, flies a circle around me, and then stops a few feet from my face, hovering in place, staring at me. There are no pupils to lock onto, but I know it's looking me in the eyes. And somehow, I sense an intelligence that wasn't there before.

"So, you're going to make me smarter?" I ask.

"We are going to allow you access to our mind, but you must also grant us access to yours. Our knowledge and experience will be available to you. In a sense, you will be one of us, and we, one of you."

Not sure how I feel about this. The benefits are clear—access to a mind greater than the sum of humanity. The downside is that I'm pretty sure that if I tick the Europhids off, or if they get tired of my presence in their infinite trans-dimensional brain, they could just give me an aneurism and be on their merry way.

"All of that is accurate," Max says. "The potential danger to yourself is real, including our ability to terminate your life, or take it over. To earn our trust, you must first put your trust in us."

"Any chance you can tell me what the grand plan is, first?" I ask.

"Please understand, if you are shown what is to come and turn down my offer, your life will be forfeit, here and now."

"You know," I say, "Max was much nicer about delivering bad news. You could learn a thing or two from him."

Max smiles. It's still forced and horrible.

I shake my head. "Agreed."

"Very well." Max reaches out with the same finger that he used to touch the bee. Touches my forehead. A freight train of information careens into my mind. Thoughts. Plans. Strategies. Locations. Personnel. Names. All of it is etched into the hard drive of my mind like I've been studying this subject my whole life.

And then it stops. Max withdraws his finger.

I stagger back a step, mind reeling from the influx of knowledge. It takes a moment to filter through all the tangential information Max hadoukened into my brain with his finger. But then I find what I'm looking for.

The plan.

The grand scheme to upend the Union and—

"Are you serious?" I ask, stunned.

"You are turning down my offer?" Max asks.

"No. No!" I pace a bit. "I just... Your plan? No offense, but it's fuck'n nuts."

"You believe you can improve upon it?"

I laugh. "Improve upon it? Hell, no. But...do you think it's possible? And you can do...all of it?"

"We would not be speaking if I believed otherwise."

I take a deep breath, enjoying the scent of summer, the feel of Earth's sun on my skin, and the birdsongs surrounding us. "Do it. Let's kick some Nazi ass."

Max holds out his finger again. "This will feel different."

I close my eyes. "Do it before I change my mind."

"That is literally what we are about to do."

One of my eyes snaps open. "Like physically? I'm not going to have a blue cucumber—sorry—growing out of my head or something?"

Max shakes his head. "You would describe our presence within your body as something akin to bacteria, living in your cells, occupying the space between synapses and populating your marrow. We will be a part of you from now until the moment you die."

"Cool," I say, but I don't mean it. I close my eye again, and I wait.

"When you emerge," Max says, "your path back will be unhindered. You will be able to move among us, as one of us."

"Okay, okay," I say. "Just get it over w—"

His finger touches my forehead. The universe explodes inside my mind. And then, all at once, I cease to exist.

"Ugh..." I wake slowly. The air on my face is cool. The floor beneath me is like a slab of concrete. I feel like I've been kicked in the nuts—if my nuts were in my skull. "Not cool, Max."

My voice is deep again. My body two feet taller. The scent of summer has been replaced by an eggy funk.

I open my eyes. Despite my blurry vision, I have no trouble making out the vast field of blue Europhids surrounding me. In every direction. The path ahead—the only thing not lit up like an all-blue Lite-Brite—beckons to me.

Need to get out. Need to get back.

I stand and rub my eyes. My vision clears as I stagger away, feeling weak. The wall of Europhids behind me just undulates slowly, indifferent to my presence. All around me, the strange beings just waggle. No sense of impending doom. No urgency or panic.

I've been betrayed. If the Union isn't already here, they will be soon.

"You're about to get fucked in the ass, you know that, right?" I increase my pace as my mind and body continue to wake up, fueled by rising adrenaline. The Europhids don't respond, visually, or in my head. I don't know what I was expecting, but nothing wasn't it.

Move your ass, I tell myself, and I break into a run.

A few steps into my sprint, blood pumping, I feel myself return to normal. Fully awake. Fully aware. It's not just the Europhids that are about to get wiped off the map. The Minutemen, including my grandson, my brother-in-arms, and Chuy...my best friend and maybe my future something-or-other.

Navigating my way back is simple. I remember the path like it's the route I take for a morning run. I slip through dark tunnels free of Euro–phids, each step planted without vision, but with full confidence.

I slide to a stop, emerging from a tunnel into a field of red Europhids. I catch my breath for a moment, looking over the vast cavern, remembering the anus-faced beast that guards it. "We're friends now, right?"

No response.

Fuck it.

I charge through the cavern. The red Europhids are as indifferent to my presence as the blues. It's a welcome change. Whatever Max did to me, it's far less dramatic than I expected, but it seems to be doing the trick. At least with these hyper-defensive little pricks. I extend my middle fingers at the red cucumbers as I run down the path.

I realize it's immature in the extreme to do the adult version of 'nana nana boo boo,' but who's here to see me? Other than a billion-year-old, universe-sized super brain... "Sorry," I say to the field. "Old habits." I lower my fingers and pour on the steam.

Ten minutes later, I'm through and at the elevator. I expected to find Brick and Chuy here, but they're nowhere to be seen. The elevator awaits. The doors open.

A quick scan of the area reveals no hiding spaces, and I somehow know there aren't any Brick could fit into. Just to be sure, I call out their names, "Brick! Chuy!" My voice echoes through the massive chambers, bouncing back several times before finally fading. I wait ten seconds for a reply and then I step into the elevator and hit the only button.

The doors close, and I'm whisked upward.

It's not until my ears pop from the ascent that I realize I could see the whole way back, even when there were no Europhids present. On the way in, we needed a flashlight for a good portion of the journey.

Holy shit. I can see in the dark!

The elevator jerks to a stop.

Will is here, I think.

I don't know why. I can just...*sense* him. The doors whoosh open, revealing Will, holding my gear. He's also petrified.

"What's happening?" I ask.

Will hands my things over, one at a time as he walks and talks. "Union. They're outside." He's breathless and terrified.

"Need a bit more info than that." When I first encountered Will, he was cocky and confident. Probably because he knew who I was. Knew my character. Grew up hearing stories about me. But now... He looks ready to pass out. Having a genocidal regime come knocking will take the bluster out of a guy. And he's probably not alone. These people have been preparing for this moment, for hundreds of years, but how many of them have seen combat?

I suppose that's why I'm here.

Will stops when I do, confused, but still trying to answer my question. "There's, ah, two...two of them. Fully armored."

"Slow down, Will," I tell him. "Take a breath."

He breathes deep. Lets it out. Hands me my knife.

"How about I guess," I say. "And you tell me if I'm wrong?"

"The two people outside haven't found the entrance, but it won't be long. There's a ship in orbit. The *Zorak*. No sign of the Union fleet?"

He hands me my rifle. I sling it over my shoulder. Pistol comes next. I holster it on my hip.

He nods at me. "All correct."

"Peachy," I say, and I clip the PSD back in place. "Where are Brick and Chuy?"

"Control deck," he says.

I'm about to ask where that is, but then I realize I already know. Just like the tunnels below, I'm now aware of every nook and cranny of this base, and all the people in it—including where they are and how they feel. For a moment, it's overwhelming. Then controlled, and that has nothing to do with me.

They really are inside me now.

Gross. And cool.

Am I psychic now? I wonder, and the depths of my mind make sense of it for me. The Europhids are everywhere, populating the deepest recesses of Beta-Prime, but they've got what best can be described as *roots* all over the planet. Not to mention wildlife allies on the surface. I'm just aware of what they are. Far away from the Europhids, I won't have this kind of mental reach.

I focus my attention outside the base and feel the Union soldiers' location.

And identities.

The first is Whip.

The second...*shit*...is Carter.

"C'mere." I pull Will against me, trigger the PSD, and rotate to the control deck.

Will and I emerge from the fourth dimension, surrounded by people who leap back at our sudden arrival. I've never met any of them, but I know them all by name. They start to salute when I say, "If you've got somewhere to be, get there now."

The thirty-odd people disperse. I snap my fingers at one of them. "Jenn."

She stops. "Sir?"

"I want every slew drive in the fleet ready to fire on my mark," I tell her. "Coordinates to come. Get it done."

She finishes the salute I interrupted the first time, nods, and then bolts from the control deck.

With the crowd missing, I get my first look at the control deck.

Everything in the Union is dark and utilitarian. Things aren't designed. They're built for functionality, and that's it. If it's ugly, but it works—like a poop-shaped starship—so be it. The Minutemen control center is a different beast. Whoever designed this had an aesthetic eye. The lines are smooth. The surfaces white and gray, but a stripe of orange cuts through the monotone workstations, creating a pleasing look that might make working in this room, day and night, a little less monotonous.

The space is built like a theater in the round. Screens line the back walls. The people at each workstation have a view of what's displayed, and if they need to, of each other. Brick and Chuy are center stage, along with Drago, Adrik, and BigApe...still wedged deep inside the hairy Russian's body. They're surrounded by a circle of holographic displays, but they're focusing on the screens around the room. One displays an image transmitted from space. A satellite feed. At the center of the black void is the *Zorak*, orbiting Beta-Prime. The rest of the screens show a series of shots from the jungle outside the base's entrance.

Carter led Whip to the LZ, but she doesn't know where the base's entrance is.

"These cameras have sound?" I ask, walking down the steps.

"You made it!" Brick says, relieved.

"Was there ever any doubt?" I ask, shaking Brick's hand.

"A lot," Chuy says. "He's been pacing like an expectant father."

"And you?" I ask.

"Vete a la mierda, cabrón." She follows the insult with a smile, and I return it. We've run through routines like this a hundred times in the past. Feels different this time. How could it not? The fruit of our combined loins populate this base—literally dozens of descendants, and more in other bases around the planet. Chuy isn't aware of the grand scale of our personal effect on this future world—but the folks with my genes in them stand out in my now-very-full mental filing cabinet. Some of them even look like her.

"Good to see you, too," I say, and I acknowledge Drago, Adrik, and BigApe with a nod. There's a lot I'd like to say to all of these people. To Chuy about...you know, stuff. Apologies to Brick. Sympathy to BigApe. God, I can't even look at him. But there isn't time for any of that.

"Someone give me audio on those two," I say to the room, knowing that one of the people at workstations will get it done. A moment later, audio from the feed fills the large room.

"You sure this is the right place?" Whip asks. Sounds annoyed.

"This whole planet is the right place," Carter replies.

They're both wearing head-to-toe, mechanized body armor, but the size difference reveals who's who.

"You need to call in the fleet," she says. "Now."

Whip shakes his head.

"I'm not calling in a mass deployment until—" He holds up a finger. "We confirm this is the right place." Holds up a second finger. "And I'm sure this isn't a trap."

Letting them wander around in the jungle is tempting, but they'll eventually stumble on the entrance.

"We could kill them," Brick says, voice low and serious. "Right now."

"I understand why you want to," I tell him, "but that wouldn't solve anything, and that's not the plan."

"What *is* plan?" Drago asks.

"First," I raise an index finger, "I'm going to say, 'Hello'. Let them know we're here."

"You can't be serious?" BigApe says.

I ignore the comment, in part because I can't bear to look at him.

"I'm coming with you," Brick says.

"No," I say, "you're not." Feels weird giving elder Brick orders, but that is why I'm here. "I need you to get everyone on-planet in a ship and ready to rotate the hell out of here."

"You want us to *abandon* Beta-Prime?" He sounds disgusted by the idea. "We didn't bring you here to retreat. We can't leave the planet undefended."

"It won't be," I say. "Trust me. Just be ready to rotate on my command."

He takes a moment. Simmers down.

"Where to?"

I head for a console and motion for the woman seated at it to move. She steps aside and waits. My fingers work the keyboard like an old pro, maneuvering through software, typing in a string of letters and numbers, and then dropping it all into the holographic feed.

I've never done any of that before, and the celestial coordinates I just punched into the system came from the part of my brain that is glowing blue. When I look up, no one is looking at the location displayed on the celestial map, they're staring at me.

"What?" I ask.

"Your eyes," Chuy says. "When you were typing. They were blue."

"Not just blue," Drago adds. "Like headlights. Glowing."

"Long story," I say. "For another time. Right now, I need you—" I point at Brick. "—to get every ship in the fleet, and every person on-world, to those coordinates."

Brick finally looks at the hologram. His eyes widen. "This is Union Command. What do you expect us to do?"

"The Union is paranoid. All data is centralized and stored on Union Command. Find the data centers. Burn them to the ground."

"What good will that do?" Will asks. "Our home will still be under attack."

"Beta-Prime was never humanity's home," I tell him. "It's theirs." I look to the floor. "But if the Union's data is destroyed, the Predictors can't do their job, and if that happens—"

"The Union will be divided," Brick says, making sense of it all.

"Every planet in the Union will be lost to the others. No way to communicate. No way to rotate from one place to another. They'll have to start over, on their own."

"They won't last a hundred years," Chuy says.

I nod. "Rabbits on an island. They'll hump themselves into extinction."

Drago shrugs. "Not bad way to go."

"But a good way to start over." I punch in a second set of celestial coordinates. "Here."

The new planet appears in the holographic display.

"Earth," Brick says, disappointed.

"The planet is recovering," I tell him. "Slowly. But with some TLC, future know how, and a good ol' 'can do' attitude..."

Brick sighs.

"It's where we belong," I say. "We're not ready to be anywhere else."

Saying it stings. Means I'm giving up Elysium, too.

Ah well.

I reach my hand out to Chuy. "Ready?"

She steps into my grasp.

"What are you going to do?" Brick asks.

"First...parley. Second...we'll get creative. Whip showing up without the rest of the Union fleet wasn't part of the plan. So, I'm improvising."

"Improvising?" Brick says, sounding concerned. "I don't think—"

Before Brick can finish expressing his concerns, I fire up the PSD and rotate into the fourth dimension, emerging a few seconds later, right in front of Whip and Carter—all by myself.

Whip and Carter do a good job hiding their surprise at my sudden arrival. Whip takes a single step back, raising his weapon. Carter doesn't even do that. She kind of just looks at me. I can't see her eyes through the armor, but she's putting off a coiled snake vibe.

"Whip," I say in greeting, not offering a hand. Then I turn to Carter. "Judas."

Whip's facemask snaps open as he chuckles. "That's a good one. I missed your sense of humor, boss."

"Likewise," I say, trying to hide my inner conflict. Like Brick, Whip is older, but he still wears the face of my friend and trusted brother. It's his heart that's changed.

"You enjoyed every second of it," Carter says.

"Wait," Whip says, smiling. "Hold on. You did the horizontal mambo with him? *Him*, but not me?"

Carter shrugs. "I fuck who I want. Got us here, didn't it?"

"Look," Whip says to me. "I know you're angry at me. I get it. For real. But the status quo is different now. A guy like me can rule the fucking galaxy. I have a damn harem, man. You know I'm not down with the racist Undesirable bullshit, but I'm living the life. Unfortunately for you..."

He swirls his hand around his face, but I get his meaning.

I'm black.

"You killed Brick's wife."

I motion to the electric whip he still carries.

"Whoa, whoa," he says. "That's a gross exaggeration. I don't know what Brick told you, but—"

"I was there," I say.

His face scrunches up. "No...you weren't. Don't know if you've figured it out yet, but we've been tracking you since you hijacked that piece of shit you've called home for the past five years. You weren't there."

"Whatever it is you think you know about me...is wrong." That's not entirely true. He probably had an accurate picture of my life up until today. But I'm not the same person I was an hour ago. What I need, is for him to believe that everything he thinks he knows is wrong.

It'll put him off balance.

Make him feel isolated and exposed.

When that happens, he'll call in the fleet. With the Union hard up for real estate, I don't think they'll lay waste to the entire planet. They'll put boots on the ground and plan to slaughter the Minutemen up close and personal.

"I'm not the person you think I am," I say, almost growling the words out and willing the Europhid presence in me to do me a solid. I can't see it myself, but the confusion on Whip's face lets me know that my eyes are, once again, glowing blue.

I raise two fingers toward Carter. Fire an imaginary gun.

Carter is struck in the head, hard enough to flip her like a pancake. Her armored body hits the ground hard. This time, Whip reels back. His facemask snaps down.

The sound of a distant sniper round catches up to the bullet, rolling through the forest.

No idea if Carter is dead. I honestly hope so. But that armor they're wearing looks tough.

Whip looks from me, to Carter and back again. "Ho-lee shit. That—seriously—that was awesome. People in this time don't appreciate thea-ter. But that... Don't take this the wrong way, but I wish you were white."

"Wouldn't change anything," I say. "I'd still be standing here, and you'd still be shitting yourself."

He goes rigid.

Whip is a lot like Marty McFly. Call him yellow and he sees red. Tries to hide it.

"C'mon out, Chuy! Let me see that fine Mexican—"

A bullet explodes into the bark of a tree just a foot from Whip's head. He looks at the bullet hole as the rifle's report echoes around us.

"I'm going to give you one chance," I tell him. "Repent. Come home. Fight the good fight."

"You don't stand a chance," he says, and he means it.

"Would with your help," I say, but I don't mean it.

"Brick would kill me, first chance he got," he says, and I wonder if he's considering coming over to our side.

And if he accepted the offer? What then? Forgive and forget? He's committed atrocities. Murdered people. He's about to launch a planetwide genocide.

There's no coming back from that.

And both of us know it.

"Thanks for the offer," he says. "Going to make killing you a little harder. Well, just a little."

Remembering the way Whip struck down Brick's wife, simply because she wasn't one of the Union's pale desirables, fills me with rage. I don't want to let him go. With a point of a finger, Chuy could drop him. We could take him and Carter inside, dismantle their armor, and make them answer for their crimes. But I have no choice. The plan doesn't work if he's dead.

But I *can* whup his ass first.

I rotate behind him, grasp hold of his whip, plant a foot on his ass, and shove. He topples forward, but he turns the fall into a roll. Comes up on his feet, aiming his weapon toward me.

I've seen what his rifle can do. Not wanting my face melted, I focus on disarming him.

The whip is easy to operate. Button on the handle. It comes to life with a crackle. Before Whip can pull the trigger, the weapon is severed in two with an electric snap.

This thing is powerful. Might even make short work of his armor.

He confirms it by taking a step back, just out of range. No way the rifle is his only weapon. The armor probably has hidden lazzer weapons, maybe even mini rocket pods.

No way to tell who would win if we went toe-to-toe right now, and I don't want to find out. I want him to leave.

I point my fingers at him the same way I did Carter. "Last chance."

"That's a fancy trick," he says, motioning to the PSD on my belt. "Sure wish I had one. Oh wait."

Whip rotates away.

What the fuck?

He appears again, crouched over Carter. Hoists her up. "When you see your boy, Porter. Thank him for the tech. Adios, assholes."

He rotates away with Carter. Just as he slips from the third dimension, a bullet slaps into a tree, right where his head had been.

I don't have time to care that Chuy lost her patience. "Chuy."

"I heard. Come get me."

I rotate through the jungle, reappearing just long enough to grab Chuy.

"Know where you're going?" she asks.

Takes just a moment of thought to access the Europhids' planet-wide awareness and locate the *Bitch'n* in orbit. I don't answer with words. I just hold on to her and rotate off world, appearing on the *Bitch'n*'s bridge.

The seats are empty.

I activate my comms. "Porter. You copy?" No answer.

"Morton. You copy?"

Chuy moves to a control panel. "Local comms are offline," she says, and with the press of a button, she turns them back on. "Porter. You copy?"

Still nothing.

"Fuck... Burnett. You copy?"

"D-Dark Horse?" He sounds terrified.

"Where are you, Burn?"

"Locked in...in a supply closet. H-Hildy is with me." His voice is shaky. He's fighting to stay coherent. Breaks my fucking heart. "We're okay, but...but..."

"There's a bomb," Hildy says. "In the hangar! Said they were going to activate it when you got back!"

"Go!" Chuy shouts, and I rotate to the hangar.

Takes a fraction of a second to find the keg-shaped bomb, but several seconds longer to fully comprehend what I'm seeing.

Porter and Morton are bound to the bomb, arms outstretched as though embracing the device, though I think they were trying to embrace each other around it. They're both stripped bare. Morton is covered in the kind of wounds a lazzer whip might cause. He was tortured.

That's how they got a PSD from Porter...

My legs go wobbly as I approach.

Emotion bubbles up, raw and unhinged.

Flashes of their final moments are assembled by my imagination. The grief. The shame. They hadn't been strong enough to withstand Whip's and Carter's assault, and in the end had given our enemies a tool that could help defeat the Minutemen.

But I don't blame them.

I blame myself. They're not soldiers, but I brought them into a war.

I drop to my knees, tears flowing freely.

The Union sucks. It's pure evil. But people are still people. The future might be so dark that the folks can't see the truth about their lives, but these two...they were stars. Not a trace of hate in their hearts.

They didn't deserve this.

"I'm sorry," I say, putting my hands on their heads, covering the lazzer holes that took their lives. A sob escapes my lips. "I'm so sorry."

A red light atop the bomb begins blinking. Sobers me fast.

I wrap an arm around the device and rotate away, leaving Morton and Porter behind. I'm not thinking when I rotate. I just do it, trying to get away from *Bitch'n.*

The moment I emerge from the fourth dimension, my skin burns. I catch a glimpse of the bomb floating away into a black void, realize I'm in space—without a suit, and I clench my eyes shut. Searing pain grips my body as the vacuum of space decreases the boiling point of my bodily fluids. If I didn't routinely exhale before rotating, the air in my lungs would have expanded, popping them like a pair of balloons inside my chest.

I've got a few seconds before the damage is irreparable.

Maybe fifteen seconds to live.

But my heart is broken.

My thoughts confused.

My nervous system overwhelmed.

I know what I have to do, but I can't think of how to do it.

And then, the bomb detonates.

42

Orange light pierces my eyelids, and I brace for oblivion.

Explosions in space don't make sound, or produce shockwaves, but I'm close enough to the bomb that the momentary combustion will likely atomize me.

My stomach churns. I feel a tug, like gravity. And then, I collide with something solid.

Did Chuy maneuver *Bitch'n* between me and the explosion?

Did she *hit* me?

Doesn't make sense. Mostly because I don't feel like I'm dying anymore.

Because I'm not in space.

There's a floor beneath me.

Warm air scorches my skin as it thaws. My lungs scream in relief when I take a breath.

I lie on the floor, curled up like a newborn, wracked by pain and the confusion of life, breathing desperately.

This is *Bitch'n*. Has to be. But how did I get here? I don't remember activating the PSD, never mind navigating the fourth dimension and rotating back out.

I'm alive, though. But Porter and Morton are not.

I force my eyes open. They burn, but I can still see. Another few seconds out there and the damage to my body would have been permanent. Because I'd be dead.

"Chuy," I say, my voice weak and rasping.

"Where are you?" she asks. Sounds like she's running.

I scan the space around me. Really confused now. "My quarters. I'm...in bed?"

Fueled by rage, I push myself up, shouting in pain. My body resists, shouting back, 'lie back down, asshole!' But fuck that. I'll lie down when this is done, or when I'm dead.

The moment I get my feet beneath me and I'm standing upright, the door slides open. Chuy rushes in, an awkward look on her face.

"I'll be okay in—" She throws her arms around me. Squeezes hard. Never has something simultaneously hurt so bad and felt so good.

"Asshole," she says, still holding me. "That was the dumbest thing you've ever done."

"Wasn't going to let anyone else die," I say.

She leans back to look me in the eyes. "You could have—"

"What?" I ask.

"Your eyes."

"Blue again?"

"Flickering," she says. "Fading."

"That explains how I got back," I say. "I was a dead man. Don't remember triggering the slew or rotating."

"They can control you?" She sounds horrified.

"If I'm ever not myself, and you think I'm lost for good, I give you permission to put a bullet through my glowing blue brains."

She looks at me like I'm a moron until she realizes I'm being serious. Then she sobers, steps away from me, thinks it over, and nods. "I can do that."

Not exactly the words you want to hear from your best friend/possible future wife with whom you'll sire the backbone of a future intergalactic insurgency. No pressure. But if I go rabid and need to be put down, there's no one I trust more to take me behind the proverbial barn and put me down.

"You're alive!" Hildy is in the doorway, beaming. Her curls are chaotic. Her face dirty. But she's joy personified. And like Chuy, she doesn't stop to think about my condition before throwing her arms around me.

Doesn't hurt as bad this time. I'm either feeling better, or Hildy simply can't generate the PSI Chuy did. I squeeze back. "Glad you're okay, kid."

"Sorry I didn't—"

"Nothing that happened here was your fault," I tell her.

Behind her, Burnett lingers in the doorway, looking at the floor. His eyes are red-rimmed and swollen. Bottom lip quivering.

I'm broken up about Morton and Porter. Going to be haunted by their deaths for the rest of my life. But Burnett was with them from childhood, when they were segregated from their better-looking counterparts and predestined for salvaging jobs far from the Union's eyes.

Hildy glances back, sees Burnett, and then whispers. "He saved my life."

I step around Hildy and stand in front of Burnett. "The weight of what happened here today is not yours to carry."

No response.

"I put you all in harm's way. I trusted the wrong person. Porter and Morton...that's on me and no one else. You hearing me?"

A slight nod is all I get.

"Hildy says you saved her," I say.

He sniffs back some tears. "I was a coward. I *hid*."

"Some of the bravest people in human history have done nothing more than hide, and keep others hidden."

"I could have done something," he says. "I could have tried."

I understand how he's feeling, but he's not me. "Carter, and the man who was with her..."

"It was your friend," he says. "Whip. He—he told us that you sent him. That y-you wanted him to—"

"I would never," I say, voice choking with anguish and rage.

"I know," he says. "We all know."

I put my hand on his shoulder. My forehead against his. "There is nothing you could have done to stop them. What happened was my fault, and I'm going to make it right."

His forehead rubs against mine when he nods.

Now the hard part.

"But I'm going to need your help to do it. After that, if you want out, you can—"

"No." He stands up, looking pissed. "I want to fight. Whatever it takes. I'm with you until the end, no matter how far we have to go, or how dangerous the mission, even if that means dying."

"Well, *shit*. Wow." I say, genuinely impressed by his zeal.

"We watched some action movies," Hildy says. "Before Carter...you know... Thinks he's John McClane now."

Burnett huffs an embarrassed laugh.

"I like it." I squeeze Burnett's shoulder. "It fits."

He sniffs back his emotions. Stands a little taller. "What do we need to do?"

"Step One," I say. "You three get to the bridge. Make sure they didn't mess around with *Bitch'n*. Then we're going to teach the Union what happens when you screw with Exo-Hunters."

"Toughest of the tough," Chuy says, and we thump our fists together. She offers her raised fist to Burnett, who is momentarily taken aback.

Then he smiles. "Toughest of the tough." He thumps his fist against Chuy's and winces in pain.

"Fuckin-A," Hildy says, and bumps her fist against Chuy's.

Had the words come from anyone else, they wouldn't have had much effect, but coming from a pint-sized blonde with pom-pom hair, it strikes a chord and gets me smiling.

"Fuckin-A."

Then she spoils it by asking, "What are you going to do?"

A sigh sneaks out. Then I say, "Going to take care of our friends."

"If you're ejecting them..." Burnett says, but doesn't get to finish.

"They'll get a proper burial," I tell him. "Someplace nice. They deserve it. Now go."

Before they can leave, I activate the slew and rotate back to the hangar bay. It's exactly as I left it, except that the bomb is gone. Porter and Morton have slumped over, their bodies not yet claimed by rigor mortis.

When my emotions swell again, I choke them down, strangling them into submission. I can weep for the fallen when the enemy is defeated. It takes ten minutes to wrap the bodies in tarps. Then I rotate them, one at a time, to the freezer. Feels weird leaving them here. My instinct is to pull them out of the frigid air, but there's nothing I can do to ease their suffering or save their lives.

All that's left is vengeance.

I close the freezer and rotate back to the bridge, shifting as I go, so that when I appear, I'm seated in my chair.

"That's a new trick," Chuy says.

Rotating feels different now. I have a better sense of where I'm going. Where I'll wind up. And I'm pretty sure that has nothing to do with me and everything to do with the Europhids in my cranium. Unlike me, they have a perfect memory—of their experiences...and mine. Access to that lets me pinpoint where I'm going. If I've been there before. Or they have.

"Any contacts?" I ask.

"Not a one," Chuy says.

"Won't be long," I say.

Burnett swivels around. "What are we looking for?"

"Just the entire Union fleet," I say. "It'll be hard to miss."

"The entire..." He swivels forward, eyes wide. Looks at Hildy. "Holy shit."

"I know, right?" There's a flicker of a smile between them, which gives me hope for Burnett. Morton and Porter never had significant others, but they talked about it a lot. They had hope for the future. Burnett seemed happy to reserve his affection for an anime body pillow salvaged from Earth. Creeped the hell out of me, but maybe the pillow will become a thing of the past.

If we survive.

"Drago," I say. "How are things going down there?"

"Big Brick man says the Minutemen are ready when you are," he replies. "How are things up there?"

"Been better," I tell him, not wanting to repeat the news. "Ready to come back?"

"Da," he says, and I'm a little surprised. I thought his reunion with Adrik might trigger his departure from *Bitch'n*'s crew. That he's coming back means he is allied with us, and not his Soviet roots, no matter how much he pines for the good ol' Soviet days. And I'm glad for it. He's an irreplaceable pain in the dick. With Morton and Porter gone, Chuy's going to need him to operate *Bitch'n* when the shit hits the slew drive.

"Be right back," I say, and I rotate to the Minutemen subterranean hangar. Guided by the Europhids' knowledge of where every person on the planet is, I appear in what must be a flagship's bridge. It's a large space. Every station filled. There's a buzz in the air.

Drago is at the room's core, along with Brick, Will, Adrik, and BigApe.

I'm about to announce myself when Chuy's voice emerges from my comms. "Might want to make it snappy, pendejo. We got company." A moment later, an alarm blares.

It's time.

43

"Someone shut that damn alarm off," Brick shouts, and a moment later, the klaxon is silenced. "Now, has anyone heard from Dark Horse?"

"Is on way," Drago says, and then he sees me. Points. "Is here now."

Brick turns to me, his face a mixture of concern and determination. I've seen the same look on his face before dozens of missions. "Well, you got your wish. The entire Union fleet is here. The planet is surrounded, and rightly fucked. This all part of the grand plan?"

"Afraid so," I tell him. "I'm just the messenger, remember? You have a problem, you can take it up with the cucumbers."

His smile cuts the tension.

"I'd rather not."

"Are your people ready to rotate?" I ask.

He nods. "You're sure about this?"

"Hell, no. Everything about it is nutso."

"That's probably why it will work," he says.

"Wait for them to get boots on the ground. Like *all* the boots. Then rotate the hell out of here and do what needs doing."

He shakes his head. "An army of millions to attack a planet of billions."

"Most of them don't know how to do more than look at a computer screen. Get the job done and the fleet won't be able to find their way back. Then you can rotate away, safe in the knowledge that the Union will eat itself alive long before they find you again."

"Part of me wants to bomb them into oblivion," he admits. "But the more I think about it, the more I realize that the best revenge is to let them destroy themselves."

"Or not," I admit. "The new colonies might pull through. But they'll have to do it on their own, cut off from the Union's support, and knowledge. But they won't be a threat to you, or the Europhids. And you...-won't be a threat to them."

Brick's brow furrows. "How's that?"

"Final request from our friends, downstairs," I say. "When the Minutemen return to Earth, you need to erase your celestial data as well. You can keep the slews. The fleet. Use it to start over. Mine the solar system for resources. But leave the rest of the universe—and Europa—alone."

He thinks on it for a moment and nods. If he didn't mean it, the Europhids would know. I take their lack of reaction in my mind as confirmation that he's being sincere. "I don't like it, but I get it."

"Good," I say, and then I turn to Drago. "Time to go."

He nods and steps closer.

I turn to Will. "Keep your old man out of trouble. And thank you."

"For what?" Will asks.

"For doing the family proud. My parents would have liked you."

His smile is contagious. "Really?"

"Really." I offer my hand. He hugs me instead.

"Okay," I say, patting his back. "About to go to war. Let's try to keep it manly."

He laughs and steps back. Tears in his eyes. Definitely my kin. The military isn't fond of men who cry, but fuck that. Better than bottling it all up, cracking from the pressure, and committing some kind of atrocity.

When I turn back to Brick, he looks concerned. "This doesn't sound like 'See you later.'"

"It's not," I say. "Europhids have a different plan for me."

"You won't be fighting with us?" He's surprised.

"I will," I say. "Just not in the same place."

"The hell does that mean?" he asks.

"Means they told me not to say." I don't like keeping secrets from Brick. Doesn't feel right. But the Europhids have their reasons. There's no way to know how Brick would react to the truth, and its potential ramifications.

"Also means you won't be coming back," he points out.

"Probably not," I admit.

He sighs. "Can't say I'm going to miss those little assholes."

"They can hear you, you know," I say.

"Damn right, I know." He wraps me in his meaty arms, smacking my back with his oven-mitt-sized hand. "It was good to see you again, old friend."

"Same," I say, and then I turn to BigApe, who is still a fright. "Ape... I'd shake your hand, but..."

He laughs. Hard. Shaking Adrik's belly. After slowing down, he says. "No need. We're coming."

"You're coming? *With us?*" Drago asks Adrik, unable to conceal his excitement.

"Da," Adrik says. "We desire to stand alongside our old comrades again." Then to me he adds, "If you approve, of course."

Looks like I'm going to have to get used to BigApe's sorry condition after all. "As long as it's okay with—"

"I would never ask someone to be where they didn't want to be."

Brick shakes Adrik's hand. "Good luck. Both of you."

"Right then," I say, and I clear my throat, choking back my rising emotions. Never thought I'd have to leave Brick behind after finding him. Never thought a crew member would have a second face on his chest, either. "Time to go. Remember, *all* the boots on the ground. Then go."

I put an arm around Drago, and I tell Adrik to hold on. When we're huddled up, I say, "Chuy, incoming." And then to Brick, I say, "Proud of you."

"Likewise," he says, and then I rotate away before I become a blubbering mess.

We appear on *Bitch'n*'s bridge. Burnett spins around. "Sir, the Union fleet has arrived."

"I'm aware," I tell him, heading for my seat. Drago makes a beeline for his station. "You can take one of the empty seats," I tell Adrik and BigApe.

"But sir, they're..." His eyes drift to Adrik, and then his open shirt. "...coming...right... Oh my God, what the hell is that?!"

His high-pitched shout turns Hildy around. When she sees BigApe, her reaction is different. She smiles wide, excited to the core. "Holy Kuato! You have a face in your chest!"

"Name's BigApe," he says, not taking offense to Burnett's and Hildy's opposite reactions. "The guy whose body I'm fused to is Adrik."

"Privet," Adrik says, with a wave, sitting down in what once was Porter's spot. He notices my consternation. "Is okay to sit?"

I nod, and I force myself to move on. I turn to Hildy. "First. What the hell is Kuato?"

"Movie reference. *Total Recall.* Arnold Schwarzenegger movie. A year after your time. Kuato was a little baby dude fused to the body of a grown man, but with arms. Totally gnarly." To BigApe she says, "Sorry."

"Sweet," I say, "We'll watch it later." Then I turn to Chuy. "Give me a sitrep."

"As Burn was trying to tell you," she says, "before his testicles ascended, the Union fleet is here."

"Annnd?" I ask.

"They're headed our way."

"How many?"

"Ten ships," she says.

"And the rest?"

"Headed to the surface," Burnett says. "Looks like a mass invasion."

"Good," I say.

"How, exactly, is that good?" Hildy asks. "These guys are killers. Anyone down there doesn't stand a chance."

"Feigned weakness, and a whole lot of deception," I say. "Back in 1066 a guy named William the Conqueror invaded England. In what became known as the Battle of Hastings, old William feigned—"

"Dark Horse," Chuy says, interrupting my history lesson. "Bad guys incoming. ETA, one mike."

"Right. Sorry." I focus up. Not a lot of time. "Drago, Chuy, I need you here. Keep those ten ships busy. Blow them out of orbit if you can. But if things get dicey, use the slew and evade."

I slide my keyboard into place and start tapping keys. I'm normally a hunt-and-peck typist, but I'm not controlling my fingers at the moment. "Burnett, this was meant for Porter. I'm hoping you can fill his shoes."

"Oh... I don't know about that. He was the engineer. I just—"

"I am engineer," Adrik says.

"Ever worked on a slew drive?" I ask.

"All the time," he says.

"Okay, then, Burn and Adrik, I want you to make these changes to the slew..." I turn to Chuy, "preferably before you start bouncing around the planet." She nods, and I hit Enter, sending the information to Burn's and Adrik's consoles.

Adrik studies it for a moment. "I do not understand. What is this supposed to do?"

"Just get it done," I say. "It's time for me to go."

"Where the hell are *you* going?" Chuy asks.

"Back down," I say.

"Why?" Her stare demands my answer be good.

"To oversee the counterattack," I say. "And to make sure Whip and Carter don't survive."

I think she's about to argue against it, but she says, "Don't forget a gun this time."

I smile at her and say, "This time, I won't need one." Then I rotate back to the surface, not far from where I first encountered Whip and Carter. As predicted, a large number of Union vessels are coming my way. Leading the way is the *Zorak*.

The jungle rumbles as hundreds of Union ships touch down, toppling trees, chasing away wildlife, and destroying everything they touch. It's just a taste of what is to come if this all goes sideways.

A strange urge to attack roils inside me, but not *from* me.

"Not yet," I say, speaking to the red Europhids I can sense all around, coiling through the earth like roots.

WHY?

The question is primal. Agitated. Eager. And from a mind that is not my own. The red Europhids might be all instinct, but they're not unintelligent.

"If they're still in the ships, they can rotate away," I say. "If they do that, we're screwed. All of us. We're going to wait until it's impossible for them to retreat."

I take their silence as begrudging agreement.

Feels weird to be speaking to an alien species over whom I have authority because some of them are living in my brain.

"So," I say. "We can talk now, huh?"

No response.

"What's it like?" I ask. "Being immense...and small at the same time."

QUIET.

"C'mon," I say. "We're brothers-in-arms now. I'm just joshing. This is how humans bond before battle."

EXPLAIN.

"I've got your back. You've got mine. We're brothers-in-arms. Like family. At least during the battle. You can go back to hating everyone when we're done, but for now, I'm one of you, and you're one of us. Get it?"

WHEN THE BATTLE IS OVER, WE WILL CONSUME YOU.

Accompanying the statement is a twisting sense of impending doom, exploding from my mind and out through every cell of my body.

"What the fuck?" I say, horrified that I've misread the situation and the blue Europhids' influence over the reds. "I'm not sure you understand. I—"

JOSHING.

"What... Oh...ho...Wow." I start laughing. "Holy shit. That was good." My laughter stops. "But seriously, you're not going to consume me, right?"

There's a long pause. And then...

NO.

My relief is short-lived. The *Zorak* descends into the jungle just fifty yards away.

"It's go-time, Red," I say. "Can I call you Red?"

NAMES ARE IRRELEVANT.

"I'll take that as a 'yes,'" I say. "You understand what I want to do?"

IT IS...UNCONVENTIONAL.

"Unconventional as fuck," I say. "And that's the point. Just be ready."

I stand, shaded by the thick canopy above, and lit by the glowing blue blobs growing from earthen spires. There are ten of them here, each one emitting mind-bending pheromones to which I am now immune, thanks to the Europhids in my head.

"This supposed to be your Leonidas moment?" Whip asks, stepping into the clearing. "One man against an army. Though I suppose Chuy is out there somewhere."

"I'm the only person here," I tell him.

"What?" Whip says, holding a hand to his armored heart, feigning a wound. "You don't think of me as a person?"

"Not you," I say. "And not them." I nod to the soldiers stepping into the clearing behind Whip. Carter, whose lithe armor is recognizable, leads the pack, breaking away and joining Whip. Her masked head is on a swivel, no doubt looking for Chuy.

"What are we waiting for?" she asks. "Just kill him, and let's get on with it."

"Really?" he asks. "You think he's out here for shits and giggles? This is part of a plan."

"Yep," I say.

"Have you *seen* how many of us there are?" Whip asks.

"I see them all," I say. Best guess, the landing ships are about half empty now. Just need a few more minutes—long enough to cut off their retreat.

He cocks his head to the side, trying to figure me out.

THIS IS FOOLISH. ATTACK.

Wait, I think.

Red sounds a lot like Carter. Eager to fight, and overconfident.

"You know," he says, "in the grand scheme, none of your lives matter. You're standing in front of a tidal wave, and no amount of bitching, moaning, or sneaky plans are going to make a difference. By this time tomorrow, every single person on this planet will be erased."

"On that," I say, "we agree." Before he can make any sense of what I've said, I add, "I'll make you a deal. Fight me. One on one. You can keep your armor. Keep your whip. Just let me see your pretty face so I can punch it in."

"Single combat, huh? Two leaders determining the fate of their armies. I like it, but you know that even after I kick your ass, we're going to roll through here like—"

"They'll surrender," I say. "If you can take me down, the Undesirables will lay down their arms and come out."

"You know we'll still kill them, right?"

I shrug. "Quickly, though?"

"Sure," he says. "I can do that."

"I have one condition."

"Oh, yeah? What's that?" he asks.

"If you win...kill her." I point at Carter. "For Benny."

Carter raises her rifle, about to shoot me down. Before it comes all the way up, Whip catches it. "Now, now, let's hear the man out."

"We were family," I say. "You, me, Benny, Brick, and Chuy. And you let her carve out his head like a fucking melon. You've got the uncaring tough man act down, I'll give you that, but Benny's death has been eating you up. She did that to you. She killed your brother."

"He's trying to turn us against each other," Carter says. "Shut him the fuck up. Now."

"He ain't wrong," Whip says. "You did kill Benny."

NOW.

Red is getting insistent. The Union army has left the fleet, but they're still too close to ensure no one escapes. "Almost," I say, and I freeze.

I said it aloud.

Whip's face mask snaps up. He's got a shit-eating grin on his face. "Who you talking to, Dark Horse?"

I honestly don't know how to answer. I just need to keep him talking for another minute. "You want the truth?"

"I'd expect nothing more from a man of your integrity," he says, and then he chuckles.

"Okay, here's the deal. You all pissed off an ancient, alien intelligence, and now they want the Union gone. Best way to do that?" I point at myself. "This guy. I'm the reason we're here. The reason we were brought to the future. All of this was planned, right down to this exact moment, where I keep talking, and you keep breathing."

"What alien intelligence?" Carter asks, while Whip looks somewhat stunned, and amused. "We have found no evidence of—"

"They look like little red and blue cucumbers," I say. "Ring any bells?"

Her silence says that it does, but even then, who would believe that a field of glowing vegetables could be sentient?

"Stay away from those," Carter says, pointing at the spires, talking to the men framing up around the clearing.

"Oh, they have nothing to worry about," I say. "Whip, on the other hand...he's pretty well fucked."

At that, Whip busts up laughing. "Little Einstein cucumbers! Pff! Oh, wow! Oh, man. You are too much!" He's delirious. The pheromones are working their magic.

"Moron," Carter says, slapping the side of Whip's helmet, dropping the face shield back down.

NOW?

I smile. "Now."

Carter's head whips toward me, her weapon coming up, but she's too late.

The ground beneath us shakes, throwing her off balance. Her lazzer blast punches a hole in the tree canopy, allowing a beam of sunlight to slip through.

All around, armored Union soldiers shout in confusion. The land beneath them roils.

Carter finds her footing.

Takes aim again.

About to put a hole through my torso.

Earth explodes into the air. A wall of coiling red tendrils fills the space between us. I feel Red's pain as the lazzer blast intended for me strikes its body instead. But Red is a planet-sized organism. This world's immune system. The blast is less than a pinprick.

The tendrils split apart, revealing Carter. "Surprise," I say, as she stumbles. The ground beneath her rises several feet, lifting her up. I hold up an index finger. "First, fuck you. Second, fuck the Union. Third..." I smile at her. "Four!"

A tree sized red appendage snaps out of the ground, whooshes through the air, and strikes Carter's side, launching her up and away. She punches through the thick canopy a moment later, still climbing. I don't care how tough their armor is, no way she's surviving a fall from a mile up. I give her a wave as she disappears from view. "Adios, bitch."

DOWN!

What happens next catches me off guard, despite my connection to Red. A tendril wraps around my ankles and yanks me off my feet, just as a lazzer blast cuts through the air where I'd been standing.

"Thanks," I say.

WE HAVE YOUR BACK.

Can't help but smile. Red is a brute, but he/it/whatever gets it. We're in this together.

Whip is back on his feet. Cackling with laughter, but now it sounds maniacal.

I reach out with my thoughts, driving Red to act in the same way I did with Carter. A roar rips through the air, as a bus-sized Basil pounds through the forest, shredding Union soldiers as it plows toward Whip. The creature's mandibles snap shut, on target to crush Whip, but he's no longer there.

He rotated, I realize just a moment before he emerges from the fourth dimension behind me, wraps his arms around my torso and rotates the two of us away.

We appear ten feet over the solid stone cliff top above the Minutemen base. Whip positions me beneath him, manhandling me with his suit's robotic strength. Then we topple to the ground and collide like a wrecking ball in free fall.

Air coughs from my lungs. My body feels like a pressed panini. Stars swirl in my vision.

When Whip rolls off me and stands, all I can do is watch.

I can feel Red coming, twisting coils climbing the cliff face from below, stretching out of the jungle atop the cliff. But Red can't move through solid stone. For the moment, Whip is free to act.

He aims the lazzer rifle at my chest. "You had a good run, boss. Going out like a fighter. I respect that..." He laughs. The pheromones haven't worn off yet. "And Carter? Holy balls. That was awesome. *Pi-chuuuu.*" He looks up into the sky like he can see her again, toppling away. "Good on you. She had that coming."

His laugher fades. "What's up with your eyes?"

While I've been lying here, the Europhids inside me have been hard at work clearing my mind. Not sure what they're doing, but I feel pretty good. For the first five seconds, I was genuinely stunned. Since then, I've been faking it.

"You know what?" he says, sounding more like himself and less drugged. "Fuck it."

I trigger my PSD and rotate away, just as he fires. The lazzer blast grazes my shoulder blade. Pain lances from the cauterized wound, but quickly fades. The Europhids aren't healing me, they're dulling the pain receptors in my mind.

Going to suck when they stop, I think, and I rotate back out, in the air behind Whip.

I land on his back, hands wrapped under his chin. I throw my weight back, catching him off guard and stumbling him back toward the cliff. When we careen over the edge together, his rifle falls away. I push off his back and activate my PSD. A moment later, I return to the cliff's edge.

Peering over the edge, I watch Whip pinwheel toward the ground, gaining speed.

Then he disappears into the fourth dimension.

Shit.

I scan the area. *Where the hell is he?*

WE CANNOT SEE HIM.

"I was asking myself."

WE DON'T CARE.

During the momentary reprieve, my senses reach beyond myself, experiencing the battle around the planet. What started as pinpricks have evolved into serious, very painful wounds. The Union is armed with lazzers, energy weapons, rocket pods, and flame throwers. All around the planet, Red is coming apart, oozing its insides into the Earth. Hundreds of Basils are dead.

But the beatdown Red is receiving pales in comparison to the counterattack. Armor be damned, Red strikes with shocking savagery, crushing men, rending them into pieces, and in some cases, invading their minds and turning them against each other. It's a kind of determined savagery that Blue is incapable of, but exactly the right kind for taking down a bunch of Nazis. The Russians did the same during World War II, sacrificing untold numbers in defense of the Mother Land. Red is doing the same for this planet...and all the others that Europhids call home. It frightens me, but I'm also glad to be fighting alongside them.

My hope is that our alliance will last when the war is won. That we won't enter into a kind of Cold War hostility...partly because I'd be the first casualty.

Motion in my vertical periphery throws my body into motion. I dive and roll to the side, just as Whip crashes down, using all the momentum from his hundred-foot fall to pound the ground where I had been standing.

Solid stone cracks.

If I hadn't moved...

How did *I move so fast?*

OUR SENSES ARE YOUR SENSES. YOU ARE FASTER BECAUSE—

"You going to take credit for everything I do?"

YES.

Can't help but laugh. Not sure if the Europhids have a sense of humor, or if they're just being bluntly honest. Either way, it's funny.

"What're you laughing at?" Whip asks.

The cracked cliff behind him crumbles and falls away. He looks back at it. "Not so funny now, eh?"

Rocket pods in his shoulders and sides, and even under his ribs, snap out. Dozens of projectiles fire, spiraling through the air, forcing me back into the fourth dimension.

Exactly where Whip wanted me.

He rotates in unison, closing the distance between us in a blink.

He punches my chest, throwing me back.

I fall.

Ribs broken. Lungs empty.

I don't know where to go, I think. Rotating now would most likely drop me in space, or worse, inside a star or a black hole. I'm cut off from Red here, so I relinquish control of my body and let Blue guide me. The Europhids are no stranger to Slew technology, and they have a good portion of the known universe mapped. It's like having my very own predictor in my head.

Lost in a sea of white, Whip pounding toward me, I trigger the PSD and rotate back to the third dimension.

I fall several feet, land on my stomach, and I'm surprised when the impact is soft. And wet. I press my hands down, attempting to push myself up, when I notice water seeping up around my fingers and the purple earth compressing beneath my weight.

I know this place...

I've been here before.

And it's not Beta-Prime.

It's—

STAY DOWN.

The voice in my head is different. Where Red is more like a Klingon, Blue has more of a Vulcan vibe. The lack of emotion makes Blue easier to trust. But will the logic-driven mind be as good in combat as Red?

Whip appears twenty feet away. Takes in the purple-hued, puddle-pocked landscape. His heavy armor sinks his feet into the spongy ground. He lifts one foot at a time.

"This like a greatest hits tour?" he asks, revealing that the Union really was tracking my every move. "Ain't nothing here that—"

The sound of wet flatulence announces the puddle-jumper a moment before it collides with Whip's back.

Thin tendrils snap out of its maw and wrap around Whip's face-mask. Its mouth opens wide, consumes his head, and starts grinding on the metal.

The naked, winged sloth grasps Whip's arms, fighting against his robotic strength. When the pair spin around, grunting and struggling, a detail jumps out. Something I missed last time, or maybe something that simply wasn't present on the creatures I encountered—a spine of small red Europhids running down its back.

Red!

HAVE YOUR BACK. STILL.

As dangerous as a Europhid-controlled puddle jumper might be, no way it's chewing through that armor. But it's bought me a little time.

Blue, I think. *We need to disable his slew drive.*

UNDERSTOOD, Blue responds.

Then my mind is filled with views of Whip from the past few minutes. I see his every move in slow motion. I can move in and out of focus. I watch his body the moment before he rotates. While I need to smack the device on my hip to rotate, Whip's PSD has been integrated into his armor. But he still needs to activate it somehow.

There! I think, focusing on his left hand. He squeezes his fist twice before rotating. *That's the key. We need to disable his left hand!*

AGREED.

A second puddle-jumper surges out of a nearby pool, catching both me and Whip off guard. It careens into his metal gut, holding and clawing. But it's still not enough. The mechanized armor is too strong.

That's when I see three more puddle-jumpers incoming, arms spread wide, stretched skin warbling in the wind. I stand by my original assessment of these things. They're freakish spazzes, but at least they're on my side now.

Just as it appears Whip will get the upper hand, three new puddle-jumpers join the fray, colliding with him en masse. All six of them fall to the spongy ground, sinking in, as water flows around them, forming a new pool.

It's hard to tell what's going on under the water. There's a lot of thrashing, the occasional fart-roar, and a whole lot of froth.

A puddle-jumper explodes from the water. Its arms don't open. It doesn't glide. It just crashes down to the ground and slides to a stop. There's a fist-sized indentation in its forehead.

They can't win.

NO.

"I need to help them," I say, trying to think of how, but jumping into that mess of claws and machine would be like dropping a Gremlin into a meat grinder.

WAIT.

"For what?!" I can feel the puddle-jumpers' pain through my connection to Red.

Whip is slowly dismantling them.

A plan unfurls in my mind. It's simple, bold, and absolutely insane. I like it.

Froth explodes as Whip launches out of the water, landing on the pool's far side. His armor is scratched up and dented, but is it enough?

Four injured and bleeding puddle-jumpers burst from the pool, charging Whip. I sense that the fight is over, but Red is incensed, lost in bloodlust.

"That's *it!*" Whip shouts. He grasps the whip on his side, snaps it out. It crackles to life, sweeping through the air with an electric snap.

The puddle-jumpers are undeterred—

—until the whip cracks and slides through their bodies, one at a time, severing them in two and ending their lives. I flinch back, feeling their lives end.

Whip catches his breath. Motions to the dead with his free hand. "That's what you've got? That's your big fuckin' play? I'm disappointed, boss. I thought you'd do better than that."

"Just getting warmed up," I say.

Whip senses the puddle-jumper gliding toward his back a moment before it hits.

His fist squeezes twice.

Nothing happens.

He looks down in time to see that his armored left hand is a mess, the armor shredded, the trigger for his slew drive, decimated. "Aww, fu—"

The puddle-jumper collides with Whip's back like a linebacker, knocking him on his face. The impact with the ground is soft, but face down is exactly where I want him.

When the puddle-jumper is clear, I rotate into the air above Whip and drop down on him. With one arm wrapped around his metal throat, I rotate away, leaving the wet ground, the puddle-jumpers, and the sponge world behind.

We rotate out of the fourth dimension, appearing a mile up in the atmosphere of a different world. A wall of white gives way to blue sky as we plummet out of a cloud and descend toward the massive jungle below. The air is cold. It's hard to breathe. But with some help from the voice in my head, I stay on task.

"Only one of us can survive this fall," Whip says, grasping my arm with his hand, ensuring that I can't rotate away without him.

"That's the point," I tell him. "But first, I have a friend I want you to meet. You remember this world, right? It's where you planted Carter and sent me to find her. But it's also home to—"

A massive turtle head pokes out of the forest below, red eyes locked onto our tumbling bodies, mouth opening wide.

Whip sees Beatrice rising up to greet us—and screams.

Whip stops fighting. Instead, he's clenching his fist over and over, trying to activate his slew drive.

"Moses," he shouts. "Don't! Please!"

The terror in his voice—something I've never heard before—hurts my soul.

"I don't want to die like this!"

"A life of killing will eventually get you killed," I tell him. We're twenty seconds out from being consumed. "You knew that when you signed up for the Marines. You knew that when you joined the Fourth Reich, and when you decided it was okay to commit genocide against people whose only difference from you is skin tone. I'm sorry, but this was the death you chose."

His face mask snaps up. He looks me in the eyes. The panic is gone, replaced by hate. "I never liked you, you god-damned n—"

Beatrice's jaws snap shut, clamping down on Whip's armored body and cleaving straight through it. Whip's scream of pain is short-lived, not because he won't survive long enough to be swallowed, but because I've rotated back out.

I appear two miles away, standing on the branch of a six-hundred-foot-tall tree. Beatrice swallows while Whip's torso tumbles to the ground. Then I see what I'm looking for. Beatrice's red eyes. Easy to over-look before, but now...

The Europhids call this planet home, too.

Beatrice roars, victorious. The sound bends trees and moves through my every cell. For a moment it feels like I'll come apart.

Then, she stops.

She turns her massive head toward me.

Is that a look of concern?

Worry swirls through me.

"What's happening?"

YOUR VISION OF THE FUTURE.

I'd nearly forgotten the vision I'd had upon being whisked to the future. The details are like a dream. I remember a walkway. A space-suit. A massive vessel of some kind. Destroyed. Bodies everywhere. And a planet.

A black planet. Back then, I didn't recognize it, but now...

Union Command...

A final detail snaps into place. A red X on the spacesuit's chest. The Minutemen's symbol.

IT WAS NOT A VISION OF YOUR FUTURE.

"Brick," I say.

IT HAS NOT YET COME TO PASS.

THERE IS STILL TIME.

"Where's Chuy?" I ask.

The Blue inside me doesn't answer with words, just a feeling. I can sense that they're in orbit around Beta Prime, on the run with ten ships in pursuit. I can also sense that the Union army on the surface is almost completely wiped out. Red took a lot of damage. Will take years to heal. But the subterranean colonies made it through untouched.

Back to the *Bitch'n.*

It's moving at a ridiculous speed, taking and returning fire, and twisting with evasive maneuvers that a Lincoln Log-shaped vessel could only pull off in the vacuum of space.

She's not an easy target. Without the Europhids' help, I could try a hundred times and not make it inside.

But with the Europhids...

I give myself a moment to process—squelch really—my feelings of regret regarding Whip. Then I rotate off world, slip through the fourth dimension, and rotate back out—

—on *Bitch'n*'s bridge, sitting down at my station.

"Swing us around!" I command.

"Yobanaya blyad!" Drago shouts in surprise.

Despite Drago's shock at my return, Chuy goes with the flow, following my order so that we're facing the enemy.

"Drago!" He snaps to attention. "Whip and Carter are done. The ground forces are KIA. These assholes are all that's left."

"Okay..." Drago says.

I motion to the windshield, through which I can see ten vessels incoming, "Kill them all."

"Da!" he says. We've been holding back. Keeping these ships occupied and distracted from what was happening below, and back home. Now...they can go to hell with the rest.

Our eight railguns fire in unison.

Tungsten rods rocket out faster than any ship could avoid, even with a slew drive. They move faster than human thought. The moment Drago fires, eight projectiles slip through the front and punch through the back, leaving massive exit wounds. Debris and crew are launched into space.

The two remaining ships turn tail in a panic.

If their slew drives functioned like ours, they'd no doubt have rotated the hell out of here. All they've managed to do is give Drago an easier target. He fires just two more rounds, each of them finding its target and finishing the Battle of Beta-Prime.

"Burn," I say, activating my comms. "Where you at?"

"Engine room," he replies.

Hand to my head. "I didn't mean physically. I meant where are you at with the slew drive? We need to go. *Now.*"

"Adrik says one more minute. Also, that whatever this change is supposed to do might also kill us."

"Awesome," I say, oozing sarcasm I know Burnett won't understand. "Let me know when we're good to go. Out."

I look back at Chuy. "Take any damage?"

Hildy swivels around. "Scoring on the hull from twenty-two lazzer blasts. A small puncture in the outer hull from shrapnel, and a dent or two in the front end from where someone—" She gives Drago a stare. "—crashed into another ship."

"They play chicken with Spetnaz." Drago shrugs. "They lose at chicken."

"That's a fair point," I say. Never play chicken with a man whose training involved breaking concrete with his forehead and being beaten by two-by-fours. "But we're good for a fight?"

"There's no one left to fight," Chuy says.

"Not here," I say. "Brick needs our help."

"Da," Drago says. "We have ten less rail projectiles, but still ninety-two more. Plus rockets. And bullets. And lazzer cannons on *Lil' Bitch'n.* Enough to secure victory."

That has yet to be determined. I have no idea what we'll find at Union Command. But I appreciate his confidence. "Drago, if I haven't said it before...I'm glad you're here."

He smiles at me. Genuine. For just a moment. Then he says, "Stop molesting me with eyes. Fucking creep."

"Fuck you too, buddy," I say with a chuckle.

Hildy spins around, facing the rest of us. "Fuck all of you guys!"

We just stare at her.

"That's like a macho way of expressing affection, right?" Hildy asks. "You fucking assholes..." She grows nervous and a little less confident. "Right?"

I raise my middle finger and hold it out at her.

Chuy does the same.

And then Drago.

Hildy glows. Gasps for joy. "You're 'fuck you'-ing me! Yes! I'm so in!" She spins forward, ready to work.

"Dark Horse." It's Burnett on the comms. "Adrik says that we're as ready as we're ever going to be. To activate the new function you—"

"I know how to do it," I say. The information is locked in the part of my mind that isn't my mind.

"He also says it will only work once," Burnett says.

"Once is all we need," I say. "Ask Adrik if he can pilot a starship."

A moment later, he replies. "Yes. Why?"

"I need both of you...sorry, all three of you, to get to *Lil' Bitch'n*, ready to fight. And I want you, Burn, at the guns."

"Seriously?" He's excited, and nervous.

"Never been more serious. You up to it?"

"You know I am," he says.

"Yeah," I say, feeling proud. "I do. Out."

"Taking control," I say to Chuy. "For the rotation. On the far end, she's all yours."

"You going to disappear again?" she asks.

"You know me," I say with a shrug. "But I always come back."

"You better," she says.

I turn my attention to the ship's controls, prepping the slew.

"Wait!' Hildy says, working the keys on her console. She taps a final button and a fast beat begins tapping out.

I recognize it instantly.

Bonnie Tyler.

Holding Out for a Hero.

Fuck, yes.

Hildy flips me off with a smile. I give it back to her and then get back to work.

Our target is distant, and full of obstacles. Union ships. Minutemen ships. Debris from both. But if I can park my ass in this chair while the ship is in combat, I should be able to...

Rotate the ship into the fourth dimension...

Slide through the empty white void...

And emerge...

Bitch'n rotates into orbit above Union Command, just as Bonnie Tyler belts out the first 'I need a hero!'

...into a shitshow of epic proportions.

Space is normally empty. Short of an asteroid field or a planetary ring system, we don't think about collisions very often. But there are ships and debris everywhere.

A body slaps against the windshield. His face is frozen in eternal surprise, his uniform Union. That's a relief, but there are several Minutemen ships in the process of silently exploding.

The Union sent a massive fleet to Beta-Prime, but that was just part of the whole. And they're making short work of the Minutemen ships too big to land on the planet.

"Chuy, take us in!" I shout. "Drago, light them up!"

Bitch'n launches into the fray, plowing through debris like the spacefaring tank she is. Explosions fill the space in front of us as railgun projectiles, rockets, and tungsten bullets fire in every direction. Some of it is automated, the targeting computer locking on to Union ships, but Drago has control of the Phalanx chain guns, gritting his teeth as he twitches the controls back and forth. A smile slowly spreads as he unleashes Mother Russia's dormant fury.

"Look out!" Hildy shouts, pointing at a damaged Union ship spiraling toward us.

It would be easy to avoid, but Chuy does the opposite. She steers *Bitch'n*'s hard-as-fuck front end directly into the much smaller craft. It explodes against our hull, shaking us up a bit, but nothing more.

Might be a few dents to work out, but the scars will help make this turd-shaped ship look a little cooler.

"Great," Hildy whispers, shaking her head. "Now *she's* crashing into ships."

"Connect me to the flagship," I say to Hildy, watching the big Minutemen vessel as we approach. I rotated onboard the ship, but never saw it from the outside. Like *Bitch'n*, it's got an old-school Navy-vessel vibe, but it's more like a battleship. And it's massive. The crew must be in the hundreds of thousands. And it's currently unleashing hell on the Union, but also taking a beating. The Union ships might be individually small, and not very tough, but they're everywhere. And fast.

They also fly in formation.

"Drago, adjust the railgun parameters. Target formations. I want multiple kills with each projectile."

He releases the Phalanx controls and stops the rail system. Takes him just a few seconds to make the change and activate the system again. The projectiles fire far less quickly, but when they do...

A string of eight Union ships are turned inside out by a single shot, the projectile's momentum carrying it through the vessels like they were marshmallow fluff. Problem is, they're quickly replaced by a dozen more. We'll put a dent in them, but a straightforward fight is unwinnable.

This is where it happens. My vision. The bodies. The destruction. That will be Brick's future if we don't change it, here and now.

"We're on with the flagship," Hildy says.

"Brick, you copy?" I ask.

"Dark Horse," he replies, sounding cool, despite the situation. "Glad to hear your voice. How did things go with our friends?"

I'm not sure if he's talking about Whip and Carter or the Europhids. But the answer is the same. "Beta-Prime is clear. Justice has been served. For Benny, and for Sara."

"Glad to hear it. Could use some help," he says. "If you're not bugging out."

"Bugging out?" I say. "Bitch, I'm just getting warmed up."

He chuckles. "Good. And as long as you're here..."

Shit.

I forgot about this part.

"...you're in charge."

Being in charge of millions of people takes a toll. Probably why most U.S. presidents with an ounce of empathy go gray in their first term. Every decision, especially in war, costs lives. Even if the battle is won. It's a horrible responsibility, but if what the Europhids showed me is true, this is just the beginning. "Gimme a sitrep."

"Assault on the surface is underway, but there is heavy resistance. We might not be able to breach the central data core."

Hildy perks up. "If they don't destroy the core, all of this will just slow them down."

"For how long?" I ask.

"A week. Maybe."

"As for the fight up here, you can see it for yourself. Their planetary defenses are...impressive. Best guess, we've got five minutes until our in-orbit fleet is FUBAR. Less, if word gets out before the data is destroyed and reinforcements arrive."

"I just need you to keep on keeping on," I tell him. "*Bitch'n* is going to back you up. If things go sideways, rotate out."

"Not leaving until the job is done," he says.

I expected nothing less, but I had to try.

"Pull your people back from the core. Focus on the data centers. I'll handle the core."

"Copy that," he says. "Godspeed."

"See you on the other side. Out."

"Burn," I say, activating my personal comms, "did Porter have prototypes for the PSD?"

He responds a moment later.

"I think he had more than just prototypes."

"There are other working models?" I ask, surprised.

"He thought it wise, given your proclivity to...break things."

I smile.

Sounds like Porter. Also explains how Whip was able to get one from him so quickly. No idea if Porter gave him more than one, but right now, that doesn't matter.

"Just sitting down in *Lil' Bitch'n*. One second." There's a five second pause as Burnett accesses the system. "Storage unit, P-0115. Should be one in there."

"Copy that," I say, and I rotate from the bridge to Porter's personal storage room. It's a massive space that looks more like a futuristic bank vault full of safe deposit boxes. I scan the numbers, quickly find 0115, and pull it open. Inside are...holy shit...a dozen PSDs, just like mine. Burn wasn't kidding.

I'm tempted to take one for everyone, but they need to be trained first. Rotating between dimensions outside of a ship is dangerous. For now, they're stuck being ferried by me.

With one PSD in hand, I rotate to the armory, grab a rifle and a handgun, and then rotate back to the bridge.

To Chuy I say, "Stay mobile. Give the railguns good angles."

She nods. Stays focused on her job. I don't need to tell Drago what to do. He's already doing it.

"Burn, you boys ready to launch?" I ask.

"Opening bay door now," he says.

"*Bitch'n* is going to be hopping around, fucking shit up. You boys might be on your own for a bit. Don't hold back. Push the weapons system to the limit, and if the guns burn out, call Chuy for a pick-up."

I glance back at Chuy. She nods, letting me know she heard.

"Hildy," I say.

She spins around, eager to help.

I toss the handgun to her. She catches it, eyes slowly widening as she looks it over. "You're with me."

She leaps to her feet. "You need me to find the core?"

"Actually," I say, "I just need you to shoot some people."

Thanks to Minutemen sympathizers and spies, the Europhid knowledge of the Union Command is extensive. I already know where we're going.

Hildy's enthusiasm falters.

"You okay with that?"

She chambers a round, gives me a squinty glare, and says, "Yippee ki yay, motherfucker."

Drago bursts out laughing. "Is *Die Hard*, yes?"

"Da," Hildy says.

"Okay, Bruce Willis." I hold out my arm to Hildy. "Time to go."

She steps into my grasp. I take one last look at Chuy, who is too focused to notice. Then I rotate into the fourth dimension and...

...into the data core.

The space is a vast orb, hundreds of feet high. At the center is a black sphere, attached to the curved ceiling and the floor. The space is toasty and smells like warm electronics.

I twist toward the sound of shouting voices. Overseers guard a doorway, weapons aimed out.

"They're falling back!" one of them shouts, confirming that Brick's people are withdrawing.

The Overseers begin to pursue, but as they're leaving, a stocky woman sees me and Hildy, and she double-takes.

"Gonna need some cover," I say, taking out the second PSD and cracking it open. "Just point and—"

"I've played video games," Hildy says.

"Using a gun is *not* like a video game," I say. I fail to see how a side-scrolling inch-high character can prepare someone to wield a weapon of war.

"They're inside the core!" the stocky woman shouts. She storms toward us, as three more Overseers stream in behind her. None of that is good, but none of them are visibly pregnant—and that is.

Hildy unleashes six rounds, each of them a hit. All four women fall to the floor. The first two might be dead. The second two are clutching their legs.

"Okay," I say. "Maybe it *is* like video games."

"VR games, beyond your time," Hildy says. "Now, hurry up! I might be good at this, but I don't like it!"

Just as I turn my attention back to the PSD, a searing pain cuts through my thigh and drops me to the floor. The PSD falls from my hand and skitters away. I reach for it, but I pull my hand back when a lazzer blast strikes the floor between my outstretched fingers and the device.

Three more Overseers stalk toward us, weapons raised. Behind them, a small army of grumpy looking ladies swarms into the core. I think they understand what's at stake, and they look ready to do anything to stop us.

Hildy has her weapon raised, but she isn't pulling the trigger. "I don't think I have enough bullets."

"No," I say, grimly. "You don't."

48

This is gonna get messy.

And I'm not opposed to mess. Sometimes, as a soldier, a little John Rambo behind-the-machine-gun action is called for. The gun feels good in your hands. The power makes you feel like a man. But if you watch the effect it has... The destruction, the blood, and the pain...

It leaves a scar.

And Hildy is about to get her first taste of that if she can stomach it.

We duck behind a control console on the inside of the large, circular catwalk that's surrounding the sphere. Lazzer blasts scorch the far side.

Luckily, the Overseers are proceeding slow and carefully, waiting for us to expose ourselves rather than trying to rush us at the expense of their own lives.

Gives me a few seconds.

"Take this." I hold my rifle up to Hildy.

She looks unsure, but after a lazzer blast burns a trough in her hair, she takes the weapon. A *Spaceballs* quote flits through my mind, but I don't bother saying it.

"Works same as the gun," I say.

"I know how it works," she grumbles. "Point and pull the trigger."

"This has two triggers," I tell her.

She looks at it, and she's confused.

"Well, what's the second one do?" The Overseers are nearly upon us. Time is running out.

"Grenade launcher," I say. "Three rounds. Just aim it at the floor, near your targets. The shrapnel and shockwave will do the rest."

"Shrapnel?"

I can see her imagination hard at work, giving her a taste of just how horrible it will be.

"But they could be pregnant."

"I don't think so," I say, glancing at the nearest Overseers. Not a baby-bump among them. The Overseers might be fond of pumping out new bodies for the Reich, but those guarding the core are lean, mean, non-pregger fighting machines. "If this works, none of them are going to survive anyway, but millions more will live." I focus on the PSD, still out of reach. If one of the Overseers hits it with a lazzer blast, our mission is—

Sparks explode from the PSD. My eyes snap shut. When I open them again, the device is gone. The grated floor where it was is now charred.

Fuck, I think.

"Fuck!" Hildy shouts. "Now what?"

"Same plan," I say, plucking the PSD from my belt.

"But we won't be able to rotate... Oh. You already know that." Sadness washes over her, and I feel it, too. She's young and recently freed. Had a whole new and exciting life ahead. I had a mission. One I believed in. One I would have died for, but I never thought it would be now. I still had so much to do.

Sorry, I think to the Europhids in my head.

No reply.

No intuited feelings.

They're just silently observing.

"What's this called?" Hildy asks. "Doing something you know will get you killed?"

"A noble death," I say.

"A suicide mission," she says.

"That, too. But I like mine better."

She nods. "Noble death it is."

A lazzer blast strikes the console, just missing her. She ducks down a little further. "Thank you for it. Better to die like this than at a hundred and fifty after a lifetime of breathing this shit air, staring at screens, telling ships where to go, and pumping out babies for someone I don't love."

"You'd have made a hell of a Marine," I tell her.

She smiles. "A Space Marine? Like Vasquez? From *Aliens?*"

"I know who Vasquez is," I say. "But not quite. That's Chuy's job."

"Then Ripley? Can I be Ripley?"

"More like Newt," I say.

"I'll take it."

"But you can be Ripley if you go to town with that rifle and buy me the time we need. Like, now."

"Deal," she says. Then she stands, levels the rifle toward the Overseers, and holds down the first trigger.

The Overseers, who no doubt thought we were done for, are caught off guard, and then overwhelmed by Hildy's barrage of tungsten rounds.

"Let's rock!" Hildy shouts, still angling for the role of Vasquez.

My instinct is to watch the battle play out. To give advice. To take part. But for the first time, I need to be the brains behind the scenes.

I don't like it, my inner bitch says.

Shut up and get the job done, my Marine self says, backhanding the other voice into submission.

I crack open the PSD and get to work. I've seen the inside of a PSD just twice. Porter felt the need to explain how it worked, and how to change the settings. I mostly tuned him out, but the Europhids have access to the memory and everything Porter showed me. As I focus, I feel my control slip away. My fingers are moving, but I'm not moving them.

I take the opportunity to say goodbye. "Chuy, give me a sitrep."

"Kicking ass and taking names," she says. "Why are you— What's wrong?"

"Things are going sideways down here." The words hurt coming out. "Don't think I'll be coming back this time."

"Are you hurt?" She sounds worried. Not like herself.

"Well, I'm shot. Again. But that's not what's stopping me."

"Then what the hell is?!" Sadness morphs to anger.

"The second PSD was destroyed. We're stuck here."

"Get out on foot," she demands.

"No can do. We're pinned by a small army of angry ladies."

"You can't just—"

"Chuy…" I don't know what to say. "I know that we were supposed to have a future together. That our children and their children are destined to fight this war for a thousand years. I started looking forward to that life. I mean, don't get me wrong, it's still weird. That's a paradigm I'm not sure either of us considered before. But it sounds like it worked, and I wanted to give it a shot. What I'm trying to say is…"

Her letting me get through a meaty slab of dialogue like that, without interrupting, is odd. "Chuy?"

No response.

"*Chuy?* You copy?"

Did she cut our connection? Is she pissed at me for dying? Blind-sided by what I said? "Chuy?"

I'm dragged out of my thoughts by two things. One, the Europhids are done. The PSD is in my hands, reassembled. Two, Hildy shouting, "Fire in the hole!" followed by the *poonch* sound of a grenade being launched.

Arms to my head, I duck down just as the round detonates. The explosion feels like a nail, driven into my ear. The shockwave shakes the platform. The chaos is followed by shouts of pain.

I lean to the side, and I look back. There are several Overseers on the floor. Some dead. Some on their way. But what I linger on is the platform itself. The grenade tore it up. Created a hole.

I pocket the PSD and grab hold of the console, hauling myself up. Leg hurts like a motherfucker, but I'm about to die. I can handle the pain.

I hold a hand out to Hildy. She gives me the weapon, happy to be rid of it. I chamber a fresh grenade, take aim and fire. As the grenade detonates, I load the last round and fire. When the smoke clears, the platform is in ruins. On the near side, the dead and dying, on the far side, a mob of very angry Overseers who can shoot all the lazzers they want, but they won't be able to hit us behind the console.

A handful of them—the fast ones I'm guessing—sprint in the opposite direction. They look like black-clad Olympic runners, rounding a track. Their weirdly perfect posture, long strides, and speedy limbs carry them around quickly, but it will take a good minute to reach us.

And by then...

I slide down against the console. Hildy is beside me.

"Glad to have met you, kid," I say. "If I was going to have a daughter, I'd want her to be like you."

She smiles at me, tears in her eyes. "If I ever got to meet my father, I'd want him to be like you."

I put my arm around her, and she leans the pom-pom hair against my shoulder. I hold the PSD out, activate it, and toss it into the air. It tumbles away, out over the open space between us and the black sphere.

Then it disappears.

A moment later, it reappears, its momentum ceased.

It flicks out of reality again, reappearing for just a moment before disappearing again. It rotates in and out of the fourth dimension at a faster and faster rate, building speed, racing toward an unknown limit, where it will unleash a devastating explosion of unknown force.

The device starts to glow.

A hum fills the air.

The sprinting Overseers arrive faster than I would have guessed. I tense, waiting for them to blast us into steaming piles of meat. But they see the shimmering PSD hovering in the air and wisely choose to bug out. I don't think it will matter, but it gives me a few more seconds to—

"Moses!"

What the hell? That's Chuy.

I push myself up, but don't see her. She must be on the sphere's far side.

"Chuy?" I shout. "We're on the other side!"

A shout of surprise tears through the air above us. Chuy falls ten feet to the floor. Coughs for air and holds out her hand. She's carrying one of the other PSDs. "How the hell do you use this thing so well?"

I blink in shock, watching her push herself up.

"Don't just stand there, pendejo!" she shouts.

I snap out of my surprise, grasp Hildy by the waist, and step in to Chuy, so she can wrap her arms around me.

The floating PSD's hum shifts to a high-pitched whistle. The light glows brighter, but it's flickering now.

I trigger the PSD and rotate away.

We emerge a moment later, in my quarters. *Bitch'n* is moving fast. There are ships and debris everywhere. The space battle is still underway, but the planet below is still visible.

And the explosion...

It's impossible to miss. A white-hot sphere billows from the surface, growing and shifting to yellow and orange. The fireball expands for ten miles. A visible shockwave expands in every direction, scouring the surface clean.

The cost in lives will be enormous, and I'll have to live with that. Knowing the universe is free from the Union will make it a little easier. Nothing about war is good, but now maybe the future can be.

"Drago," I say, activating my comms. "Let Brick know that the core has been destroyed."

"I think he knows," Drago says. "Minutemen forces already rotating away. Union vessels seem...confused."

"Where is Burnett?" I ask. "We need to—"

"Already here. Took damage. Had to come back. But all okay."

"Awesome," I say, slowly absorbing the fact that we not only won, but also survived. "Good. Rotate away with the Minutemen."

"Would if we could," he says. "But we took damage, too. Power is failing. Slew drive is primed for one jump."

One jump. Those two words carry a lot of weight. Feels wrong to bail in the wake of a successful mission. To not say goodbye again.

But this is the mission, too.

The real mission.

And there is nothing to say that hasn't already been said.

"Everyone," I say, letting me broadcast to the whole crew. "I need you all on the bridge, seated and buckled, ASAP. Let's move, people!"

"You okay?" Chuy asks, giving me a 'What's up with you?' stare.

I hold my arms out to the pair of women. "Could just be a bumpy ride, is all."

They step into my grasp and the three of us rotate to the bridge. Burnett, Drago, Adrik, and by extension, BigApe, are seated and buckled.

Burnett smiles at me. "We were already here."

"Go," I say to Chuy and Hildy, nudging them to their stations. As I sit in my chair and buckle up, I ask, "You're all in this fight for the long haul, right? No matter where it takes us, or what the risks are?"

The group collectively turns toward me like I've asked them all if they prefer their thongs made from spider silk or bologna.

"Just fuckin' punch it!" Hildy shouts.

So, I do.

The rotation starts like any other, slipping into white. But the moment that happens, I'm overwhelmed. The changes to the slew drive are too much. The distances involved. The fucking math. It's more than I can handle on the fly.

So, I relent and give my blue brain control.

And things don't get much better.

A typical rotation feels odd. It can be nauseating for the uninitiated. But it's never painful.

This…this feels like I'm being stabbed to death by a thousand maniacal Smurfs.

Through the pain, an overwhelming, almost crushing gravity pulls me down. An elevator in free fall. I scream, but I'm moving faster than the soundwaves. My voice is silenced. My vision is white. My body ceases to exist. Reality is coming apart.

This can't be right.

Something's gone wrong.

I become immaterial. The seatbelt's pressure slips away. Nothing of *Bitch'n* remains. And my crew… Lost in a sea of white or destroyed.

Pressure builds around my head, crushing out another silent scream until—

I wake up on the floor. I'm still in *Bitch'n*. Still on the bridge. But I've slipped out of my chair despite the buckle being fastened.

The important thing is that we're no longer in the fourth dimension, or whatever the hell dimension that was. I push myself up to my hands and knees. My head feels like a dingleberry wedged between Andre the Giant's ass cheeks. The room spins.

I take a deep breath. Then another.

Little help, I think to the blue in my brain, and then I open my eyes again. The pressure remains, but the spinning has stopped. I glance through the windshield. Outside—stars. No debris. No Union ships. We're clear.

The question is—

Did we make it?

"Chuy?" I pull myself up, using my seat to hold my weight. "You okay?"

"Ugh..." comes the response, but it's not in the room. It's in my comms. "I'm in a closet, I think."

"On board *Bitch'n*?"

"Well," she says. "I'm staring into the crossed eyes of an anime babe with baseball tits, pink braids, her tongue out, and stains I don't want to know about."

Burnett's closet. Gross. "Get back to the bridge as soon as you can walk."

"Already on my way," she says, proving once again that she's tougher than me.

Back in my seat, I scan the bridge. Burnett and Hildy are still seated. Drago is on the floor and starting to stir. Like me, his body somehow slipped through the seatbelt. Adrik is on the floor, too, mostly out of view. All I can see are his feet...

Four of them. And two are bare.

The fuck?

I stand, unsteady, but I really don't like the idea of a stowaway. Clinging to consoles, I work my way closer. One of the bodies is naked, tall, and white as snow, like it was some cave-dwelling creature. The other...is Adrik.

Or used to be.

A husk of a body barely fills his clothing.

If Adrik is dead, then who…

A tattoo on the man's blazing white shoulder stands out. It's a bald eagle, clutching the Earth in its talons, but the globe becomes an ape's skull. Clutched in the skull's jaws is a dagger, blood dripping from the tip. Above the image is 'USMC.' Below it, 'Semper Fidelis.' It's a one-of-a-kind tat, and I've seen it before.

"BigApe?" I step over Adrik, legs shaking, and I grasp BigApe's arm. With a grunt, I roll him over. His face is pale and pruned, like he's been in a pool for a few days, but also from age. He's still thirty years older than me. I check for a pulse. Strong and steady.

"What happened?" It's Drago. He's clinging to the wall, fighting to stay upright. Saddened by the sight of his old friend.

"They separated," I guess. "When we rotated."

"Was not normal rotation," he says.

I shake my head.

"Hope it was worth it," he says, and he rolls Adrik over. His face is missing, smoothed out like a mannequin.

"So do I," I say, taking off my outer shirt and laying it over BigApe's nakedness. He'd always been a little ashamed of his small stature…down below. Claimed to a be 'a grower, not a show-er.' I'd feel bad if he woke in his own body for the first time in thirty-plus years only to remember he's not well endowed.

"I feel like Grimace just gobbled me up and shat me out," Hildy says, rubbing her temples. I'm about to question her knowledge of McDonald's, but then I remember she's watched a lot of media from my time. And apparently, she didn't limit herself to sci-fi and action movies. She watched commercials, too. Weird.

Burnett wakes with a gasp. He slaps his body all over, checking to make sure all of him is there. When he's convinced he's whole, he sighs with relief, and then he feels the discomfort of waking.

"You okay?" I ask him.

"There were two of me," he says, "when we were rotating. Felt like I was being torn apart."

"Turns out that's not impossible." I motion to BigApe and Adrik.

Burnett unbuckles, stands, nearly falls over, but then sees the pair of men lying on the floor. "Adrik is…"

"What's wrong with Adrik?" BigApe asks, his voice groaning. His eyes blink open. He's staring at the ceiling. "Are we dying? I feel like we're dying."

"Only one of you," Drago says, sullen. He returns to his station, eyes on the floor.

"What does he—" A spasm rolls through BigApe's body. His eyes go wide. "I felt that. *All* of that." His arms come up. He makes fists. "I'm back…" To me, he asks, "Am I back?"

I nod and attempt to smile, but he sees through it.

"What's wrong? Where's—" He turns to the side. Sees Adrik's weird, faceless body. Pushes himself away from it, jumps to his feet, and stumbles back against the wall. He's disoriented from the rotation, but probably also because he hasn't had full control of a body in a long time. He manages to hang on to my shirt, though, keeping it held in place.

Before he can say anything, his left arm juts up. His pinky flails around like a worm on a hook.

What the…

"Oh my God," BigApe says. "He's here. He's still here."

"Like a ghost?" Burnett looks around the bridge like he might be able to spot Adrik's specter.

Drago is back on his feet. "What do you mean, still here?"

"We're still bonded," BigApe says. "But now…he's inside me. In my head mostly. And…" He holds up his hand. The flailing finger points toward Drago. "He says not to mourn him. That he had his time. And now it's…"

BigApe tears up a bit. "Thank you, friend," he says to the man inside him. He nods like he's hearing a response, then turns to me. "We want to know what the hell happened."

"We all do," Chuy says, entering the bridge. She's covered in some kind of strong-smelling cleaning liquid. And she's not happy about it.

"Better if I show you," I say, taking my seat. I take control of *Bitch'n* and with a subtle burst of the port thrusters, I turn us toward…

Hildy snaps to her feet, excited. "Is that Earth? Are we at Earth?"

"But…" Burnett is confused. "Isn't this where the Minutemen went?"

"It is," I say. "About a thousand years from now."

Chuy grabs my shoulder. Spins me around. "We're home?"

"We traveled through time, *again?*" Drago asks, taking a seat as he looks at the view.

"Yes," I say to Drago, and then to Chuy. "Almost."

"What do you mean, almost?"

"We left in 1989. If the Europhids didn't miss the mark by thirty years this time, this is 2026."

"That's when things kick off with the early Union," BigApe says. "When the revolution began, and you became their leader."

I nod. "But this time, I'm thirty-two years younger, I know what's coming, and I've got a God-damned spaceship and the best team of badasses anyone could ask for. We won the war for the future, but the fight for the past is still a goat that needs fucking."

"Hell, yes!" Burnett says. "We're going to fuck some goats!"

Chuy has a laugh. "He knows the goats aren't literal, right?"

I shrug. "Hard to say, because, you know, the pillow. Also, goats aren't extinct yet."

"No," she says. "They aren't." And then she catches me off guard with a kiss. It's tense at first. Strange and unknown. But then I relax into it, slip my arms around her waist, and pull her closer.

When we separate, Burnett and Hildy, now on their feet, start cheering and clapping.

"Yes! I've always hoped!" Burnett says.

Hildy grabs his cheeks, pulls him in, and gives him a puckery kiss on the lips. It's not long, or particularly sexual—closer to something a grandmother would lay on an unwilling grandchild—but Burnett swoons back into his chair, a funny smile on his face.

"I think I speak for all of us," BigApe says, "when I ask, can I have some fucking clothes, please?" His pinkie goes bananas. "Right, also, we're with you. Whatever you need."

I thought this moment would feel better. A recognizable Earth without the Union. The human race a bit saner. Confined to the one and only planet we call home. But the cost to get here was great. Porter,

Morton, Whip, Benny, and even Carter are dead. I had to leave Brick behind. And now, instead of a happy victory lap, I need to root out the source of an impending evil empire and cut it down.

The weight on my shoulders is heavier than ever.

Chuy seems to read my mind, hands on my shoulders, head beside mine. "It's not your burden to carry alone. Let us help you."

I smile, slip an arm around her waist again, and then say, "We'll get started in thirty minutes."

Chuy calls bullshit with a raised eyebrow. "Fifteen at best."

Before the others can question what we're talking about, I trigger the PSD and rotate away with Chuy. We land in my bed, already removing clothing. Motion in my periphery freezes me in place.

It's outside my porthole.

In space.

I do a slow turn, and reel back when I see a man in a spacesuit... behind the wheel of a red and black sports car.

"Fifty bucks says a rich white guy did this," Chuy says.

"I don't have fifty dollars."

"Then I'll just have to find another way for you to pay me back." She tackles me back into the bed, straddles me, and pulls off her shirt, undeterred by the lifeless peeping Tom sailing past.

EPILOGUE

It's been six months since we arrived in the future-past. Took us that long to reestablish ourselves back on Earth, not as ourselves, who disappeared thirty-seven years ago, but as new people, with new names and histories.

Technology in 2025 is sleek and sexy, closer to the Minutemen aesthetics, but Union tech is still far more advanced. With Hildy behind the keyboard, we've been able to fabricate detailed backstories, get social security numbers, degrees, and bank accounts with enough money to start a revolution.

While all that was happening, we scoured the planet's rich and powerful, searching for signs of racist bent. Found plenty. Some of it was painfully blunt and systemic—the kind of thing I thought relegated to the years before MLK. But we're not looking for a loud, blunt instrument. We're looking for a keen mind who knows when to strike, when to stay quiet, and how to start a white supremacist movement without anyone noticing—until it's too late.

Haven't found him yet, but when we do... Well, let's just say it's not going to be a fun day for the Fourth Reich. We're going to abort that shit before it can ever leave the womb.

But first...

The six of us are gathered on a man-made green hillside. At the top, where the view of the ocean is best, are two gravestones. The first reads, 'Porter — A loyal friend, a dedicated soldier, and a mind without comparison.' The second, 'Morton...' which is followed by his favorite quote. 'I went through shit, and came out clean on the other side.'

Took us a long time to bury them, because I wanted to do it right. Waited until we were 'real' people. Until we had money. And a home. And land to put them in.

Burnett spoke. About brotherhood. And friendship. And sacrifice. Nearly broke my damn heart. Even Drago was wiping his eyes.

Now all that's left is to shovel the dirt over them...a task I demanded I do alone. Burnett, Hildy, Drago, and BigApe head back to our compound hidden in the trees of what was previously Anastasia State Park in St. Augustine, Florida. To get the land, we simply had to fake an environmental disaster, and then buy it from the state on the cheap, with a promise to clean it up. The sixteen-hundred-acre peninsula is populated by moss-filled trees that hide what's going on beneath. Also: alligators. Walkways cross the dunes, leading to our very own private beach, where, if you swim deep enough, you'll find what looks like a submarine parked on the ocean floor.

It's a nice place to live. Light years better than the inside of a space dump. *Bitch'n* served us well, and still does, but I hope to never call her home again.

Burnett puts his arm around Hildy as they walk away. They're officially a thing, and they still represent the kind of innocent, loving people I hope the world can achieve. Seeing as they were both from a future where Nazis were in charge for a thousand years, it gives me hope for the people of this era. If a couple raised in the Fourth Reich can see me as just another person, maybe the rest of the world can, too.

A shovel digs into earth. It's Chuy.

I'm about to complain. That I want to do it alone.

"Don't even say it, joder aliento."

"Fuck breath? Classy." I pick up the second shovel, happy she's here.

Then we move dirt in silence for an hour. It's a sad moment, but I'm at peace.

For now.

This morning we launched a Minutemen website. There's a questionnaire. A manifesto. A FAQ.

All of it's anonymous, but it allows people to send us tips, to sign up for the newsletter, and join the not-yet revolution. It's also a place where those who oppose our vision can lash out and put themselves front and center on my radar. It's a big pain in the ass, but the future Minutemen, and even the Europhids, don't know who launched the white power movement that's been building steam for a few years now, into an established government superpower. So, it's up to us to find them, and hopefully stop them before America finds itself in another civil war. No idea if the website will work. From what I understand of the Internet during this time, these things are hit or miss.

But Hildy is 'doing the socials' and advertising. All of it under a shell company owned by people who don't exist. The rest of us are prepping for the future we all hope to avoid—amassing guns, ammo, and a shit-ton of canned beans. Because: Wolverines. Those beans always looked good to me.

By the time I tap the soil flat and lay down the carved-out grass, the sun is setting. Wispy clouds overhead glow pink and orange. Out over the ocean, the sky is dark purple.

Chuy stabs her shovel into the ground and stands beside me. Links her fingers with mine.

"They would have liked this," she says. "I'm glad you waited."

I turn to her. She's lit by the sunset, covered in dirt and sweat. The moment is perfect. Our happy-for-now ending. I reach into my pocket. Pull out my phone.

"What are you doing?" Chuy asks.

"You know how I like everything to have a soundtrack..." I tap the play button. The happy guitar rift of *I'm Gonna Be* by the Proclaimers fills the air, followed by a foot-tapping beat and lyrics that make even the grouchiest person smile.

Chuy wraps her arms around my neck. "Would you? Walk five hundred miles?"

"I'd cross the galaxy." We lean in, to kiss.

"Oh, God, I think I'm going to be sick. Like a couple of horny teenagers, you two." It's a gray-haired woman in a tight-fitting, very colorful power suit that suggests she's far more comfortable with her body-type than she should be. The sass in her eyes makes it work, though. She motions to the graves. "Sorry for your loss."

"The park is closed," I tell her.

"That's cute," she says. "Saw your website."

"Our *website?*" Chuy asks, trying to sound casual, but failing horribly.

"Sounds like you might be up to no good," she says.

I tense. The woman is old, but confident. Powerful.

And white.

She chuckles at me. "Oh, come now. You look like you've got a dick in your ass."

"Huh?" is all I manage to say.

She shakes her head and *tsks.* "You need to work on your communication skills, or this is going to be the shortest damn revolution ever."

"Lady," I say. "I don't know what you want, but—"

"I'm here to help."

"How can *you* help?" Chuy asks.

"Aside from satiating the troops' carnal needs?" The woman smiles. Offers her hand for me to shake. "Name's Winnie."

I stop the music and shake her hand.

"We just put the website up this morning," Chuy says. "How did you—"

She rolls her eyes. "We've been watching you since you thought it was a good idea to steal a car from orbit, and then drive it around St. Augustine. At least you stole one of the prototypes. The publicized car Elon launched is currently coasting past Mars."

Chuy backhand slaps my shoulder. "Told you that was stupid."

Winnie gets a look in her eyes, like she's hearing God speak to her. Then she says, "Look, I represent some folks who are interested in what you're up to, where you came from, and what you plan to do with that shit-shaped spaceship out there in the water. We're not the bad guys, but we need to make sure you aren't either. Then we can talk about la revolucion. Agreed? Estupenda."

Before I can reply, she's walking away. "I'll be in touch."

A helicopter roars overhead. Looks fast. Like it cost a lot of money.

"That's it?" I catch up to her. "You can't just drop all this on me and bail."

She stops. Looks me in the eyes. "Sure I can, Moses." She smiles as the helicopter descends. "Looking good for a man my age." She gives me a quick up and down. Gives me a different kind of smile. "Let me know when you get bored of G.I. Jacinta over there. For now, I need to introduce myself to some folks in Boston."

She ducks down as the helicopter lands twenty feet away. I watch her go, feeling beyond confused. Then she stops suddenly. Turns around. Shouts over the loud rotor and the whooshing wind. "Hey! I'm not your only visitor! There's someone in the lodge!"

The lodge was once a visitor's center. Now it's where we all live while the rest of our facility is being built. It's also where the others went.

I sprint away as the helicopter whisks the strange woman into the sky. No idea if she was telling the truth about anything. She might very well be the brains behind the Fourth Reich's rise. But the Europhid presence in my mind, which occasionally flares when danger is near, had no reaction to the woman.

"What's wrong?" Chuy asks, as I run toward her.

"Intruder in the lodge," I say.

She's by my side a moment later, both of us drawing the sidearms we keep with us at all times. We rotated together, emerging just outside the lodge's front door, which we shove open. We step into the large living space—leading with our guns. A quick sweep reveals only surprised familiar faces seated in the room's leather furniture.

"Whoa!" Burnett says, raising his hands.

Drago laughs at me. "Looks like little mouse, afraid of cat in house."

"Stand down," BigApe says, placing a hand on my weapon. Lowering it. "We're all friends here."

"Speaking of that," Hildy says. "We have—"

Motion draws my eyes to the kitchen.

A man in a Stetson steps into the doorway.

He's got two revolvers hanging from his hips.

My gun comes back up, as I shove BigApe to the floor. Chuy takes aim as well.

Before either of us can consider whether to take a shot, the stranger has drawn both revolvers and fired—one bullet from each. My gun snaps out of my hand, landing beside Chuy's on the floor.

He disarmed us both, faster than I could think.

Chuy and I give each other a 'How the fuck?' look, and then I rotate from the living space to the kitchen, emerging from the fourth dimension directly behind the man. I draw my knife, slip it against his throat, and say, "Who the hell are you?"

He slowly raises his hands, letting the revolvers dangle.

"I was *trying* to tell you," Hildy says, a little angry. "He's here to help. Saw the website, apparently."

"The website doesn't give our location," Chuy points out. "You said it would be a secret."

Hildy frowns. "It was."

"Kind of feels like you put us in the yellow pages," I say, and then to the man, I ask, "How did you find us?"

The man shrugs. "I have my ways."

The accent is... "Russian?" I ask. Maybe he's a friend of Drago's.

"Czech," Drago says, sounding bitter. "Apparently, Soviet Union decided to remove troops from Czechoslovakia."

"Czech Republic," the man corrects.

"Whatever," Drago says. "Is now independent country, like other Soviet states. Blah, blah, blah, America. Freedom. Apple pie."

"His name is Milos Vesely," Burnett says, "and he's really nice."

I decide to trust my people. If Drago and BigApe thought the man was a threat, they'd have shut him down. I remove the knife from his throat and step around him. "Okay Milos, why the hell are you here?"

"Same reason you are. I am gunslinger. Am Cowboy." He gives a lop-sided smile. "And I hunt Nazis."

```
[info] Scenario: JR-00073 - Exo-Hunter - Complete

[info] Runtime 537382 Complete

[info] Process 766.23 Iteration Complete

[info] Reaping Environment...

[debug] Environment Reclaimed

[info] — INITIALIZING —

[info] Genomic Matrix: 6385-H26

[info] Loading Scenario: JR-00107 - Nemesis Rebirth

[info] Environment Selected: H26-Terra

[info] Rendering Environment...

[info] Runtime 537383 Starting

        ... 3

        ... 2

        ... 1

        BEGIN.
```

POSTSCRIPT

If you're not sure who Winnie is, check out THE OTHERS. If you're not sure who Cowboy is, read SECONDWORLD, followed by NAZI HUNTER: ATLANTIS.

AUTHOR'S NOTE

Before we get started... In the tradition of Dark Horse, let's fire up a song for the credits. "Heroes" by David Bowie seems appropriate. Head on over to bewareofmonsters.com/playlist for all the songs referenced in the novel. "Heroes" is the last song on the list.

Music playing? Great.

The first question you might be wondering is whether this novel was influenced by the COVID-19 virus, as well as the protests spurred by the death of George Floyd. After all, this is a novel about a black man fighting white supremacists after a virus wiped out a large part of the human race. While I finished the novel two months into lockdown, and a month after the protests began, I started writing long before both. The subject matter in this novel has been weighing on me for a long time, as it does most people watching the news for the past few years. White supremacy is a virus, as deadly as COVID, and I look forward to a future where we've all be vaccinated against it.

What about the Europhids? Was I planning to bring the gelatinous wangs from *Beneath* back some day? Yes...and no. I've always wanted to revisit the Europhids, but I never felt I had a good concept to bring them back. When I was writing the scene with the seductive flesh-eating bacteria, my description of them brought the Europhids front and center in my mind. And...they fit. In fact, it was like I'd been writing the novel for them, without even...

Hold on—

Jeremy checks to make sure his eyes aren't blue.

Okay, I'm good.

Even details like Beatrice's red eyes were there before I consciously thought of using the Europhids!

And now, the big questions for you long time readers. Why is Winnie here? She appeared in *Flux*, too. She mentions going to Boston. That's where *Tribe* takes place. And *Tether*! And what's up with Cowboy?! Is this the start of a crossover?

Maybe. I'm laying down the groundwork for a potential crossover, yes. It would involve characters from *Exo-Hunter*, *The Others*, *Flux*, *Tribe*, and *Tether*. And yes...Cowboy. Because: Nazis. Can't leave him out! BUT, as always, it depends on sales of *Exo-Hunter*–whose characters will be central to the story. So, if you want that to happen, or you want to see a sequel to *Exo-Hunter*, be sure to post reviews on Audible, Amazon, and Goodreads. Posting reviews not only lets people know you enjoyed the book, but it also helps trigger recommendation algorithms that suggest books to people who have not yet read the novel. This is the primary method for marketing books, and the power is all yours.

I hope you enjoyed *Exo-Hunter* as much as I did, writing it. The subject matter covered is bleak and heartbreaking, but I hope we can all have a laugh together and look forward to a better future— sans Nazis! Seriously. Nazis?! In America?! Ugh.

—Jeremy Robinson

ACKNOWLEDGMENTS

Big thanks to comrade Ian Kharitonov for making sure my filthy Russian is accurate. And to Rian Martin, Rene Ramirez, Heather Zingiberis, Omar Munoz, Marie Gándara, Maurits van Eersel, and Christiane Alemão for making sure I can curse *en Español* like a champ. Como se dice, "Thank you," en Español? RobinsonFest 2021, cervezas en mi!

Big thanks to Kane Gilmour, for his masterful editing, to Roger Brodeur for his proofreading and fact-checking, and to Kyle Mohr for his relentless knowledge about everything I know nothing about. We had an amazing team of proofreaders this time around. Jennifer Antle, Brandon Burnett, Julie Cummings Carter, Elizabeth Cooper, Dan Delgado, Dustin Dreyling, Dee Haddrill, Becki Tapia Laurent, Rian Martin, Kyle Mohr, Jeff Sexton, and Kelly Tyler—you guys help keep me from sounding like a dotard. Thank you!

Also…thank you to Alex Maddern (aka bigAPE) and Brandon Burnett for having a sense of humor over horrible things I do to your namesakes. If you ever feel wounded by your characters' fates, I'll pay for that dolphin therapy you both talk about all the time…

And thanks to you, the reader, for supporting my habit of writing about crazy-weird things. Wouldn't be here without you.

ABOUT THE AUTHOR

Jeremy Robinson is the *New York Times* bestselling author of sixty novels and novellas, including *Apocalypse Machine, Island 731*, and *SecondWorld*, as well as the Jack Sigler thriller series, and *Project Nemesis*, the highest selling, original (non-licensed) kaiju novel of all time. He's known for mixing elements of science, history and mythology, which has earned him the #1 spot in Science Fiction and Action-Adventure, and secured him as the top creature feature author. Many of his novels have been adapted into comic books, optioned for film and TV, and translated into thirteen languages. He lives in New Hampshire with his wife and three children.

Visit him at www.bewareofmonsters.com.

CPSIA information can be obtained
at www.ICGtesting.com
Printed in the USA
LVHW092027170121
676726LV00024B/635/J